Niagara Falls
All Over Again

THE DIAL PRESS

Niagara Falls
All Over Again

Elizabeth McCracken

T H E   D I A L   P R E S S

Published by
The Dial Press
Random House, Inc.
1540 Broadway
New York, New York 10036

Library of Congress Cataloging in Publication Data

McCracken, Elizabeth.
    Niagara Falls all over again / Elizabeth McCracken.
        p.   cm.
    ISBN 0-385-31837-5
    1. Comedians—Fiction.   2. Male friendship—Fiction.   I. Title.
PS3563.C35248 N5 2001
813'.54—dc21   2001028314

Book design by Lynn Newmark

Manufactured in the United States of America
Published simultaneously in Canada

August 2001

10   9   8   7   6   5   4   3   2   1

BVG

For Samuel & Natalie Jacobson McCracken
My favorite comedy team

"Haven't I always taken care of you?
You're the first one I think of."

—Oliver Hardy to Stan Laurel in *Atoll K,*
their last movie, 1950

1

Dearly Beloved

This story—like most of the stories in the history of the world—begins far away from Des Moines, Iowa.

It starts with two men—one thin, one fat—dressed in tuxedos, walking down a black-and-white street arm-in-arm. The fat man keeps stumbling. At one point he falls and manages to land on his high silk hat. The fat man will always land on his hat, and the thin man will always help him up, whack him over the head, and replace it.

"I don't want to do this, Professor," the fat man pleads in a childish voice.

"You'll be fine," says the thin man, who, befitting his name, wears a mortarboard instead of a top hat. He drags the fat man up a set of stairs into a white church and through the flung-back doors and down the aisle to a sudden wedding march. Though both men are rotten marchers, they make it to the altar, where a minister opens a Bible in a chiding way: there's no good reason to be late to your own wedding, even if your bride is a pony. Which she is, a chubby, swaybacked roan pony whose hindquarters keep shifting—she's not thrilled about the match either. In this world, everyone wears a hat; the pony's is straw, trimmed with a net veil thrown over her shoulders. The fat man sneaks sugar cubes to his intended. The pony has a history of bolting.

"We are gathered," intones the justice of the peace, which is when the fat man howls, "Oh my fucking God!"

The cameras—there are cameras here, and a boom mike, and a director who hates the pony, and a script girl and a prop guy and dollies and grips—stop rolling.

"What *is* it?" the director asks.

"That fucking pony!" the fat man says. "That fucking pony bit me!"

"Okay, that's it," the director says, but he laughs. "We need a new pony."

"Jesus Christ." The fat man is trying to shake the ache out of his hand, but he's milking it. "Get me a better-looking one this time, will you? I want a Shetland. I'm sorry, sweetheart," he says to the pony, "but a pony like you, and a guy like me—take my word for it. I'm saving you a lot of heartache down the road."

The director shrugs, but it's 1946, and the fat man is famous. He can hire and fire any pony he wants. Already he's walking off the set, doffing his white gloves, tossing his high silk hat at the wardrobe girl, who carries a torch for him. Everyone on the set carries a torch for him; either he doesn't care or doesn't notice. "Come on," he tells the thin man. "I'm hungry."

The thin man follows. (When the cameras stop, the thin man always follows.) "Don't insult the pony. The pony is high-strung. You try being a pony in this town."

"That fucking *pony*," the fat man says gravely.

"Oh, Rocky. We both know the pony only wants to make you happy," says the thin man, the other man, the straight man: me.

Here's what I think: when you're born, you're assigned a brain like you're assigned a desk, a nice desk, with plenty of pigeonholes and drawers and secret compartments. At the start, it's empty, and then you spend your life filling it up. You're the only one who understands the filing system, you amass some clutter, sure, but somehow it works: you're asked for the capital of Oregon, and you say Salem; you want to remember your first-grade teacher's name, and there it is, Miss Fox. Then suddenly you're old, and though everything's still in your brain, it's crammed so tight that when you try to remember the name of the guy who does the upkeep on your lawn, your first childhood crush comes fluttering out, or the persistent smell of tomato soup in a certain Des Moines neighborhood.

Or you try to recall your wedding day, and you remember a fat man. Or the birth of your first kid, and you remember a fat man. You loved your wife, who died decades ago; you love your kids, who you see once a week. But facts are facts: every time you try to remember anything, the fat man comes strolling into your brain, his hands in his pockets, whiskey on his breath.

At which point you decide to write your memoirs, hoping to clear space for the future, however long *that* is.

Maybe you've seen our movies. A chubby guy in a striped shirt whose head is a magnet for coconuts, shot puts, thrown horseshoes, upside-down urns, buckets of water. A thin man in a graduation cap and tweeds who is afraid of everything but his partner. Carter and Sharp, briefly the number-one box office draw in the country, now an answer to back-of-the-magazine quizzes. I don't think we even show up on late-night television these days. In the 1940s, you couldn't avoid us. We made twenty-eight movies in thirteen years, every one a love story, no matter what anybody says. We were two guys who so obviously belonged together you never had to wonder whether we'd end up arm-in-arm by the final frame: of course we would, we always did. Even with Astaire and Rogers, you had to wonder. Not with us.

Here's What You Do

His regular straight man turned up drunk, is how it started. I was a young man backstage of the Minneapolis Pantages Theater in the second year of the country's Great Depression and the third of my own. It was 1931, and I was a vaudevillian, though vaudeville was dying. I hardly noticed. Everything was dying: it was hard to figure out what would rise from the ashes, and what was sputtering out for good.

I'd been summoned to Minneapolis to sub for a Dutch comic with a bum appendix. When I arrived, the stage manager handed me a bright red wig that smelled like the tail of a golden retriever. I painted freckles on my face and went on in a borrowed checkered jacket. I looked demented, not Dutch, and told jokes in my usual mournful way.

Some audiences liked the deadpan delivery. Not this one. I could hear several hundred programs opening, several hundred fingers sliding down the bill to see who was next; I could feel the damp leavings of several hundred sighs of boredom, puffed up from the house one at a time to pop like bubbles on my cheek. So it wasn't a surprise when I stepped off the stage and the manager handed me my publicity photos, which was how you got fired in vaudeville.

He was a parsnippy-looking guy, scraped and pale, but he wasn't heartless. He saw the look on my face. "Listen, kid," he said. "God never closes a door without opening a window."

Good news if you're a bird. I was twenty years old and out of work; I believed that if God opened a window, He meant me to jump. A flash act had taken over the stage, a bunch of pretty girls dancing as they warbled some song about the weather: they predicted rain, and wore cellophane slickers and carried mustard-colored umbrellas, which, of course, they twirled.

I rolled up my pictures and stuffed them in my jacket pocket. Then I felt a finger tapping my shoulder.

My first impression was of an overwhelming plaidness. The guy's suit looked like a worked-over full-color crossword puzzle, smudged and guaranteed to give you a headache. His face was worse: he'd applied his makeup in the dark, apparently, pancake layered on so thick you could've stuck candles in it, rouge smeared in the neighborhood of his cheeks. I couldn't tell what he really looked like. Heavy. Snub nosed. Agitated. Still tapping me with one hand, rubbing his stomach with the other. Behind him, a sharp-faced man was vomiting into a lady's purse.

"You a straight man?" the tapping guy asked.

"Sure," I said. Of course I was. I was whatever he needed. If he'd been short a poodle for his trained-dog act, I would have dropped to the ground and wagged my tail.

"You know the Swiss Cheese Bit?"

I nodded.

He continued to tap my shoulder. Suddenly I reached up and snagged the offending finger with one fist. I was an Iowa boy. I knew how to catch pests. I could feel his finger wiggle in my hand, trying to tickle my lifeline.

"You'll do," he said.

"I'll do what?" I asked.

Then I saw that beyond all that pie-brown makeup, his dark eyes shone like the rich, sweet filling in a Danish pastry: poppy seed, or prune. He gave me a lopsided smile, as though he already believed I was funny, and right then I began to believe it myself. At least we both knew my reflexes were quick. Rocky Carter, I would find out soon enough, was one of those people who could will light into his eyes, make them gleam and twinkle and shine and glint and sparkle, any number of otherwise indescribable clichés, a knack I now think of as nearly the definition of charisma.

Later, in the cartoon credits of our movies, they always drew me much taller, but that's because he slumped and I wore lifts. We were about the same height, which is to say short. I let go of his hand, and he snatched the red wig off my head and stuffed it behind the rolled-up photos already in my pocket.

"I'm Rocky Carter," he said.

I'd studied the bill. I knew who he was. "I'm Mike Sharp."

"You are *not*. What's your real name, son?"

"Sharp," I said. "Mose Sharp."

"We're old friends already," he declared. "So I'll call you Mose. Do you drink, Mose Sharp?"

"No," I lied.

Clearly he heard the deceit in my voice, because he smiled pretty wide when he said, "Wrong answer."

Carter and Fabian—Freddy Fabian was the guy vomiting into the purse—weren't the headliners, but they were better off than I was. I tried not to think of this as my big break. I'd had that thought too many times over the past two years, ever since I'd left Valley Junction, Iowa, for what turned out to be the big lights of Duluth, Davenport, Toledo and Wichita, any number of two-bit towns with two-bit theaters. Minneapolis was a step up. By 1931, I'd done everything: acrobatics, eccentric dancing, juggling, ventriloquism. I'd played both juvenile and geriatric roles in tabloid shows, full-length plays cut down to size for the vaude circuit. I'd appeared as a woman and a little boy; I'd tried on accents of every nationality. And I'd told the truth to the first question Rocky ever asked me. I'd been a straight man for a couple dozen acts: a group of hard-boiled kids, a frail old-time comic whose arthritic pratfalls caused the audience to gasp in horror, a temperamental seal, a pair of French brothers, and, for an entire season, a troublesome nineteen-year-old Dumb Dora comedienne named Mimi with whom I'd been horribly in love. I'd thought she'd been in love with me too. When Mimi—her real name was Miriam—handed me my pictures, I thought about getting off the circuit and going home to run my father's clothing store. Instead, I kept plugging away.

It's not something that people understand so much these days, how a comedian needs a straight man. They see one funny guy, and then another guy who isn't so funny. They don't realize that the comic (Rock, for instance, his pants so baggy they drape like an opera gown) needs a straight man (me, for instance, in my tweeds and mortarboard) standing still, telling him to act right. Getting him into the right kind of trouble. Making him look so dopey he's adorable. Most people in this world want to be the comic, and why not? You get laughs and love and attention. You get all the best catchphrases. Used to be that a good straight man could get the lion's share of the salary, sixty–forty, a little money to salve his ego and keep him in the act. I was nobody when I joined up with Rock, so with us it was the other way around. Not that I was thinking of money that first night in Minneapolis. I just followed the guy out onto the dark stage, rubbing my painted freckles off with my thumb, happy I had somewhere to go. The light hit us like a bucket of water, and I said my first line—"Here's what you do"—and we were off.

It's like this: Rocky has just been hired at a cheese factory. He's in charge of making the holes in the Swiss, but he doesn't know how. I'm the foreman, I say, A hole is nothing! You're bothering me now about nothing? (Maybe it doesn't sound funny on the page, but Beethoven on the page is just black dots.) Rocky gets nervous, and more nervous, and downright panicked about the holes, the nothing.

Onstage with Rocky, I was handsomer, funnier. If anyone in the audience recognized the Dutch comic made over into the fierce foreman, they forgave me. The crowd was no longer a squawk box worked by a crank—turn that crank harder!—but what they were: a bunch of gorgeous people who happened to find us very, very funny. Then suddenly Rocky ad-libbed in a big way: he jumped into my arms, all the way off the floor, so I was cradling him. *Oof.* Like a lady scared of a mouse, and so I said, "What are you, a man or a mouse?"

"Mouse," he said in his squeakiest voice.

"You're a mouse in a cheese factory," I told him. "You're living the life of Reilly." I didn't put him down. I was twenty years old, I could lift anything if an audience was involved.

"I'm scared," he said.

"Oh, Rocky," I said dotingly. "Poor Rocky. Shall I sing you a song?"

"Uh-huh," he said.

So I started Brahms's lullaby.

"Not that one," he said.

"Okay." I tried Rockabye Baby.

"No!" He thumped me on the chest.

Rockabye Your Baby with a Dixie Melody? No. Beautiful Dreamer? Worse. You Made Me Love You? Out of the question. Abba-Dabba Honeymoon?

A sly nod, a settling in.

It's almost impossible to hold on to 180 pounds of snuggling comic, but I managed. "You better sing with me, folks," I told the audience, "or we'll be here all night." So they joined in, and that night five hundred people sang Rocky Carter to sleep for the first time. That's the bit we became famous for: Why Don't You Sleep? We did it a million times, in the movies, on radio, on TV. Veronica Lake sang Rocky to sleep, and Dan Dailey, and Bing Crosby. Always a different ridiculous song. Rocky said it was our funniest bit. Rock was educated—Harvard, he said sometimes, Princeton others, School of the Street, he told reporters. Anyhow, he studied things. What made Chaplin great? Keaton? A kind of tenderness and need, he said, not like these jokers everywhere. Why Don't You Sleep would be how people remembered us, he said. It would be our signature.

He was right, of course, but mostly I think he just liked being sung to.

After we got off—four curtain calls, the real thing, no milking— Rocky used the house manager's phone to call up Freddy Fabian at his hotel. Midnight; Fabian was probably in the middle of the start of his hangover. Rock stuck a finger in his free ear, as though the applause was still deafening, and swiveled at the waist to wink at me.

"Freddy," said Rocky. "Freddy: remember how you said your father wanted you to take over the grocery store?"

12:30 A.M.

"To us!" Rocky said.

"To you!" he said.

"To me!" he said.

"Especially to me!"

12:45 A.M.

"Look," said Rocky. "I want you to listen. Are you listening? Pay attention. This is very important. Stop laughing! No, I mean it! Okay, laughing boy. Keep on laughing."

1:00 A.M.

"How many sisters you got? What? You lucky son of a bitch! Listen: I'm an only child. Six sisters, you ought to be able to spare one. Pick me out a pip, okay? We'll send her a telegram in the morning."

1:25 A.M.

"Miriam who? Veblen? Oh, yes, yes, yes: Mimi and Savant. That act's bullshit, you know that. Really? Let me shake your hand. No, the other one, your *empty* hand. The guy I saw in the act was a nance. I'm sure you gave it a je ne sais quoi. Mimi, on the other hand: tout le monde sait her *quoi*. No kidding? Really? Well, I'm sure you gave that some class too."

1:50 A.M.

"Didn't they teach you to drink, wherever it is you're from? Oh. Well, no, they wouldn't teach you to drink *there*."

1:55 A.M.

"Hey, kid, how old—your glass is empty, here—how old are you? A youngster! I'm twenty-five, fourteen years experience in show biz. My parents—are you kidding? Who do you think packed my bag?"

2:00 A.M.

"Let me shake your hand. No, I'm serious. I *am*."

We drank in my boardinghouse room, and the landlady came in to shush us once an hour, like a cuckoo in a clock. First Rocky and then I flirted with her—that's probably why she kept coming back, she liked the flattery. Also I threw my Dutch wig out the window, to signal that I would never need it again, and only afterward did I remember that it was borrowed, and this seemed like the funniest thing in the world, and though it was the middle of the night we discussed who it fell on: the landlady, a dog, a cop. Rocky spoke in his childish stage voice all night, I think. Maybe he wanted to convince me that our spot that night wasn't a fluke.

No. I'm wrong. Back then there was a slight difference in his voice onstage and off, but he didn't start to squeak full-time till some years later, when we guested on the Rudy Vallee radio show and listeners complained that they couldn't tell us apart. Rocky knocked himself up an octave to solve that problem.

Still, that's how I remember it: Rocky in falsetto describing a Dalmatian in a little Dutch-boy wig discovering he's lost his appeal to all other dogs. I do know that we believed we would become famous, a thought that had never strictly occurred to me before. I believed because Rocky was positive, and though many a lost lamb has thus been led to slaughter—maybe he'd said the same thing the night before to Freddy Fabian, maybe he said it to anybody—the most curious thing of all was he turned out to be right.

"So," he said. "How'd you get into show business?"

"Oh," I answered. "One of my sisters pushed me."

2

The Sharps of Iowa

I grew up in Valley Junction, Iowa, a little whistle-stop town just west of Des Moines, the only boy among six sisters. Annie, Ida, Sadie, Fannie, Hattie, Rose. (There was another list, too, of the brothers and sisters who hadn't lived: Samuel, Libby, Sarah, Abie, Louis, Hilla. This was a list we never said aloud.) I came sixth, two years after Hattie, almost to the day. *This one we'll coddle*, said my father, who loved his daughters but longed for an heir.

Hattie, aged two, had other plans. She looked into my crib and decided that Mama and Papa had finally brought home what she really wanted for her birthday: someone to boss around. "Mine!" she told our sisters. She slapped their hands away from me. "Okay," the older girls said, laughing, "see if *you* can stop his crying." My oldest sister fished me out and sat Hattie down and plopped me on her plush little lap. What do you know? I shut right up.

I swear I remember staring up at her on my first day on earth. I was—there's photographic evidence—a good-looking baby, with a full head of black hair that Hattie stroked with the back of her wrist. Did she even know my name? She cooed, "Mine, mine, mine."

I cooed back, thinking the same thing.

From my crib, from the flowered carpet in the living room, from the back steps where I staged plays with root vegetables stolen from the bins in the pantry: what I remember is Hattie's face looking back at me, Hattie's voice singing lullabies, Hattie scolding me for dreaming when we could be climbing trees or fording puddles. Our mother was always pregnant, shut away in her bedroom. Mama's breath was hot and inky;

her hair was black; her voice was sandy and kind; we were told to leave her alone until she felt better. She never did. She finally died after our sister Rose was born. I was four, and Hattie six.

The morning of Mama's funeral, confused by the gloom indoors, I stepped outside and directly into a casserole dish. The neighbors had brought us food, which they left on the back stairs of our house. Cold navy beans slid into the sagging cuff of my sock, and this was an unhappiness I understood: I felt myself about to cry, a ticklish feeling around my nose. I stood ankle-deep in the casserole, and then, suddenly, Hattie stepped down beside me, into a loaf of bread. Then she stepped into a lemon cake. Then—the bread stuck on her foot like a boot—she stomped into all the other dishes, a roast chicken, a crock of butter, some thoughtfully sliced pot roast. She did this soberly, as though she were rending a garment, or covering a mirror.

I stamped my foot into an apple crumble, breaking the glass pie plate beneath. Mrs. Combs, our next-door neighbor, might have wondered about the noise that came from our backyard, but what could she do? Besides, she'd heard Jews broke glasses at weddings. Why not pie plates at funerals? We trampled all the food. In houses around us, north, south, across the back lot, neighbors pulled back curtains and wondered whether this is what Jews did, when their mothers died.

The older girls watched us from the kitchen windows. Such waste, they thought. Such ingratitude. Fannie and Ida and Sadie wanted to stop us, but Annie, the oldest, rocked the baby and kept them from the door.

"Let them alone," she said. "There's time enough for crying."

The other girls agreed. Soon enough we'd miss our mother. Soon enough we'd weep. They'd be ready for us then. They had examined their own grief and decided they couldn't use it, not when the littler kids suffered, so they folded it up, and ironed and scented it, and tried to make it look like something else entirely, offered it to us as though it was plain, brand-new, original concern. Hattie, savvy, recognized sympathy for what it is, hand-me-down love.

Get that away from us, she thought.

Oh, the older girls wanted to mother us. They tried to wrestle us onto their laps; they tried to order us around, but it was too late: I belonged to Hattie, and she belonged to me.

Some days I forgot my mother was dead and went looking for her. Was she in her bedroom? The pantry? No. I'd hide on the back staircase then, exhausted. Hattie would find me. "There you are," she'd say as though I was the one who'd been misplaced, and she'd thrust her arms under mine and bear-hug me to my feet and pull me, my toes bumping each step, through the kitchen and out the door. She must have missed Mama too, I realize now. But she kept me busy so we could both forget. Like Annie, she knew there was all the time in the world for crying, and so it was best never to start.

She tried to teach me things: I made a fine audience but a miserable student. I applauded lessons. When I refused to learn to tree-climb, Hattie tossed me into the arms of the elm in front of our house. I bounced once, then sat down to see what she'd do next. I was a composer of songs as a child, though often I merely sang opera—

Potato! Potato, Potato!
Potato. Potato. Potato?
Potato potato potato potato.

—and Hattie could join in on the harmony, even if I was making up the lyrics right then. *Harmony* was what we called her inability to carry a tune.

All of Valley Junction knew us, the little Jewish kids, two of Old Man Sharp's brood: the tall redheaded girl and her short black-haired swarthy brother. We didn't look like each other, but we didn't look like anybody else in town either. Together we wandered everywhere in Vee Jay, fearless. Our sister Annie, who was afraid of everything—smallpox, the nearby river, the slightest cough, birds, fire—thought this was a sign of muddleheadedness. She told us so.

"Keep on that way," she warned, "and you'll come to grief."

My Father's First Stand

My father's store, Sharp's Gents' Furnishings, was a long narrow store that differed from the other long narrow stores on Fifth Street only in what it stocked. The floors were composed of wide unfinished boards that had been seasoned with dirt that sweeping couldn't budge and mopping turned to a stubborn paste. Floor-to-ceiling shelves of stock made accessible by sliding wrought-iron ladders stood against each wall—denim coveralls so stiff you could spread butter with them, union suits in bright red and speckled cream.

That was where my father went, after he was widowed. He'd buried six children by the time his wife died, and would live with that sorrow for the rest of his life, but he did not believe in mourning, which to him was a kind of idleness that could kill you. Like my sisters, he believed that grief was a fact. You put it in your pocket where you felt it at all times, and then you went back to work.

In 1891, he'd been a peddler in the Iowa countryside, selling to farmers and farmers' wives. Then he heard that the Rock Island Line planned to open a roundhouse in Walnut Township, just west of Des Moines. Why not become one of the settlement's first merchants? Within days of arriving, he'd cast off every detail of his old life, like a cowboy in a Western who'd shot a man, except in this case the last bad place was Vilna, and what he threw away was not, he thought, of much consequence: an unpronounceable name, a careful adherence to his religion, a bushy red beard that had kept him warm while he traveled, and his childhood languages—Lithuanian and Yiddish, neither of which I ever heard him speak more than three words of. His sentimental tongue refused to assimilate: he heard the words in American but they came out Yiddishe.

The boat hadn't landed on the shores of Des Moines: he must have started on the East Coast or the Gulf Coast and worked his way to the center of the country, where he met my mother's father, Rabbi Benjamin Kipple. We had a portrait of Rabbi Kipple in our parlor, a bearded man wearing a hat as round as an ottoman. A peculiar man, said our father—he had a hard time keeping a pulpit: he quoted Milton in sermons, for instance, and was known for springing onto chairs to make a point, and then tumbling off them. A slapstick man of God, in other words. When the rabbi arrived in Des Moines, invited by the Children of Israel shul, he leaped from the train in front of a woman waiting for her sister. She took him in—dark beard, pink cheeks, and large blue eyes— and fell to the platform, screaming, "Jesus Christ has come!" Rabbi Kipple stepped over her feet. He murmured, "No, madam, just His *mizpocah.*"

My father, a new arrival to Iowa himself and a congregant at Children of Israel, had a weakness for smart men who were willing to be foolish. Every summer of my childhood, my father brought us to the state fair: he'd never missed one all his years in Iowa, he told us. He'd gone the first time with his future father-in-law. What would the natives have made of the two of them, one small deliberate man of commerce, one tall gawky enthusiastic man of God?

I imagine them walking the fairgrounds, black-clad but happy in the Iowa heat. A comedy team, absolutely. The prize bull is as big as a building. The hogs seem mean and sunburnt. My grandfather (I like to think) cannot meet an animal without doing an impression—strutting like a rooster, lowing like a cow, sneezing like a horse with his whole head. My father the peddler has met plenty of American livestock, but the rabbi is transfixed. Best are the goats, so lovable and pushy he wants to climb in their pen and butt heads with each one in the jostling way of little boys. He has one leg slung over the corral before my father catches the back of his coat to talk him out of it. (Actually, the rabbi is relieved. His sense of humor depends on reasonable people like my father keeping him out of trouble.) The goats stick their anvil heads through the rail-and-post fence like salesmen, and nibble at the knees of the rabbi's trousers. In the company of goats, he suddenly realizes, it is easy to ask a favor. So he turns to Jakov Shmuel Sharensky—as my father is still known—and explains that he is dying. No, my father says, as though that will change the rabbi's mind. The rabbi straightens my father's collar fondly, and makes his request: please marry my Goldie, let me worry less. She's seventeen, you can teach her anything.

That much is true, anyhow: my father married my mother because his dying best friend asked him to; then he took the child home and found that they loved each other. Duty, he explained to us, is always rewarded.

They stayed in love despite everything: the age difference, too many dead children, so many live ones. Nobody has an imagination anymore: they figure an older man, an orphaned teenager, she always pregnant—a brute, that man. They picture the nineteenth-century sex, like sex is furniture and changes styles with the years, like sex is transportation or weaponry, something that has been around since the beginning of time but only recently has acquired any panache.

I don't think that's how it was at all. My mother was young; my father was her slave. He agreed to anything she asked, even all those children.

"But you have three already," he might say.

"Not enough," my mother would answer.

"And me."

"And you," she'd say kindly. "I don't want another husband. Husbands I have enough of."

He'd never imagined outliving her. Once she died, my father turned to me, the thin boy among all those girls, and thought: my little businessman, let us begin.

To start with, he changed the name of the store to Sharp and Son's. This he had painted in red-and-black letters on the window. Then he brought me to the store and set me on the glass counter out front and introduced me to his customers, the railroad men, who shook my hand and called me Boss. They told me how honest my father was, as though I, too, had once suspected that all Jews were crooks, still suspected the rest of 'em but not my father. Jake Sharp, the men of Vee Jay called him, like he was an Irish tough. He sold them clothing and cashed their paychecks and acted as banker; in the flowered safe in the back room were dozens of envelopes full of cash, accounts kept on the back flaps in pencil.

At four I slept among the inventory; at six I learned to straighten; at eight I restocked the shelves from the storeroom; and when I turned ten my father began to talk of me taking over the store, and Hattie decided she needed to put a stop to the nonsense. She hadn't raised me up by hand so that I could become a shopkeeper. For my tenth birthday, she decided, she needed to give me something larger than even Sharp's, and so she did: she gave me vaudeville.

"Okay, kid," she whispered in our front hall. She wound a scarf around my neck. The lapels of her brown coat, a favorite of mine, were fur trimmed; she wore a fur hat that nearly matched, like a black-bearded man with a chestnut mustache. My other sisters were a matched set: short, narrow-hipped and busty, with small hook noses and pale distracted cat-eyes. Hattie was tall and wide across the hips and there was nothing the least bit subtle about her nose; her hair shone like a mesh coin purse, coppery and, like copper, both warm and cool. She tucked another scarf into the collar of my coat, though already I was sweating.

I don't remember the streetcar ride from downtown Valley Junction to downtown Des Moines; I don't remember the marquee. We must have bought tickets at the booth outside; we certainly had to climb the stairs to the balcony. Still, I remember the day as though Hattie smuggled me inside, wrapped in her coat, until the moment we stepped into the house of the Des Moines Orpheum.

Ribbons and ribbons of gold, and velvet, and silk cord. The seats were pink velveteen. I grabbed Hattie's arm, dizzy with the real perspective of the distance and the forced perspective of the railings and sloping floor. Beyond and below the balcony, more seats. The drawn curtains were darker pink; on the ceiling painted angels were made modest by floating scraps of fabric. Gap-mouthed organ pipes stood against the wall to the right of the stage. I thought of a jewelry box my mother owned, with a celluloid ballerina who popped up when you lifted the lid, and just at that moment—as though the building itself could read my mind—the organist appeared on a platform, rising from the orchestra pit, and began to play.

"From up here we'll be able to see everything," Hattie explained. She unfolded a seat for me.

I sat. "A movie?"

She put a gloved hand on my neck to shush me.

While people around us took their seats, the organist descended, still playing, and a troupe of five Oriental acrobats began to fling themselves around onstage in time to the music. First just grown-ups, who I took to be siblings. The tallest acrobat sprung offstage and then sprung back carrying two carpetbags, and then someone in the wings threw him a third, which he caught and set down next to the others in one swinging motion. He undid the brass buckles—in my head I can still hear them ping, though maybe the house percussionist simply struck the triangle— opened them up, and out stepped the contents: a medium-sized child, a small child, and a child so tiny it seemed like a trick, a dog in a toddler suit. Applause. The Fujiyama Japs, the program called them. Somehow, they made the way they tossed each other around seem like good manners. Pass the salt, pass the potatoes, pass the twelve-year-old, pass the baby, thank you, don't mention it. At any moment, they might have started flinging each other into the audience. Would you like the baby? Here, sir. Hand him along the row when you're done.

"Vaudeville," Hattie whispered in my ear, as though that explained everything.

That one act would have been enough. But the acrobats were followed by a singer, a shrunk-down version of a play about a crooked politician, a dog act, a man who folded paper in complicated ways, a stout lady who sang about the man she loved who then pulled her hair right off her head—she was a man herself!—a comedy trio, a pair of eccentric dancers who weren't the Fujiyamas but not bad either: they were brother and sister, which made sense when you watched them roughhouse in time to the music. While they danced they were effortless, but they panted like spaniels when they took their bows. (We did not see a young comic from Boston named Rocky Carter, though years later this myth would slip into my official biography: *bitten by show-biz bug, aged ten, when he saw his future partner perform at the Des Moines Orpheum.* Rocky started that rumor.) I don't remember who the headliner was that afternoon, but my favorite act was a girl who came out on a horse and warbled a song (I've never heard it since) called "My Navaho Love." All I knew was a horse inside a theater was the most astounding thing I'd ever seen, though outside I didn't care for them one way or the other.

Most city boys of my generation were brought up on vaude. Not me. A whole lifetime, it seemed to me then, wasted. Real people on a stage, just for us! My older sisters remembered life before the movies, had seen silent film for the first time projected on the side of a building in downtown Vee Jay, the actors made haggard by bricks, and a miracle. Me, I believed in the Nabob Theater the way I believed in any geographic phenomenon. Who had installed the Raccoon River, two blocks away? God, and then He thought the place could use a movie palace too. (No doubt when Noah filled his Ark some years later, he made sure to include among his couples one straight man, one comic, who'd try to get through the door at the top of the gangplank at the same time, when even the elephants knew better.) I knew all about moving pictures: the people in them only mimed singing, and there was never a chance, when you came back the next day, that a dancer could slip or a dog jump from the stage or a girl on a horse notice a dark-haired boy in the balcony, and address a verse up there, to the rafters.

When the Indian Maid lifted her arms in the air at the end of the song, I thought I could see, just under the arch of her armpits, a margin of white skin between the brown of her body makeup and her sand-colored buckskin costume. I wanted to get up close, so I could count the beads on her bodice.

Afterward, Hattie asked me who my favorite was. We were back in the real world, Des Moines, walking streets called *Walnut* and *Mulberry* and *Grand*. The sun had come out just in time to set. Already I wanted to run back to the theater, set up camp on one of the velveteen seats. I thought it was the only place in the world like that. *Vaudeville*, Hattie had said, and I thought that *vaudeville* meant only this one theater with this particular handful of performers on this solitary afternoon. Had I understood, I might have died of pleasure, there on Grand Avenue on the afternoon of my tenth birthday.

"I liked the Indian girl," I said.

Hattie snorted. "Her? She's no more Indian than I am."

"I liked her," I said, aware of my treachery.

The day had gotten too warm for Hattie's fur hat, so she gave it to me to carry. Behind us, the sun bounced off the gold dome of the State Capitol building. "I think I'll be a dancer," Hattie said. Then she took the hat back from me, and stopped.

"Hmmm," she said. She set her hat on my head, then angled it rakishly—she had to hook it on my ears so it wouldn't fall down around my nose. "What will you be?"

I felt transformed by my new headgear, foreign, ursine, despite my own everyday noggin underneath. Well, wasn't that the point? Like the man who sang dressed as a woman. Except I knew the right answer as I looked at Hattie. A sister-and-brother act, and Hattie couldn't sing. She tilted her head in the same direction that she'd tilted my hat. "A dancer," I said. "Me too."

"We'll have to practice," she said, and I said, "Sharp and Sharp."

"Sharp and Sharper," she answered. "Partners?"

My first contract.

The Comic Baby

Comedians rarely have happy childhoods. Cue the violins: they should be whining "Laugh, Clown, Laugh" right about now.

For instance: Rocky. All of his childhood stories were about brands of misery, even when presented as high slapstick. He was, he said, the only child of college professors in Boston, and he'd worked in various capacities in burlesque houses from the time he was eleven. His first burley house was the Old Howard in Boston's Scollay Square, where he'd been allowed to occasionally touch the dancers, a gift he described so vividly I could feel it: small hand on a big thigh, half your palm on stocking and half on skin, your middle finger ticking along the border like a metronome, not being able to decide which version of leg you liked better.

When he drank, Rocky would speak fondly of the women he met then. Sometimes he made it sound as though he'd slept with plenty; sometimes he claimed his cheeks had permanent slap-burn, so clumsy and sudden were his advances. A childhood in a burlesque house! I was skeptical.

"Safest place in the world for me," he said when he was outlining his show-biz life the day after we met.

"But you were *eleven*," I said. "Didn't your parents go looking for you?"

He shook his head as though my foolishness in thinking so was sweet. "There was dancing there," he explained. "My parents never went anywhere there might be dancing. You think they'd been brought up on an island where the locals performed human sacrifice in tap shoes. As a kid, I was punished if I even walked too enthusiastically. No. I left. My folks let me go."

"And that was the end of it?"

"Oh, we write," he said, "but they are sorely disappointed in their only offspring."

"What did they want you to be?"

"A disappointment," he said. "They'd *planned* on that. They just figured I'd be a disappointment in a field they understood. That way they could have written a monograph on the subject. My mother was a sociologist. She'd studied me all her life, and she never saw *that* coming, her kid becoming a burlesque comic. I refuted all her research."

There are books that talk about Rocky, but they're filled with the stories he liked to tell just to hear them. How he boxed as a kid. (He told me himself this wasn't true. "I like to scare reporters," he said, "except girl reporters, but they never send me girl reporters.") How he'd briefly been a cook in the navy, a story I believed until we filmed *Gobs Away!* and he proved himself to be completely ignorant of anything shipside; the writers incorporated some of his more boneheaded misunderstandings into the script: "The waddyacallit, top floor, penthouse, *deck*." He had a tattoo he said was from his service days, a so-called anchor that looked more like a fishhook. I don't know where he really got it.

When I first met him, I loved his lies. Mental exercise, I thought,

warming up for the stage: he'd lie to see how far he could get. He'd tell a
pretty girl he'd gone to the Cordon Bleu, and then inform her how you
got the butter on the inside of chicken Kiev—you took a live chicken,
see, and fed it cream, and then you picked up the chicken and shook and
shook. . . . He liked best the moment some tender soul frowned and
said, "That's not true. Is it?" Oh yes, of course, completely true. He could
cite facts for hours by making them up on the spot, but he knew some
things for sure. He could read both Latin and Italian: I saw him do it. I
might have thought he was snowing me (I read English, that's all) until
we made a European tour in the forties. In London, he translated the
Latin off the tombs in Saint Paul's with such passion and cleverness that
even the tour guides shut up and sidled over. During our week in
Barcelona, he caught Spanish like some tourists catch colds. He was talking up shopgirls and bawling out cabdrivers by the end of the week.
From the look on their faces, he must have been saying *something*.

In Paris—where he spoke a burbling fast-paced French—I asked him:
where did he learn his languages? He shrugged, and slapped me on the
back, and said, "Didn't I ever tell you I was a child prodigy?"

We were in a basement jazz club that looked like a catacomb, and sat
at a bar tended by a thin man who looked like a corpse taking advantage
of the short commute. Rocky was ordering various drinks for us, happy I
had no idea what was in them. The guy put a pink concoction in front of
me. "Drink up," said Rock.

"What is it?"

He menaced my drink with a lit match. "Le Sterneau."

"No, really," I said. The drink tasted of peaches and peppers. "Like,
French. When did you have time to learn French?"

"Would I lie to you?" he asked. "I was a failed child prodigy." Which
led to this version of his childhood:

"I'm still not sure my parents know where babies come from—they'd
married late, they'd been clumsy about romance all their lives—runs in
the family, Professor—and I doubt they believed that the outcome of
sex would be for them what it was for other people. They probably
thought babies came from flirting, and they never flirted. So there I am,
a baby, completely bored by childhood, and so's my old man bored, and
he figures, Ah! something in common. Why not make himself a child
prodigy? It was all the rage among his colleagues. Now you know, Professor, that real-life professors make the best straight men: they just can't
see that cream pie coming. So my father the straight man says to me, the

comic baby, *Look here. You will learn Latin,* and he drills me through noun declensions. I declined until I was old enough to decline, if you know what I mean. When I turned five, my father gave up. 'Bright kid,' the neighbors told him. Ha! He'd taught me so much in my first five years it took me until I was eleven to forget it all. Every day I forgot a little until I was stupid enough to make my way in the world."

"You remember the languages," I said.

"That's about it," he said. "I'd give them up if I could." He gestured silently to our ghoulish barkeep. Apparently he could do even that in French, because two poison green drinks arrived. Then Rock laughed. "I learned one other thing, one very useful thing that I call upon often in my comedy career. How to take a punch."

Now I ask you, is this true? A child prodigy? But he could speak those languages, and he could take a punch. *Hit me harder,* he told me during our earliest years onstage. *I can't,* I said, and he said, *Learn. Don't you want it to be funny? Learn, kiddo.*

You're Not Dancing

I believed, as I said, that vaudeville was Hattie's clever invention, my birthday gift. She explained to me the hundreds of theaters across the country, the thousands of performers inside, and the trains that brought them to the theaters. Every Saturday we went to the matinee, then we came home to practice. Our sister Rose sat on the back stairs or on the grass, and watched. (Our little audience: we tolerated her presence, because she regularly gave us standing ovations.) Hattie could do anything: backflips and backbends and one-handed cartwheels. She could hold still as a mannequin until I begged her to move, to blink her glassy unfamiliar eyes. We were vaudeville stars, and then movie stars, and then movie stars touring vaudeville houses. I always pretended to be a particular person—Harold Lloyd, for instance—but Hattie played Hattie, except famous. She despised Harold Lloyd; she hated everything in a thrilling way, except Buster Keaton. Rose had a crush on Charley Chase, which made Hattie crazy. "Charley Chase isn't even funny," said Hattie, and six-year-old Rose swoonily said, "But he's handsome."

"A comedian doesn't need to be handsome," said Hattie. "It's better if he's not."

(Years later I'd argue with Rocky over who was funny and who wasn't. He loved Charley Chase, as it happened, though he loved anyone who came to a bad end, and Charley Chase had drunk himself to death. His doctor told him he'd die if he didn't lay off the stuff, and Chase declared he'd rather be dead than sober, and soon enough while on a bender he got his wish.)

So we threw each other around the backyard, and slunk through the alleys of downtown Valley Junction looking up to the windows of pool halls so we could hear accents to imitate. We hooked our knees over tree branches to see how long we could bear our own blood beating away in our faces, the bark biting at the backs of our knees. Hattie's idea: she was crazy for tests of stamina. She could last longer, always. All my life I have partnered up with people funnier than me, smarter, better. Hattie was only the first. *What's the secret of your success?* Live off the glory of others. They won't mind as long as you admire them.

We did not tell our father of our true ambitions. Let him think we wanted what he wanted for us: good grades at school, the admiration of the neighbors, marriage, children. Hattie would find a nice husband. I would find a nice wife. Eventually I would become Sharp, of Sharp and Son's, and my own son would assume my old role, and so it would pass on for centuries.

By the time I was eleven I was sent to the front of the store after school one afternoon a week to apprentice with Ed Dubuque, my father's right-hand man. Ed insisted that his name was real, that his father had been French-Canadian, but there was a rumor around town that he'd been brought up a ward of the state, in an orphanage that named its charges after the duller-sounding Iowa towns—Davenport, Bettendorf, Solon—names that made the orphans sound like solid citizens or gamblers. (Oh, to be named Oskaloosa, or What Cheer, or Cedar Falls!) Poor Ed Dubuque did seem orphanish, abandoned and busy, and he looked like a puppet: weak chinned, spindle nosed, with blond hair that stood upright. He even moved like a marionette, as though his center of gravity was somewhere around his shoulders: his hands floated down to pat children on the head, and when he was startled—several times a day—

he jumped straight in the air, knees bent. At slow times he stood behind the counter, his head swaying. I loved him. "Master Sharp," he always called me. I couldn't tell whether he was kidding or not.

"Watch Ed," my father directed, and I did. I could have watched Ed Dubuque for hours. He was a careful, sweet guy who knew all the customers by name, including, it seemed, those he'd never met before. Maybe he'd memorized the census. Sometimes, when he asked a man for his pant size, the customer would look suddenly abashed, as though Ed had asked his grandmother's maiden name: he didn't know, God help him; if only he'd paid better attention. And Ed would shake his head deferentially—*No, of course, too much in this life to keep track of*—and get his tape measure. He gently encircled a customer's waist and then offered a pair of pants; he knelt at a customer's feet to pin the cuffs, his face turned up. *How's this?*

And so I let both Hattie and Pop plan my future: the wood floor of a stage, the wood floor of Sharp's Gents'. Upon one set of boards or another, I was destined to tap out my days.

100 MPH

When I was twelve, I came down with a sore throat and slight fever, and Annie promptly sent me to my room, where she bundled me up in bed. She blamed the store, which, in catering to railroad men, invited sicknesses from as far away as Philadelphia. To Annie's mind, a hangnail was as bad as malaria. The diseases that had killed our invisible and unspoken-of dead siblings, after all, had started as coughs so slight they could have been mistaken for sighs, and so she prescribed bed rest and quarantine for everything, believing that germs couldn't possibly muscle their way through a bedroom door. On this day, she tucked the quilt beneath my mattress so tightly I might as well have been tied at the stake. Then she went to Sharp's Gents' for her bookkeeping duties.

I couldn't pull my arms out from under the covers to read, which I wasn't allowed to do anyhow: according to Annie, even the funny pages were too heavy for an invalid to lift. That left sleeping and thinking. I tried to combine the two by hypnotizing myself with strange vivid thoughts (here I am floating down the Raccoon River in a giant felt hat; here I am like my Biblical namesake, being lifted from the river by a princess) in the hopes that I could influence my dreams. That sometimes worked when I had a fever.

I dreamt I was in bed; I dreamt I couldn't move; then all of a sudden I *was* in bed, I *couldn't* move, and I looked at the window and saw a face. Slowly it resolved into Hattie, who pushed up the sash and stepped into the room.

"Shhh." She was always shushing me.

I tried to sit up while Hattie closed the window. Finally I had to box my way out of my cocoon. "Were you *outside?*" I said stupidly. "Did you climb the tree to get up here?"

She was wearing a green and pink silk dress that looked like part of one of my fever dreams. The belt around her hips had come undone, and she tied it. "I went out my window. How do you feel?"

"*Why* did you go out the window?" I asked. The bedroom she shared with Rose was all the way over on the other side of the house.

She sat on the bed, near my feet. Annie would have been furious: Hattie might as well have guzzled a glass of my spit. I slept in an iron sleigh bed, a terrible piece of furniture that under normal circumstances discouraged loitering: you'd need dozens of pillows to make leaning on the curved headboard tolerable. The footboard was just as bad. Hattie lay the wrong way around and set her feet on my pillow. "I was up on the roof," she said. "You can see everything from up there."

A vague petty feeling sunk into my neck, and at the moment I believed it was jealousy: behind my back, while I was at the store, Hattie was working on some act I'd never be a part of. Rooftop walking. I was terrified of heights. I lay down so I couldn't see her face. All these years later, I picture myself—yanking the pillow out from under her feet and throwing it into her face at the end of the bed—and I think maybe I had a premonition, though of what I'm not sure. Maybe that's all jealousy is, the ability to look into someone's future or past and see your own absence.

"You'll get caught," I told her.

She slipped the thrown pillow under her head. She didn't have to warn me not to tell anyone; she knew I never would. "Next time you can come with me."

That won me over, though we both knew I got nervous standing on a chair. "Aren't you scared?" I asked. I stretched one leg out so I could stick my foot in her armpit.

"Stop that," she said idly, but allowed it. "If I stood up, I might be scared. Mostly I just sit."

"Why?" I shifted my foot to her neck. I was twelve, and as determined as a dentist to find the spot that would cause her to flinch. She just tucked her chin down on my toes, and considered the question.

"The first time," she said, and already I was amazed: more than once, then? "I wondered how much I could see."

I could feel her voice buzz on my hot toes. The sock seemed to conduct the sensation all the way to my ankle. "And?"

"A lot. Next time I'll show you."

I shrugged, though she couldn't see that.

"I'll show you how not to fall," said Hattie, as though not-falling was a piece of information she'd picked up.

"Annie would faint," I said.

"So we won't invite her."

Our town would look like a map from up there, Des Moines like Canada, except east. Maybe off in the corner there'd be a compass; I had an idea they were actual things, municipal constructions that told you where north was. Here's city hall, here's the high school, here's the municipal compass, a contraption like a metal merry-go-round.

On the roof, said Hattie, the view was mostly trees. You could see a little bit of Fifth Street, three blocks away. Not Sharp and Son's Gents' Furnishings—well, maybe one brick or two, among the nearer leaves. She could see the river, though, and the railroad tracks which, I now decided, were made of the same stuff as my dreamt-up north-pointing dials, except they didn't tell you where to go, they just went there.

"Can you see the racetrack?" I asked. There had been a wooden racetrack on the far west side. We'd never gone, but we heard stories: they broke the hundred-mile-per-hour mark. A barnstormer dropped flour bombs in the middle of the track, and you could see the plume a mile away. Barney Oldfield raced there once. And on opening day, two men died in crashes, which wasn't enough for the rest of the cars to stop racing.

"No," she said. "They tore that down years ago. Don't you remember?"

"Maybe."

"They used the wood to build some houses."

"Really?"

"I can't remember which ones."

We were quiet then, imagining living in a house upon whose walls cars had driven a hundred miles per hour. Upon whose walls, on opening day, two men had died in crashes.

"You know what I used to pretend?" she asked. She threw off my feet and sat up. "I used to think that Mama was a race-car driver at the track, because that's when she got sick. She's not in her room, I told myself: she's racing. She'd come home in her duster, driving one of those cars that looks like a canoe. I thought she would have broken the record, and she'd have the prize money, and I'd be on the front porch—"

We never spoke about our mother, Hattie and I, and now I understood why: at this moment, I could almost feel through the floorboards the slight tremor of our front door opening, the soft spot just over the threshold that made a footfall audible all through the house. No everyday ghost, she'd snuck up on me the way she snuck into dreams: she'd been away, and now she was home. All these years later, I still dream about the people I have lost: Hattie, my mother, my wife, Rocky. They are always travelers, always home with a suitcase, mildly surprised at how much I love and miss them. Then I wake up, and it takes minutes for me to realize they've left for good. It's a common dream among survivors, I'm told. I never know whether it's the meanest trick God plays on us, or the purest form of His love.

Now Hattie dreamed for me. "And she walks up the steps," she said, "and sets down the money, and she shakes my hand. To congratulate me. Because I'm the only one who guessed. And when I'm on the roof, I think, 'She's home now, but by the time I get down she'll be gone.' "

These days, sometimes, I picture Hattie sitting safely astride the roof. The shingles shine, as if sugared. So does the sky, ringed by clouds like meringues. I want it sweet up there, because she loved sweets: rock candy, anise balls, chocolate babies, chocolate Easter bunnies, anything you could bite the ears or toes off of. I think for her, in her voice, *Mama will be home soon.*

I still avoid heights, but I imagine that people scale them to make where they've been more beautiful. Look at that green, look at that blue water. Look at Valley Junction as the sun sets, the sky full of light, the clouds rimmed in gold like china cups. Blue and gold and pink. Valley

Junction is beautiful in it, a gray-faced lady in an evening gown, elegant and unlikely as Margaret Dumont. From up here, you can believe that your mother, who you know is dead, might come up that walk, past that flagpole, up those stairs, and under the roof of the porch. As long as you stay up here, she might be in the kitchen, singing to your baby brother.

3

Who Needs Hattie

Years passed. My father joined Temple B'nai Jeshurun, the Reform congregation in Des Moines, and though Fannie was already married and Annie (according to Hattie) seemed determined to stay a spinster, Ida and then Sadie met and married nice Jewish boys. I worked at the store one or two afternoons a week, a good son, dutiful, deferential, my necktie precisely knotted, my hair perfectly combed. I asked questions, customers answered. I grew taller (though not tall) and, according to the local gossip, handsome. Good looks are an asset for a businessman. At home, I practiced with Hattie, learned to lead while dancing (though we made it all up; my father would not pay for dancing lessons), learned to watch and guess what would come next.

In other words, I was brought up a straight man.

But then, at the start of Hattie's senior year of high school, the principal came to the house. Mr. Blaine was a young man with a flat, round face and matching silver-rimmed spectacles: the only color to him was whatever the lenses caught and reflected. The kids at school liked his childish nervousness; we thought we could always outwit him. He walked into our parlor holding his hat, and said, "Mr. Sharp, sir, I've come to talk to you about Hattie."

Pop nodded. "Hattie, Mose. Why don't you wait in the yard?"

So we went outside and sat on the back steps. "Has Mr. Blaine come to propose marriage, then?" I asked.

Hattie smirked. "Of course. We were planning to run away together, but—" Her gray cotton dress had a rash of roses stitched near the collar;

she felt them with the tips of her fingers. "No. He's talking to Pop about college. For me."

"Oh. He thinks you should go?"

She shrugged. Not many Valley Junction girls went to college in 1924. Nobody in our family ever had, except for Rabbi Kipple, smiling from his portrait. We read always. But college?

"You don't need a degree to dance," I said.

"No," she said. Then suddenly, "Don't get mad."

"I won't," I answered, already starting.

"I think college isn't such a bad idea. For me. We'll go somewhere afterward. Mose?"

I had thought I'd be getting out of Iowa soon. Vaudeville would surely take me out; the only problem was it might keep bringing me back. But that would be okay, playing Des Moines. We'd be written up in the paper. When the *Titanic* went down, a boxed item on the front page of the *Register* announced that there were no Iowans on board. It went on and on about no Iowans being on board. Surely if *that* was news, two local kids headlining at the Orpheum Theater would be. There was another Iowa vaude act, the Cherry Sisters, four girls from Indian Creek who were famous—really—because they sang so terribly, and so obliviously. The local papers *loved* the Cherry Sisters.

"Iowa City," said Hattie. "That's where Mr. Blaine says I should go. He says"—here Hattie used the voice she'd made up for all dull grown-ups—"'there are Jewish girls there, Ha-aa-Hattie.' He figures Hattie *has* to be a nickname, but what's the full form? He says I'm a pioneer. He means I'm Jewish. They call me the little Jewish girl. That *bright* little Jewish girl."

I turned and looked at her. "So why do you want to do what he says?"

She was quiet. The roses on her dress looked inflamed from her scratching. "I just do," she said finally.

Now I think: she wanted to get away from us. I understand. It's why I eventually left myself. In Vee Jay, she was a Sharp girl, part of a famous family. My sisters were the Sharp Girls, I was the Sharp Boy, my father was Old Man Sharp. We weren't the only Jews in town—there were the Brodies, who owned the grocery, and the Jacobses, who ran the dime store, and Old Man Soltot, the cobbler, and in Des Moines there were enough Jews to sustain four congregations—B'nai Jeshurun, plus two

Orthodox and one Conservative shul—but we were visible. We had been taught to keep our hands clasped behind our backs whenever we visited someone's house, to wait until we were invited to sit down, and to not look at *anything:* not down at rugs or straight ahead at paintings or up at dishes on plate rails, for fear our curiosity would seem like avarice. It was hard to do this and not appear stupid. At home, we could run wild, but out in the world, our father said, people would be examining us, wondering what Jews were like. We had to be good.

Why wouldn't Hattie want to try out what it was like to be just Hattie?

Now, though, I left her on the stairs and lay on my back in the grass. "If that's what you want," I said, wounded.

After a while, we heard Pop show the principal to the door. Then he came through the house and out the back. My fastidious father never loosened his tie except when he undressed at night; even now he wore his jacket and vest.

"Sweetheart," he said to Hattie. He sat down next to her on the stairs. Then he sighed almost happily and clapped his hands. "So! What will you study in school?"

I could see her shiver: who knew it would be this easy? "English?" she said.

He nodded. "And Mose—"

I sat up. I thought he'd say something to comfort me, because I sorely needed comfort.

"—when it's your time, you can go, too. Iowa City has a fine business school. My smart children." He smiled, as though the principal had come to the house to give him this gift: a son and a daughter capable of learning. It was so odd to see them together, Hattie and my father, the two halves of my life at last conspiring over my future. My father had his arm around Hattie's waist.

I'd thought I'd known everything about Hattie. How could I not? My favorite sister, my best pal: of *course* I knew her. I knew, for instance, the matter-of-fact syncopated feel of her hip beneath my hand as we waltzed, first dignified, then faster and faster, till one then the other of us lifted off the ground; eventually we got airborne at the same time, a trick we imagined looked both easy and impossible. I knew, when we tried some little piece of patter, dancing side by side, how to wait until she was done, first with the joke and then with the step, before I answered with another joke, and then another step. After practice, while she plot-ted our career—we'd go to Chicago first, a big city but still midwest-ern—I knew not to interrupt her as she scratched a map with the toe of her shoe in the dirt, or wound her hair on the back of her head in an at-tempt to look older. In other words, I understood her timing, and I be-lieved that meant I understood her soul.

Now that I've been in the business for seventy years, I know the dif-ference.

I don't remember what became of Hattie's diploma, though her gradua-tion dress was ruined. "I hate it," she said after we got back from the cer-emony at the high school. She looked wonderful. Clever Ed Dubuque had made it out of white silk; it had a dropped waist and a boat neck that showed off her throat.

"I feel like a doll." She nibbled on the edge of a cookie.

"You *look* like a doll," said Annie, thinking this a compliment. We sat in the parlor, the three children left (Annie, me, Rose) and the one who was leaving. The married sisters had come to the ceremony and fussed over Hattie and then gone off to their families. My father had already re-turned to the store.

"So," said Annie. "What will you study?"

"I'd like to be a lawyer," Hattie said, not looking at me.

"*I'd* like to be a bird," said Annie.

A lawyer? She'd been promising me: after college, vaudeville. Maybe even before: I'd come to Iowa City in two years and then we'd make our escape without having to run away from home.

I looked at Hattie, but she stared up at Rabbi Kipple. She looked ready for a portrait herself, a graduation portrait, which in fact she in-tended to pose for the next day at the Stamp and Photograph Gallery in Des Moines. She frowned, as though already wrestling with a tricky legal question. A lawyer? I tried to catch her eye the way I always did, by sim-ply wanting her to look at me. Suddenly, I knew the truth. She *would* be-come a lawyer, and if I complained, she'd say that I could become a lawyer too. Like Annie, I'd never heard of a lady lawyer before—that's why she said she'd like to be a bird; to her it was as unlikely—but I knew that Hattie would do it. She would forget about me. She would leave me to run the store.

I hadn't even wanted to be a dancer before her (a ridiculous thought, because when did I ever have a *before Hattie?* She had a *before Mose,* but

I had been born into the partnership). She'd come up with the whole plan. She'd taught me. I had been a boy who never gave a thought to the future, except I didn't want to be a shopkeeper, and I knew *that* because Hattie told me. I was sixteen years old. Now I don't know which is more ludicrous: that I had thought, before this moment, that my future was assured, or that I thought, after this moment, that it was destroyed.

"Excuse me," said Hattie, and left the room.

If I opened my mouth I'd burst into tears. I felt babyish there on the sofa, dressed up for Hattie's graduation, a cookie crumbling in my hand. My shoes were polished, and I wanted to muddy them. A lawyer? Yes, we can be partners, Sharp and Sharp. (Would Sharp be a good name for a lawyer, or bad?) Hattie was smarter than me, of course she was: I just hadn't realized how clearly she knew that.

Forget it. I'd be a single. I'd tap-dance and sing. I'd put together a minstrel act just to spite her, because she hated minstrel acts. The Sharp Boy. A *lawyer*. What snobbishness. We'd always said we'd be hoofers. Well, I still would.

Rose, sitting on the sofa next to me, said, "I'll be your dance partner, if you want."

The front of her dress was flocked with powdered sugar from the cookies. I patted her hand absentmindedly. "Maybe," I said, but who could replace Hattie? Not my twelve-year-old sister, she of the bad eyesight and knock knees. No, I'd have to work the act over into something I could do alone.

First, though, I'd take the shine off my shoes. Outside it was a cloudy June day; I walked into the backyard and looked at the elm and thought about climbing it, to prove that my fear of heights had to do with Hattie, and now that we were no longer partners I could do anything. I have since learned that this theory is sound: if someone is willing to be brave for you, you are less likely to be brave yourself.

"Who *needs* her?" I said aloud. "Not me."

From behind me: a soft scraping. I turned around.

There was Hattie, on top of the house. Behind her, the sky was gray, the sun a silk patch on a wool blanket. The birds who flew by were birds; they wanted to fly, so they did. Hattie walked along the peak of the roof as though it were a tightrope. She must not have heard me; she didn't glance down. Maybe she was just looking east to Iowa City. Maybe she wanted to be a bird, too.

I forgave her, mostly. That is to say, I recognized her. She was still a person who was willing to climb out a window onto a roof. Still up for a stunt. Still Hattie, not a lawyer yet.

"Hey," I said.

At the sound of my voice, she turned, then wobbled. For a minute I thought her clumsiness was a joke. She wheeled her arms in the air. In her white dress against the gray sky, she looked like a movie, dappled and imprecise, clearly an actual person but not really moving like one.

Then she slid. She fell to her knee, to her stomach. Then her whole body flipped onto her shoulder. I'd seen her do things like that before: a body is an object you can throw around from the inside, like this—then she'd cartwheel or somersault or she'd just stand and pick me up by my ankles and hoist, and before I fell to the ground I'd think I could fly. She said when I was bigger I'd have to catch her.

Now she was the one who flew. She came to the edge of the roof. Her hands kept scrambling to grab hold of something. I watched her without understanding: at any moment I thought she'd manage to stop and save herself; she'd get her fingers around a shingle, or she'd come to rest sitting at the gutter, or she'd grab a limb of the elm like a trapeze. Then she wailed, a noise I can still hear, she was calling for help, and that unstuck my feet: I was supposed to be doing something. I ran to the edge of the house and put out my hands to catch her, the way she'd been trying to teach me. I waited for her to land in my arms. I waited to learn the trick.

Give Him the Business

In all our years together, I never told Rocky what killed Hattie. Sometimes it almost felt as though he planned to win her away from me, he asked so many questions. He wanted every detail. I'd shrug as though I hadn't heard the doctor's diagnosis.

I told him everything else, just not that.

When I was exhausted with wishing that Hattie was still alive, I wished at least she'd had a different death. I wished she had spent some time dying, in other words: I wished I could have sat on the edge of her sickbed, that I could have climbed the roof—

No. Even if I try, make myself over into Harold Lloyd or Douglas

Fairbanks, Sr., my fantasy self puts one knee on my bedroom windowsill, looks down, and climbs back inside. Okay, I would sneak past Annie, then, into Hattie's room, ready to risk some killing germ, weighed down with a board game and bagfuls of candy from the dime store. Her arms would worm out from under Annie's fierce tucking, ready for presents.

I believed then—part of me still believes—that I had killed Hattie. I had called out, knowing she would always answer me. It must have been windy up on the roof, said Annie; it must have been slick; she must not have known how tricky it was to walk on slanted shingles. I never explained that she had plenty of practice. When Rocky asked what Hattie had died of, I wouldn't say, because I believed that if I put it into words, it would be true. But my version of her death, the one in which I killed her, became true anyhow. Secrecy turns the slightest worry into your deepest fearful belief; over time, it builds up, a pearl inside an oyster, and that's how carefully you guard it.

Now it seems to me that Hattie was never quite a Sharp, though I know that any of my sisters, magnified under the glass of time and regret, might seem so. Each one, you might have said: the youngest, the oldest, the kindest, the best mother, the middle girl of all those girls— she was the one we couldn't spare.

Or me. Years later, if it had been me, someone would have said, The only boy. Surely his father's favorite. Look, here he is among the girls in his Battenberg lace collar. He was going to go into vaudeville, you know. Uncle Mose could dance like a dream.

In all of my memories of Hattie, forever and ever, I'm looking up at her chin and dreaming of the day I'll be tall enough to look down on the curve of her nose. (I never would have been.) She looks like an allegorical figure, like Liberty, or Grace, or the Pride of the Rock Island Line, or the Woman at Home for Whom You Fight.

She's Hattie, though. She's a long-nosed, curly-headed, acid-tongued, too-smart-for-her-own-good Jewish girl from Iowa, and every day I wish she were still here to boss me around.

The morning after Hattie died, my father helped me dress. That was a dance in itself, Pop holding out first my pants, then my shirt. I hopped as solemnly as I could, tried to sneak the casts on my wrists down sleeves without touching the fabric. Then I tipped up my chin to make room for his buttoning fingers.

"Sad life, sad life," said Papa. "Sad life, Mose."

And I thought, I am the ruined one.

Two steps closer, and I would have caught her. I was certain of this. She fell into my hands, and then my wrists gave way. I tried to remember the feel of her silk dress rushing past my palms, but I couldn't.

That afternoon, my family sat in the sanctuary of the temple, nearly braided together on our bench: Rose lay across my lap, my father had his hand on my back beneath my jacket, Annie leaned on his shoulder, Fannie had her arm linked with Annie, then Sadie, then Ida: there was no air between us at all. My sisters' wise husbands kept their distance: when a mother dies, a husband can comfort, can present himself and your life with him as a kind of substitute, but after the death of a sibling, a husband and children seem skimpy compared to the grief. The rabbi recited the Twenty-third Psalm, the one that told you not to be afraid of death because God walked with you always.

It wasn't God's company I wanted.

At home, my living sisters fussed till I had to run up the stairs and slam the door and roll in my bed with guilt for hating their kindness. You'll miss her most, they said to me. I didn't want that job all to myself. I fell asleep and dreamed of Hattie's weight landing in my cradling arms, my knees bent to cushion my sudden burden, the flourish I took to display her to the neighbors: *you will note that the young lady is completely unharmed.* On the sidewalk, a crowd applauded. Then I dreamt that she landed right on top of me, safe, and I was the one who was killed, and I thought, as I woke, *I'm happy to die.*

This is how it starts, I thought: your dreams are smashed and so you stay at home and accept only what life hands over. You might as well become a shopkeeper. So I tried to take my father's cure. I worked afternoons at the store. Men came in, a little shy over how shabbily life had treated Old Man Sharp. They shook his hand, they shook their heads, and then they conducted their business. They did not even look at me, the boy who'd failed to save his sister. I held a feather duster between my forearms and pushed stock around. The doctor had set my wrists so my hands tipped back, as though I was about to applaud.

At home, I set my wrists on my knees and stared at the casts. I'd loved my hands, though I'd never said that aloud. I'd thought them heroic. They'd rested at the small of Hattie's back when we danced; they rose in front of me when I delivered a monologue. When I sang I let them point at my invisible and adored audience, to let them know who had broken my heart: that woman there, and that one three rows behind, and you, the blonde in lavender in the balcony. Now, locked away in plaster, they seemed small people I'd let down, friends of Hattie's who'd always preferred her company to mine.

These things take time, I heard my sisters whisper to each other. *He'll come around,* Ed Dubuque told my father. *Shows what they know,* I thought to myself. I did not plan on coming around. I did not plan on letting time change me at all. I spent the whole summer this way, a silent, shattered kid, three months of bad thoughts and grieving for Hattie.

In August, just before school started, I sat in my usual spot in the parlor, on the edge of our elderly horsehair sofa, the curtains shut against the afternoon sun. Rose came in and switched on the radio. She was strange, a little miniature Annie except more cheerful, and she loved the radio more than anything.

"Turn that off," I told her. "I have a headache."

She sat cross-legged on the carpet in front of the radio cabinet and fiddled with the knobs. "It's time for the Fitch Shampoo Hour."

"I don't care."

"*I* do," said Rose. She turned and looked at me, squint-eyed. Somewhere she owned a pair of eyeglasses that she hated. "I'm going to have my own radio program," she said.

"No kidding," I sighed.

She said, grandly, "I am going to introduce great musicians. Some will be live, and some will be on records. If you make it big as a singer, you can be a guest."

Hadn't anyone told her? I wasn't a singer. I was a sixteen-year-old shopkeeper's assistant. It irked me, as if she was really going to be in show business while I stayed in Vee Jay to man Sharp's Gents'. "That's great, Rose," I said. "You'll be a success. You've got a face for radio."

She was almost pleased before the insult hit. Then she just stared at me, and I realized who she was: our audience. *My* audience. Whenever Hattie and I danced or sang or tumbled, there was Rose, watching. Sometimes she asked to join in, but mostly she listened and applauded and called for encores. She might have been good on the radio. The live musicians I wasn't so sure of; Rose was not so awfully good with people. But the records themselves—I could see her. There's Rose, in her hands a record as black and slick and grooved as a bandleader's brilliantined head. She's by herself in the studio; maybe there's someone else on the other side of the glass, but she can't see him for the glare. She holds the record flat between her palms, as if it's a face she's about to dreamily kiss. (Maybe she does kiss it, just off center of the label. If it's French, she kisses it twice. She can almost smell the pomade.) Then she sets the record on the player. Then she sets the tone arm on the record. Then in homes across the city, maybe across America, living rooms and kitchens and Hollywood bathrooms with starlets in bubbly tubs, Rose's one action takes place.

"Did you like that one?" she asks at the end. "Here's another, folks." And she sends them to sleep, to sex, to dinner, to work.

"I wanted to ask Hattie," she said icily, staring at the speaker, "but you know she couldn't sing."

That was true.

If you make it big, Rose had said, and suddenly I burned to be on my sister's radio show. She was a tough kid; she wouldn't cut her brother a break. I'd have to work. I could feel something strange kicking up at the base of my skull: possibility.

"Do you promise?" I asked Rose.

"Do I promise?"

"Do you promise I'll be on your show when I hit it big?" I said.

She appraised me. "That'll be nice," she said skeptically. "I imagine I'll be happy to have you."

The Scarlet Ampersand

I began to hatch a plan. Chicago, where Hattie and I had always planned to go. Vaudeville. I could sing; everyone said so. A foot in the door. I'd talk to Ed Dubuque, who'd lived in Chicago as a young man and told me he had friends who were performers. "You should hear Paolo play piano," he'd told me once. "He plays hymns like they're honky-tonk, and honky-tonk like hymns." I was sure Ed would help: he loved me, and besides, with me gone he'd surely inherit the store. We both knew that. I worked out a whole speech, and I had my mouth open to deliver it a week after I'd insulted Rose, my father in his office at the back of the store, me and Ed by the painted window in the front of Sharp's. The late afternoon

sun dropped a banner of shadow across us: SHARP & SON'S GENTS' FUR-
NISHINGS. The ampersand fell right on my face: the scarlet punctuation,
the mark of a straight man.

What I said was, "Ed, I can't breathe."

He put his hand to my chest solicitously. "Sit down," he said.

I tried again. "I can't breathe *here*. In the store. In this town. Probably
in the whole state of Iowa. Ed—"

"Shhh," he said. "Okay, Master Sharp. Hold your horses." He looked
to the back of the store, and then at his wristwatch, a Hamilton that had
been a gift from my father. "After closing. We'll talk."

I nodded, though then I really couldn't breathe: all my plans swelled
my throat. But we stood there silently for fifteen more minutes, and
then Ed went to my father's office and came back with both of our hats.
"Follow me," he said, and we walked out and crossed the street and up
the stairs into one of the dark pool halls that downtown Vee Jay was famous for. They sold bootleg beer and Templeton whiskey, named for the
nearby town that distilled it. Ed walked in like he owned the place. The
bartender waved him over and the two of them gabbed and laughed for
a minute, and then Ed brought over a glass of beer for me, my first ever.

I took a sip and felt it in my collarbone, then all the way down my
arms and to my fingers. Ed raised his eyebrows. Okay, I thought, but
then a barrel-bellied man in railroad coveralls ambled up behind Ed and
stared at us. He tapped Ed on the shoulder. Oh, God, a fight.

"Schmidt," said Ed.

"Dubuque," the guy answered. He picked up a cue and a block of
chalk.

"Pay attention," Ed said to me. "Here's where your education begins."

He doffed his tweed jacket and hung over the pool table, defying
gravity the way he did, and they began to play. Everything I knew about
pool I'd learned from a W. C. Fields short, which is really all you need, as
long as you're a spectator. Ed murdered the guy. They shook hands and
the railroad man handed over a dollar bill.

"Good grief, Ed," I said. "Where did you learn that?"

"Chicago." He picked up his glass.

"That's where I want to go."

He waited for me to explain myself. I couldn't. My plans—I'd been
planning continuously since talking to Rose, more efficiently than I ever
had with Hattie—were as precise and unlikely as a house of cards, and to

disturb a single piece, I thought, would topple them over. I counted on Ed to read my mind.

He took a swig of beer. "Why Chicago?"

I whispered, "Vaudeville."

"I adore your father. . . ." he said.

"I know you do."

Ed frowned. I readied myself for a lecture on Duty and Business and Courage. Instead he picked up his jacket and put it on carelessly, so he looked like a bum in a scarecrow's too-tight duds. Then, with an elegant shake of his shoulders followed by a small finesse of his wrists, he re-aligned it. (That was the most valuable move Ed ever taught me. I practiced for ages, to get from fool to dandy with one shrug. It was a great sight gag. I never got as good at it as Ed.)

"Dubuque!" yelled one of the men. "Don't leave!"

Ed flashed a salesman's smile. "Stephens!" he yelled back, in a deep voice I'd never heard before. "Gotta leave!" He turned to me. "That's why your father and I are a good team. Half the men in town won't trust a fellow who won't shoot billiards with them. The other half won't trust one who does. Chicago." Ed sighed, as though he hated the thought. "Vaudeville. Well, I can give you some names."

We had stopped on the steep stairs of the pool hall down to the street; a man who looked as though he'd been sleeping in a field, flossy with straw and cornsilk, passed by us. I grabbed Ed's hand and shook it.

He looked even more pained than he had before. "I'd try to talk you out of going, if it'd do any good."

"It won't."

"I'm aware of that," he said. "I've left places myself a few times. You'll need some clothes."

He took me back across the street to the alley entrance of the dark-ened store. "Mr. Sharp?" he called, unlocking the door. No answer. I'd been in Sharp's thousands of times since childhood, but never when it was empty of my father.

Ed moved through the store, pulling shirts from shelves, a suit from one of the storage cabinets, a straw boater from a hatbox in the back room, a pair of brown oxfords. In five minutes he'd put together a pretty snappy outfit, snappier than I would have thought possible from the stock at Sharp's. My father would have been happy to carry nothing but coveralls and funeral suits, but Ed talked him into buying a few things for the odd local college boy. I pulled on the suit's vest, which had so many pockets it made me look like a chest of drawers. I loved it.

"You'll break your father's heart, you know," said Ed.

"I know."

"When are you going to tell him?"

"I wasn't planning to," I said.

"Then I guess you better start planning," snapped the normally deferential Ed. "Don't be a coward. It's too hard to live with yourself. Your father deserves a good-bye. More than that, but at least that much."

I stared at the floor. I could not imagine a world in which I would jauntily tell my father, So long, I'm off to seek my fortune. He'd tell me no, and I'd have to sneak out of town anyhow. "I'll try," I said.

"Mose," he said. He gave his head a tiny, tragic shake. "You're too young to have so hard a heart."

The problem was, it wasn't hard. The problem was, the minute my father looked at me, I was ready to kick off those oxfords, hem my pants instead of cuffing them, give up all those clothes no workingman would ever consider even trying on, and assume my position behind the counter at Sharp's Gents'. If I did that, my heart would harden for real. People who manage to turn things down, jobs and marriage and children, love and steady meals, have hearts soft as velvet, hearts—like my new fine duds—never meant for work. These people cry at movies and weddings and funerals. They compose sentimental songs crooned across country, and letters to long-gone lovers. (But only lovers who will stay gone.) They paint. They write poetry. They star in movies. Believe me, I know. Their voices make fun of their own bad habits—a love of money or liquor or pretty girls in skimpy dresses—on living-room radios turned louder by strange teenage girls who laugh in all the wrong places.

History remembers the velvet hearted. I hoped to remain one of them.

But the Cow Wasn't Armed

Two days later I worked at Sharp's Gents' for the last time. Ed had taken the day off. He might have worried that he'd suddenly blurt out the details of my escape. At five, my father and I closed the store. Something had gone wrong with a shipment of gloves: the factory had thrown them in a box, all sizes, each glove separated from its partner. So for an hour after five, that's what we did; we sat in the back of the store and married gloves. I had to open each glove to find the label, but my father could judge size by a glance. He sorted them as though he was shaking hands with dozens of strangers, as quickly as a politician at a campaign whistle-stop: good-bye, good-bye, good-bye.

"Who teaches the business course at school?" he asked. "You'll take it?"

"Miss Kemp," I said. The school year started in a week. Of course he assumed I'd be there.

"A woman," he said. "You could teach it better. Ah, well."

The brown canvas of the gloves dried out my fingers. "Miss Kemp's smart."

"She is not a businessman," said my father. "She is not like us. Well, you'll get an A, and then after college, maybe you'll teach the class."

I tried to break the news. "I don't know where I'll be in four years," I told Pop.

"Here," said my father.

"I'll go to Iowa City," I lied. "And then maybe—"

"Listen." My father looked at me. He never wore glasses a day in his life, though he lived to be ninety-four. His brown irises were gold flecked. "This is your store."

"No, Pop, it's your store."

"It is not. This store belongs to you. Do you know how old I am? I am seventy-eight years old. There is nothing on the earth that belongs to me. I am done with it: this store, this town, this life. Anything now I use, I borrow. I borrow from you. Do you understand?"

"You're fine, Pop," I told him.

"Today, yes. Tomorrow, who knows? I have come a long way, Mose. I am nearly finished. You are just getting started. Don't let this go to waste."

"I don't know how to run a business."

He stopped matching gloves for a minute and touched me on the shoulder. "You think you don't," he said gently. "You'll meet a girl. You'll get married, you'll have children. You have this store, then your son will have this store. You needn't wander around."

"But if I want to—"

"Don't," he said. He picked up another pair of gloves. "I did. It's no life."

He did not look like a man done with life: he'd outlived his much younger wife and seven of his children, but nobody would have guessed his age; he'd grown to be a cute old man, his creamy skin kept smooth by morning shaves at Carson's barbershop, his mustache and hair trimmed several times a week. He could have shaved himself, of course, but how else would he get to know the men of Valley Junction? By leaving me Sharp's Gents' of Vee Jay, he imagined he was bequeathing not just a job for the rest of my days, not just the chance to support my sisters when he was dead, but something much better: the love he had cultivated in this tiny town bordered on one side by the state capitol, and the other by cow barns and cornfields. Not as good as a mother's love, he knew, but more durable. The girls could take care of each other. A motherless boy needed something else.

If I was going to break his heart anyhow I'd rather not watch. That night, I added him to the list of people I'd miss for the rest of my life: my mother, Hattie, and now my father. I wrote him a long letter that explained, because wasn't I my father's favorite? Wouldn't he understand? Like him I had to leave my hometown and travel; like him I needed to make my own way among strangers. I begged his pardon and his sympathy. Then I realized my father would read such an apology and tear it up, so I beat him to the punch and shredded it myself; instead I left a brief note, explaining how I loved everyone, how I'd promised Hattie we'd be vaudeville stars and I had to make good on as much of that vow as I could. Maybe I'd get booked into Des Moines and I'd take them out to dinner downtown. The next day I snuck out of the house for an early train, Ed's cardboard suitcase full of clothes in my hand, a few family photos filched from the sideboard.

In Chicago I found Ed's friend Paolo, who played piano in a Bucktown vaude house. He said, "I got enough advice to discourage a dozen guys like you," and then told me I had to start even lower than I'd planned, at amateur nights, if I could get on at all. I got on, and then I snagged a job across town as a juvenile in a melodrama: my qualifications were that I looked capable of breaking my parents' hearts. Terrible stuff and almost no money and five shows a day, but good enough till I got a real break. The melodrama went on to play some cowtowns in Minnesota, and soon enough a letter that had been following me for some time—from Paolo to the first, second, and third theaters I appeared in—finally found me in Lawrence, Kansas. It was from my father, though in Annie's perfect penmanship. Ed must have told them where I'd gone.

November 27, 1927
For my dear son—

You say you do not want to be a shopkeeper. You have grander plans for yourself. People who have grand plans are starving to death. I am only a shopkeeper. But in my family nobody starves. I take care of Annie and Rose. And you. You have always had money, a shopkeeper's money.

Remember your family. I don't know what will happen to all these people I pay for when I die. They need you. If you do not come to take your place at Sharp's you must not love them, or me.

If you do not come home to run Sharp's, do not come home.

May God bless and strengthen you, my dear son, and that He may lead you back into virtue's path is the earnest prayer of,

yr. loving father

That night I went on, stunned and stiff, perfect for my role. After the last show, at two in the morning, I took a walk to the outskirts of town. Then I kept walking, past the houses, into the field. The sky was full of starry fizzy lights, but the roads were black: I couldn't really see where I was going, though I tried to both remember and forget the forgettable little town and its vaude house behind me. Maybe I was just trying to figure out how it would feel to lose a place, to completely remove my own carcass and look back to see how much I'd miss, how much I was missed myself. No matter how far I walked, I couldn't get enough distance. I leaned against a fence and heard noises in the field behind me. A farmer, come to shoot a trespasser. I stuck my hands in the air, waited for a shotgun to hit me in the back. Instead, a cow lowed.

Was this a sign? If in real life you are acting out ludicrous bits of business, well, why not get paid for it?

I'd heard of guys trapped by girls, but not their own fathers. I suppose I'd known that I was giving up my family when I left, but I didn't realize that *they* would give up me. I imagined they'd forgive me anything.

I tried to see myself years in the future, an orphan. The dresser top would be bare of photographs. If I ever married, I'd have to explain: my family was as good as dead, because I did not wish to spend my days helping strangers in and out of clothes. That night, when I made my way back to the boardinghouse, I looked at the pictures I'd nabbed, one of my parents, one of all us kids. My mother has that distracted old-photograph look: her eyes have lost their focus, though she's gently smiling. But Pop! He is not looking at the photographer, he is not looking at the camera, he is looking into the camera, past the glass lens, past the sliding shutter, so ready that he can see the brief appearance of the film itself, staring back at him. *Remember your family, Mose,* he had written, and I thought, *As if I could ever forget.* I tucked him and then the rest of us in my suitcase, and told myself I would travel alone and be happy alone.

But my father knew, better than I did. He wanted to save me from a life of restlessness. Traveling on foot in the Iowa snow was the earliest story he told about himself, back when he was fresh off the boat from Lithuania. "It was so cold," he would say when we were small, "I dreamed of sleeping in a cow. Must be warm inside a cow. But the snow, it turned out, was a good thing, because in one bad blizzard, I was stranded for a week at a farm with a schoolteacher, and she taught me English. I might not have learned otherwise."

In a week? We didn't believe it.

"Isn't this English I'm speaking?" he asked.

I don't know who that schoolteacher was, young or old, beautiful, plain, kind, or merely bored. Was she unmarried, looking to make over a young man who came up the walk, feet frozen but still clanging his pots as if to prove their worth—*Look, lady, fine pots, good pots?* Was she married but lonely, like a wife in a dirty joke? Was she simply a woman who always needed a student? What did my father think, the next morning, when they opened the door and were met by a wall of snow?

Men who travel dream, it's unavoidable. I don't know what my father dreamed of then besides bedding down in a cow. He was so far away from home that even in fields where the snow had blown away into drifts, he could not drop to his knees to the frozen ground, lumpy like the underside of a familiar calloused foot, and know that he touched something that eventually touched people he loved.

My mother believed in curses, my father once told me. She believed in a vindictive God, a vicious practical joker, an eavesdropper who killed children. I don't know what she would have made of Hattie's death.

But my father believed that God was good. He saw before I did that God makes bargains, and he believed that my presence in the store was part of a tragic, already sealed bargain. He had his son. He had five fine daughters. And he knew why Hattie had gone up on the roof: God had put her there, to deliver me. God knew that it was necessary, and so He whispered in Hattie's ear.

My father loved and missed Hattie. He said so. He wept for her in his office off the stockroom; he prayed for her at B'nai Jeshurun. He would not have bargained her life away, he would not have considered it for a moment. God makes his own bargains. God is a businessman, and God loves those in His store, and God does not give things away. You may go from one end of this world to the other, from the plains by the Nemen River in Lithuania to the plains by the Raccoon River in America: there are prices for everything. You do not live without paying terrible, terrible prices for the flimsiest of pleasures, the smallest rewards. So your bargain with God is arranged by God, and afterward you can only walk away, and look at what you have closed in your fist, and use that as best you can.

4

Enter Mimi

I was fired from the melodrama when the middle-aged lady who played my disappointed mother fell in love with an out-of-work actor who wanted my role. "He's too fat," she said, "he's too old, but love is blind, eh?" It surely is, I told her. Then I worked for three weeks as a straight man for a trained seal named Boris—its owner had wrenched his back and needed a sub—and I tossed chopped fish into its humid mouth and tolerated the baleful looks and occasional nips it gave me when I missed a line, not to mention its body odor: you could hardly believe a live thing could stink that badly. Then the seal fired me with a chomp to my fingers and a slap of its tail. "He doesn't like you, I guess," said Boris's owner, lying on the floor next to his boarding room bed. "But at least your hand won't smell of fish. After a while"—he sniffed his own fingers, wincing at the effort—"it's permanent." Boris and I were appearing in a small theater in Duluth, and I convinced the house manager to give me a spot by myself. "What do you do?" he asked, and I told him I could sing and dance. Well, I could, even though for years all I'd sung was duets. He was dubious, but let me finish the week because he hated my old partner, the seal.

What kept me going was Hattie. In the few moments before I stepped on the stage, I imagined she was in the audience. Somehow, my journey had brought me here, to this midwestern backwater where she'd moved instead of dying. She'd seen my name on the bill or had spotted me going through a stage door or had simply been bored and had come to the theater. I could see her, amid the alien elbows of the audience. The woman behind her is upset to be sitting behind such a tall girl, with such distracting red hair, but Hattie doesn't notice. She is waiting for her only brother to step onstage. She is ready to applaud.

And then, every night, I would lose heart, because she was supposed to be beside me onstage. Even Boris was better than no one. Though in-human and hateful, at least he looked in my direction once in a while, for herring and straight lines. I needed a partner. I had always needed a partner.

So I found one, or she found me.

Hattie had been my first partner, of course, and later Rocky and I would claim he was my second, that I wandered lonely as a cloud until he appeared by my side. We said this the way long-married parents never mention first loves to the children, or if they do, as a joke—*Your mother was set to marry Chuck O'Neill, bucktoothed kid, ears out to here, nice enough, did I mention his nose?* I always felt bad about that, because before I had Rocky, I had Miriam.

We met in Duluth, at the end of my disastrous week as a single act. For all I know, Boris pointed me out to Miriam: *See that guy? He's lonely. He smells of fish. Chances are he'll do anything for you if you're nice to him.* She was a child comic, a woman dressed as a girl, à la Baby Snooks ex-cept sexy: miles of crinolines, corkscrew blond curls, glossy Mary Janes that she stared at, toes in, when she started to say something tinged with innuendo. By the punch line she looked up, all smiles. A guy named Ben Savant was her straight man, a dark-hearted rogue trying to talk her into a kiss. Basically it was a Dumb Dora act. *Mimi, what do your parents do at night? They put out the cat. Well, what does your father do in the morn-ing? He lets in the cat. No, no: forget about the cat, the cat's run away from home. Wa-ahah!*

She carried an enormous lollipop that, though she only mimed lick-ing it, got somehow sticky anyhow and picked up pieces of fluff, so it had to be replaced every few days. (If she'd kept the cellophane on, the stage lights would have flashed off.) The act was mostly Savant leering and her acting innocent. Like so many things, funny then, unacceptable now. His suit was as black as his mustache, which was as black as his hat; her blond hair matched her dress. Only the lollipop was lively.

I had a habit of watching other acts from the wings; green as I was, someone else's talent could cheer me up. It was the only thing that did. That Saturday night, I saw Mimi and Savant lay 'em in the aisles, which was almost as interesting as their transformation as they stepped off the stage. Savant was a kid, probably not much older than me, and his villainous mustache was blackened cotton wool spirit gummed to his upper lip. "Hot," he said to me, peeling it off. He stuck it in my hand, like he was tipping a bellboy. Miriam followed. Up close you could see she was no kid. I figured she was at least ten years older than me. You could see how wide her real mouth was, blotted out with pancake, a tiny cupid's bow pout painted over it like a ribbon on a wreath. Same with her nose: it was a fair-sized hook, but she had it shaded into buttonhood. I'm sure it was convincing from the house. As Mimi, lost child, she kept her eyes wide open, her upper lashes hitting the bottom of her eyebrows; she applied the mascara with a heated pin, to make it thick. Each lash ended in a round ball, like a drawing of a crown in a children's picture book. It must have been an effort to keep so wide-eyed, because in real life she had the heavy-lidded look of a vamp, sleepy and cynical. The lids came down the minute the curtain did.

She noticed me clutching another guy's used mustache and smiled. One of her incisors had come in crooked; it made her look extra delighted.

"Hello, son," she said. "Hungry?"

I shrugged. Six months on the road alone had made me a lousy conversationalist. Miriam didn't care.

"Come to dinner," she said.

I shrugged again.

"You're about to be handed your pictures," she said accurately. "I'm offering you a free meal. Don't be dumb." She extended her hand, and I took it, and she dragged me across the street to a Chinese restaurant, my first. Dark red walls and dark green booths, Chinese tchotchkes everywhere, and a woman dressed as a toddler who sat across the table and seemed to be flirting with me. Despite the costume, I couldn't reconcile the kid who skipped onstage with this languid creature.

"Hey, boy wonder," Miriam said.

"Who, me?"

She'd filled in the rest of her lips the minute we sat down; now they matched the scarlet rickrack that trimmed our emerald-green booth. Her elbows were on the tabletop, her hips all the way back on the seat. Though I could not see down her high-necked dress, somehow I felt like I could. "I collect boy wonders," she said.

"Like your partner?"

"Ben? Ben has a crush on the saxophone player."

I tried to remember a lady saxophone player.

"Don't look so shocked!" she said, though at the moment I wasn't. "He's a nice boy. They all are."

So then I began to get shocked. But she reached across the table and fingered a button on my jacket cuff. She smoked. She swore. An old-timer, she'd been playing six years old for ten years. "I've tried other acts, but this is the only one."

"What will you do when you get too old for it?" I said.

"Hey! Who says?"

"No," I said. "I—Never. Of course never."

"That's right." She had her fingers in my plate. I had ordered chop suey, because it was the only thing on the menu I'd ever heard of. "You don't think I'm too old, do you?" she asked, and she reached across the table with her sticky fingers and fiddled the button again.

"For what?" I asked. I was trying to flirt. Now I suspect flirting on my part would have been beside the point.

"That remains to be seen."

I was eighteen years old, but before this night—this memorable night, as it turned out—I'd never so much as kissed a girl. In the most abstract way the female sex was not a mystery: I'd grown up in a house filled to the rafters with it. I'd had passing crushes on girls at Valley High, but they were not Jewish. There were no nice Jewish girls my age in Vee Jay; my father sent Hattie and me to dances at the Jewish Community Center in Des Moines, where we took to the floor with each other. We picked out couples to mock. Hattie could mimic any-one's shuffling step. If Pop had wanted us to meet our future spouses, he should have sent us without each other. Now here I was in a Chinese restaurant, some strange woman tickling me on the wrist, and I realized I could have gone with any of those Valley Junction girls, if it hadn't been for Hattie. She had taken up all my time. These days any psychiatrist will tell you that it's normal to feel anger at someone who dies—first for being dumb enough to quit living, then for every other transgression—but I didn't know that. There I was, invigorated with rage for Hattie. I turned my hand around and caught Mimi's.

"He lives!" she said. She stubbed out her cigarette and blinked at me—a movement so deliberate and lash heavy I thought I could feel the wind from it on my cheek. I brought her knuckles to my mouth and kissed them.

Nine hours later, after the second show, in her hotel room, I said, "The only thing you're too old for is this wig." It was a wig after all; it had shifted under my hand.

"How old do you think I am?" she asked.

Well, I may have been underexperienced, but I wasn't a lost cause. "I don't know."

"Sixteen."

I laughed.

"Sixteen," she repeated, and suddenly I saw it: she *was* sixteen. Six years old for ten years, six plus ten. Maybe it was her lovely large nose that made her look older, or her cigarettes, or the way she'd seduced a lonely young man as though she were a vaudeville cliché. Later I got so good at guessing women's ages—not out loud, of course—that I could have done it as an act. At the time, though: *sixteen?*

"You're still too old for the wig," I said.

"Ah," she said. "Well, the wig." She got up and went to the chair by the window to smoke a cigarette. She had a swimmer's figure, lovely to me, tiny through the torso but wide hipped and perfectly suited to her costume: nothing to tape down above, concealed by petticoats below.

"Why?" I asked. As the boys in the band would say, I had already discovered that she wasn't a natural blonde. The way she was sitting, I could see the major piece of evidence.

She looked at me, and sighed. "Because this," she said, and pulled off the wig. What was underneath was not exactly hair: it was flossy blond in some parts, and white in others, and ragged and peaked; underneath you could see its original dark brown, like tree bark in a snowstorm. "I've been peroxiding for . . . Last week some chorus girl did this to me. She said she knew how I could go real. . . ." She tossed the wig around on her fist, and then regarded it, as though she were on the edge of a sentimental wig-induced monologue, a sweet vaudeville Hamlet. "It'll grow out eventually, but in the meantime . . ."

"That's not so bad," I said. "You should just cut it short."

"The wig?"

"Your hair. I could do it for you."

"You know how?"

"I cut my own. That's harder. Do you have scissors?"

"In . . ." She gestured toward a bag on the vanity. I found them: they were shaped like a long-billed bird.

"You're sure?" she said.

"Uh-huh."

And so, in Duluth, Minnesota, shortly after sleeping with a girl for the first time in my life, I cut her hair short, and tried to comb it back. I was so grateful to Miriam that I would have done anything: after the haircut, I could clip her nails, or iron her dresses, or polish her shoes.

"It bristles," she said.

"You need some greasy kid's stuff." She had Vaseline in her bag; that would do, though a few moments later I would wrestle her back to bed and we'd get the pillowcases and sheets so greasy they turned translucent. Now I took a glob from the jar and combed it through her hair, which was actually nearly mahogany.

"I think I'll keep you around," she said. "You're handy."

And so she did, and so I was.

The Disappointment Act

"You're going on in Indianapolis tomorrow," Miriam said the next morning over the room-service tray. She had ordered me coddled eggs and dry toast, like the invalid I was. "With me," she added. "Okay, Savant?"

I'd never meant to be a comedian, but as always my breaks came when I rode on someone else's coattails, in this case Miriam's frothy yellow skirt. Ben Savant said he wanted to take some time off. He knew that Mimi had been eyeing me that week—that's why he'd handed over his handlebar mustache—and before he left town he handed over everything else too: his costume, his supply of cotton wool and spirit gum, even his name and glossies, because there was no point in throwing out perfectly good pictures. Turned out the guy I met wasn't even the real Ben Savant; he'd stepped in so seamlessly everyone, including Mimi, had forgotten his real name. The first Savant had drunk himself to death some years before, and had been, in fact, Miriam's father. The mustache, as advertised, was hot, and the spirit gum tasted awful.

There was something about seeing Miriam close-up onstage that unnerved me, too many layers of what-age-was-she and where-had-we-met. I could see the girders of brown makeup meant to bend her nose into something less Semitic; I could see a bruise on her neck, free of makeup because only someone standing right next to her could peer past her collar and see it. Good God, did I do that? The wide-open eyes and the simpering giggle seemed designed to drive me crazy, not to amuse the audience.

Mimi, who do you like better, your father or your mother?

Why, I don't have anything against either one of 'em.

The shorn hair turned her from a cutie to a beauty. I'd never noticed that a hairstyle could make such a difference. There, revealed, her arching nose, her newly huge brown eyes. The neck so long it seemed impossible. Cheekbones. A profile. Her dark oiled hair showed comb marks like the grain of dark oiled wood, and entirely changed her complexion from slightly ruddy, under the blond wig, to roses-and-cream. Her eyebrows matched the rest of her, instead of looking like a proofreader's fatheaded correction: insert eyebrows here.

I was eighteen: of course I loved her. She'd rescued and renovated me, and in return I kept proposing marriage. How else could I keep her around? She turned me down every time, which I took to mean she loved me but hated convention. Years after we'd broken up, I'd tell myself: you were a kid, you didn't really love her. In the months afterward, though, I walked the streets of every new and old town, saying, you loved her, you loved her, you loved her, that was love. She always faced the audiences, and I faced her.

She was a nice Jewish girl, like me from somewhere unlikely: Louisville, Kentucky. She was a little confused when I brought her a Christmas stocking filled with candy and dime-store presents; she was totally flummoxed three months later when I presented her with an Easter basket. "I hate to break it to you," she said, "but we're Jewish. You know that, don't you?"

"Some Jews celebrate Easter," I said.

She stared at me.

I tried to explain that I'd always thought of Easter as a secular holiday: chicks, candy, bunnies, cards. My mother and then Annie bought us Easter baskets from the five-and-ten. I don't know how old I was before I realized it all had something to do with the death of Jesus Christ, but I know exactly how old I was before I realized it was *entirely* connected to the death of Jesus Christ: eighteen, at the Monroe Hotel in Chicago. Thereafter, we sometimes went to Saturday-morning services, if we were in the right town and awake in time.

Miriam was the least serious person I'd ever known. She laughed constantly, at my jokes and my foibles: the time I tried to iron a pair of pants and left a cathedral-shaped burn on the seat without realizing, my first unpleasant encounter with a pickled egg. She seemed always to have just bitten me somewhere, about to run away from the scene of her mischief. She had teenage skin, by which I mean beautiful, and even then, when I ran a hand down her back, I realized I would never sleep with anyone that young again. She decided she'd educate me in everything. "Now, pay attention," she said, leaning over me in bed. "I'm only going to show you this once.

"What a sweet, sweet boy you are."

She was a beautiful girl. Sometimes she drank too much—always after the shows, never before—and then she did seem a little like onstage Mimi, because she cried and then laughed immediately afterward. Sometimes she even talked in her baby voice. I hated it.

"You're a grown woman," I said, even though this wasn't exactly true, and she would pout, and come over and sit on my lap—she was quite a lapful—and say, "You're supposed to help me *forget*."

So: we weren't married, but I assumed we somehow were. Miriam didn't. She still flirted with an occasional boy wonder, praising him for his youth as though she herself was seventy-five. Then she said, one morning when we'd finished a week in Madison, "I think it's time to break up the act."

"Okay," I said. "Well, that might be easier. The agent can get us work—"

"No, no," said Miriam. We were surrounded by room-service trays again; she had a terrible weakness for bellboys. "Everything, I meant. No act. No romance."

Oh.

Despite the wig and the cupid's bow mouth, she never saw life onstage as separate from life off: to her, that would have been as ridiculous as claiming you were one person while taking a walk, and another while sitting in a restaurant, and then someone else again while bathing. But, see, I *did* feel that way. Even standing up from a chair I felt suddenly changed, now a standing man, a man who stood, and if I put my mind to it, I could be a man who walked, and a man who sang. This is why I always loved to dance: everyone wanted to know a man who danced.

Turned out my predecessor in the Ben Savant biz had decided to make a comeback, and they were going to try something new, a reverse drag double, where she'd play the male part and he the female. With the short hair—which I had cut for her every two weeks—she could go wig-less.

"Finally I can get out of these petticoats. Good-bye," she said to me, and walked away into the sunset—actually, we were in our hotel room and she didn't move. Still, I see her in men's pants held up by sus-penders, her coat hooked over one shoulder on two curved fingers, a boater tucked under her arm. She tries to swagger away like a boy, but she's still my girl, though smaller and smaller, till she disappears at the end of the road where the sidewalks clap together and there's no room for anyone. She hasn't bumped her nose on the backdrop, she's just gone.

Aha, you might say to me: she left you, and so you hated her. I toyed with hate, and then chose something harder. I decided I wanted to be her pal. Other people who'd left me had managed by dying, and it seemed a shame to let a whole living woman go to waste. I wanted her to think well of me, which seemed a kind of revenge in itself. Look what a reasonable fellow you just left! Look how you can't forget him! So I courted her—for the first time—I wrote her letters, which she returned with postcards, and once or twice, though I couldn't afford it, I called her on the telephone (I tracked her new act's progress with the week's *Variety*). She seemed fresh out of love, but I was sure that somewhere in her luggage, among the makeup and the worn-out shoes, was a tiny package of affection for me, which I kept petitioning for. It *belonged* to me. Hating her wouldn't have been so awful, so constant, but that might require *her* to hate me, and that, I realized, I couldn't bear.

We'd parted at the Madison Orpheum, after ten months on the road together. I refused to say good-bye; I had a horror of the word. I had not said good-bye to my sisters, I had not said good-bye to my father, I would not say good-bye to Miriam. That last night, I could hear her call my name backstage, but I'd gone to hide among the blades in a sword-swallower's dressing room. "You're safe here," the sword swallower as-sured me, laughing because he believed I was the heartbreaker. Eventually, Miriam gave up, and went back to the hotel room to pack her things alone. Will I ever see you again? I'd asked, and she'd shrugged. But that's the thing about the circuit: what you once lost—on purpose, by accident—is delivered to your doorstep sooner or later. And make no mistake: you are delivered, too, even to people who'd like to refuse you. Maybe especially.

The Genuine Article

So I was back to being a single, a comedian, I decided. I figured what most people figure: a comedy act is a business, the comic is the boss, the straight man's just the hired help. Surely after my time on the road with Miriam, I deserved a promotion. I tried to write some patter songs. One—inspired by my eleventh-grade English class—went this way:

> *I'll be a satyr that's wiser but sadder*
> *   if you're not my nymph anymore.*
> *All of the patter I had wouldn't matter*
> *   if you walked away from my door.*
> *Wasn't it bliss when we kissed in the mist?*
> *It wasn't a myth, then, my lips on your wrist.*
> *Insistently kissing my kissable miss.*
> *Mad as a hatter, but what would it matter*
> *   if you aren't my love anymore.*

(To write a song, you walk down the street with your head thrown back, hoping some rhyme will trickle down your throat like a nosebleed. Kiss, bliss, sis, bris?

Probably *not* bris.)

I got some photos made up, captioned Mike Sharp, glad to get my old name or some facsimile back under my own face. Miriam and I had shared her agent, a faceless guy named Maurice who worked out of New York and didn't care anything about this year's Savant; he wouldn't return my calls and telegrams. A juggler I met in Milwaukee said he knew a hungry agent in Chicago who I should cable. So I did, with the words "Find me work!"

Theater bookers didn't care about this year's Savant, either; maybe that's why last year's Savant had come back to Mimi. I became what was called a disappointment act, a trouper who'd step in anytime someone got sick or drunk or arrested or divorced. For two years I did everything: tap-dancing, singing, tab shows, flash shows, juggling. I was the guy who was merely sufficient. You hired me, or you had a hole onstage: I caught the tumbling Irish acrobat; I sang harmony to the chubby ingenue's declarations of love; I was the husband who opened the door at the end of a scene to catch my wife caressing the handsome stranger. Mike Sharp: the thumb in the dike.

That was onstage. Off, I looked around and saw: no one. Not my family, not Miriam, and especially not Hattie, who I almost expected to pop up now that Miriam was gone, I'd ignored her for so long. I was a single, an orphan. And *lonely*. For ten months I'd had someone to say things to. Not serious things, just *I wonder if these shoes will last another month* or *I saw the funniest baby on the street today* or *My stomach's upset, but I don't think it's serious*. In a bar you can discuss politics or women or money, but you can't tell a stranger that your stomach's upset but you don't think it's serious.

Everyone in vaudeville was strange to me: men and women, slack-rope walkers and animal trainers, Russians and Catholics and Negroes. You couldn't tell from an act who was real and who'd put on an accent, the counterfeit from the actual. The female impersonators, for instance: some of them were perfectly masculine, big knuckled and ready to fight. Others out of costume still seemed girlish, not like real girls, but like the most pampered eerie fairy-tale girl there ever was. They stood on the sidewalk with their unlit cigarettes, waiting for someone to approach with a match. Someone always did.

I learned as much Yiddish from Gentiles as Jews; for years I wasn't sure what was actual Yiddish and what was backstage slang. Sometimes I did a Dutch act, sometimes Italian. I even did a Hebe act for a couple of weeks, with a guy named Farnsworth who played an Irish tough trying to wheedle me into a bargain. Already it was appallingly dated, but I waxed my teeth so they looked pointed and worked up a Yiddishe accent modeled, I am sorry to say, on my father's. Still, being Jewish myself wasn't really an advantage. For a Hebe act you played smart and stingy, for a Dutch act, stupid and lovable. Anyone could do it.

I don't know how I got through those years after Mimi left me, except through a combination of pride and rage, the cocktail that young men guzzle down until they either wise up or die from years of consumption. They're delicious together, pride and rage. I would not go back home. I could not fail Hattie, sometimes because I loved her and believed I was fulfilling her wishes, sometimes because I hated her and wanted to show her what I was made of. I had the worst of all worlds: I was a solo act, except when I was acting.

I'd been doing the Hebe act when I landed in Iowa again, Cedar

Rapids, about 130 miles from Vee Jay. Farnsworth, or whatever his real name was, horrified me: he smelled worse than Boris the Seal, and told me every day that he was looking for my replacement. It had gotten to where we only spoke onstage. In Iowa, I moped and thought of my sisters: Rose and Annie in Valley Junction; Ida in Des Moines; Fannie in Madrid; Sadie in Cascade, not far from Cedar Rapids. I sent money home, though I couldn't afford it. Annie wrote back, care of my agent: *Scribble a little note next time.* I hadn't. Now I composed telegrams in my head. Not to Pop: of course he wouldn't come. But Rose loved comedians, and Annie loved Rose: they could be coaxed, couldn't they?

To see their brother do a Hebe act?

I was so miserable that week everyone on the bill stayed away from me, except for a blackface tramp juggler and eccentric dancer named Walter Cutter, who played the deuce spot. We nodded when we passed each other backstage. He shook my hand once when I came off, like a critic who'd just been grudgingly impressed with a young upstart's talent. Nice of him, since he—though not the headliner—was the guy who brought the house down, every single time. He could juggle fourteen balls and make them look like six dozen. He did a stair dance that rivaled Bill Robinson's (and that's saying something), rubber-limbed and elegant.

The only thing Walter Cutter didn't do was talk. Not onstage, not off.

"You know why, don't you?" Farnsworth said to me, breaking his own vow of silence. "He's a nigger. He keeps his face blacked up and thinks he'll get away with it, doesn't talk 'cause that'll show him up as colored."

Plenty of genuinely black acts wore greasepaint onstage. Walter used burnt cork to cover his skin. Farnsworth was right: he never took it off. He had removed his white glove to shake my hand, and I could see that he was light-complected; I myself was swarthy. In other words, we were about the same color. If he'd wanted to, he probably could have passed and worked the theaters in the south where they wouldn't hire colored; most northern theaters booked whoever audiences wanted to come and see.

I'd been on the same bill as plenty of Negro acts, and I'd seen anger and disdain and occasional violence and matter-of-fact friendly mixing and indifference—this was 1930, after all—but I'd never run into anything like what Walter stirred up in our Cedar Rapids colleagues, all without saying a word. Some people, like Farnsworth, just hated his race. Some people—this was Farnsworth's problem too—hated him because he was a showstopper they had to follow. Mostly I think his silence got to them, the comics especially. They didn't trust a guy who didn't talk, talk all the time, brag and kibbitz and insult. They told jokes and Walter didn't even smile, never mind laugh. Oh, they hated him. No one playing the Criterion would speak to me, because I had shaken his hand. Somebody tried ratting Walter out to the house manager. It didn't make any difference: the theater booked plenty of black acts, plus he'd already gone on and killed. Only a fool would take an act like that off the bill and send him down the road.

By the end of the week we were best pals, though all we'd done was nod and shake each other's hands and play some pinochle backstage. Walter kept score on a piece of paper with the tiniest stub of a pencil. When he won a hand, he smiled, and I saw that he was missing half his teeth. He didn't talk, so I didn't talk. We mimed to each other. Saturday between shows I gestured at him: *a drink?*

He shrugged agreeably and beckoned me through the stage door. Not till we got to the speakeasy did I remember he might have trouble getting served, but the bartender seemed to know him. Even so, Walter hadn't washed his face, though wherever he had the hint of wrinkles you could see his skin under the cracked cork. There we were: a black guy made up to look black and a Jewish guy dressed up as an old Jew. I almost laughed. I could taste the wax on my front teeth.

We carried our drinks to a table and sat down to play pinochle. Between hands, he wrote things on a notepad. Our first conversation. His handwriting was ornate. *Where are you from?* Iowa, I told him. *Home!* he wrote, and then he dealt the cards.

"After a fashion," I said.

Lucky you. Haven't seen my people in thirty years.

"No? Why not?"

He grimaced. Then he wrote, *They won't.* He put the pencil on the table and pointed a long finger at his temple and shook his head.

"What?" I asked.

He tapped his ear, and shook his head more empathetically.

"I'm sorry," I said. "I don't get you."

He sighed, silently of course, and picked up the pencil. He held it for a few minutes like it was a burning match he wanted to let singe his fingers, and then wrote, in big block letters, with none of the usual elegant flourish:

DEAF.

He pointed to himself.

I said, "You don't seem so."

Eyebrows up. A shake of the head. On the page, *I read lips. Have since I was a child. A teacher showed me. Scares people.*

"Scares people? Why?"

Either I can hear and am just pretending or it's magic. So says my parents. They were frightened of me. He went back and crossed out *were* and changed it to *are.*

From his suit pocket he drew out an old picture on a gray cardboard backing, a theatrical shot from the end of the last century: himself, in full tramp dress, including what must have been a red nose, no cork, just a big shaggy false beard and a matching wig bristling out from under his stovepipe hat, the familiar look of educated seriousness on his face. His hands were full of rubber balls, and he offered one at the camera, as though it was the fruit of knowledge and he thought you better not take it, in case you became as wise and desperate and down at the heels as he. At the bottom of the cardboard it said, CUTTER THE GREAT COON JUG-GLER—THE GENUINE ARTICLE.

He wrote on the pad, *Me at fourteen.* Then he picked up the picture and put it in my hand and gestured, For you.

"No," I said, "I can't take this."

He pulled out several from his pocket, to show that he had plenty. I don't know whether he'd sold them once upon a time or they were lobby cards, but it's true they were outdated now. It was a weird gift, but one I wanted.

He wrote on his pad, though I hadn't asked, *Through my feet I feel the drums. That's how I dance.*

Farnsworth finally fired me that night, onstage—he made it a joke, I think to see if I'd go off in character. The audience figured I got axed this way every night. "Go back to Des Moines!" he bellowed, and I exited stage left, vowing that I wouldn't. A local reference! The audience applauded. I walked straight out through the wings to the stage door and kept going, even though Farnsworth owned the dusty Hebe suit.

I thought of myself like Walter Cutter then, proud and downtrodden. I was so proud I would not take Walter's advice, which came in the form of *Lucky you.* I wouldn't go to Des Moines until vaudeville took me closer, and I could show my father I hadn't made a terrible mistake. I planned my return, honest to God I planned it, but pride—

—not pride. I know that now. In my case it was cowardice, and in Walter's case it was necessity, and that at twenty I thought we were going through similar things shows you what being twenty does to the brain. I isolated myself. I cast myself out. The tragedy of Adam and Eve, the reason we can love them, is their eviction. They had to leave, and they left weeping. They didn't pack up and sneak away. That's the ugliest thing in the world, I've come to believe, though at twenty I wasn't done trying.

There's an old bit—Abbott and Costello did it later on film, and the Three Stooges: two guys onstage, one of whom is driven insane by some words. Sometimes it's *Susquehanna Hat Company*, sometimes *Floogle Street*. In the most famous version it's *Niagara Falls*. When the straight man hears a certain set of unlikely words, he gets hypnotized and violent. He repeats the phrase in a strangled voice, and then he beats the comic. Then somehow the straight man catches hold of himself and pulls away. But the comic is a comic: if there's something he shouldn't do, he can't help doing it. He says, "I ain't gonna say those words again." Straight man says, "What words?" Comic: "Niagara Falls." And the beating starts again, and stops again, and starts.

When you travel alone, you pick up your own set of words. If asked, you'd say you never wanted to hear them again: *Niagara Falls, Miriam, Mimi, Savant, Louisville, Valley Junction, Iowa*. But that's not true. You wish some innocent stranger *would* say them, so you can act in self-defense. You stare at people; you dare them to say the words. Comedy is not realistic: the straight man stops and lets the comic live, three, four, five times—he beats him silly but not bloody. In real life you wouldn't stop, you'd keep pummeling until you'd thrashed those words right out of the world. They'd be gone, and you'd be the one who banished them.

I took the train back to Chicago, to try my luck at another talent show. From there, I got a job assisting a morphine-addicted magician who seemed bent on setting me on fire. Then suddenly I was in Duluth again, dancing alone in my boardinghouse to keep my legs up. Someone knocked at the door, and for a moment, still dancing, I imagined who it might be: Miriam, come to ask my forgiveness. Boris the seal, honking that fish tasted sweeter from my fingers than anyone else's. Florenz Ziegfeld and George White, fighting over whether I'd be the headliner in the Follies or the Scandals.

It was the landlady, a red-nosed woman in a striped housecoat. "You're keeping everyone awake," she said. Then she thrust an envelope into my hand, a telegram from the hungry agent that said, *Can you dance? Learn Pantages Minneapolis tomorrow.*

Could I dance? I could fly. I packed my case and caught a train that night. "Lucky guy," I told myself as we pulled out of Duluth, and then wondered when I'd started talking aloud. That is, I said, aloud, "When did you start talking to yourself?" The guy next to me sighed, then changed seats.

All the way to Minneapolis, I shined my shoes. When I got there, I had to dirty them up again, because the skinny guy in charge of the tab show wanted a Dutch comic who could dance—the one they'd booked had a bum appendix. He'd been taken to the hospital in his costume but left behind his wig. Afterward, I was fired again. The beginning of the end, I thought. Time to listen: vaudeville was dying. I should leave before it killed me too. I stood in the wings and watched the girls onstage, lovely in their skimpy costumes, the light off the umbrellas they turned hitting my face like rainwater. Maybe that's why the agitated comic behind me—his straight man vomiting in somebody's purse—noticed me. Probably I was just close up. He was a stout man whose suspenders seemed in danger of pulling his pants to his chin, and he was doing a small dance of impatience in the wings.

"You'll do," he said to me.

Remember: the Pantages, Minneapolis, September 1931?

This is where you came in.

5

Good-bye, Freddy, Good-bye

The morning after we met, like a couple who gets drunk in a strange town and wakes up with rings on their fingers and a few faint happy memories of the evening before, Rocky and I went out to breakfast to take a gander at what we'd gotten ourselves into. What had roused me from bed was rolling over and getting stabbed by a pin that affixed a note to my shirtfront: *Meet me at the Busy Bee 10 A.M. Your partner.*

My partner!

Said partner, I had thought, was a dark-haired clown in makeup and baggy pants. A patsy. An overexcited fat man. I looked around the Busy Bee, and all I saw was a blond guy in a good suit, puffy from drink but handsome, who waved at me. Then he waved a little harder.

When people ask me what he was like, I always want to say the one thing they won't believe: he was good-looking. They have eyes, these people, and they've seen the party in question plenty. Dark hair sticking up, sloppy fat, useless with his hands and feet, squeaky, breathless. With rare exceptions, if you wanted to make it in the movies you had to choose between funny and handsome: Fred Astaire and Stan Laurel could be brothers, but which one's the heartthrob? Even a voice makes a difference in how good-looking you are, and Rock's real voice was knowing and slow. He could have made a living off of it, if things had gone differently. The stuff he colored his hair with washed out. (Rubbed off, too, I learned later. I was the one who told him to either dye it or give up: I was tired of finding bootblack on my good clothes.) He was handsome the way Babe Ruth was handsome, a combination of confidence and being glad to see you. A backslapping man. A handshaker. A kisser of babies and pretty girls. Just like Babe Ruth, he'd peek past a curtain at the one old lady who hadn't smiled for anyone and point: *She'll be laughing hysterically by the time I'm done.*

So there he was, my sandy-haired partner with the big hands.

"Hey!" he said. I couldn't believe that anyone who'd drunk as much as we had the night before could look so pink and bright: healthy, really. He stood up and gave me a quick hug, surprising both me and the waitress, who had arrived with his breakfast. "How do you feel?"

"Like a wrung-out sponge," I told him.

"You need to eat."

"I need not to."

"That's okay too." He sat down in front of his just-delivered plate, which was filled with a jumble of food. "Do you mind," he said, picking up his fork. He took a couple of quick bites before I replied. Each time he lifted the fork with his left hand, he brought his right hand up delicately, palm down, beneath it. After the third bite I realized he did this to protect his shirtfront.

Then he set the fork down. I thought he was formulating some elaborate question—he had an expression of concerned concentration on his face—but all he said was "So?"

"So?" I answered.

His deep-set eyes—on film they looked comical, like buttons on an overstuffed mattress—were round and complicated, halfway between brown and green. He tapped his fork on the edge of his plate. "So. Still a good idea, the two of us striking out?"

"We have a contract," I said seriously.

"I know *that*." He smiled and patted his shirt pocket. "I was just wondering whether I'd have to take you to court."

We did have a contract, drawn up at some point overnight. The terms: Rocky would get sixty percent, I would get forty, but on the tenth anniversary of our partnership the terms would reverse, and then reverse again ten years after that. Rocky put that clause in: he claimed it'd give us incentive to stick together. For all I know, the percentages were nothing but misdirection—*Pay no attention to* this, *which says you'll get less, but to* this, *which says you'll get more.* Later I found out that for Rocky, the future was like Mozambique: he believed in it, he just had no interest. What were the chances he'd get there?

Now he took the sorry thing out of his pocket. Even the paper had a hangover: it was crumpled and mottled with whiskey, nearly illegible.

"You think it's valid like that?" I asked.

"It looks like the Magna Carta. If anything, it's *more* valid." He read it over nostalgically. "Someday," he said, "this will be an important historical document."

"Aha," said a nearby voice, but not loud enough that I thought it was directed at us. Then louder, "A-*ha!*" Fred Fabian. I felt like a correspondent in a divorce case. Who knows how he found us. Maybe Rocky had pinned a note to him too. He had the look of a man who had slept too much or too little.

Listen, before you feel sorry for Freddy Fabian, I insist he wouldn't have had a career anyhow. Though in real life his face was unobjectionable, it would have photographed terribly, all dark circles and sunken cheekbones. Also his teeth were awful: they looked like they'd been carved out of a block of cheese. What's more, he had no ambition. He was always trying to talk Rocky into traveling less, and solely around Chicago, where his family lived. An itchy man, Fabian; he constantly pulled his clothing away from his skin, first at his wrists, then at his shirtfront, then, hands in pockets, from his hips—a sideways flick of the wrist—and his crotch—forward. Maybe he could have found work in the movies as a heavy, I don't know. He certainly looked like a two-bit mobster as he stood by our table.

"Signor Fabiano!" Rocky said. "Sit down."

Freddy wouldn't look at us. Instead, he spun one of his square cufflinks, occasionally lining it up with his shirt cuff. "I'm not sitting down," he said. He had the kind of accent you get from an Italian neighborhood.

"Get some gravy and biscuits," said Rocky. "That usually settles your stomach."

"No," Fabian said, in a voice that meant *You know nothing about me and gravy and biscuits.* Even standing still, he wobbled slightly. Maybe he'd started to drink again when he'd gotten the middle-of-the-night call from backstage. "I hope," he said. "I hope." What did he hope? He was hopeless, a man—like all spurned men—who did not know whether he wished that we'd be happy together, or that we'd choke on our breakfast, or that somehow he'd be asked back as part of a team, even an overcrowded one. He shook his long bony head, and then tried to steady it with trembling fingers. "I thought we were funny," he said plaintively.

Rocky slid over in the booth, but kept one arm on the back. "Sit down, Alfredo. You're making me dizzy." Fabian collapsed on the seat.

Rocky's hand settled on his estranged partner's far shoulder. "Look: You don't even like show business. You throw up before every curtain." Fabian nodded sadly. "And there's nothing wrong with that, but then you drink so you'll forget how much you hate it, but that's not all you forget. So what's the point? You got money, I know you do, because you're cheaper than hell, so why not go home and sell that cheese you like so much?"

"Boof-falo mozz'rella," said Fabian in his soft accent. The name alone made me want to throw up, but it seemed to calm him.

I regarded the two of them, and tried to decide that Rocky and I looked funnier together. Close up, the recently dissolved team of Fabian and Carter came off like a pair of toughs, one Irish, one Italian, both a little hangdog and worked over.

"Hey," said Fabian to me. "New guy."

"Mike," I told him.

"Mike," he said. Then he stared. "So. You're Jewish?"

Not the question I'd expected, especially since I was usually mistaken for something more exotic, but I was game. "Yes. You?"

"Not." Fabian picked up a fork and began to eat directly from Rocky's plate, halfhearted bites. "We're Catholic," he said, pointing at Rocky and then himself with the butt end of his fork. He turned the plate a quarter revolution, and examined what the orbit had brought him. The fork he held in the air, as though it was an instrument with which to repair Rocky's breakfast.

"Okay," I said agreeably.

Rocky slapped Fabian on the back. "Jews are funny," he said.

"Maybe," said Fabian. "Sometimes. I was just wondering."

"Why do you care?" I asked.

"Did I ask to see your horns?" he said with some real meanness. "I'm just trying to figure out what's funny about you."

"Jews are funny," Rocky repeated, "as long at they're not too *frum*."

"Too what?" I asked nervously.

He smiled broadly. Then he laughed. "Very good," he said, though at the time I didn't get my own joke: *frum* was Yiddish for observant.

Fabian didn't get it either. He was staring me down. "Barney Sullivan," he said. "Manny Lane. Ted Mathis—"

"*Freddy*," said Rocky.

Freddy eyeballed him. "Joe Hatch. Lee Schmidt. Harry Ray. That everyone?"

"That's it, sure," Rock said wearily.

"His straight men," Fabian said to me. "Of the last two years. Don't get comfortable. Every time he meets someone new—that's it."

"I'll chase after anything in a nice suit with good timing," Rocky said. "Freddy, Freddy. Do not pin this on me. You—"

"Remember this," Fabian told me. Now I really felt like I was busting up a marriage. He rubbed the side of his face. I couldn't tell whether he was preparing for tears or preventing them. He said, in a small voice, "Please, Rock. Where else am I going to get a job? As a friend—"

"A good straight man can always get work," Rocky told him.

You could hear in the silence that followed a full report on Fabian's merits as a straight man.

Rocky slapped his ex-partner's arm again, this time cajolingly. "You'll do okay. You'll do fine. Do you need money?"

Fabian was still holding the fork, which he stared into as though it would show him his future. Beg more? Beg less? He let his shoulders drop. "Do *you* need money, is more like it," he said, a little too late to be cutting.

"I'm set. Boof'lo mozzarella," Rocky said musingly.

Fabian dropped the fork and stood up. "Look." Now he tried to play the big man. "I wish you much success. All the success in the world. This is disgusting. See you around."

"We'll call when we're in Chicago," Rocky said.

Fabian raised himself to full height, and I thought, Yeah, now I can see it, he's got something. "What," he said, "makes you think I'll be there?" He pointlessly threw some dollar bills on the table, for the meal he'd never ordered, and muttered, "I always wanted to be a singer, you fat idiot." Then Freddy Fabian exited the Busy Bee, trying to look significant. The bell jangled when he left, same as it had when he walked in.

Rocky turned to me, smiling. "Ah, Freddy," he said. "He's been calling me that since before I was fat. You nervous? Don't be. You got talent. He didn't."

"What about the other guys?"

"Let's see." He closed one eye and thought. "Barney Sullivan: died—of old age—in Cleveland. Manny Lane. Married a hoofer and wanted to put her in the act, but there wasn't room for three of us. Ted Mathis—can't remember what happened to Ted, exactly. Hatch became a junky. Probably not my fault. Lee Schmidt stepped on my lines. Lots. Really

not a straight man, more of a singer or monologist or something. Harry
Ray suffered from stage fright. Freddy Fabian: couldn't hold his liquor.
Plus whenever we play Chicago, the guy works days in his father's store
and comes onstage smelling of groceries. He figures the customer's always right, but it's not *funny* if the customer's always right. What are
you worried about? You're good. You got some things to learn, sure, but
you'll learn them. I mean, Freddy wasn't all wrong: I *will* be famous. I'm
funny, and I will succeed, and I'll tell you right now, Mose Sharp, that I
am not someone who sticks with a lousy act just because I like the other
guy. I'll be his friend forever, but I am a comic, not a captain. I will not
go down with the ship. You and me, we won't have that problem. You're
good. Stop! Don't worry. You're good, and I'm good, and together we're
better, and that's all you need to know."

I nodded.

"This would be a fine time to say something," Rock said.

"Right you are," I said, "but I'm speechless."

"You'll have to get over that. Now listen while I tell you of the future," he said, and began to. We'd become headliners, we'd hit the big
time, we'd move to New York. Movies, probably, though Rocky said he
needed an audience to work. If you can't hear 'em laugh, how do you
know you're funny? Carter and Fabian had a route—they were booked
into houses for the next eight weeks—and Rocky figured it didn't matter
who he showed up with. He'd drunkenly wired his agent the night before.

I watched him. He'd say something deadpan, and then laugh out
loud. He was a slob, and yet he had fancy etiquette-book manners; he
found a napkin and touched it to the corner of his mouth after every
bite. Somehow he never spoke with a full mouth, which he managed
more through efficient consumption than waiting things out. Every now
and then he'd ask a personal question. "You're not married?"

"No," I said.

"Close, ever?"

I thought about Miriam and then I shook my head.

He threw his napkin in his plate and then rested his chin on one
hand. "I imagine you're lucky with girls. Right?"

What could I say? I said, smiling, "I wouldn't call it luck."

"Okay, okay then, you *understand* women."

Well, I had a lot of sisters, that was true. He was looking at me as though I could teach him things. I never lied, mind you, I just implied that he was right. "I wouldn't say that either. Let's just say I've studied the issue."

He nodded, still leaning into his hand, wistful. "I've studied it myself, with no success. I had a feeling about you. Here's my theory: good straight man is good with women. It comes from the same part of your brain. Charm. I always wanted to go on the road with a guy who had a talent for meeting women. Me and Fabian, we sat in bars and played hearts. But that's not good enough for guys like us," he said, indicating me, then him. "We have to be ambitious in everything, even girls."

Guys like us, I thought, tickled to be a guy like him. Already I was wondering how I could become a ladies' man. "You ever been close to married?"

"You should eat something." He lifted the napkin from the plate to see if anything edible had escaped his notice: no. "I've never had a near miss, but I do have a distant missus. I'm married."

"Where's your wife?"

"A good question. Florida? I think that's what the note under the milk bottle said. Plus it said: Don't try to find me. Personally I think she ran away with the milkman. I never did get a bill for that bottle."

"I'm sorry," I said.

"It was easier with the second wife. The next one, number three? That'll be true love, whoever she is. See what I mean? Ambition."

He flagged down the waitress for a plate of pancakes and some toast. "I'm trying to gain weight," he said. "While you've been studying women, I've been studying comedy, and I think fat men are funnier."

"Not always," I said.

"Not always," he agreed. "Not Chaplin. But Chaplin might be funnier if he got heavy. There's no telling."

"No," I said, fascinated.

"Don't you gain weight, though," he said. "You look fine. Wouldn't be funny, you being fat. But you're going to need a wig."

"What?" I'd been so happy, flinging that wig to the sidewalk below.

"A piece," he said. "You're losing your hair. I mean, you don't need to do anything about it *today*. Just keep an eye out."

My fingers were in my hair, trying to find what he was talking about.

"Right here," he said, and he reached across the table and touched my forehead where, if I'd had horns, they would have sprouted. "Look, you're not bald, but one day?"

"I have a widow's peak," I said. "It just depends how I comb it."

"You can fool the mirror," he said, "but you can't fool the balcony. Okay, Sharp, if everything goes right, I'll buy you a mirror and you can see what I'm talking about. Get your fingers out of your hair."

"Sorry." I set my hands down on the table so he could watch them.

"You're still worried," he said. "About what Freddy told you. Don't be. Please don't be. I don't remember how long you've been on the circuit, but take it from me, six partners in two years is nothing. That's what you do. You switch around till you find someone who matches up. That's us. On my honor. Thirty years from now there'll be books about me and you. Movies. National holidays. I promise. Believe me, I never promised Freddy a national holiday, or any of those other guys. This meal's on me, by the way, so order something. Come on, eat something, don't be so delicate. Do you cook? I learned in the navy, myself. I'd offer to make you dinner sometime, but I can't cook for less than two hundred."

He paused here, and ate some toast thoughtfully.

"If it's a matter of the math," I said, "I can help you with it."

"No, Clever Hans," he said, "it's not a matter of the math."

If all of this sounds like romance, it was, in its way. I'm not talking about any kind of funny business. But an act is a marriage—years later, when I met my future wife, I thought *Yes, I remember this*. You meet someone, and you take all sorts of things on faith, but it doesn't *feel* like faith. You have to be a little faithless to talk of faith; if you believe, it's all facts. We will be together forever; the two of us will be a smash. If you had any inkling of the odds against you—and I'm talking both of show business and Wedded Bliss—you'd break up the next day and save yourself a lot of trouble.

I loved the guy. It's hard to describe it, exactly; it's even hard for me to remember, what with everything that came later. I'd idolized Hattie, but I'd known her all my life. Rocky was bluff and sometimes mean and funny and smart and a stranger, so I couldn't take any of it for granted. All day long, he surprised me.

He took a shine to me, too. Who is so adorable as a devoted fan with a nice personality?

Dogs Like Eggs

But I wasn't transformed, not yet. I was still myself, a nice Jewish boy from Iowa who'd stumbled from one act to another. My transformation came the next week, when we'd moved on to the Milwaukee Palace to play on a motley bill: Archie Grace and Sammy, a ventriloquist act; Dr. Elkhorn and his canines, all of them, man and dogs, fancy and stump-legged and mournful—I wouldn't have been surprised to see the doctor baying at the moon with his pack; and the headliner, Jack Robertson, the human cobra, a monopede dancer from Aberdeen who'd somewhere misplaced his right leg and left arm. Back in my Mimi-and-Savant days, I'd played the Kalamazoo Magestic with the admirable Robertson: he shimmied up a rope and twined himself around it so fast it was hard to tell what was man and what was rope. "I used to have a tank act," he told the audience, "a big tank filled with water, but I kept going in circles." He'd gotten even more muscular since Kalamazoo, and had added a bit that involved bending backward, grasping his ankle, and rolling around the stage like a thrown hubcap.

There was a bad flash act, a big musical number featuring one juvenile singer who seemed composed of slightly chewed candy (licorice hair, jelly-bean lips, round gumdroppish feet that stuck to the stage) and five unpretty girls dressed up as flowers. Sisters, I realized when I looked at them, and he was probably the sole brother, creepily singing to each one, "My violet, my daisy, my Irish rose/My buttercup, I'll eat you up. . . ." The opener was a zaftig contortionist who called herself the Indian Rubber Maid, by which she must have meant that she looked like she'd bounce.

The stage was so uneven we had to watch where we put our feet. Well, I only had to stand still. Rocky kept tripping, on purpose, and when he jumped into my arms at the end of the act it was a flying leap. How I caught him I'll never know, but I did, and the audience roared: they thought we'd made the whole thing up just for them. "Where did you come from?" I asked my armful, and he answered, "Daddy says from heaven, but Mama says the Sears, Roebuck catalog."

After the second show, around 10:00 P.M., Rocky said, "A drink? I know a place." Jack Robertson was still onstage; he'd left his crutch, as usual, in the wings. His simplest running hop was worthy of applause.

We caught a cab, I figured to a downtown speakeasy, but instead we drove till the buildings petered out and we got to a large white house on a good-sized lot. "Here we go," said Rocky. He caught me by the arm when I headed for the front porch. "This way, darling boy."

Around back was a slanted cellar door, which might have seemed furtive if it hadn't been painted bright red. He knocked with the heel of his shoe. After a moment, one side of the door flew open, and a round head poked out, which belonged to a lady with white curls that looked like they'd been combed with a pillow.

"My favorite!" she said. She reached up and grabbed Rock's ankle, then kissed the toecap of his shoe. "Come in!"

We followed her down the stairs into a room that looked ready for a family dinner party, the chairs and tables borrowed from a variety of neighbors: oak and wicker and wrought iron. A bar ran along one wall, fronted by red-leather-topped stools.

"My favorite!" said the lady of the house again. She was a plump middle-aged woman dressed in a man's suit, black, a crumpled shirt of impressive whiteness open at the neck. Rocky picked her up, kissed her pink nose, and then set her down to see what she'd do. She socked him tenderly in the stomach. "Ouch," said Rocky. "I told some other guys on the bill to come over."

"A party!" she said, as though we were throwing one in her honor. "Hooray!" Ladies' clothes might have made her look stout and mannish; the suit gave her a kind of end-of-the-night glamour. She grabbed me by the shoulders.

"You!" she said.

Me?

She leaned in, and kissed me on the lips. I felt like I'd been hit in the face with a whiskey pie. Then she let me go so she could sock me in the stomach. "Who are you?" she asked.

"This is the Professor," Rocky told her, which was news to me.

"Ah! He knows things."

"He knows a few things."

"But will he tell us?"

"You might persuade him, Christine."

She touched my cheek fondly. Her fingers felt like rose-filled cannolis. "I'm very persuasive, Professor. Aren't I persuasive, Mr. Carter? I'm very persuasive," she said to me.

I could see it might be some time before I'd be speaking.

"Listen, *I* know," said Rocky, "but careful you don't spend all night persuading him, and forget about me. I like a little persuasion myself."

She laughed dirtily and leered at him.

"Christine!" said Rocky. "And me so meek and mild. The Professor's the one you need to watch out for. He's a heartbreaker."

"Lucky for me, I got an anthracite heart. Hard and black." She rapped her breastbone to prove it, though she had to push her knuckles through her cleavage to manage.

I cleared my throat. " 'Says Phoebe Snow, the miners know, that to hard coal, my fame I owe, for my delight, in wearing white, is due alone, to anthracite.' "

"Poetry!" Christine clapped her hands. "He's a professor of poetry!"

Rocky said, "You know, I've been here five minutes and I haven't seen a bottle yet."

Someone knocked on the door behind us. "That'll be Jack, I bet," said Rocky, and it was, our friend the monopede dancer. He jumped over five stairs at once and grabbed Rocky's shirt collar.

"All right," Robertson said.

Rocky assumed a pose of fraudulent innocence. "Jackie! Jack, my lad! What brings you here?"

"What doesn't bring me here, more like. Where is it?"

Rocky opened his mouth. Robertson's hand began to gather more and more of Rocky's shirtfront. "O-*kay*," Rocky said. He pulled Robertson's crutch from under the back of his coat. I could not figure out how he could have stolen it without me noticing, never mind sneaking it here. "We just wanted to be assured of your presence."

Robertson tucked the crutch under his arm. "There's liquor here, is there?" he asked in his Scottish mortician's voice, as if politely wondering the location of a corpse. Christine kissed him; that was the toll she demanded of everyone. She didn't punch him in the stomach though. I thought he'd push her away, but suddenly he smiled shyly. They looked like initial letters in a book of fairy tales, Jack for *In the day of kings*, Christine for *Once upon a time*.

"Excuse my manners," Jack said. "Pleasure to meet you. There's liquor here, is there?"

Onstage he wore an acrobat's unitard, tailored to minimize what was left of his leg and arm. Now he had on a tight single-legged pair of pants, a one-armed sweater, one pull-on boot. His red hair was shorn in a military brush cut that showed the base of his skull but got thicker over his ears. He looked like an aging college football player caught in a stripe of light. He nodded at me.

"You lose your limbs in the war?" Christine asked.

"No, miss. I knew their exact location the whole time. Stepped on a mine." Somehow, he made it seem like he was just a different model of man, a coupe instead of a sedan.

"And they couldn't be saved?"

"Probably were," said Jack. "Probably stuffed like a trout over some doctor's fireplace. A drink?"

I don't know when the night began to get out of hand, though I do know that it grieved Christine to see a guest with an empty glass. She served good smuggled Canadian whiskey and bad home-brewed beer that tasted like pound cake, and a little absorbent food so her guests could keep drinking. Eventually half the bill showed up: the entire house orchestra, several of the flash-act sisters. The basement filled up with cigarette smoke, which must have floated though the floorboards to the mysterious house above, climbing the spirals of bed springs, filling coffee cups. Rocky and I sat on stools at Christine's bar; Jack Robertson lifted himself onto the bar top.

"Didn't your mother teach you manners?" Rocky asked him.

"She did na. She taught me this—"and then he started a long song that mostly had no words but involved knifing a man in his sleep. When he finished, he said to Rocky, "Yeh don't know how to drink."

"I don't?"

Robertson shook his head and stretched out on the bar. "Backache," he said to me as he reclined. Rocky set his whiskey glass in the space where Robertson's right leg should have been.

"Tell me," he said thoughtfully, fingering the fabric over Robertson's leg stump.

"Yeh dirty bastard," said Robertson. "I'm missing what it looks like I'm missing, and that's all. Don't go looking. You," he said to me. "Where did you find this thief? Last time I saw you, you had a girl. Pretty big-nosed girl."

"She's a boy now," I said.

He nodded and polished the bar with the back of his head. "I heard. What did this one used to be?"

"Sober," said Rocky, waving his glass at Christine, who had for some reason pulled Jack Robertson's boot off. "But that was a long time ago."

Christine fingered Robertson's toes. "Only five," she said sadly.

"I have an average of five toes," he answered. "Less than most, more than some."

Archie Grace the ventriloquist came in with the violet sister instead of Sammy. The other girls—Daisy and Rose—had changed, but Violet hadn't; when she sat down, her crinoline-filled skirt flounced up in front like a broken accordion. She must have been under the impression that Grace had been beguiled by the outfit, and was afraid that in street clothes she'd look like what she was: a chapped-looking teenager, no better or worse than the rest of her sisters.

"Hello," Grace called to us.

Jack Robertson pushed himself up on his elbow. "Yeh know I don't talk to yeh when you're alone. Where's your little friend?"

"At the hotel," said Grace.

"Asleep!" said Robertson.

"*Stored,*" said Grace.

"*Asleep,*" said Robertson, "and you shouldha stayed there, and Sam shouldha come with us."

"His body's in a box," Grace said, "and his head's in the chest of drawers. Well, *one* of his heads."

"Jesus," said Robertson, as though Grace had just confessed to a particularly grisly murder. I shivered myself. Grace, despite his name, was graceless, a man with a terrible temper and no talent for small talk, but Sammy—I feel dumb even saying this—was a panic. He wore a tweed cap and painted eyeglasses, like Bobby Clarke; he could do a great double take; he laughed like a bird. He chased after girls, and liked a drink now and then, and movies and nightclubs (or so he said), and I realize that I am talking about a couple of pounds of wood, but you never met him. Sammy was a star. It was a shame he had to work with such a dullard. Imagine what he could have been with the right partner!

"Listen to me, Professor," Rocky said in my ear.

"Okay," I said, though it was hard. Grace was talking to Jack Robertson in Sammy's voice, and Robertson had hopped off the bar and coiled and hissed, "Now yeh're just mocking him." I wanted to see what would happen.

Rock kicked my calf. "First thing we do, is we work on your concentration."

"Uh-huh."

He grabbed the rim of my barstool and turned it. "Here I am." He had a cigar in his hand, which he smoked in a series of short sudden puffs. Mostly it was a prop. He brought the cigar up, parked it a quarter of an inch from his lips, and said, "Listen: I'm Annie Sullivan, and you're Helen Keller."

Another night, I thought, I wouldn't understand it, but tonight! No. Wait. I *didn't* understand it. "Sorry?"

"You're Helen Keller. We're starting from scratch. I'm going to teach you everything I know, so the first thing to do is forget everything *you* know."

"But, Rocky." I elbowed the bar in an attempt to prop myself up. "I don't *want* to be Helen Keller."

"Neither did Helen Keller, but look how well that's turning out."

"I've been around awhile," I said. Where was that bar? I kept missing it.

"I know." Rock grabbed my arm and set it on the bar for me. My stool turned and I wobbled and he caught my other elbow, and set that next to the first. Then he slung his arm around my shoulder. I could feel the heat of his cigar by my ear. "You've learned things, Professor," he said. "You're not the green kid you used to be. But you have two choices. Either you remember everything and I have to disabuse you of one fatheaded notion at a time, or starting now you develop amnesia and I don't have to talk so much."

I nodded. I had that sudden drunken belief in transformation. I was the Professor. A man of style. A *vaudevillian*.

"And another thing," he said. "You need some new suits."

I looked down to examine my jacket and gripped the lapel as tenderly as I could. Inside was the label that said *Sharp and Son's Gents' Furnishings* in black cursive. I'd worn that jacket hard, out of nostalgia and thrift: I spent my money on costumes, not street clothes.

"You are not a tramp comic," said Rocky. He took his arm back. Ashes fell like snow past my nose. "Small guy like you, it's even more important to dress the act. You gotta look sharp, Sharp."

We'd only been together for five days, and I'd already observed Rock's personal sartorial style, half vanity, half slovenliness. He had some silk ties, and some that seemed made from funeral-wreath ribbon. He owned one fine-fitting pale blue suit that made him look like a prosperous prizefighter, but he'd outgrown the rest of his clothes. Jackets pulled across his shoulders, shirts parted in a triangle above his belt. Right now he wore a windowpane tweed coat over a V-necked sweater and a pair of pale gabardine pants gone glossy at the knees. He looked like a pile of kicked-off blankets. And he was giving me advice?

Of course he was.

"Tomorrow," he said, "we'll talk timing."

Across the room Jack Robertson pounded the table and said to Archie Grace, "Sam's twice the man you'll ever be!"

Grace looked at him, then closed his eyes for a long moment. "Oh, Jesus," he said. "I *know*."

Rocky turned me back on my stool so we could watch the proceedings. "Girls," he pointed out. Yes, he was right: girls. All the flowers from the flash act had arrived, along with the Indian Rubber Maid, who sat at a table by herself. Rocky sighed. "Pretty, pretty girls. How do you talk to them, Professor?"

It might have been the drink; it might have been Rock's teacherly insults. I said, "Watch," and jumped off my perch. My knees bounced; I was lucky I didn't keep going till I was sprawled out snoozing on the floor. Go for the girl who's by herself. It's all a matter of asking the right question. This is just an act; you're just playing a part.

I arrived at the Indian Rubber Maid's table grinning. She looked at me, then looked away. I sat down in the chair across from her, and put my hands in my lap, playing shy. That is, I was a shy person pretending to be a bold person pretending to be shy. Finally she said, "Hello."

I said, "I think you're wonderful."

She smiled and revealed dimples and a set of tiny china-doll teeth. "No, you don't."

Thank God she hadn't recognized the line: it was what Sammy had said, leaning off Grace's knee, to a woman in the front row. "Now, Sammy," Grace had said, and Sammy interrupted: "But I do. I think she's wonderful." I'm not saying that every woman would fall for a strange man who'd picked up romantic tips from a ventriloquist's dummy, but there are worse ways to go about it: Believe yourself lovable, confident. Know that it's a miracle you can even talk to a girl.

"But I do," I said to the Indian Rubber Maid. "I think you're wonderful."

I could feel Rocky watch us from across the room. For his benefit—and mine, naturally—I took her plump hand in mine. She was a pretty dark-haired girl, though how she'd gotten into the contortionist racket was anyone's guess: onstage her breasts kept getting in the way; she almost had to tuck them in her armpits for the most rigorous stunts. We'd rented separate rooms, Rocky and I, at his insistence: as hail-fellow-well-met as he ever got, he needed time to himself, and besides, we could afford it. I leaned forward and suggested that she come back with me, and she nodded, still playing coy.

Then the cellar door banged open. "Hello?" Dr. Elkhorn called, his fist full of leash handles. The dogs jumped down the stairs sideways, like mountain goats.

"Buy those animals a drink on me!" said Jack Robertson, who sat on a chair across from Archie Grace's Violet, his leg thrust under her skirt. She wore on her face a sleepy-eyed expression that might have been the start of pleasure, irritation, hunger, amusement, deep thought, any number of things that look identical at the start, though unlike at the end. Grace himself was crawling across the floor toward the bathroom, muttering, "Don't get up, please don't get up."

"In America, the dogs are teetotalers," Rocky called from the bar.

You could see the long muscles in Robertson's lone leg flex. "Till now they are." Violet let one gloved hand fall to his calf.

"Do dogs drink milk?" Rocky asked Dr. Elkhorn.

"Cats drink milk," offered Robertson.

"Dogs'll drink *anything,*" Archie Grace said miserably into the floor. He'd stalled out near the back of the room.

"Milk?" said Christine, as though this were some newfangled invention.

"Scramble 'em some eggs," said Rocky. "Dogs like eggs?" he asked Dr. Elkhorn. "I'm only guessing scrambled. Poached, maybe."

Christine slammed her hand on the bar. "I am not poaching eggs for seventy-five dogs."

"You're exaggerating for no reason again. There are not seventy-five dogs. There are . . ."

And then Dr. Elkhorn let go of the leads, and it sure felt like there were seventy-five dogs. They ran under chairs, they came snuffling up to ankles. One approached Rocky and began barking, for no reason I could figure, unless he thought he'd treed some weird animal in some weird chrome-trimmed elm. Another grabbed hold of my sock, didn't pull, just bit down. One dog jumped onto a table and ran around the perimeter circus-ring style. The biggest tried to molest Archie Grace in an offhand way, as though making a pass at a crawling man was part of the theatrical canine's code. Love, I mean to tell you, was in the air. I couldn't imagine how such professionally well-behaved dogs could be so badly behaved off-duty, except to say that they were vaudevillians. In six months I would read in *Variety* that Dr. Elkhorn had poisoned those strange dogs and himself, that they'd all been found together in a hotel bed, the dogs tilting their muzzles up to their master's chin. Well, they said Elkhorn was the murderer. Maybe it was one bright angry dog.

That night some of us knew and some of us didn't, but vaudeville was sinking already. A few people made it out; a disaster always has survivors. I did, and Rocky, and Fred Allen and Burns & Allen and Cantor and Bert Lahr and Baby Rose Marie. More drowned. Where could Jack Robertson dance when vaudeville was over? Who'd hire an inept but buxom contortionist? And as for ventriloquists, there really was only room for one, and Edgar Bergen stepped in. There are memorials, as there should be, for soldiers killed in every war, for those who died in camps in the Holocaust, for those lost at sea. There should be one with the names of all those who disappeared when vaudeville finally died. Dr. Think-a-Drink Hoffman. The Cherry Sisters. Patine and Rose. Maybe the best of us survived, but I don't think so.

Now, Dr. Elkhorn clapped his hands, and the dogs suddenly sat. They didn't even pant. "Seven," said their master in a soft voice. "Scrambled will be fine."

By then I'd stood up, hand-in-hand with the Indian Rubber Maid, whose actual name I can't remember. I found her coat and helped her on with it. Across the room, Rocky raised his glass to me. Helen Keller was never so suave, I wanted to tell him, but instead, still playing the dummy-about-town, I winked and walked out into the night with a sweet tipsy girl, and that, no matter what I might later tell reporters and fans and my own curious children, is the moment I knew I would be a success in show business.

The Education of a Straight Man

A fan of Carter and Sharp—and we have them still, a fan club even—would recognize the boys in our earliest performances, but just barely. Rocky wore a suit, not his trademark striped shirt, and his voice was deeper, and though you could call him fat—plenty of people besides Freddy Fabian did—he was a mere shadow of his future self. (We had terrible fights when I could no longer lift him: was he too heavy, or was I too old? Probably we met in the middle.) My offstage moniker, Professor, was still strictly offstage. What's more, my character was a mean fop, a confidence man who saw in the poor guy an easy mark. Later I became a stern but addlepated academic.

We did our act in-one, meaning in front of the drawn curtain. Behind us, scenery shifted and scraped. Rocky threw himself around that stage, first like a feather pillow, then like a sack of potatoes, then like a ballerina who hasn't noticed she's gone to seed. Me, I stood still and smoked a cigarette and leaned against an imaginary lamppost, upright and nonchalant. When we were bored, we did dialect. Sometimes we sang, me seriously, Rock in mock opera. We did everything two young men could possibly do to make the audience remember us, but our material didn't make us funny, Rocky did.

Also, I hit him a lot.

It was called a knockabout act, and the slap was our tag, the way the audience knew when to laugh. George Burns took a puff on his cigar, Will Rogers twirled his lariat, I hit Rocky: over the head, across the face. Sometimes I delivered a kick to the seat of his pants. I hated it. Rocky insisted it was hysterical. What really amused him, though, was running into someone on the street who'd seen our show and wanted to hit *me*, for treating that fat little fella so rough.

I learned all of his gestures: the tilted head with the hand to the ear, listening; the tilted head with the clasped hands near his knees, wrist touching wrist, deep love; hands clasped behind the tilted head, one leg cocked out, an impression of the girl who inspired this passion. The man could not hold still. There he goes sliding across the apron of the stage on one knee—two knees if it's a tough crowd. There he is falling in a dead faint, because I've scared him. He hugs the proscenium arch. He hugs his straight man—briefly, because the straight man is scowling at such mush: there's serious work to be done. When all else fails, he hugs himself, so tightly it seems like his elbows have swapped sides, so needfully one leg comes around and embraces the other. He turns to look at me—he's *terrified*—and with the upstage eye, the one the audience can't see, he winks. Then he scuttles away in his own arms, limping with crossed legs. The poor little man, don't you love him, love him, love him?

A straight man is the fellow who spins the yo-yo. The yo-yo's the fun part, you keep your eye on the yo-yo, but you lose interest the minute it doesn't come back.

PROFESSOR: So here's your salad fork, your meat fork, your fish fork, your oyster fork, your salad knife, your meat knife, your fish knife, your soup spoon, your fruit spoon. What's the matter?

ROCKY: All this hardware, and nothing to stir my coffee with.

PROFESSOR: Pay attention. (SMACKS HIM) Coffee comes later.

ROCKY: Good. Can I have some cream?

PROFESSOR: Sure, sure.

ROCKY: And some sugar.

PROFESSOR: Okay, but pay attention.

ROCKY: I like sugar in my coffee.

PROFESSOR: Sure, who doesn't?

ROCKY: And a doughnut.

PROFESSOR: A doughnut?

ROCKY: A cup of coffee's sad without a doughnut.

PROFESSOR: (SMACKS ROCKY) Are you going to pay attention?

ROCKY: And maybe another doughnut.

PROFESSOR: Another doughnut?

ROCKY: To keep the first doughnut company.

PROFESSOR: You're being ridiculous.

ROCKY: Poor lonely doughnut.

PROFESSOR: Rocky!

ROCKY: I feel sad for that doughnut.

PROFESSOR: Look. You come into the dining room. Here's the beautiful table. What do you say to your hostess?

ROCKY: What, no doughnuts?

PROFESSOR: Now why would you say a terrible thing like that?

ROCKY: I don't mean to be rude.

PROFESSOR: You'll hurt her feelings, you say something like that.

ROCKY (NEAR TEARS): I'm sorry.

PROFESSOR: Okay.

ROCKY: This is the saddest story I ever heard.

PROFESSOR: What are you talking about?

ROCKY: That poor woman, and no doughnuts!

PROFESSOR: Now, look. It's time to sit down.

(ROCKY SITS. PROF SMACKS HIM.)

PROFESSOR: Not yet! There are ladies.

ROCKY: There are ladies?

PROFESSOR: Yes, there are ladies.

ROCKY: Maybe they're out back eating the doughnuts.

PROFESSOR: No, no. I mean imagine there are ladies.

(ROCKY WOLF-WHISTLES)

PROFESSOR: What's that for?

ROCKY: I got a good imagination.

Success seemed always around the corner. We got reviewed in *Variety*. We became headliners, our salaries grew, people in the business knew our names. Any minute now, we'd hit it big. We barely felt the Depression, if only because we had struggled all our working lives for jobs and lodging. *What are you complaining about?* I heard my father say. *You have a job when many do not.* I knew that. And still we wanted more. We worked and worked—winters in vaude houses, summers at beach and lake resorts. If there were a movie version of our life—there hasn't been, just a lousy TV special starring guys who looked like us if you squinted—our ten years in vaudeville would be described by all the usual clichés: the pages falling off a calendar, footage of a locomotive racing diagonally at a camera, us onstage doing the act, a spinning news-paper announcing the stock market crash or FDR's election, calendar (year change), train (other direction), stage (same old team, new cos-

tumes). I kept waiting to show up at the theater to see Rock shaking
hands with some keen-eyed straight man in a good suit. He had a history
of leaving, I had a history of being left. But he didn't: he stuck it out.

Our agent forwarded letters from Annie, who wrote me weekly letters full of news. Rocky read them aloud admiringly. "What a family you
have!" he said. "Let's visit them."

"Visit your own family," I told him.

"That's different."

"Why?"

"I'm in love with *yours*," he said, sticking the latest missive in his
pocket. We were a team: my letters were his letters. "Rose especially.
She's my dream girl—"

"You leave her alone," I said.

We played all kinds of theaters. Some small-time vaudeville took
place in mildewed tents. The audience sat on wood benches, and you
could hear them shift their weight. In the right kind of quiet you could
almost detect seats of pants prying up splinters. Applause sounds different in a tent: not so good. It doesn't have that rising, heated sound.

In real vaude houses, the velvet seats were the color of the insides of
bonbons, cherry red or yellow cream. Some houses were painted like
Versailles, some in the newest Deco designs, celluloid green trimmed in
black. Chandeliers big as bedrooms—bigger!—hung in the lobby. I liked
touring the houses themselves, sitting in the seats, pretending to be part
of the audience. The balcony was my favorite, of course: I'd never seen
vaudeville from the orchestra. Up in the cheap seats, I could hold still,
and imagine the dark, and then the girl on the horse taking the stage,
and finally, Hattie fidgeting beside me—she hates that horse, and that
fake girl covered with shoe polish to make her look Navajo—and so I
worked to take up only my rightful half of the armrest, and when I
turned and she was gone, I could pretend she'd just stalked out and was
waiting for me, fed up, in the lobby. "I got somebody you *have* to meet,"
I wanted to tell her, because Rocky made me miss Hattie more than I
had in ages, more than Miriam ever did.

"Stay out of the seats," he finally told me, when he caught me wool-
gathering there. "This isn't amateur hour. Time to stop thinking like an
audience."

Ixnay on the Uckfay

Rock talked me into drinking more than I might have, but since I went on the road I'd picked up the habit of a drink now and then. We were young, we believed all the alcohol gave us more energy. I still do. How do you stay up until five in the morning without a drink in your hand? Sober, I'd go yawning into bed after the second show, but drunk I was always up for an adventure. These adventures usually meant chasing after more booze, it's true. Where's the next drink? It's in some chorus girl's purse, and I hear she's got a crush on you, Mose, so let's go. It's in a private club downtown. It's in the backseat of a car that's driving south to Missouri, we'll get back somehow, we'll find another backseat and another bottle. One of my oldest pals in the world lives just outside town, and he's always up for something; one of my biggest fans runs a restaurant here, and so what if this is a dry county—for me it isn't, for me this county is sopping wet.

Why do you fellows drink so much, some girls wanted to know. Well, it depended on what time of day you asked us. I never drank in the morning till I teamed up with Rock, and then only sometimes, and if I hadn't been drinking too much the night before, but it was one of my favorite things, a drink before lunch, sweet brandy cut with coffee or cream. It makes you feel like a kid snowed out of school: no rules, just something syrupy to soothe your throat. You feel like your fever's breaking. You're idle but hopeful and fooling your mother, who, wherever she is, is giving you sympathy you don't deserve, the best kind. If you drink in the afternoon, you're trying to stretch the hours out. Think lazily about the dinner that will sober you up before your first show, there's plenty of day ahead of you. If you drink in the evening, when decent people drink, you're just trying to get drunk. For us, anyhow, it meant we weren't working.

We only got fired once. This was 1934, and we'd finally been booked in New York, but first we had to play Providence, Rhode Island. Rock and I were having a conversation backstage about a certain dancer in a flash act that I had just taken out between shows. There was a list posted by the stage door of all the words you weren't allowed to say inside the theater, backstage, onstage, anywhere. The manager, a hatchet-nosed high-waisted college boy, was a stickler. He had knocked on dressing-room doors after the first show with a list of changes: the aforementioned dancer had to replace her flesh-colored stockings. The monologist had to cut a joke about a softball game between the Ku Klux Klan and the Knights of Columbus. Rocky and I never worked blue; the manager warned us to keep it that way. This may have been why Rocky, in full sight of this kid, loudly asked me a question that he should have known I'd never answer.

"Did you fuck her?"

"Rocky," I said. I was a rogue, but I was a gentleman.

"Educate me, Professor," he said. "I'm a young man trying to make my way in this world. In this *particular* world. Did you fuck her?"

I saw the manager scowling at us, tapping his foot in a near parody of disapproval. A kid that young ought to know not to fasten his belt that tight. "Listen," I said to Rock, "ixnay on the uckfay."

The manager advanced on us. We'd shown our lack of class at last, he thought. Some in-one act was playing, so there were layers of velvet and canvas and comics between us and the house. *"Gentlemen,"* he said, and Rocky said, amiably, "I'm just asking my associate Professor Sharp, who is keeping company with a young lady—*that* young lady"—he found her flexing her shoulders in the wings, warming up, and pointed—"whether or not—and I think you'll find the answer educational too—he fucked her."

"Out," said the manager. "I don't care how funny you sons of bitches are supposed to be."

"Such *language*," said Rocky, tipping his prop hat.

"We'll go to the club," he told me, once we'd sent our stuff to the hotel in one taxi and climbed into a second. (I was always shocked by his willingness to hail a cab. Why not a streetcar? Why not a bracing walk? "Because we make enough money," he'd say, his fingers already on their way to his mouth for a whistle.)

"What club?" I asked. We passed a distant ostentatious white-domed building. I missed the flash-act dancer, a sweet nonsensical Polish girl who did not wear underwear of any kind; the manager had only worried about her flesh-colored stockings because he lacked imagination. She had a beautiful habit of pronouncing "think" as "sing": *I sing you are handsome. I sing you are funny.* In bed, in the coarsest language possible, she repeatedly demanded that I do to her what I thought I was already doing anyhow. We weren't at the theater, so she didn't get in trouble. I'd planned a week of meeting her between shows.

"The club," said Rocky. "My club. The Swans. What, you think we got canned by accident? I'm thirsty."

We'd been fired around 10:30; now it was 11:00. Even if I had to sleep alone, bed did not sound like such a bad idea. "Next time you get fired on purpose, could you ask me?"

"Relax. It's *Providence*. Next week we're in New York, and who'll care about Rhode Island?"

"I guess."

"Don't guess," he said. "Believe."

The club was a local chapter of some kind of vaudeville fraternity, one of those dark-doored joints with no windows, filled with smoke and drink and an exhausting forced hilarity. Some of the guys I recognized from the circuit, but Rocky seemed to be bosom pals with every last one. "This is Mike Sharp," he said, dragging me by the neck. "Be nice."

"I'm always nice," I said, and everyone laughed.

"*We* aren't," said some guy in a chalk-striped suit. There was a game of billiards going, and I watched and realized that Ed Dubuque could have made a fortune here. Also there was a cat, the president of the club I was told, and when the cat jumped up on the billiard table the game had to stop until he felt like getting down. It was a club with rules like *that*. Now I can say it: I never really cared for theater people. Theater men, anyhow. I was fond of merry oddballs like Jack Robertson the monopede dancer, or quiet geniuses like Walter Cutter. Essentially I didn't like comedians, except Rocky. I thought he was the funniest guy in the world, and there was nothing I liked less than watching him in a room full of funny guys, trying to claim his title.

The membership at the Swans had armies of ants in their pants. Every story, every bit, involved springing up at the very least, and possibly balancing on a chair or the bar or the billiard table. You had to grab sleeves or shirtfronts or pant seats; you had to feign anger or terror or a fainting spell. This crowd fainted more often than a cotillion of corseted debutantes. I wasn't the only one who noticed.

"Siddown!" said the ham-faced bartender. "Sweet Jesus, you lot are up and down like a whore's nightgown." They all applauded. He must have said this every night.

Late in the evening Rocky, pink cheeked with drink, rolled up his shirtsleeves. He leaned in and grabbed my shoulder. His breath had that gin smell, rotten sentimental flowers.

"I am going to teach you how to tango," he said.

I said, "Rocky, I hardly know you."

"Nevertheless." He suddenly scratched his nose with the flat of one palm, and then shouted, "Somebody give me a rose!" For half a second he attempted to hold a pool cue between his teeth. On the bar, the club president napped in a furry ball on top of a discarded newspaper, the tip of his tail schoolmarmishly tapping a headline. Rocky removed him— surely a breach of the club charter!—and commandeered the paper. He rolled up a sheet and artfully tore one end into petals: a rose.

"Tastes terrible," Rocky said, giving it a nibble. And then he began to dance by himself. We all pom-pommed in an Argentinean way. At first it was a joke, and then it wasn't. Rocky held the air, and you knew exactly what his imagined partner weighed. Small, especially compared to him, and so he was deferential; he danced on his toes, his feet back, to give her room. You even knew that she tried to get away from him, and then she got more forgiving and passionate. He loved her; she had a temper, she was still making up her mind. Well, I thought, this was worth getting fired for.

He tilted her into a dip. I swear I could see her hand wrinkling the back of his shirt.

Later, he showed me how to cultivate that newspaper flower. I hadn't noticed that the actual fashioning of it was part of the trick, like Charlie Chaplin making do with a shoe for dinner, two dinner rolls on forks for entertainment, a gag he'd stolen from Fatty Arbuckle anyhow. "Here," Rocky said to me. He inclined his head toward the rose that emerged from the local editorial, petal by petal, his face undisturbed, curious, watching it bloom.

The All-Girl Cure

Middling success gets exhausting, take my word for it. Rocky ate more, drank more. Fatter was funnier, so he claimed, but really he was just hungry. He couldn't get enough. He'd clean off his plate and then look at mine, hopeful. At first it was a request, but soon enough it might as well have been written into the contract: once he'd demolished his meal, he got to eat whatever was left of mine. Sometimes he ordered two meals at once, the only man for whom the fried-clam platter was a side dish. You passed an ice-cream shop with Rocky, and two doors down you suddenly realized you were walking alone. Go back, peer through the window, and there he was, instructing the help on how to lay on the whipped cream, the maraschino cherries, like a pharaoh overseeing a pyramid.

As for me, I became a ladies' man. I'd discovered the secret, which was mostly just deciding to be one. Wasn't Rocky right? I needed the practice for the act. The more girls I saw offstage, the more my timing improved: I learned the uses of the long look, the pause, the sudden twinkling smile. How could I think I knew anything about comedy, back when I knew nothing about sex? Waiter, another girl please, we're booked in Chicago next week and I have a piece of business I need to polish. What the hell, I'll take all the girls in the house. Girls like that never harmed anyone.

I spent my money on clothes, slick plaid jackets and light wool pants. In other words, I became a dandy, a religious affiliation I still cling to. I took up smoking, so I could carry a lighter and a case. I wore my hat at angles that my father would have considered a thumb in the eye of society: the way you wore your hat was not a joke. Nothing, thought my father, was more serious.

Now I was seeing lots of girls, chorines and dramatic actresses and tumblers and hoofers and soubrettes. Not all of them were as eager as the Indian Rubber Maid to come back to my room, but plenty were. Lots and lots of girls. This one smells like roses and that one smells like cake. This one knows the words to the Iowa fight song and will sing them; this one likes to drink; this shy one will surprise you by slipping the cigar from your hand and taking a puff. This one is just your size; this one is smaller; this one outweighs you in a pleasant, daunting way.

I had a lot of fun. What can I say? I made them laugh.

Rocky, though he'd seen it happen, could not understand. He loved women, but he was inept, so romantically amateurish he'd ask anyone for advice. Sometimes I watched him trying to talk to a girl. If he was sober, he came off too brisk and busy. Drunk, he bumbled, overaffectionate, a dog wanting nothing but to lay its head in your lap. He'd go to kiss a girl's hand, and she'd end up damp to the elbow. He spent endearments like nickels, called everyone Baby and Sweetheart and Darling and Little Friend and Cutie. This worked until he called the bartender Doll Baby, and the girl he had his eye on suspected that Rock's affection was for the world at large, not her in particular.

"There must be some tricks you're not telling me," Rocky would beg.

"What can I tell you?" I'd answer. "It's love."

Not that I didn't have my methods. Ever since the start of the world, girls have been told by their mothers: a certain kind of man is only after one thing. A suspicious mother is almost always right. Some guys (Rocky, for instance) believed that this meant a guy on the make should act innocent, interested only vaguely in the girl's company, and not at all in the One Thing. But girls didn't care. All you had to do was convince a girl that it was Her One Thing that you were angling for, hers and hers alone, surrounded as it was by all her charms. Of *course* you wanted to sleep with her—how will you ever get there if you don't make that clear?—it's you, my darling brunette, my beloved redhead, my most glorious bottle blonde. You with the three brothers, or the father with the butcher shop, or a love of Bach. Let me kiss you, because your butcher father writes you letters that quote Tennyson. Come back to my room, because you love Bach.

So you find your girl and sit down next to her between shows, in a restaurant, or a sitting room, or best of all a park, on a bench. Courtesy and courage. You rest your right elbow on the back of the bench, near her shoulder, make a bow of your arms, hands clasped in front, your left elbow pointing at your left hip. Maybe a bow of your legs, too, your ankle crossed on your knee. Smile as though she has just told nine tenths of a long joke that promises to be the funniest thing you ever heard, you can taste the punch line. Don't touch her, but keep close. Ask her questions. Look her in the eyes, sure, but look away, down to her lap, at her shoulder—you're either a confident man made shy by her beauty, or an emboldened shrinking violet; either transformation'll charm her. If you hold still enough, she will be the one to put her hand on your nearby knee, and then slide it closer to your hip, and then, on a good day, she will spread her overcoat across your laps. Better still, a newspaper, which will rattle but is disposable, and makes more sense as a prop. You are theatrical people, after all. Tabloids are too small: you need something respectable and full sized. You are only sitting with your girl, reading the paper together— is the right movie playing at the right theater—and you look at the paper, and then at your girl, your free hand holding your side of the daily news, and hers hers. The prim pigeons will fly away, but squirrels are worse perverts than old ladies, and will loiter. One set of her garters has come undone (Oh, you men who care nothing for fashion, let me tell you a story about the days before pantyhose!) and the pale stocking has fallen around her pale shoe on the dark grass like a ring around the moon. If you are a good actor, and a quiet careful polite boy brought up in a houseful of girls, only those local squirrels will wonder why you don't run a finger along the newsprint, why the far left columns crumple in your grip, why she folds the horoscope nearly in half, her thumb threading it between her fingers, her tongue between her teeth. Why it takes so long for the two of you to fold the paper up, neatly, as though you are making the bed.

6

Ah! It's You!

We were playing the Casino Theater at Coney Island when Rocky became enamored of a nearsighted chanteuse named Penny O'Hanian, a pretty girl with a great deal of nut-brown hair who specialized in love-gone-wrong songs. Maybe she was just a good singer, but despite a thin voice she sounded like she meant every stepped-on word. Her eyesight was so bad (she refused to wear glasses) that she had to sidle stage right and feel for the curtain with her fingers. Then she whipped it around herself like a cape—that was her exit—and whipped it back for her bow. Sometimes in the whirlwind of velvet, she nearly toppled over.

Even backstage, she made noise: she sang under her breath so people would know she was coming. Years later, when I heard about the way bats navigate, I thought of Penny, singing out as she groped her way through life. She fixed on her face a standoffish expression because she didn't want to smile at strangers, and you could get quite close to her before she could make out your features, and this was her charm. The minute you came into focus, Penny would suddenly look delighted, relieved, nearly heartsick. *Just the person I was longing to see!* She'd grab you by the forearm. She wouldn't let go.

You had to love Penny for that, and Rocky did. He never noticed that she did it to everyone she knew.

"She's adorable," he told me.

"She is," I answered, and I thought, Right up until she opens her mouth. I found her—forgive me, Penny, I didn't know you well then—maddening. Completely. She couldn't shut up. Spending time with Penny was like walking into a crowd of chickens: that noisy and that meaningful. Or like she'd been having a conversation with herself all day, and there was no way you'd catch up. Rocky, no mean talker himself, watched her babble, happily shaking his head. He started keeping company with her. At least I think he did. It was hard to tell. Maybe *I* was keeping company with her. All I knew was that for a week at the Casino, followed by a week at Loew's Majestic in the Bronx, then finally in Manhattan at the Eltinge (named after the famous female impersonator), she was around all the time, at dinners, in taverns. She'd reach out and snag one of our forearms and say, brightly, "Where will we dine tonight, boys?" I'm still not convinced that Penny wasn't just desperate for a couple of seeing-eye friends. It must have been a great relief to her not to totter into a burlesque house thinking it was a department store.

For instance: at a midtown chop house, Rocky was telling a story about Julian Eltinge, the theater's namesake: he'd once punched Rocky in the nose.

"Why?" I asked.

"He thought I made a comment about his virility."

"Did you?"

Rocky looked theatrically sheepish. "No. No words were exchanged at all."

"So why did he hit you?"

"I patted him on the keester. I thought it was a compliment, from one professional to another."

"What a beautiful dress," Penny said.

We had manners, we were game: we looked around to see what dress Penny meant.

"The one I saw Eltinge in," she said. "He was fat already, but, my God! I wish I looked that good." Then she said to Rocky, "I mean, you've never patted *my* keester."

"I'm a gentleman," Rock explained. "That was my problem: so was Eltinge."

"I could use a nice dress." Penny sighed. "I like blue." Then, moments later, "I like cut flowers in a vase." She sensed movement in the room, and called out to the man who was approaching our table, "I could use a fresh napkin."

The guy in question was a tall blond young man in a tan suit with oversized shoulder pads and a dizzying checked yellow tie. The waiters, on the other hand, were all puny Jewish fellows in short red jackets and black bow-ties. "Couldn't we all?" the guy said amiably, and kept on going toward the Gents'.

"Was that the maître d'?" Penny asked.

I laughed. "For Pete's sake, Penny, why don't you get glasses?" Maybe I was just a glasses snob, having gotten my first pair at age twenty-five. I admired myself in the mirror constantly, though I don't know whether that was because they suited me or because I hadn't clearly seen my own face for several years. Or because I had also just purchased my first toupee, and I was working on not noticing it.

"I don't need them," Penny said. Then, to Rocky, as if I'd suggested she should wear a mask to cover her puss, she said, "Mike thinks I should get glasses!"

He said, "Not till we're married, sweetheart," and slapped me heartily on the back.

That was a joke, I was sure. He thought she was pretty sweet—it was all he could do to resist picking her up and carrying her around so she wouldn't bump into things—but he wasn't even sleeping with her. I thought he should give it a try. Penny was so eccentric, not to mention free with her fingers, that it would at least have been an interesting experience.

Niagara Falls the First Time

Penny saw us off at Penn Station—we were headed for Buffalo, then Canada, the first time I'd ever leave the States. She stood on the platform and waved at all the passing windows, just in case someone she knew was on the other side, waving back.

"Nice girl," I said to Rocky, hoping for some information. He shrugged, and shouldered his suitcase onto the luggage rack.

"Very nice girl," I said again.

He nodded absentmindedly. "Listen," he said suddenly. "I want to stop and see Niagara Falls. We'll go?"

"I guess."

"You *guess*?"

"Water running downhill," I said. If he was bored by Penny, I was bored by some dog-legged river. "What's the big to-do?"

"You'll see. Don't play jaded, kid. It doesn't become you."

He was right. Good God: I'd only known the Falls as part of that old bit. In real life the river poured and poured and poured, rainbows woven in at the bottom, the giant plume of mist floating up, water giving into gravity and then finding a loophole. I could see how the mere memory could drive someone insane. I felt unstable myself.

"Rocky," I said in wonder. "Why don't they take a *breath?*"

"They don't have waterfalls in Iowa?" he asked casually.

I didn't know the answer to that. Anyhow, it sure wasn't Duluth.

There was a guy there who engraved drinking glasses with names. He used a pneumatic drill tipped with a diamond, and the glass chips rained down, beautiful as the diamond, beautiful as the finished glass, beautiful as the Falls themselves. I thought about getting one, but didn't know whose name to put down. In my father's house, there were seven ruby glass cups, souvenirs of some fair from some cousin, one for each of us living kids, our names and birth dates written on the side. By now my sisters had plenty of children whose names might be engraved in glass by a fond uncle; Annie, my dogged correspondent, had cataloged them for me. I fingered a bill in my pocket.

"C'mon," said Rocky. "Let's go."

Souvenirs everywhere, mostly for the fabled visiting newlyweds and their spendthrift sentiment. I examined reverse-glass painted brooches, change purses made of tiny seashells, etched aluminum cups. We stood on the Canadian side of the border and Rocky read aloud from a pamphlet about all the people who'd ever gone over the Falls in a barrel. Not all of the barrels were barrels: one guy rode over in a giant rubber ball, another in a tin ship that crumpled like foil on the river below.

"Here's someone," said Rocky. " 'His capsule bounced behind the great curtain of the Falls, out of the reach of rescuers. Despite all efforts to save him, Stathakis suffocated behind the rush of water.' "

"Well, then he lived longer than he deserved to."

"You wouldn't go over?" Rocky asked. "You'd be a hero if you lived."

I turned to him. The wind had pulled his hair into chunks. He looked at the Falls as though they were a particularly worthy adversary, and I decided not to tell him that in June of 1927 I'd lost my stomach for acts of pointless, gravity-tempting bravery. That man who starved had had a family, and they'd never forgiven him for what he'd done.

"We're booked for weeks," I said. "Please don't go over Niagara Falls in a barrel."

"Well, if that's how you feel, I won't. Otherwise I'd go. Coverage in all the papers whether you make it or not. Rubber. Big rubber enclosed ball. It'll bounce, it'll float, it'll be watertight. Made of old girdles, maybe: nothing can get through a girdle. And can you imagine the view?"

"Yes," I said. "I can imagine it right here where I'm standing, thanks."

For his sake I tried to see it: the tiny enclosed ship, a single window for its single passenger. Furtively, you bring it to the top floor of the Falls. You look around for the authorities, set it in the water, and anchor it to shore. You get in. Any minute you'll be facing your death, but right now, even though the current is knocking you around, you can think: any leaks? No. Breathe in. Pull the anchor from the shore. Shoot forward.

Stare out the window to the spot where the bottom drops out of the river. What's that: fear? Exhilaration? Belief that God has time to save idiots like you, when everywhere people die through no fault of their own? No, He'd wash His hands of you, here was the sink He'd do it in.

What you think, just before you plummet: *You know, I'm sure the view is actually much better from dry land.*

Back to New York to play the boroughs. In my spare time, I picked up girls. If I ran into a girl I'd slept with, it was like I had to bed her again, to make sure she still thought I was a nice guy. The ones who'd changed their minds made me crazy, though almost none of them did. Two or three, maybe, and they'd married, and even then that didn't seem like a good excuse. I tried flowers, songs, whatever might work. One recently wed former paramour said, "Why me? There are plenty of girls," and I scratched my head and said, "You know? You're right," and let go of her hand and fairly skipped off.

That worked.

I'd always been taught that love went something like this: There is a girl out there for you, and you find her, and then you work endlessly to keep love around. "Your parents loved each other, Mose," my father told me more than once, "better love because harder work." And so I came to understand: love is an animal that can—with a great deal of patience—be taught to sleep in the house. That doesn't mean it won't kill you if you're not careful.

Really, do you want it in your house?

Maybe I liked some of those girls better than others. A girl named Gwen, maybe, and an Italian girl named Carlotta. Maybe sometimes I was glad to get away, and other times not, but mostly I remember being full of love while lying down with every girl, and then less so when I stood up to leave, as though my brain was a bowl tilted to collect a stingy serving of something that, when I was upright, drained to my feet, where it did no good.

But before then I felt swell, I felt fine, I felt perfectly cheerful. The cure for unhappiness is happiness, I don't care what anyone says. The guys in vaudeville, they took all sorts of cures, you only had to watch what they ran to first thing in the morning to ease the last bits of their night terrors: a bottle, a needle, a bookie, a Western Union office, a stage, a wife, a child, a giant meal, a strange pretty girl. Would we be ashamed later? Sure. These days, when shamefulness and shamelessness are both sins, I don't know how people operate. Back then, only shamelessness was: we were ashamed, and so we buried ourselves in the thing that shamed us, because it was the only thing that might make us feel better. And then we repented. And then, flush with repentance, we sinned again.

Tansy's Discovery

Carter and Sharp were weary. Vaudeville wheezed all around us, milking its deathbed scene worse than, well, a vaudevillian. By 1937 we played as many nightclubs as vaude houses. Summers we worked in the Catskills or out near the Minnesota lakes. It got so Rocky wouldn't go to a movie or listen to the radio. He couldn't stand all those guys with less talent than us who nevertheless got big breaks.

And then we met Buddy Tansy.

We were in New York again, playing a run-down theater in the Bronx that had quit booking vaude acts in the early thirties in favor of movies, and was now adding a few performers to warm up the audience before the pictures. I think we opened for *The Good Earth*. The dressing rooms were in the basement and smelled like one hundred years of trained-dog acts. When we walked into ours after the show, there was a tiny man sitting on the old daybed, reading a newspaper. He squinted at us when we came in.

"I'm Buddy Tansy," he said, trying to wrestle the paper to the ground. It seemed to be getting the better of him.

"Good for you!" said Rocky.

"I want to represent you."

"We have representation," I said, reaching past him for my case. After the act Rock was cheerful and filled with the milk of human kindness. I was filled with a burning need to hit the cold cream. The towel by the sink had, like the shroud of Turin, the impression of someone's face.

"I'm better," said the little man unconvincingly.

"So talk to us, Buddy Tansy," said Rocky. "Tell us how you will change our life."

"Really? You won't be sorry. You sure?" He wrung his hands, as if this invitation was too much to bear.

Rocky and I weren't tall men, but Tansy was minuscule. He had the exasperated dignity of a man who'd spent his life being shut up in dumbwaiters and theatrical trunks as a gag. I'd never had such leanings in my life, but even *I* wanted to find out what unlikely place I could cram Tansy into. His given name was Edward, and he tried to get people to call him Buddy, but everyone called him Tansy, an elf of a name for an elf of a man. He hated it. Good old Tansy. He had a small head with small features, and pointed teeth that showed when he smiled, which made him look nervous and cornered. All in all, he resembled some avid little animal, one who'd spend all its time nibbling on things it shouldn't—the lettuce in your garden, the wiring under your house.

"I want to get you boys famous," he said to us in that Bronx dressing room. "I want to do great things for you."

"Yeah?" Rocky said. "How."

Tansy bared his teeth; we didn't know that was his smile. He hopped off the daybed and sat on the counter in front of the mirror. "I know some people. I could get you in a Broadway show."

"Really," I said.

"I don't know about Broadway," Rocky said. "Right now, we can work all year round if we want. That's secure. A Broadway show closes, and we're out of a job."

"Nothing's secure," said Tansy. "But I could get you a thousand a week."

"We get that," said Rocky.

"A*piece*," said Tansy. "You'd each get a thousand."

No, I thought, I'd get eight hundred and Rocky would get twelve. Still, it was quite a bit more than we had been making—which, by the way, was not a thousand dollars. Well, as far as I knew, it wasn't.

"Minus ten percent," said Rocky.

Tansy showed us his alarming teeth again. "I have to eat." He looked at me. "But I'll earn you more than the extra ten. I'm good."

"Yes," I said.

Rocky turned and looked at me—what was I doing, making a decision? Rocky handled those, and career ambition, and nearly everything. For the first time I saw something he'd left out, something he'd failed to aspire to.

"Broadway," I said helplessly. I hadn't realized it until this very second, but I'd always wanted to play Broadway. I'd only dreamt of vaudeville because it seemed possible. There hadn't been Broadway in Iowa.

Rocky whistled. "Broadway, huh? Okay, little one." He patted Tansy's shoulder. "Whatever jobs you find us, ten percent."

Tansy nodded seriously. "I'll send you the paperwork. You won't be sorry. You want movies?" he said, as though offering coffee.

"Sure," said Rocky, as though offered coffee while longing for something stronger.

Within a week Tansy asked us out to dinner at his favorite joint, a dark Italian restaurant in midtown called DelGizzi's, famous for a series of bloodred murals of fairy-tale characters done by a hungry artist who'd always been short of cash. Tansy was already at a booth in the back when we came in. He'd made sure to arrive early; he probably figured he looked taller when he was sitting down, and he was the one man in the world for whom this might be true. He'd chosen the wrong painting to sit in front of, though: Cinderella seemed about to snuff him out with the heel of her glass slipper. "Over here, boys," Tansy said. "Sit down, sit down, this meal's on me. So. There's a Broadway show, maybe. What I want to do is book you into Grossinger's as part of a revue. Money's not great, but the backers of the Broadway revue will see you there, and by October you'll make your debut in the legitimate theater."

Rock perused the menu like it was his family tree. "If I wanted to play the Catskills for no money," he said, "I could book myself."

"Aw, come on!" said Tansy. "Fellas! Don't you trust me?"

"I do," I told him.

"See?" he said to Rock. "The kid trusts me."

Rocky shook his head and gave me a dirty look. Clearly I was drunk with power. "What's the Broadway show?"

"Oh, *they* don't even know yet. The Grossinger's revue's kind of an old burlesque thing. Up your alley, right? Old times, right? And here's how sure I am," said Tansy, looking more terrified than competent, "if it goes wrong, I'll give you back my commission. I'll write you a check."

Rock tossed his menu to the far side of the table. "How's about this: We don't pay you in the first place, and if it goes okay, we write you a check."

"Oh," said Tansy.

"No," I said, thinking Broadway, Broadway! "Rocky, we'll do it. Tansy, we'll do it."

"If it goes wrong," said Rocky, "you're *both* writing me a check."

It was just as Tansy foretold: we played Grossinger's and important people saw us. Now, instead of being ignorant of the act, they were merely skeptical.

Radio people said we were too visual. Movie people said we were too verbal. Broadway backers declared our comedy too low. *Low comedy*, two words I despise. The only thing worse is *light entertainment*. Still, we got a reputation in the city, which meant we could work nightclubs exclusively. Mayor La Guardia had been closing the burlesque houses, and dozens of comedians were out of work. We couldn't play the clubs forever. We didn't know what would happen to us.

But the guy who booked the Rudy Vallee radio show thought we might have something. Vallee went up against Kate Smith, the First Lady of Radio, who'd recently cozied up to Abbott and Costello (after having been burned by Bert Lahr, who'd flattened her with his ad libs). Vallee's booker didn't like low comics himself, but he saw how they went over with the audience, both live and listening in—Vallee's show had introduced Joe Penner, of Wanna buy a duck? fame, though Penner's fame had pretty much peaked by 1937.

We were summoned for another dinner at DelGizzi's. This time when we walked in, Tansy was already sitting next to a giant man who wore a pair of tiny glasses. What a bad idea, I thought, to have such a fleshy face with those glasses: they looked ready to sproing off his face if he raised his eyebrows. His hair was already sproinging, his pomade no match for his cowlicks. Lucite wouldn't have been a match for Neddy Jefferson's cowlicks. He looked like a cartoon of FDR, with a face bunched up between the wide plains of his jaw and forehead.

"This is Neddy," Tansy says. "He's your writer."

Who knew we had a writer? Who knew we needed one?

Neddy was the most neurotic guy I ever met, which is saying something. A smaller guy might have ripped handkerchiefs and scraps of paper to bits; Neddy destroyed steno notebooks and entire packs of cigarettes in seconds, tearing them apart. He was always turning something to confetti. He didn't laugh. If you told a joke he thought was a keeper, he nodded. "That's good," he'd say. "That'll go over." He and Tansy were great pals, both similarly obsessed with comedy without either one having a visible knack for it. They talked about the big laugh the way Pierre and Marie Curie must have discussed radium. Together, they looked like an old portrait of an inbred Spanish king and the court dwarf. They were with us till the end, those two. I miss them both.

Neddy was a scholar. He owned every joke book ever written, from Joe Miller to Clason's Budget Book, and his talent was for rewriting jokes and bits. With Neddy on the payroll, Carter and Sharp hit the boards with comedy unseen since the sixteenth century. "Nobody's ever played it in pants," was how Neddy put it, if asked if a sketch was brand new.

How could we complain? Though ad-libbing was giddy fun, doing the same bits over and over was only good if you were obscure. What if we were a hit and Vallee asked us back? We wanted to go on with "Why Don't You Sleep?" but Neddy convinced us it was too visual. Instead we went with a sketch we'd been doing for years called "Love Advice," in which Rocky had broken up with a girl and I tried to talk him into getting back on the horse, so to speak. Neddy shored it up for us.

PROF: So your girl left you. What do you want to do?

ROCKY: What I'd like to do is: put on my best coat—

PROF:—yes—

ROCKY: A nice pair of shoes.

PROF:—yes—

ROCKY: Some swell cologne.

PROF: Of course.

ROCKY: And climb under a rock and die.

PROF: That's no good. What do you want? You want your girl to come back in town some day and say, "Hey. I wonder whatever happened to Rocky," and have somebody tell her, "See that well-dressed, sweet-smelling boulder over there? Lift it up and you'll see."

ROCKY: Depends. What does she say after that?

Other than the complaints about not being able to tell our voices apart, we were a hit, and got asked back in two weeks, and we did "Why Don't You Sleep?" despite Neddy's misgivings. Rudy Vallee, the Vagabond Lover, sang, "Let's Put Out the Lights and Go to Bed" (except of course he had to change "bed" to "sleep" for the censors). Leaning over the mike, Rocky added a few percussive, national snores. Me, I kept quiet. I suffered from terrible mike fright, worse than any stage fright I ever had, because where was my voice going? I imagined it swelling electric wires all the way to Valley Junction, where it would switch on the radio like a poltergeist and demand to be heard. "Mose?" my father would say, but my voice—now separate from my body and making its own bad decisions—would dial up the volume and natter on.

Still, radio was easy. All I had to carry were my script and my nerves. "Don't flutter," Vallee said to me kindly while the announcer did a commercial for Fleischmann's yeast; Vallee's show was *The Fleischmann's Hour.* I thought he meant that somehow my shaking body was audible over the airwaves, but he pointed at my script. That was good: something to concentrate on.

Pretty soon we were regulars on the Vallee show, we who'd never done anything regularly in our lives. And soon after that, we were called into DelGizzi's again, this time to a booth in front of the three little pigs, pink bellied and blithe despite the smell of seasoned pork chops in the air. Tansy played dumb for the first half of dinner, but then he couldn't contain himself.

"You doubted me," he said.

"We never doubted you," said Rocky.

"You doubted me," Tansy repeated. He was trying his best to look downtrodden, but he giggled. In fact, he couldn't stop.

"What is it, little one?" Rocky asked.

Tansy was steering his steak around his plate with a fork. "Broadway," he managed to squeak out. "A revue. In the spring."

Rocky reached out with his own fork and stopped Tansy's steak. They sat there a moment, fork to fork, and Rocky gave a whoop, and speared the steak and brought it to his own plate, where in celebration he began to carve it in thirds the way a dreaming general slices a map of enemy territory.

"Tansy!" I said, because it was all I could think of. "Tansy!" My first instinct was to run to the phone and call—well, who? Annie. Miriam. My father. Hattie, who would have been flat-out stunned. It was the first sudden success I'd ever had that didn't involve a girl.

Rocky said to Tansy, one hand over his heart, "We never doubted you." He put a piece of meat on my plate and a piece on Tansy's and began eating what was left, as though through this ritual he and I, like the little man with the pointed teeth, would be able to see into the future.

How We Became The Boys

The Money Show, like our Grossinger's appearance, was a burlesque-style review—one of those shows that was like *Hellzapoppin'* but wasn't *Hellzapoppin'.* Some dancing, some singing, a couple of knockabout comedians. We had two bits, a comic skit and a song-and-dance number in which I played a cop trying to arrest a comely young lady who was, of course, Rocky in drag, trying to escape a couple of mobsters. Rocky didn't like the song we were given, so he rewrote the lyric. It was called, "Stop! You're Under Arrest." I still sing it around the house:

ROCKY: But aren't you married?

MIKE: Aw, she's an old battle-ax.
             I'll keep you in diamonds
             I'll keep you in Cadillacs
             I'll keep you in caviar
             Up to your elbas.

ROCKY: What, no dessert?

MIKE: A dozen peach melbas!

ROCKY: Officer, darling,
                You're sweet, I'll confess,
                But I'm spoken for—

MIKE: —Stop!
                You're under arrest!

Plenty was different, now that we were in a show with actual backers, but the best of it were the costumes. My cop's uniform was real, not
a dark suit dressed up with silver buttons. Rocky's dress was heavy cotton accented with black lace. Beneath it he wore a kind of padded union
suit to make him curvy.

"Wouldn't you marry me?" he asked, swooning at himself in the mirror. Though he'd already applied his giant red lipstick and his giant red
wig, all he wore was his voluptuous undersuit.

"Well," I said, "I'm thinking it over. No."

He put down his powder puff. "Why not?" he asked, hurt.

"Because you're too good for me, sweetheart."

He blew me a kiss.

How long had it been since either of us had stayed anywhere for
more than a month? What luxury, to really live somewhere. We got
apartments in the same building on East Sixty-fourth Street—nothing
grand, just one-room places in a turn-of-the-century building with a
view of the river. I unpacked my suitcase, went to see movie matinees,
ordered telephone service in my own name. By now Penny and Rocky
were an absolute item. She came backstage after the show every night,
trying to find Rock. It must have been an unpleasant surprise for Penny
to make out, down the hall, the blurred figure of a dowager, only to discover upon her arrival that it was in fact her steady beau. "I don't like
you like this," she said.

"Why not, darling?" Rocky put his arm around her and patted his siz-
able bosom. "You scared? Just rest your head here and tell me all about
it." He kissed her cheek. She scowled and tried to scrub the lipstick off
with her knuckles.

"What's the matter?" he asked. "I thought you liked female imps. You
liked Eltinge, didn't you?"

She tried to pull off his wig, but he wouldn't let her. "Eltinge," she
hissed, "didn't look like my *mother*."

The Money Show tried out in Providence and opened in New York in the middle of September 1938. The show was a modest hit, but Carter and Sharp, all the reviews said, were a real find—Rocky Carter never played his scenes the same way twice, and Mike Sharp kept up with every turn he took. Brooks Atkinson said we were the only reason to go. Between that and spots on the Vallee show and a few late-night club gigs, we did pretty well for ourselves. Before 1938, if we'd broken up, nobody would have noticed. Now we were The Boys. That's what people called us. Where are The Boys? The Boys are headlining at the Steel Pier next month. The Boys won't work for less than two thousand a week.

We had more money that we'd ever had in our lives. Rocky spent every dime, on fresh flowers for his buttonhole, on good suits and good food and drinks for everyone in the house, no matter what the house was. Rocky loved gratitude. Gratitude from strangers was even better. *The Money Show* closed after two months, but we didn't care. We'd been called to California, by a big studio, for a *feature*.

"We'll stop in Valley Junction this time," said Rocky. I was helping him pack up his apartment, which in two months he'd managed to fill with outgrown-clothes and half-eaten sandwiches. He was rewarding himself for his industry by taking sips from a silver flask that Penny had given him.

"No," I said. "Are you saving these magazines?"

"Why," he asked, "are you so pigheaded about this? You got a family who loves you. I want my sixty percent of that love. Course, I'm willing to take all of my cut of the love from Rose—"

"Stop that. I'm not pigheaded. I want . . ." Even talking about going to Valley Junction terrified me. My fear, I know now, was a brand of homesickness so thorough you feel helpless, and so want to stay away from the thing that infected you in the first place.

I've lived a long time, and so people ask if longevity runs in the family. Now I can say yes: my sister Annie lived to be more than a hundred, my sister Sadie ninety-two. Various nieces and nephews who are about my age still walk the earth, and by walk I mean actually *walk*. But if you'd asked in 1939, I would have said no, sadly. My mother had died young; so had Hattie. I did not know any forebears other than my parents and Rabbi Kipple, and I always thought of Rabbi Kipple as exactly the age he was in his portrait, in his forties. Everyone else was dead;

everyone else had died before I was born; therefore, everyone else had died young.

When I'd left town more than ten years before, I'd reconciled myself to the fact I'd never see my father again. My sisters, I figured, would show up in my life eventually. They'd come to a show, or I'd walk into a train car and there one would be, or—this was most likely—I'd get a telegram informing me of my father's death and if I got it in time and wasn't on one of the coasts, I'd go to the funeral. But my father would die. Who survived old age?

Sometimes I thought: surely he's dead by now, and nobody's told me. Then I'd get a letter from Annie, bless her heart, filling me in on the news of the family. How could it be that a man who died in my head once a month could live so long? Understand: I wanted him to live forever. Thinking about his death was how I punished myself. Heartless boy (I would always be a boy in my father's presence) to have left a father who loved you. Heartless brother, to leave your sisters weeping in the parlor. People in Valley Junction knew my mother, but they *loved* my father. I imagined the back steps piled high with offerings. Soon the steps would fill, and the neighbors would hang the branches with tureens of soup. They'd line up as many pound cakes as would fit on windowsills. There's a loaf of bread in the mailbox. There are pies in the bushes, their meringues dusted with snow. Someone has slipped a stack of pancakes under the doormat. Candy like fallen leaves lies in heaps everywhere, everywhere.

But he didn't die. Over and over he didn't die.

Now Rocky shook his flask at me. "I've already cabled them," he said. "I signed your name. It's all set."

"Oy *vey*," I said. My hands and feet began to prickle with fear. "No—"

"You've already said yes. You can't just change your mind. You promised me."

"When did I ever—"

"We were thirty-two miles southeast of Chicago, sitting in the dining car of the Wolverine. You said, 'Next time. I promise.' It's next time. You *promised*. Me, and now the rest of the Sharenskys."

"Goddamn your memory." I massaged my eyebrows, which for some reason usually calmed me. "Rocky. Rocky. I'll—"

"Don't break our hearts, Mosey," he said quietly.

I sighed. He had me. It was one thing not to go home; it was another thing to say I would and then not show up, even though I *hadn't* said I would. I sat down on the sofa. Something broke beneath the cushion—a plate, maybe. I held out my hand for the flask. "Okay. Good God. Why on earth? I guess we could."

"Sure!" said Rock. "And I'll stay in a nice hotel—the Corn Cob Arms, that the best one?"

"The Fort Des Moines," I said.

"The Fort Des Moines. And maybe you can invite poor *goyishe* me over for dinner so I can meet your sisters. I've been dreaming about those sisters for a while now. I mean, I'd never be unfaithful to Rose, but I'd like to get a gander at the whole sorority. How many are there? Thirty-six?"

"Five," I said.

He said, "Annie-Ida-Fannie-Sadie-Hattie-Rose."

"Five living sisters," I said, "and three of those are married."

He took back his flask and toasted. "Many a fine woman is."

7

An Orphaned Girl Is Hard to Marry

Rocky and I got separate sleepers for our trip West. "No more berths for us!" he declared. In Chicago, we'd change for the the Rock Island Rocket.

"You'll get off in Des Moines," I said, consulting the timetable in the dining car. "And I'll—"

"We'll both get off in West Des Moines," Rock said.

"There is no West Des Moines," I explained, but there it was in print, the next stop after Rock Island Station, right where Valley Junction should be.

"Annie *wrote* you," said Rocky. "They changed the name last year. And I'm coming with you."

"That's not—"

"Yes, it is. First West Des Moines née Valley Junction. Then I'll investigate the fleshpots of Des Moines, and you'll reconvene with your sisters." He thought I'd bolt. I'd keep going west till I got to Nebraska.

You would have thought he was the one going to meet his family, whom he loved. In the dining car he wondered what Annie would cook.

"Green beans," I said. "And cookies that taste like pencil drawings of cookies."

"I can't wait." He sighed. "And to see little Rose, all grown up. Do you think she'll remember me? Do you think she's been true?"

"Rocky."

"Little Rose Sharensky. I do love that girl. . . ."

"Why did you do this to me?" I asked. I swiveled to sit sideways in the booth, then got a little motion sick and swiveled back.

"You're not mad, are you? You're going home a hero!"

"Of course I'm mad," I said. "I don't want to do this. You're making me."

"You know what I've never understood about you?" said Rocky. "I'm being serious now. Tell me why you left home."

"You know why," I said.

"Okay, so let me tell you why *I* left home. My father once beat me because I left my homework on the sofa."

My father, a shopkeeper, wanted me to inherit his store.

"My mother once refused to talk to me for three weeks because she thought I'd taken more than my share of sugar. I was eleven," said Rocky.

My father wanted me to work beside him every day, to be his right-hand man.

"My parents once went on a research trip to Ontario. They left me at home with a list of things not to touch. I was nine."

My sisters wanted to see me become, like my father, a pillar of the community. They wanted me to marry a nice Jewish girl and have children and never leave Iowa.

"My mother told me I had ruined her education. My father told me I had ruined my mother. My mother said she hated the sight of me. My father said he despised my voice."

My family worried, worried, worried about me, until I couldn't breathe.

"And you know what? We write. We talk on the phone. They can't stand me and I love them, and what's kept me on the road is that someday they'll go into a movie theater and see my face and maybe for a moment think, Look at the kid! Who *wouldn't* love him? But you," he said.

"Me."

"You ran away from home because your family loves you too much!"

I tried to smile at every single person in the dining car: Nothing wrong here, folks. An olive-skinned girl in a violet blouse gave me a sympathetic look before turning to gossip with her friends. I wanted to go and join them. "Sshh. That's not it."

"Right, right, right, your sister died and she would have been a star and you made a promise and you'll kill yourself to keep it. But she never would have made it in vaudeville, you know that."

"Rocky—"

"Look, I'll leave Hattie alone. She's dead, she's wonderful—I'm sorry, it's just that your cowardice on this subject, it gives me a headache. I don't understand it. And the reason I sent that cable was because I knew—don't fool yourself, I know everything about you, I know every stupid secret—is that once you see your sisters and your father and that store, which, I assure you, you have escaped for all time, you will be happier and less fearful. And that will make me happier. And possibly less fearful. For Christ's sake," he said bitterly, "I'm tired of your moods."

He pushed away his china dinner plate and glared at me. There was a trail of grease down his shirt from where he'd dropped a piece of ham steak. Then he got up from the table. "Please, Professor," he said. "Don't fuck this up for me." He turned and left for his sleeper.

I didn't know this before, but it is comparatively easy to pick up a girl in a dining car if she sees you being bullied by a fat man, even if she doesn't speak English.

In the morning he was contrite. He knocked on the door of my room—the sympathetic Portuguese girl (I think she was Portuguese) had gone back to her friends before dawn—with a plate of scrambled eggs in his hands, which he managed to eat standing up, despite the train's shimmying. "I got things on my mind," he said. "I don't mean to take them out on you."

"What things?" I asked.

He waved his fork dismissively in the air. "You know. Everything. I just don't want you to worry. You'll see your family. We'll have a nice meal. Rose and I will make our wedding plans. Then we'll all go out to California and make movies."

"All of us?"

"Sure. Annie play the oboe or something? We'll find a spot for her. She'll give ZaSu Pitts a run for the money. We'll invite all the Sharps into the act."

That's what I was afraid of.

We stepped off the train into an ice-blue afternoon. There would have been frost on the ground that morning. West Des Moines, huh? It was as though Valley Junction had been forced into a bad marriage, and decided to put on a brave face. I was wearing one of my old Sharp's Gents' suits out of nostalgia and realized, for the first time, that I'd gotten a little taller and a little wider since I'd left. My wrists hung out of the sleeves and the wind bit at them.

"Okay," I said. "Come on."

I looked up Fifth Street.

"Well?" said Rock.

"Strangest thing," I said. "Store's not here."

"It moved."

"What? It was right here—" I pointed at a dubious-looking restaurant.

"It *moved*," Rocky said. "Do you even read Annie's letters? Five years ago, your old man moved the store. Come on." He grabbed the back of my coat and towed me up the street till we got to the slightly more genteel two-hundred block, my suitcase bouncing against my leg. Our trunks had been sent on to California. That's what a small town it was, one block and you were in a better neighborhood. There was the store. Across the new window painted letters spelled, *Sharp and Son's*, which broke my heart and made me happy.

The Depression hadn't missed Valley Junction. Ten years after the crash the town looked rearranged and abandoned. The Rock Island line had moved its roundhouse. The trains still came through, but few of them stopped. No good to the town unless they stopped. The men who'd banked with my father were smart. Old Man Sharp paid no interest, but he charged no fees and he'd never fold.

The new store was clean, with linoleum floors and bright hanging light fixtures and signs on the walls that pointed out departments, if you could call them that: *Shoes, Suits, Hats*. They'd kept the sliding iron ladders, I was glad to see, and the big front counter, and the man who stood behind the counter, his hands held an inch above the glass top.

"Well, good grief," Ed Dubuque said to me. "The fatted calf has come home."

"I don't think it's the calf that comes home," I said, but he was already throwing his long puppetish arms around my neck. Ed's hair had thinned and his face had picked up a few lines, but then so had mine, so had mine. He looked wonderful. Did I have to go to the house? Couldn't the three of us spend the afternoon in a pool hall, drinking beer and making bets?

"I hear you're a star of stage and screen, Master Sharp," he said.

"Stage, I guess," I said, "and not a star. Other than that, you've got it right. Is my father here?"

He gave me a head-swinging appraisal, his forearms still resting on my shoulders. "No," he said. "He doesn't come in anymore. He's not at home?"

"We're on our way there. Never comes in?"

Ed grimaced and smiled at the same time. "He's ninety. He's not so good, Mose. Figured that's why you were here."

"It is why," said Rocky from the back of the store, where he was leafing through a stack of folded shirts. He walked over to the counter to shake Ed's hand. "Pleased to meet you—Ed? I'm Rocky Carter, Mose's partner."

"A pleasure," said Ed.

Rocky clapped his hands together. "So. Let's go. Let's go to six twenty-five Eighth Street and see your father."

"You know the place?" Ed asked.

"Oh," said Rocky, "I imagine I'll know it when I see it."

Ed turned to me. "Master Sharp," he said delicately. "Your suit."

"You recognize it?"

Ed inclined his head in sorrow. "You can't see your father like that." He fingered the lapel, which was shredding at the edges. He was right: nothing would count if my father thought I looked shabby. Well, I had a suitcase full of fine clothes, I'd just go in the back and change—but Rocky, always helpful, had started undressing a mannequin who leaned in the doorway in the back.

"We can find something—" Ed began. He must have thought I was down on my luck, dressed as I was.

"No," I said. "Rock's right. I'll wear what that guy's wearing." So we stripped the dummy of his herringbone jacket and I put it on, and Rocky and I set out.

At least the house was where we'd always kept it, at Eighth and Hillside at the top of the hill. Rock and I walked there in silence. Every now and then he gave me a pat on one shoulder. Four steps up the porch; red door; chipped black knob. Was I supposed to knock? I didn't know. Rock reached around and did it for me. I looked down at my new clothes: that dummy must have been in the window, once, and for a long time; the jacket was sun-damaged.

I swore I would remain my grown-up self. Everything had changed since I'd left ten years before: people paid money to look at me. They applauded and usually laughed. Girls from every state in the nation had praised me for my kindness, my patience, my impatience. It's only your father, I thought. It's only any old tough audience.

"Knock 'em dead, kid," Rocky said under his breath as the door began to open.

There was Annie, middle-aged, fat, and gray. "You're not supposed to be here yet!" she cried, hugging me. She was soft; she smelled of boiled vegetables; she smelled like Iowa. "I didn't think you'd really come, Mosey," she said. "I thought you were gone forever. Come in, come in. Nobody's here now but Papa and me, not till dinner. Come in. And your friend! Mr. Carter?"

"Annie Sharp," Rocky said warmly. "I'd recognize you anywhere." He pushed me through the doorway. "Do I smell cookies?" he asked.

"No," said Annie, puzzled.

Then we were in the house at the foot of the stairs, the flowered blue wallpaper, the carved newel post that looked like a chess piece. Rocky was still pushing me. "Here," said Annie, and she led me to the parlor. I felt Rocky's hands leave my back.

Pop sat in a chair, his feet propped on a comically small ottoman I didn't recognize. He'd grown his beard back, red despite his age. A made-up bed had been jammed in the corner by the front windows.

"Hello," I said, and he raised his head.

Something had happened to his face. The left side had fallen like a velvet curtain caught on a prop. He looked like the thing he'd been outrunning his whole life: an old Jew, a remnant of the old country. A foreigner. In fact, he looked something like I did in my Hebe act. I'd changed suits because I didn't want to look shabby in his presence, but his own clothes were ragged, and I understood that he realized he was dying, and there was no point in being fitted for a new suit. This was not frugality—my father owned a storeful of suits—but a kind of superstition. In his old age my father believed that the Evil Eye was everywhere, even in dressing rooms. Don't tempt it with plans. The beard made him look sloppy, but his softened cheek wouldn't have stood up to a razor.

I only wanted him to invite me into the room. I only wanted his forgiveness. His blessings—Oh, I wanted everything my father had planned to give me all those years before: I just didn't want the building they were stored in. My father was a businessman and had offered me a deal: I turned it down, everything, and only now did it occur to me that we should have bargained longer, that I could have bought the stock—by which I mean my father's love—and left behind the real estate.

"Look, Papa: it's Mosey," said Annie. I took a few more steps in. "He's like this," she said to me. "Stroke. Just two weeks ago. He's fine, only a little slower. I would have written, but then we got your wire." She knelt at his chair and held his hand: I'd never seen her so tender. "It's fine, it's fine. You know who this is." If he wasn't sure it was me, who was I? Some young man in a suit that looked familiar, ruined by the sun so it seemed, in the dark room, as though he was standing in a sunbeam anyhow. Was I looking for work? A handout? His blessing to marry one of his daughters? Pop raised his arms, though one barely left his lap. I went and took that heavier hand. It felt like a prop, too, a folded dusty lady's fan, lace over cracked ivory.

"So," said Pop, in a similarly cracked voice, "you're a little late for dinner."

My father, the comedian. At last we had something in common.

Annie had left the room; I could hear her talking to Rocky in the kitchen, the clang of dishes: she was trying to make up for the lack of cookies.

"Are you married?" Pop asked me. He'd probably been rehearsing that line too.

"No."

He nodded, and then said, "Don't wait too long." Annie and Rocky appeared in the doorway to the kitchen. Already Rock was eating a beige boiled chicken leg. Then he saw my father and, thinking he should look presentable and be introduced already, tried to find a place to put it. Annie put her hand out, and he gratefully gave her the awful-looking thing. She took it with her back to the kitchen.

"Pop," I said, "I want you to meet my partner. This is Rocky Carter."

Rock knelt at my father's feet, as Annie had, and shook my father's ailing hand. "It's a pleasure, sir," he said.

"Mr. Carter," said my father, nodding. "What is it that you do for a living?"

Rock looked up at me.

"He's a comedian. Like me. We do an act together."

"But after that?" said my father. He pointed at Rock. "Not forever."

"Probably not," said Rocky, "but for now."

Pop regarded me with an expression I recognized. Hope. Sure: this was my partner, we were in some strange business together—why not stay here and take over the store? Always room for another name on the plate glass window: Sharp and Son and Friend.

"You," said my father to Rocky. "Sir. Are you married?"

Rocky scratched the back of his head, ashamed. "That's a complicated question."

"Bah!" said my father, but he smiled. "You young men! Why do you wait like this? Not good to have children late. Too much time wondering, will they be orphans."

Pop meant himself, of course: he waited, he worried. Now he looked at me. "Why I married your mother."

"Why?" I asked.

"An orphan," he said. "Now, I wonder like my friend the rabbi. What will become of my daughter? Who will marry her? An orphaned girl is hard to marry. You," he said to Rocky. "You, perhaps."

Rocky looked at me slyly. "Where *is* Rose?"

My father frowned, and hissed in contempt at such a question. "No. Not—Annie. Who will marry *Annie.*"

From the kitchen we heard the humiliated sound of someone trying to drown out gossip from the other room with running water. I couldn't tell whether Pop's eyes were so bad he couldn't see that Rocky was young, or his memory so bad he'd forgotten that Annie was old. Middle-aged, anyhow: she was nearly fifty, too old even for a slaphappy friendly guy like Rock.

"You'll stay for dinner," my father said to Rocky.

I was about to make an excuse, but Rocky answered, wincing only slightly, "Thank you, sir. Of course I will."

In the kitchen, I tried to ask Annie about Rose, but she hushed me, and pointed to the parlor. I understood only that my father did not want her name spoken. As the house filled up with my sisters and their families, Rose was not even mentioned. My sister Fannie arrived first, holding a fat pink baby I was shocked to learn was her granddaughter. "This is Great-Uncle Mose," she said, waggling the baby into my arms.

"Oof," I said. "Who are you? You're heavy."

"That's Francine," she said. "Marilyn's girl."

The baby scanned my forehead as though it were the morning paper.

That was how the night went: This is Leah's Lou; there's Sally's David. I was as flummoxed as a total stranger, my sisters and their children had been so fruitfully multiplying. My brothers-in-law—Morris, Ben, Abe—each took me aside and offered me money. Abe, Sadie's husband, actually slipped some bills into my hand. "Take it," he said. "To set you up. I'm jealous, you know."

"What of?"

We stood in the hall, and he peered into the parlor, teeming with babies and children and teenagers and wives. My God: how many sisters *did* I have? "Youth," Abe said. "You know, I was a pretty fair dancer as a kid." He gave his considerable belly a pat, as though it were a trunk that held all of his former success. "So take the money, and become famous with it, and maybe you'll give me a part in one of your pictures."

I didn't need the cash, but you know what? His pride was worth more than my pride, so I took it. Seventy-five bucks.

I talked to Fannie, Sadie, Ida. I talked to their daughters—God's fancy joke, all those girls turning into more girls, though in the next generation down there were plenty of boys, and I wanted to say to my father, See? You can leave the store to Max and David and Lou: Sharp and Great-Grandsons.

The dining-room table had been stretched to an Olympic length with leaves and card tables at either end; we all sat around it, some in the dining room and some in the parlor. My father sat at the head of the table, Rocky and I flanking him, the long-lost son and his portly *goyishe* fair-haired brother. The design on Rock's dinner plate never saw daylight, with so many women rushing to serve him. He was extra-solicitous of Annie, who avoided him till she realized he wasn't avoiding her.

"I thought *tsimmes* had carrots," he said.

"No," Abe said gravely—my God, I hope he didn't slip Rocky money!—"Elsewhere, yes, but not in this family. Carrots in a *tsimmes* are a crime. Never speak of them."

"I'm sorry," said Rocky, just as gravely. "I didn't know."

"You'll get the hang of it," said Annie, ladling more *tsimmes* onto Rock's plate.

When Abe made a reference to the European war, the sisters quieted him. Fannie, who was given to speaking what she believed was Yiddish so the children wouldn't understand, said, "Ssshh. *Der Kinder.*"

"I'm saying only that at the Settlement House—"

"Tell me, Mr. Sharp," Rocky said to my father. "When did you come to this country?"

My father turned to Rocky very slowly, brushing some crumbs out of his beard with the edge of his good hand. "Eighteen eighty," he said. "First, Wilkes-Barre, Pennsylvania, where I met my wife—"

"Sssh, sshh," I said to some teenage niece, who was whispering about a boyfriend in my ear. All around the table, the Sharp children quieted whoever was talking. Wilkes-Barre, Pennsylvania? Wilkes-Barre, *Pennsylvania?*

There is nothing the least bit shocking about Wilkes-Barre, Pennsylvania. We had simply never heard my father suggest anything but that life began in Iowa.

All sides of the endless table grew silent. My father noticed, though he continued to address Rocky directly: he just spoke louder. It was an effort for him. "Wilkes-Barre, Pennsylvania," he said, "was where I met Rabbi Louis Kipple." He pointed down the table to the portrait in the parlor. "And his daughter, my Goldie."

"Did you love her right away?" Rock asked.

My father smiled. "She did not make a good impression, no. She was not so fond of me. But she was new. I went to see the rabbi to ask a question. His wife, not a well woman, not a nice woman, answered the door with the baby, I asked for the rebbe, she thrust the baby into my arms, squalling and screaming"—my father mimed a thrust baby as best he could—"and so I met Goldie. But had I plans to marry then, no."

Have you ever wondered about what happens before Genesis? Why didn't God make Adam and Eve infants? My father had never told us this story. We had never asked.

Rocky said, "So then—"

"So!" said my father. "My question for Rabbi Kipple: How shall I worship when I travel? Shall I go to Iowa? We discuss. Fifteen years later his wife is dead, and he writes a letter: Can you get a minyan together in Des Moines, what about a shul, and then he comes, with Goldie, to Children of Israel. And then *he* grows sick, wants to arrange a wedding. Goldie prepared the meal. Awful. I thought, who will teach her to cook? A little Jewish girl, alone. Sixteen and fat. She would become a maid or shopgirl. I invited a child to live with me, I married her so no talk from the neighbors. I knew nothing of marriage. *American* marriages. They must involve love. Mine did."

"She was beautiful," said Rocky, as though he remembered her.

Pop nodded. He seemed exhausted. "So, my friend, Mr. Carter, this is why I tell you: it is good to marry. I didn't know myself. I thought I was only being kind."

Oh, we were grateful to Rocky. We were angry, too. We—I am willing to speak for my sisters, now, for any child of a close-mouthed father—could not believe this was happening. A guy just waltzes in, and the next thing we know my father is telling stories like it's nothing. He held a baby in his arms, and fifteen years later he married her. That story was my inheritance, not Rocky's!

I am an old man myself now, and I understand. Your own children and their questions! They interrupt you. Their eyes bulge when a relative in a story behaves in a way they can't imagine (and they can't imagine much). They interrupt again, though every question they ask, every single one, is the same: How exactly has this story shaped my life? Why haven't you told me this before, didn't you know what it would mean to me?

Maybe it's just a good story. Maybe you just want to tell it.

My sisters left not long after dinner; with the table set up in two rooms, it was hard to linger. Rock and I formed a two-man receiving line at the door. After Ida had kissed Rocky's cheek, she turned to me. Then she burst into tears. "You're bald!" she said. "And I'm fat!" She threw herself into my arms.

"I'm not *bald*," I said, the bratty little brother. She pinched my back to make me behave. "Sorry, sorry," she said into my shoulder, then she stepped back and dried her face with a lavender handkerchief. "It's just: next time, don't be gone so long. Don't let me only hear you on the radio. I never thought I'd be jealous of Rudy Vallee, but I thought, Why does he get to talk to my brother and I don't?"

I took her hand and handkerchief, both wet. At least somebody in the family had an idea that comedy wasn't some hobby I'd picked up. She wasn't fat, Ida, just plump around the middle, and her eyes were still purplish-blue.

"He promises!" Rocky said.

"And he's a man of his word," said Ben, shepherding his wife out.

The house felt forsaken once they'd all gone. Annie invited Rocky to stay overnight. No point going all the way to the Fort Des Moines.

"Take my room," I said. "I'll stay down here, and sleep near Pop."

My father's bed had been moved to the parlor so he didn't have to climb stairs. I didn't want to climb them myself, to wake up in the sleigh bed, waiting for Hattie to come through the window. Instead, I'd sleep on the sunporch on the old wicker settee, piled under quilts to keep warm.

It was late enough. Rock and my father both went to bed in opposite corners of the house, and I went to talk to Annie while she cleaned. There wasn't much to do, she'd had so much help in the kitchen.

"See?" she said. She sat me down at the table and poured me a cup of coffee. I could see the elm out back, and suddenly I wanted to climb it. "You've come home once. Now you can do it over and over."

"Sure," I said.

"A nice man, your friend Rocky. Tell him I'm not waiting for a proposal."

"I will. So tell me—where *is* Rose?"

"Gone," said Annie, and turned her attention to the sink.

"Yes, I know, but where has she gone?"

She shrugged and began to wash the bottom of a round pot in careful circular strokes, as though trying not to wake it. "Married. So she told us. To a man named Quigley."

"Quigley," I said. I tried to absorb this: Rose had married a man with a funny name, and so—

"*Catholic,*" Annie said quietly to the pot.

"Oh." I nodded. "Disowned."

Annie shrugged again, miserable.

"Did he disown me, when I left?"

She spun suddenly, and held the soapy pot to her chest, as though she'd forgotten what it was—a bouquet of flowers, the hand of someone to whom she professed love. "No, of course not. We couldn't forget you. You were always our boy."

Exactly what I was afraid of and hoped for. "Well, at least Rose left for love."

"Love!" Annie sniffed. "No, for love she would have stayed. She didn't even ask!"

"Ask what?"

"If she should marry him! She should have asked!"

"Would Pop have said yes?"

"No: that's why she should have asked."

I laughed. Smart Rose.

"We don't mention her," said Annie. She put the pot back in the sink. The front of her dress was damp. "So please. Don't."

"You mean Pop doesn't mention her."

"No." Then she said, more to the last of the dirty dishes than to me, "He's never said her name. Not once."

I imagined she did, though, every night: *Rose, where are you?*

In the living room my father snored so raspily it made the back of my throat ache. I was always their boy. I'd never been lost, just gone. Just away. Not like Rose, good as dead. Worse: she was dead but insulting them still, wherever she was. I don't think Rose was a thing my father had ever imagined losing; he had only seen that she would lose him. An orphaned girl is hard to marry. My father had lost other children: Samuel and Libby and Sarah and Abie and Louis and Hilla. Hattie. He'd almost lost me, too, but here I was, thanks to Rocky. My father had worked to keep hold of me, I was a fortune, but Rose was the loose change in his pocket, and he'd lost her out of carelessness. He'd never told her who she should marry. He'd never told her, Your life is here, with those who love you.

He was busy telling that to me.

A Catholic, a barbarian. He knew nothing of Catholics except the words that came to him: *flesh, thorns, passion.* He saw gilt-edged blood when he closed his eyes. And now Roseleh was married to one.

"Lots of people hate Jews too," I told Annie.

"The ignorant," she answered.

Iowa Stripped to the Waist

One memorable night in my childhood, we found a vagrant sleeping on the settee on the screened porch; he'd let himself in through the screen door. We didn't know what to do; we stared at him as though he were a dozing skunk. My father said, "Let him rest," and in the morning Hattie (the only one of us brave enough) went out with a sack of doughnuts that Annie had made that morning, which, considering Annie's doughnuts, was either charity or punishment.

I wondered whether the diamond pattern of the wicker had bitten into his skin the way it was biting into mine. I was home, but I wasn't home: I was in the transient spot, the place you could fall asleep without the honest members of the household noticing. Above me, in my own bed, Rocky snored, the guy who'd engineered this neat trick: me in Valley Junction again. What a prank that telegram had been, a harebrained, cruel, canny, kind trick. I was so grateful to the guy I hated it, and to this day—six decades later—one of my greatest regrets is I never managed to tell him so.

Rocky the practical joker snuck into the sunporch early the next morning. "Come on," he said. "Let's go look at the bright spots of your youth." We took my father's car, an old Jewett, which nobody drove anymore, and headed out for the city.

"I don't think I'll marry Annie," Rocky said. "Do you mind?"

"Who says she wants to marry you?" I asked.

"A wise woman. But Rose! Rose has forsaken me!"

I explained what I knew of what had happened.

"A Catholic!" Rocky said, and whistled. "A bad business, that bunch. If I were your father, I'd form a posse."

"That's not it," I said.

"S'okay. Little Rose, married. I never thought she'd do me this way. What's she, eleven?"

"Twenty-six."

"Oh, well, then, she *had* to settle for a Quigley. That's some story, about your folks. So, hey: where are those bright spots?"

Des Moines at first glance isn't pretty, but if you look hard and in the right places, it reveals its beauty. Look harder, and it gets ugly all over again.

We drove down Polk Boulevard, under the elms, past the grand lawns, then swung around and took Grand Avenue downtown, past George the Chili King's, over to Gray's Lake. It was 7:00 A.M., and the city was still shut down, a museum of my childhood, everything behind glass. We drove by the Jewish Community Center, where I used to go to dances, and then past the fairgrounds. I'd managed to come back home. I'd seen my family. I'd lived.

The one person I was still avoiding was Hattie.

It was like Hattie was a dear friend who I'd fallen out of touch with while I was away, one I'd thought of all the time and meant to write, and then the meaning-to-write began to eclipse the friendship itself, until the memory was half guilt, half melancholy. I'd betrayed Hattie some-how. I had the sense that she still lived in town but I'd been so lousy about everything that I couldn't bear to look her up. And so I had to avoid all of the places she might possibly be. If this had been a movie, I suppose I would have gone to her grave and wept. I didn't. I hate ceme-teries. We should all be cremated. We should all be thrown up in the air. How would *I* like to be remembered? Not as a body in a box, that's for sure.

We ended up at the State House grounds, Des Moines' grandest spot. Once there had been some slums at the western foot of the hill, but they'd been torn down. I'd've loved to take Rock into the State House itself: even an Easterner would be impressed by the glory of that building. Instead, we walked around to the south side to look at the Sol-diers' and Sailors' Monument, a solid column topped by Victory, skirted at its base with sculptures of Iowa Personified, A Mother's Sacrifice, and (at each corner) a Soldier or Sailor. A beaut of a monument when you first saw it; then, suddenly, not. The triumphant servicemen seemed on closer inspection leeringly drunk. The old mother sitting with a child at her feet was venerable, then haggard. Was that a feather duster in Vic-tory's hand? And Iowa Personified was a young bare-to-the-waist woman who held up her breasts, one in each hand, thrusting them to-ward—well, who knew? She was supposed to be offering nourishment, but she looked like a cooch dancer. The inscription above her head read, *Iowa, her affections, like the rivers of her borders, flow to an inseparable union.*

As a kid I'd suspected there was something smutty about that. Most astonishing to me then was that a man hadn't left Iowa topless: a woman had. There was the sculptress's name on the pedestal, Harriet Ketchum. I was an educated boy, and I knew that a naked sculpture implied the existence of an actual naked lady. The statue itself didn't titillate me, but the fact that it had once been near a semiclad artist's model did. Maybe Harriet Ketchum just looked at herself in the mirror.

Now Rocky eyeballed it. He said, "She looks like she's trying to un-screw her tits, but can't figure out if they come off clockwise or counter-clockwise."

He had a point.

"And," he added, "all the boys come here and give her a rub for luck."

"Could be. I've never heard that."

"I'm not asking you, I'm telling you. Wherever there are public

breasts, there are boys rubbing them for luck. See how they're a different color than the rest of her?"

"No, actually."

"So what did you do here as a kid? Sled? What?" It was windy and
bright on the hill, and Rocky looked like a monument himself, his coat
flowing behind him, the wind rattling his white shirt. Heavy men always
look handsome in a breeze.

"We took our sleds here, sure." And though I thought I'd brought
him to an unsentimental place, I remembered coming here with Hattie,
winters with toboggans, summers with sheets to spread out on the lawn.
Our sister Ida and her family lived on Ninth Street, and in August on
visits we were allowed to bundle up our bedclothes and walk here for
the breeze that hit this hill and no place else, as though it was paying its
respects to the politicians. Plenty of families would have had the same
clever idea. The side of the hill, as we walked up hugging our pillows,
looked like a ramshackle galaxy: a child beneath a bleached sheet, glow-
ing faintly, was a distant star; a fat man in his undershirt shone as bright
as Venus; look, there are the Pleiades, all seven, dozing. I can't imagine
sleeping outside these days, but we could, we did. Not all night. Hattie
would wake me. She'd poke me with the toe of her shoe, but I bided my
time till she had to crouch and put her hand on my back. "Mose, Mosey,"
she said, quiet because of the dreamers all around us. "Ida will worry.
Let's go."

Ah, God. Grief was a flood. I knew that from growing up in Valley
Junction, where the Raccoon River jumped its banks once a decade and
slunk into town like a convict come back to a favorite crime scene. The
floods soaked your basement, the rains that caused the floods came
through the shingles of the roof into the attic, the very places you saved
things. People sandbagged and waited for the water to go down. Base-
ments were worse. Your beloved belongings floated until they sank. The
water eventually dragged down everything you owned, your books, your
diaries, your most seaworthy childhood toys. When the water left and
your life was back out in the air, your things would be so heavy you
couldn't lift them to throw them away, mildew blooming like black
roses already. But before the water receded, everything you loved was
somewhere underneath, and if you couldn't clearly see it all, neither
could you see what had been destroyed. While your belongings were
submerged, you could walk among them, slowly by necessity. There was

no need to clean up. There was no need to salvage some things and burn others and arrange for replacements. You stood in the water, and though once the place dried out you could get to work, you hoped it never would: look, that chair's sound, that magazine's legible, that face in the photo album's only slightly blurred, ready for conversation or kisses. We're only separated. We still can see.

Leave that shipwreck alone.

Adam and Eve Was a Marriage of Convenience

Our train left the next morning at nine. "Stay!" said Annie, and we had to explain that we actually *were* employed, that people waited for us in California. My father was sitting in his chair when I got ready to leave. I took his outstretched hand and he reeled me in—where had such strength come from?—and I tumbled into his lap. I'm breaking my elderly father! I thought, but I felt his arm around me, his knuckles fondly knocking my shoulder. "Come back," he whispered. "Come to California," I whispered back. He knocked on my shoulder twice more and let me go. My father shared my superstition—maybe he was the one who put the idea in my head—and we did not say the word *good-bye*. I was not so sad. I'd come to Iowa and lived, and surely that meant I could return whenever I wanted.

We took a local to Fort Madison, where we boarded the Super Chief to California, an all-Pullman train, very deluxe, very Hollywood. Ahead of us, in our car, a thin woman in a suit with a fox collar stepped out of a compartment. She turned around and looked up.

"Penny!" I said.

"Mr. Sharp!" she said back, and then in a low friendly voice, "Mr. Carter."

He paused. "*Mrs.* Carter." He muscled by me to kiss her. When they turned, Rocky held out Penny's wrist, as though her hand were a flashlight he meant to shine at my face.

"Meet the little woman," said Rocky, and Penny smiled dazzlingly in my general direction. Ah. There was a ring on that hand. I tried to sort this out: Penny was not in New York. Penny was on the train. Penny and Rocky appeared to be married.

How could he have kept *that* a secret from me?

"No kidding!" I said, and gave her a kiss. We had to bust it up to let a middle-aged couple get past us.

"You haven't told me how I look," said Penny.

"You're beautiful, Pen," I said. "You don't look married at all." That wasn't true. She looked married and divorced and already facing a long future alone. "But when did this *happen*?"

Rocky shrugged. Penny said, "The night before you left. We figured, California! Why not go together? We'd've told you, but . . . surprised, right?" She laughed delightedly, as though your husband wanting to keep your marriage from his best friend was good news under certain circumstances. Rocky wouldn't look at me.

Nevertheless, the newlyweds went to their compartment and I went to mine. The bed pulled down from the wall right in front of the window: it made me feel like a failed tank act, drowned, pressed up against the glass for the audience—people at the stations we pulled into, that is—to gawk at. I couldn't get over this sudden marriage. Probably he'd been drunk, maybe they both had. I remembered how indifferent he'd seemed to Penny when we left her the first time, waving in Penn Station at our northbound train. Maybe he'd married her out of a different brand of boredom, and was ashamed.

I was a bachelor then. Now I'm sure it wasn't shame or restlessness. Rocky knew how to talk about anything but happiness, and Penny, for all her chatter and nightclub flash, made the guy authentically happy. He couldn't explain it, so he wouldn't try. In those days Rock never said anything he couldn't bluff his way out of.

Somehow I could not imagine that we were actually moving toward California: it seemed more likely that California was being pulled toward us, on giant chains run by the train engine, and that we stayed where we were while the cars rocked from the effort. Where I had picked up such a cinematic notion, I have no idea, but that's what eventually happened in our movies. No matter where trouble found Carter and Sharp—Mexico, Mars, Italy, New Orleans—we ourselves were always on a Californian movie lot, and the mountains, the craters, the Mardi Gras parade, were pulled in by chains and prettied up with paint.

In the morning I went to meet them in the red-and-black dining car.

Penny wasn't up yet; Rock waited by himself in one of the orange leather booths.

"She's a great girl," I said as I sat down. "Now, tell me the truth. Are you divorced from your *last* wife?"

"Yes!" he said. "Penny made me, actually, and there went my last good reason for not getting married. I only hope your father is right about this come-to-love business."

"You love her already, and you know it," I said.

"Yeah, sure. I'll tell you the truth, Professor. I've never seen a woman so quickly ruined by marriage." He said this as though he was not the man who instigated the marriage, and therefore the ruin.

"She looks fine," I said. I was a matrimonial amateur, but it struck me as unseemly to talk about your wife that way. Then I said it: "I know I'm an amateur—"

"That's right," said Rocky. "You'll learn. You know"—he reached across the table and flicked at my lapel—"I've never seen you look so unpressed."

"Unimpressed?"

"*Wrinkled,*" said Rocky.

Penny arrived then, yawning and smoking. She slid in next to Rocky and reached across him to grind out her cigarette in the ashtray.

"Mike's a mess," said Rocky.

"He looks swell," said Penny, for whom wrinkles were a kind of sartorial braille.

Poor kid. She was wearing a great deal of makeup, which just made her look more exhausted. I don't think Rocky really was to blame. Nightclub singers don't age well—all that smoke and liquor and nightly pining. Besides, someone who liked to flirt as much as Penny did would be miserable married: she was like a dog chasing a rabbit for years only to discover that, upon cornering the thing, she didn't much care for rabbits. I started really liking Penny, once she was married to Rock: as she put it (somewhat to my embarrassment), we shared a husband. That would get me into trouble later.

A marriage of convenience. What marriage isn't? Penny and Rocky, getting hitched in New York. My father marrying my mother so the neighbors don't talk. Love is inconvenient; marriage makes it less so. Years later, me and Jessica, my fancy dancer, as Rocky called her: I wanted to marry Jessie so that in the morning, when we woke up, there we'd be, married, convenient, sufficient. Rose on the highway with Quigley at the wheel, Rose leaving Iowa. Marry your driver, girls, and you'll get where you're going faster.

"What next?" Penny said now, which is what she always said. Once it meant she was looking forward to the next adventure; this time it sounded as though she was addressing a punishing God.

"What indeed?" said Rocky, not catching the tone. "What heights shall we soar to now?"

8

The Boys in Hollywood

By 1939, when I arrived, Hollywood had already made plenty of pictures about Midwestern bumpkins such as myself who came to the land of sunshine and either triumphed or lost their minds. We were cheerful gawkers, one hand on our cardboard grips, one holding our hats to the crowns of our heads. I was set to strike that pose, but Rock's first act in Los Angeles—we were standing on the platform of the station—was to light a cigar and suggest getting drunk.

"All right," Penny said amiably. She'd tucked herself under Rock's arm, so she wouldn't get lost. "But where are the oranges?"

Rocky pulled her closer. "What oranges, my love?"

"Oranges," she explained. "Whenever I pictured myself in California, I always had an orange in my hand."

"You thought they doled them out at the border?"

"Maybe."

"They only take away your old fruit," said Rocky. "They don't give you replacements."

"We should have oranges," said Penny. "And honey. And—what do they drink here? Is there such a thing as an orange julep?"

"I'll invent them for you," said Rocky. "Orange juleps, honey juleps, milk-and-honey juleps, grape juleps. Name your julep."

"Honey," she answered, shivering in her lilac Swiss-dotted frock, part of her California trousseau. She had a diaphanous shawl that she pulled around her shoulders, though it didn't look like it could warm a wax dummy.

The studio had arranged a couple of neighboring bungalows for us

on Melrose Avenue, and Rocky directed a taxi to take our luggage to
them: Penny had packed so many trunks we couldn't have ridden along
even if we'd wanted to.

In any case, she insisted on sight-seeing before drinking, though with
her vision that meant dropping to a squat in the front of Grauman's
Chinese so she could trace Norma Shearer's tiny footprints with her fingers. The movie palaces themselves were red-and-gold smudges to her,
and she could not see the letters on Mount Lee that in those days still
read HOLLYWOODLAND.

"It's like Stonehenge," I said.

"It's parochial," Rock answered. "It's advertising. There should be a
giant sign next to it saying when and where the local Rotary club meets."
(He was right, of course. It had originally been an ad for a nearby housing development of the same name.)

"Aha!" I said. "Mystery of Stonehenge solved. Odd Fellows meet here
third Thursday of every month. See it, Penn? Over there?"

"I only read menus. Let's eat," said Penny.

"Let's drink," said her husband, and so we did. We went to the
Trocadero, and then to the Mocambo. Rocky was looking for the brass
band he assumed would welcome him to California: if we just kept
looking, surely they would show up. "I'd settle for one lousy sousa-
phone," he said. "A flugelhorn. Anything." At three in the morning we
went to a diner to eat ourselves sober, at least a little, and at dawn we
were in yet another cab, which took us to the beach. Even Penny could
see the ocean: the size of it seemed to knock her over onto the sand,
where she sat in her lilac dress, the shawl wrapped several times around
her head.

"How very blue." She pointed at the sky, and then at the sea. "I'd like
a dress that shade," she said, and passed out.

"Whaddya think?" Rock asked.

I answered despite myself, "God is mighty."

"*I* am mighty!" Rocky said, and began to strip off his shoes and socks
and pants. Having conquered the West Coast, he'd now whip its ocean
into shape. Maybe he could work Hawaii in before breakfast.

"I've never seen the ocean before," I said.

"Yes, you have," said Rocky. "I saw you see it."

"You did?"

"The East Coast," he said. "The East *Coast*."

I laughed at my own stupidity: of course. I had seen city harbors, I had even gone across one so I could stand at the feet of the Statue of Liberty, but that wasn't the *ocean* ocean. Here it was, miles of ocean ocean, the ocean blue, slapping waves on the sand and then pulling them back like a cardplayer who's misdealt. *Waves.* That's what I hadn't seen before, the way a wave curled over and stretched and showed its underside, sea green! before it broke. I rolled up my pant legs. Rocky strode into the water in his shorts and undershirt.

Could water around your ankles make you seasick? I closed my eyes and tilted my face up; even the insides of my eyelids seemed sea-green instead of the usual hot orange. Probably I was just hungover. Despite the nausea and a pressing headache around the edges of my brain, I felt pretty terrific. For years I'd felt like I'd jumped bail in my hometown, and now I'd settled my business there and I was free and brave and in California.

We waded out farther. Suddenly Rocky dove forward and began to swim.

"Come on," he said.

"Can't. Don't know how."

He turned over in the water and wiggled his toes at me. "Everyone knows how to swim," he said, but then he shrugged his way into a backstroke, and then a front stroke, and kept going.

Behind us on the beach, Penny slumbered next to a pile of clothing shaped like her husband. I thought about covering her with Rock's jacket, but she looked comfortable enough.

When I turned back and scanned the horizon, Rocky was gone. I searched for a waterspout, the crook of his elbow slicing up like a shark fin, the backs of his heels making whitecaps on the waves. For eight years Rocky had been in plain sight. Where was he now? I looked up the deserted beach and down the deserted beach and back to the ocean, and I could only come to one conclusion: Rocky had drowned. He'd stumbled drunk into the Pacific and sunk to the bottom.

I'd talked him out of going over Niagara Falls in a barrel, only to lose him to another body of water. Do you know: I went running farther out, the surf coming up to my hips. I swear I was ready to dive in, to start parting my hands in front of me till I found him (that's what you did when a child got lost in a cornfield, I remembered), calling his name. Didn't I have to save him?

Except I couldn't. I was out to nearly my waist, the waves even higher, before I realized that swimming wasn't something you'd pick up the first time. The newspaper article would say, *one man drowned, and then another man drowned*. That, too, was a familiar Iowan story, people who went leaping into flooded rivers, hoping to be heroes but ending up as corpses.

I turned to the shore and yelled Penny's name, but she was out cold. Then I felt something brush past my ankle.

It was Rocky. He pulled me out of the water like Frankenstein with his bride, my back against the surface of the ocean. My heart had swollen so in my chest it felt rib-striped.

"Kick your legs a little," he said. "See? You can swim."

"I wasn't!" I told him. "I thought you were dead!"

"Me?" He laughed and set me on my feet. He started walking back to Penny. "If there's one thing you shoulda noticed by now: I'm buoyant. You can't drown *me*."

"No kidding, Rock, I thought you'd drowned yourself." Then I felt something else run past my ankle, and jumped again. "Something bit me!"

"Nothing bit you. It was probably a dead fish rushing by."

"I'm getting out of this goddamn ocean," I said. "Dead fish!"

He was looking at the beach, squinting at the sun. If he'd kept his underclothes on for modesty's sake, it wasn't working. His back was to me, his wet undershirt soaked to silk netting. He put his arms up, as if to dry them, and said, "Only their souls ascend to heaven."

They Also Serve Who Only Dance and Sing

"The studio's trying to find something to suit your talents," Tansy told us, and we got antsy. All we knew was we weren't working, though we did draw a small salary. I started to long for that brass band myself, something to show that Hollywood knew that The Boys had arrived.

Then the draft act passed. Why not draft Carter and Sharp? As it happened, there was an old army script floating around just made for a comedy team, intended for Wheeler and Woolsey, or Olsen and Johnson, or Clark and McCullough, or some other mismatched pair of guys who'd either broken up or died or gotten too old to make credible soldiers. "I got a guy who can spruce it up for you," Tansy told the studio, and that's how Neddy became our movie writer too. He punched up the script, took out the references to the Kaiser, stuck in a number in a USO club. A cheap and easy vehicle for its cheap and easy stars.

Red, White, and Who? was a dumb and cheerful army picture, complete with a few patriotic songs belted from the back of a jeep. Some consider it our best movie. The timing, anyhow, made it our luckiest. We played soldiers on leave from camp who accidentally fall asleep on a train and end up in New York City; for the rest of the movie we try to get back to base before our absence is noticed. An old friend of ours from vaude, Johnny Atkinson, appeared as our mean sergeant. He'd been in Hollywood awhile, playing tough guys with hearts of gold. That was Johnny, the kind of guy who smoked a stogie while pruning his rosebushes. He had a flat-nosed gangster's face and sorrowful blue eyes.

I loved the soundstages, the prop rooms, the cameraman leaning into his camera, the booms, the cars we drove in front of movie screens full of passing scenery. I loved seeing a character who'd last played a cop in a Bette Davis flick playing an army secretary for us. I loved having someone else apply my makeup for me. "Close your eyes," the makeup girl would say. "Now open. Now close."

Rocky had been right, all those years before: he had to have an audience to work. We decided to play to the cameramen, the grips, the propmen, the script girl, anyone who happened to be on the soundstage. Frank Brothers, the director, tore out his hair. He needed a silent set, but we needed laughs. So we worked even louder to cover up the laughter, and the folks on the set laughed louder, and we threw our props around—guns to the ground! suitcases on the baggage racks! ourselves onto upper berths!—and together we managed.

The picture was a huge hit. You can't imagine. We filmed it in the thirty-one days of October 1940; the studio released it in June of '41; by July, we were famous. Luck. Maybe lack of it too: for the rest of our careers, we had to make movies that resembled this one. Even if we'd stumbled onto something by mistake, that was how we'd do it forever and ever, whether Carter and Sharp got in trouble in the navy or on the moon, in the Wild West or Ancient Egypt. We filmed on the same breakneck schedule, and the budgets only got bigger because our salaries did. A rock on a dude ranch reappeared three years later as a rock on Mars; an Italian nightclub became a New York nightclub with a change of tablecloths. "It's what your fans want!" the studio said, as though the public would miss a papier-mâché boulder.

Tansy had been clever, or psychic. When we signed with the studio for a pittance, he inserted a clause in our contract that said we'd bring home a percentage of the profits of all our pictures. Nobody'd ever heard of such a thing back then, but the studio shrugged at the oddity—how many tickets could a couple of knockabout comedians sell, anyhow?—and allowed it. Plenty of other guys (the Three Stooges, for instance, no matter which Three Stooges they were at the time) made nearly nothing from their studio deals.

Carter and Sharp, on the other hand, got filthy rich.

Red, White, and Who? was still playing when Pearl Harbor was bombed. Good box office, plus a war: like plenty of guys Rocky and I wore uniforms almost nonstop in the early forties. We just returned them to wardrobe at the end of the day. *Gobs Away!, Fly Boys, Navy Blues, We're in the Army, Carter and Sharp on the High Seas* (our first title billing!), *Wrong Way Rocky*: endless, those pictures. We churned 'em out four a year, and I pretty much couldn't tell one from the other, though as I recall *Fly Boys* was the best of the lot, and *We're in the Army*, essentially a retread of *Red, White, and Who?*, the worst. None of the movies made reference to a particular war or enemy. The War raged; the Enemy would be defeated. Sometimes nonsense that sounded like Hitler or Tojo squawked out of a radio. Maybe those pictures had distinct plots; all I remember is Carter and Sharp blundering about like fools, while various second leads bounded into heroism. Sometimes Rocky got to act heroic, too, mostly by accident. I hid under a lot of beds in those pictures.

If you judge history by Carter and Sharp movies, it was a pretty glamorous war. All girls had time to style their hair perfectly for their WAC caps; all soldiers were broad shouldered and brave (with two top-billed exceptions, of course). Everyone could dance. For any battle, there were five parties, and no one ever, ever died on-screen. Battle wounds made soldiers stronger. Orphans were adopted. The jeep was invented because it made such a good little stage: it's hard to do a musical number in a closed car. Once our radio show started, we'd joke about rationing—the Professor might try to get Rocky to invest a pound of hamburger in a surefire meat-loaf deal—but in our movies, we never mentioned a lack of anything.

Days off, I called my sisters in Des Moines and got the news. Annie had planted a Victory garden; Abe and Sadie were hoping that their clothing store had been rationed enough pairs of leather shoes (Abe thought plastic disastrous for growing feet); everyone argued about how much to tell the children. My father, said Annie, refused to talk about the war at all, though whether this was old age or old sorrow, she didn't know. The WACs were headquartered at Fort Des Moines, and marched down Grand Avenue downtown, dozens of women in heavy shoes, and while some of them might have been beautiful in other circumstances, as they passed by the Savery Hotel, they looked like what they were: soldiers who happened to wear skirts. (Even so, Des Moines became a fabled place on U.S. Army bases: all those single women! Soldiers wanted to transfer to Fort Des Moines, meet a nice WAC, and get her drunk at Babe's. Des Moines, City of Romance!)

Rocky and I didn't save tin foil or plant gardens, but we joined the war effort. We went on bond drives, first locally, and then cross-country. A city had to promise a million-dollar subscription to get us to stop and perform. Eighty cities came up with the cash, and we hit them all in thirty days. Vaudeville at high speed: we'd dash from the airport to the high school auditorium, do "Why Don't You Sleep?" or some other bit, heckle the audience into buying bonds, and dash back to the airport. Starlets could bribe with kisses; we made our pitch into a giant gamble, me choosing one half the room, Rocky the other. "You gonna let *that* side of the room beat you?" Rocky would say. "Come on!" We set records that way.

Now when people talked about The Boys, they didn't mean us. The Boys were who we drummed up money for. The Boys were who we entertained at army bases and navy camps, who'd laugh at any groaning joke about KP or WACs or WAVEs. We were happy to do our part, though in this we were no better than Bugs Bunny, another bond salesman.

You could argue that I did plenty of good making upbeat films in which I impersonated a serviceman—think of the young men who would realize, while watching, *Sure, I'm scared, but who's as bad as that guy?* Sometimes I had my doubts: Annie wrote of the kids in Valley Junction who'd joined up, and I sensed some rebuke in her letters. Finally, at a bond drive on the Santa Monica boardwalk, I was climbing the stairs onto a bandstand when I heard a woman's voice at my ankles.

She said, unmistakably, "Slacker!"

Then it was a filthy name: a slacker was a coward, a man willing to sacrifice other men's lives for his own comfort. Ahead of me, Rocky was already skipping around the stage, waiting for me to stroll on and tell him to hold still. But I was on the stairs, looking for the owner of the voice. There she was. Her hair was an artificial russety orange-blond—judging by her eyebrows, it had once been black-brown—and her small round blue hat was sliding into one dark, belligerent eye. Her lipstick made her mouth look extra puckered.

"Tell me, you," she said, "why do you let boys better than you fight? And die? What's wrong with you, you don't enlist? *You*—"

Already I'd started to bend down to take her white-gloved hand, to explain myself. All my life, my only defense—against angry women, or anyone—had been my charm. But charm was not patriotic, and maybe this woman believed that in order to save my own life I'd used my Hollywood savoir faire and slipped free of the draft. She stuck her own hands behind her back so I couldn't touch her.

"My son died," she said, "to save the likes of you." I didn't know whether she meant fancy movie stars or Jews, though either way I was afraid she was about to spit at me. Except to spit she'd have to break her gaze, and that she'd never do.

"My son *died*," she said again, and I thought sadly, but didn't say, Dear lady, lots of people have died. Let's you and I sit and talk and discuss all of them—

"Sister," said an old bald man standing next to her, "he's one of the good guys." That didn't help, of course: her problem was she was surrounded by chumps who had the good luck to be alive, while the one person who deserved to be was dead. All I could do was shrug, stand back up, and join Rocky—4F because of his weight—at the microphone.

I couldn't shake her, though. Even the misguided dye job seemed brave to me: I imagined her with the peroxide bottle, weeping for her son and washing the color from her hair. My sisters would have clucked at all that artifice, the losing battle to stay young and glamorous, but I was with that lady: when someone dies, it only makes sense to do desperate things to stop the clock and then wrestle it into the other direction. And besides, I believed her: here I was, well paid, useless, a slacker.

Rocky poked me in the ribs. "Wake up!" he said. "We're fighting for our country here!" and the crowd cheered.

All through that appearance, all the way home, all that night: I argued with myself. Don't be stupid, I said, and then, That's like saying, Don't be brave. You're not a slacker, you're a morale booster. You're not a morale booster, you're a coward. You could be killed. *Rocky* would kill you—imagine quitting the business when things are going so well!

By six in the morning, I couldn't stand myself. All I wanted was a uniform that didn't come out of the wardrobe department, that didn't say, on its stitched name tag, Buzz or Flash or Percival or any of my foolish movie names. M. Sharp. Private. That'd be fine. I went to the local draft board on Cuyoga Boulevard and stood in line with all the other young men who'd been up talking to themselves or their loved ones and had jumped to the same conclusion. I didn't get far.

"Let me get this straight," the doctor said. He sat on a rolling stool in front of my chair and took my forearms and lifted my wrists so I could get a good look. "You think you can be a soldier with *these?*" He coughed a little, and tried to cover his mouth with his elbow. "You'd keep dropping things. All the jobs we have are for guys who don't drop things."

Ah. My wrists. They'd ached for fifteen years, ever since Hattie's fall not-quite-into my arms. I'm still not sure whether the Valley Junction doctor had botched setting them. Watch me smoke a cigarette in a movie, and you'll see: I lift my whole arm to my mouth, my elbow up and my cigarette dangling. I'm not trying to be debonair, I just don't bend like other smokers.

I explained to the doctor that my wrists were oddly strong, locked as they were: didn't I hold up Rocky pretty well? The doctor laughed. He bounced my sore wrists on his knees. "Make more funny movies," he said. "That's your part."

In our pictures, when the Professor got drafted, he'd pull any kind of lamebrain stunt at his inspection to get out of it: he sat on a radiator in hopes of sweating off enough pounds to be underweight; he applied an iron to flatten the soles of his feet. The movie doctor would give him the bad news: "4-A! Next!" But this doctor knew he was giving me bad news by denying me. He looked over the top of his thick glasses, and I thought: *lousy eyes, 4F,* as though there were some comfort in stamping him defective too. But he was in a hurry: there were plenty of guys waiting to see him and a newsreel crew outside, because some matinee idol—not me—was supposed to enlist later. "Good of you to come," the doctor said.

I thought, without gratitude, Maybe Hattie has saved my life.

When the Carter and Sharp radio show went on the air (Tuesday nights at seven, shipped overseas via Armed Forces Radio), Penny wanted a part. Fred Allen had hired his wife, why not Rocky?

Because he'd *never do anything that Fred Allen did.*

Okay, then, like Jack Benny.

No, said Rocky.

I don't know why he was so adamant, though it was true that Penny wouldn't have been right: our sponsors, the manufacturers of Cape's Turkish soap, wanted the show bubble light and cheerful, and Penny torch-sang everything, even "Keep Your Sunny Side Up." Compared to Penny, Marlene Dietrich was Helen Kane.

Rocky adored radio, where you could stand with your script and the audience could recognize and love even the plainest ad-lib. My mike fright was a little better than it had been on the Vallee show. Mostly, I worried about getting the giggles, then I discovered that the audience loved it when I got the giggles. They thought that was *hysterical.* The only time I became incapacitated was the night our soundman showed up drunk—his wife had just left him—and for every single sound effect clattered the hoof-beat coconuts. A visitor knocks: clippety-clop. Rocky walks to the door: clippety-clop. We're riding around in the car, and I tell him to hit the horn; Rocky extracts a kiss from the vocalist; I fall down the stairs: here comes the cavalry, every single time. I could hardly breathe after the first ten minutes, and maybe we should have sent the guy home, but it was so *funny.*

"Hey, Rocky," I said, "you sound a little horse."

"Must you always be such a naysayer?" he answered.

The radio show allowed Rocky to finally kidnap my sisters. He did it behind my back. He convinced the writers that he should be the only boy from a large family.

"Six beautiful sisters!" he said to me, breaking the news, but who was he fooling? Beautiful sisters wouldn't be funny.

"Why can't I keep my own sisters?"

"Because," said Rocky, "you're the straight man. Six sisters is a punch line, not a setup." They even named Rocky's fictional sisters after mine, though they changed Hattie to Betty after I insisted. Maybe I should have also insisted on changing the other names, but we did need the gags—if you came up with enough running jokes, your audience felt in cahoots with you, and they'd keep tuning in.

Rocky's sisters loved him. They knit him six-armed sweaters. They baked him sugarless, eggless, butterless, tasteless Victory cookies that, when you bit into them, made a sound like a struck gong. Soon enough, they were as famous as he was: they got fan mail. Reporters wrote articles about them. They assumed the sisters were real. Why would someone make up siblings, just for a laugh? On the other hand, who really had six sisters? I was, radio-wise, a guy without a family. Rocky was the guy with too much, including a protective mother who hated me. "Listen, Mr. So-called Sharp," she'd say to me, "you leave Lovey alone." (Both halves of that sentence became catchphrases.) The fictional Mrs. Carter loved her son so much that she got in fistfights (the soundman hit the pages of an open dictionary with a damp glove) with everyone: me; Bill Thomas, our announcer; Loretta Patchett, the vocalist; and a slew of guest stars, including Lana Turner, Jack Benny, Don Ameche, and Joe Louis.

Do you have to ask who won?

I felt like I was cheating on my real sisters with another pack of girls. Their letters didn't mention their radio counterparts. They said, simply, that they'd listened to the show, and that I was very funny. Would Pop listen, I wondered. Then I thought: Annie makes him, because one of the sisters is named Rose, that forbidden name suddenly spoken in the house again. And then, as it happened, Rose's ill-fated marriage to the Roman Catholic met its ill fate; Quigley-less, she'd come back to Vee Jay. If you wanted to cast a spell over Rose, of course you used the radio: her name was said aloud in the parlor, and like any ghost, she was summoned back. She sent me a letter: *you can write to me here, now. Picture me in the parlor, listening to you.* My father forgave her, because he'd been proved right.

"Rocky!" people yelled on the street. "How are your sisters?"

"Unmarried!" he yelled back. "What are you looking for? We got 'em in all sizes."

Undraftable and overpaid as I was, my own war was pretty glamorous, despite myself. In 1942, the year I turned thirty-one, I had money in the bank and money in my pockets. I volunteered at the Hollywood Canteen. I dated starlets and would-be starlets. Every Tuesday night at seven, people tuned in to hear my mockable, quavering voice say, "What will we do with you, Rocky, what *will* we do?" And in Lithuania, forty thousand Jews in the town of Vilna were killed, some shot in their homes and some taken into the Ponary Forest and exterminated there, but they were all killed, including those related to a man who had once been called Jakov Shmuel Sharensky.

I didn't know that then. As I said, in my line of work, we did not discuss killing, only rescues.

Everyone Dances Underwater

There were days when I came home, and, having spent hours going *Yipes! Duck in this alleyway; here comes the sarge!* could not shake it. I went *Yipes* through the door, *Yipes* to the kitchen, *Yipes* into bed under the covers, my shoulders up around my ears and my arms fluttering like the flightless bird I was.

So to soothe my nerves, I bought things, including—at Rocky's urging—a house. (On our radio show, we joked about the housing shortage. We just never suffered from it.) The lady agent showed me a five-year-old white stucco house in North Hollywood, with a flat-topped Spanish-style roof that seemed impractical; I told her so: what about snow? Would you have to shovel it off so it wouldn't cave in your ceilings?

She looked at me. She looked at the sky. She looked at the palm trees that lined the street.

Yes, that's right: *California.* I laughed and pulled out my checkbook. You could stroll across that roof like a park if you wanted. Safe. Anyone who wanted to hurt herself here would have to jump, I thought.

I hadn't given much thought to the house itself, which God knows was more room than I needed, but I was like someone who'd starved as a kid: all I wanted was space. I'd grown up in a house crowded with people; I'd roomed in broom closets all my years on the road. Sometimes, in vaude houses, dazzled by the space and high ceilings, I'd daydream about moving onto the stage, or even into one of the boxes that overlooked it—maybe I'd install a Murphy bed to pull down from the wall, an invention I'd only seen in movies, where they behaved like dragons accustomed to a steady diet of sleepers. My new place—not quite a mansion, but pretty close—had six bedrooms, and five bathrooms, and a whole variety of rooms in which to live and dine and recreate and play games, and all for me. Dimly I thought, Well, kid, if you ever marry you can fill the place up; mostly I judged it a hell of a spot for assignations.

There had been nothing in my childhood home newer than the nineteenth century except some of the people: I wanted a place where everything was new and modish and luminous. That was how I decorated: mirrors everywhere, setting like suns and rising like moons; slim tables with blue glass tops. A martini cart trembling with glasses.

Rocky and Penny bought a bona-fide Beverly Hills mansion that had belonged to a suicided silent movie director. The place was as fountainous as Rome: in every corner on the grounds, there was something or someone cast in concrete and spitting. They had two swimming pools and a tennis court and a guesthouse and bathrooms for days and days. Their greatest regret was that because of the manpower shortage, they couldn't build on *more* bathrooms. Happily, the place came with a movie theater already, and they added a popcorn machine and moved in a soda fountain by the main swimming pool. Rocky, fondly remembering that cellar in Milwaukee, put in a bar in the basement and hired, before any other household help, a bartender, a wonderful old Portuguese guy named Bobby who wore his hair in a dyed black pageboy and mixed weaker and weaker drinks as the night wore on. Penny wanted a Ferris wheel, though Rocky was putting that off. They threw parties downstairs, and invited everyone—crew guys from our movies, people who Penny had met in stores, soldiers on leave. Rocky vowed that he'd never forget what it was like to be a regular working stiff—though when was he ever?—which to his mind meant laying out as much cash as it took to get the working stiffs dead drunk. Sometimes the parties would start with dinner; mostly, they'd start with drinks and end with breakfast for whoever was left standing. The soda fountain had a giant grill, and we would emerge from the smoky basement and go out to the pool, the sky the color of a dress that Penny wanted. Rocky would scramble dozens and dozens of eggs.

Sometimes then, five in the morning, Penny would sing. She missed her New York nightclubs, and tried her best to re-create them in the silk jersey dawn. Band members still among the living would gamely try to play along with her. Lately, she had acquired a taste for blues numbers full of murder:

I love you like a razorblade
I love you like a knife

I love you like a Gatling gun
You love me like a wife.

Or:

Poppa, don't push me.
I've killed men before.
You'll be kissing the threshold
If you walk toward that door.

An unsavory song over scrambled eggs. It seemed just right.

Some nights I brought over a lady comic I'd met at the Hollywood Canteen named Sukey Decker. We were pals. Sukey was bucktoothed to that narrow margin of beauty between forgettable and unfortunate: with some effort she could make herself look comic straight on, but she couldn't help her gorgeous profile. Lovely figure, too, the kind that comics trace in the air with the flats of their hands, saying *zowie* or *hubba hubba*. The movies didn't know what to do with her; she would pal around with the leading lady and crack wise and only show her legs as a burlesque punch line. On radio, and later on TV, she did well. Her shtick was a kind of world-weary man-hunger. Her voice was like that, too, low and slightly soft around the edges: hearing it was like tasting expensive candy. Till then, you'd never realized how lousy most candy was.

The four of us often ended up at Rocky's basement bar and smoked cigarettes and insulted each other and drank too much. "What time is it?" Penny would ask, unable to see the clock over the bar. "Tomorrow," Rocky would answer: nine in the morning, or ten. "A little eye-opener never hurt anyone," said Sukey, who could outdrink us or anyone.

I like Sukey a lot. As far as we knew, she'd never married. She didn't even go with anyone, though on the radio she joked that she could do without silk and nylon and meat and gas and sugar, but the man shortage was about to kill her.

"She likes me," said Rocky one drunken tomorrow morning, though that wasn't true. She hated him; she only came to his parties because he had great taste in musicians. But Sukey fascinated Rocky. "What's her story?" he asked me, though Sukey was sitting next to him. He hooked an arm around her neck.

"Who knows?" I said.

"Okay, sweetheart." He pulled her in and kissed the top of her head. *"You* tell me your story."

"What story?" she asked.

"Boyfriends," he said, giving her a wobbly gesture that meant, *Do you have any?*

"I'm allergic," she said.

Sukey was like a high elevation: when she was around you, you got drunker quicker. Penny was already drowsing like the dormouse on the edge of the bar. "You're afraid," Rock said, sloppy and sage.

"Of what?"

"Men," said Rocky, in a pure imitation of how Sukey as a leading lady's best friend would have said it, equal parts contempt and longing. That he managed this was a coincidence, the way sometimes the third verse of a long-forgotten song will come cresting into your brain on too much whiskey.

Sukey laughed. "You *sadden* me," she said. "You *amuse* me. But you don't frighten me."

"Okay," said Rocky, "sex. You're afraid of."

"Oh, sex. No, I'm not afraid of sex. I'm all for sex. Sex doesn't give me a second's pause. Sex?" she said. "Sex is swell."

"Good," said Rocky, puzzled.

"But *romance,*" said Sukey, "*mortifies* me."

Sukey liked me fine as a friend, and I pretended that the feeling was mutual, that all I longed for was her company and clever wit and the occasional firm handshake. Really, I wanted to get her into bed. I mean, not just into bed, because I also loved her company and clever wit; it's just that her firm handshake tortured me with its possibilities. I suspected that the Professor had monkey-wrenched my love life: she would have gone for me if I'd been a leading man. I decided I could wait her out. She wasn't your usual girl; she required unusual tactics. But Sukey seemed quite immune to my charms. In retrospect I'd say she was immune to charm, period; she hated anything that smacked of pretense or practice. She was a devout cynic, which meant that only naïve sincerity could melt her heart. In other words, she adored Penny and her five-in-the-morning declarations of homicide. *Sweetheart, I'll stab you/Tangled up in my bedding./I want to cry at your funeral/Not at your wedding.*

"She's like a cartoon girl," Sukey once told me, and I realized who Penny had always reminded me of: certain female impersonators who'd studied girlishness. "Betty Boop," Sukey called Penny, who giggled and showed her garters. The four of us mostly palled around together at Rocky's place, because Sukey did not want to be photographed next to me at a nightclub with a caption that only said the truth, but suggested much more: *Funnyman Mike Sharp and Funnylady Sukey Decker, out on the town, insist they're "Just Friends."*

Penny finally ordered a Ferris wheel when Rock and I were out on a bond drive, and one Sunday she invited Sukey and me over for its inaugural spin. We had cocktails by the pool, under its empty turning shadow. Penny kept trying to talk me onto it.

"Keep talking," I told her.

She wore a green top with slim green pants and green shoes, and lay across Rock's lap on a chaise longue. She looked like a piece of parsley on the blue plate special. "Suit yourself," she said sleepily.

Then she rolled to her feet and put her hands out to Sukey, *Will you dance*, and Sukey took them in agreement. That was one of the loveliest things about Penny: she'd ask anyone to dance, old men and grandmas and five-year-olds and homely single women, though this might be because all of the above looked the same, to Penny; what she could see, from across the room, were shoulders shifting longingly in time to the rhythm.

"It Had to Be You" played on the portable record player. Penny was the stronger dancer, and so she tried to use her advantage to force Sukey into leading. This ploy failed, but they looked lovely dancing together, in time but out of step. Both of them wore giant Andrews Sisters rolled hairdos; Sukey had on a fascinating halter top and a pair of camel-colored bell-bottoms. Penny placed her hand on the knot that held up Sukey's top.

Soon enough, Rocky stood up and offered his hands to me. We danced. Next to each other awhile, then arm-in-arm, both of us self-conscious but not embarrassed: we were men who'd danced together plenty onstage and in the movies. According to Rocky, heavy guys were always great dancers, because they flung themselves around to music at an early age to get a laugh and found out they liked it.

He started to sing: "When Mose Sharp was booooorn, 'mid Iowa coooooooorn . . ." Then he swiveled me around and dipped me one way. Out of the corner of my eye I could see Penny threaten to untie Sukey's halter top. Maybe that's what threw me off balance when Rocky suddenly dipped me the other way. I fell through his arms and into the pool. On the other hand, he might have dropped me on purpose, for a laugh. I still don't know.

Gravity must have treated me like any other heavy object—the seat of my pants must have gotten wet before the tips of my fingers as Rocky let go of them—but in my memory I'm a character in a comic strip: panel one, dancing on the deck with Rocky. Panel two, suddenly under-water—it wasn't that I'd forgotten that I couldn't swim; I'd forgotten that swimming was something you wanted to do, if you ended up in a pool. The water yanked at my necktie, the bottom of my jacket, as though it planned to make me presentable. Panel three: a half a dozen hands slip into my various pockets to lift me up. Panel four: I'm on the deck, lying on my back, surrounded by people who want to give me arti-ficial respiration but are laughing too hard.

The sky beyond them looked as hard as the tile under me. I felt pinned down by my wet clothes, but full of life. If I'd been in a movie, I would have sat up, spit out a mouthful of water, and removed a goldfish from my pocket.

"Can't you *swim?*" Sukey asked.

"Not a stroke!" I said cheerfully. "I could have drowned!"

We were all giggling. Well, they giggled; I laughed and wept at the same time as they hauled me to my feet, trying to slap the water out of my clothes, out of my toupee, which had kept half a toehold on my head. Who cared? I wasn't vain: I was alive!

"I could have drowned!" I told Sukey.

"You didn't," she said. She removed my wig and tucked it in her handbag, which set us all to laughing harder.

There wasn't a stitch of clothing anywhere in any of the dozens of closets in that house that would have fit me. I was folded into Rock's oversized toweling robe, and then folded into the passenger's side of my Buick, a gift from the studio in late 1941, just before the manufacturers quit production on civilian vehicles.

"I could have drowned!" I kept saying. "I could have drowned!"

Rocky leaned into the car. "You would have figured out how to swim eventually."

Sukey drove me to my house, as always relatively sober. "How will you get home?" I asked her, and she said that we'd figure that out later. Meaning: I drove her home the next morning, because she spent the night with me. At first I was still shocky and sodden from the pool, and then I was shocky and sodden from Sukey. She'd helped me into the house and into my bedroom, at which point I turned to her and said, "For God's sake, Suke, don't leave me alone." "You're all right," she said, but I think she saw the look on my face that said I wasn't. "I could have drowned," I said, my hands reaching for her but lost in the sleeves of the robe, "I could have drowned," and she told me to shut up, and then she shut me up.

I felt, simultaneously, like a river being dragged for a body; like the body beneath the surface of the river, insensible but wanting to be found; like the searching heroes bobbing on the river's surface in their boat. *There you are*, I heard Sukey say, the heroes looking for the body, the drowning man pulled into the boat by his rescuers. It felt exactly that personal: a matter of life and death between strangers.

For the next few months, it would suddenly occur to me that I could have sunk to the bottom of the pool and been retrieved too late. If they'd been a little drunker. If I'd been a little drunker . . . The lesson I took from this was that I shouldn't dance with Rocky near the pool. I wasn't angry at him, exactly, more bewildered by the possibility. I would have been on the front pages of all the movie magazines, my name and the word TRAGEDY. I could still feel the scouring chlorine in my nose, could see the angling shadow arms of the Ferris wheel turning above me. You're not beyond learning, Rocky told me, but I decided that I was. A better man would have signed up for swimming lessons the next day.

Sukey, meanwhile, was doing her best to befuddle me. Her best was pretty damn good. We had an agreement, by which I mean she had demands and I met them. She did not want to be my girlfriend. She did not want to be my date. She did not want my name linked to hers in any way, by anyone. This, of course, included Rocky and Penny. In return, we'd sleep together every now and then.

Such a puzzle, Sukey, calm and expert. I never met anyone who could make her fingers so separate: a caress from her meant one finger edging along an ear, her thumb at the corner of your mouth, a third finger at your waist, a fourth . . . Sleeping with Sukey made me feel pleasantly, sexily infested. She'd call me up in the middle of the night and invite me over—after that first night, she never came to my place—and afterward she made me again pledge my silence.

"Should I be insulted?" I asked. "You think I'd hurt your career?"

"I don't want people to know about me," she'd answer. Indeed, she never told me a single story about her past. I began to miss the Sukey I'd known before I fell into the pool, who was more likely to make a joke at her own expense than this intermittently ardent woman who met me at the door fresh from the shower. Still, I thought I might be in love with her. I hadn't had this steady a date since Miriam. Then again, a woman hadn't treated me with this much indifference since Miriam. I didn't see the connection then. I wondered how to tell, as though love was a house that needed to be viewed in the right kind of light, the right kind of weather, by which I mean of course her loving me back.

Carmen of Beverly Hills

"Come meet someone, Mosey!" Rocky called to me one afternoon on the set of *Gobs Away!* He displayed with a flourish a terrible-looking little gent.

I shook the man's hand, which took some doing, because his hands were already shaking. The guy was mostly a pair of giant blue eyes; the rest of his face seemed to have eroded like a cliff. His thin lips were sparkling wet, and his black suit looked slept in. Somebody—maybe Rocky—had already stuck a round white sailor's hat on his head at an angle that might have appeared jaunty if the guy's neck didn't look in danger of bending under its weight.

"Nice to meet you," I said.

"Skipper Moran!" said Rocky. I looked confused, and he repeated the name.

"Iss goo," said the old guy. I couldn't tell whether drink or a foreign accent had robbed him of his consonants.

Then I remembered Rocky talking about Skipper Moran, years before, when we regularly had arguments about who was funny and who wasn't. I said Harry Langdon, Buster Keaton, Mabel Normand. He said Fatty Arbuckle, Charley Chase, Billy Blevan, Mack Swain, and Skipper Moran, a particularly obscure Mack Sennett second banana. Moran's specialty was getting caught in things: trash cans, fences, fat women's dé-colletés. Despite the Irish name, he was a German immigrant, and once sound came in, disappeared.

Maybe the rag-bin clothes were left over from his movies, but the smell of whiskey couldn't have been. "Funny boy," Skipper Moran said to me warmly.

"Thanks," I said, but maybe he was just giving me his job description.

"I'm talking to Neddy," Rock said. Neddy was always hired to write special material for us. "We gotta get a part for this guy." Years later, when Rock had his own problems, I wished some young comic would do the same for him.

Poor Skipper. Neddy worked up a bit of mime for him—we couldn't let a guy with a German accent speak in such times—in a scene at some big do in this picture, a good-bye bash for sailors shipping out. Rocky and I were pulling KP duty in the kitchen and complaining, and Skipper played a geriatric gob who peeled potatoes. On the first take, he sliced open his thumb. On the second his hands trembled so they blurred.

"This is a disaster," I said to Rocky.

"No," he said. "Betcha a hundred bucks it won't be."

I just nodded.

Rocky took him off set, and when they returned five minutes later, Skipper Moran sat down at his pail of spuds with a ludicrous bandage on his thumb and was—I hate to admit it—suddenly funny. He threw the potatoes in the air and caught them on the end of his knife, he hugged the pail close to him with his legs and picked up another potato with his feet. His upper limbs got into a fight with his lower limbs, spuds every-where, and at the end, of course, he'd gotten caught in the bucket, folded up in half, someone's limber grandpa with a sweet, befuddled ex-pression on his face. He asked, without a trace of an accent, "Help?"

In the next shot, I slipped a hundred bucks in Rocky's pocket. He turned his face from the camera. "Thanks," he said. His breath was whiskey-coated.

Rocky's breath. I could write pages on it. In my life, I breathed in more Rocky Air than Iowan. There the guy was, breathing. I mean, not that I blame him. All those years we stood nose to nose: onstage, and closer in movies, and closer even in publicity stills so both our heads would fit in the frame. Me the stern educator, he the truant student—for those shots, like the leading man I wished to be, I stood on a box to ex-aggerate the height difference. (The height difference didn't exist.)

"Move in closer, boys," the photographer would say. Normally Rocky's breath was like anyone's, a caffeinated meadow, though if he'd been on a bender the meadow had flooded and gone to rot overnight. It changed, though, if he were on a diet or a health kick—for Rocky, never the same thing. Fatter was funnier, but sometimes, weary of being funny, he'd decide to slim; other times, weary of being bad, he'd resolve to be good. A health kick meant fruit and water and thick steaks for protein and hard-boiled eggs that found their way into his back pocket, where he sat on them. His breath was fierce then: I think his tongue went in mourning for the bourbon. A diet meant coffee, steaks, and gin: nothing else. Then his breath smelled of juniper, with a hint of an old metal cocktail shaker behind it.

And you know, that's one of the things I miss about him, the same way I missed Iowa thunderstorms in California, Iowa ice storms, mornings you woke up and the trees had turned to chandeliers and the roads to plate glass. It's the bad weather you miss most.

Penny, when she heard that her husband had hired Skipper Moran, threw a fit. If he could give a job to old-time foreign has-been comics, why couldn't he find a part, just a little part, for his own darling, talented wife? "That's different," Rocky told her, and she replied, "I'll say it is," and announced that she was going to sleep on the Ferris wheel and skulked out the door. "Be reasonable, Penn," he said, but she wouldn't talk to him, and so he set her in motion. She rode for nearly an hour, sitting in silence. She threw her wedding ring in the direction of his head, then she threw up and he let her down.

"The silence I can take," he told me. "It's the *singing*."

He'd come over to my place, which he did only when he wanted to get away from Penny. He hated giving up hosting privileges. So we sat in my living room, and Rocky smoked a cigar and tapped ashes on the white rug. I tried to keep myself from thrusting an ashtray underneath.

"You love her voice," I said.

"When she's happy. When she's mad it's like being married to a bad musical. She gets furious, and then she *sings*. Like she's seen so many movies, she thinks it's real life—she'll yell for about three seconds, get quiet, and break into song. And I swear she gets madder because I won't sing back."

"Maybe you should try," I suggested.

"You ever try to reason with an angry woman?"

"Once or twice."

"You felt like singing? If I'm going to fight with someone, I don't want it to be like some goddamn quiz show."

"I was thinking more opera," I said.

"This marriage," he said in a suddenly fierce voice, "is giving me a headache. She's a nice girl, but who knows what she wants?"

"Ask her," I said.

"Oh, she tells me. She wants a kid, do you believe that?"

"Sure. Another drink?"

He nodded, though of course with Rocky it was a rhetorical question. I pulled the martini cart closer to my chair.

"Imagine it," Rocky said. "If the baby cries, how's she going to find it? She can't make her way down a hallway in the dark as it is. Plus I think there's something wrong with her memory. We've been in the house two years already, and she's still surprised when she opens the door. 'Oh, look!' she says. 'A bathroom!' "

"Hire a nurse," I said, rattling my shaker. I adored making martinis. It made me feel like a mad scientist.

"Well, of course she wants a nurse too. Make me a Gibson this time, will you?"

"No onions."

"Just my luck," said Rocky, though it couldn't have been my lack of onions that made him so gloomy. "She proposed to *me*, I ever tell you that? What was I supposed to say, no?"

I strained the martini and handed it to him. "You married her because it would have been awkward not to marry her?"

"She lied to me. She said it was election day, and when she hustled me into the booth, there was a JP waiting. The problem is, Professor, she's not even my type."

"What do you mean?"

"You know: I like big blondes." He drew a big blonde in the air. "She's so little." He pinched his fingers together. "A sturdy woman, that's more my type."

I stared at him. "What, your *blood* type?"

"No, you know—"

"What is *wrong* with you, Rocky?" I felt like snatching back the martini. No more gin until you behave yourself.

"What's wrong with *you*? Not everyone has your catholic tastes."

"You're being ridiculous, that's what's wrong with me. Someone's not your type, you leave her alone. She's a lovely girl. You married her."

"You say that," he said, "but I notice, looking around, that you appear to be a bachelor."

We examined my living room, empty of women.

"You notice correctly. You know why? Because I don't go around marrying people out of boredom."

"My partner the playboy," Rocky said admiringly. He angled his empty glass toward me and I poured a little more from the shaker. "You'll never get married. I'd like to think you would, but you won't."

"Of course I will," I said. "Eventually."

"Well, you might *get* married, but you'll never *be* married. You'll fuck around."

That bothered me. "Why would you even say something like that?"

"What? That historically you've spent a goodly amount of time fucking around, and history repeats itself?"

"I never did."

"Are you *kidding* me?"

"No. I mean, not the way I define the word."

"Which word would that be? Fuck?"

"Actually, no. *Around.* I've never made a promise I didn't keep. I've never been a sneak. I've never lied."

"Never."

"Never. I've been discreet, sure. Stop laughing. I mean it. When I get married, it'll mean I've stopped."

"Fucking around."

"The around part, sure."

"Well, darling boy, when the time comes, remember who to ask for divorce advice." He twirled his glass between his fingers morosely. "You know how to find them, but nobody knows better than me how to lose them."

Whose Julep?

Tansy always said that money changed Rocky, and not for the better, but I think it was just the opposite: he stayed the same as he always was. That was the problem. He'd never been humble, he'd never been thrifty, he'd never had an ounce of noblesse oblige. A man with big dreams and a brash belief in himself and no money at all has a kind of charm. The guy's got pride, God bless him. No telling how far a fellow like that can go.

Same guy, same habits, but rich? Worst jerk you ever met.

Rocky had always wanted a bar in his basement, a band playing by the swimming pool, the prettiest lady barber in town to cut his hair. Poor, he drank too much and ate too much and sometimes lost his temper with strangers and those he loved, and the only thing that changed was now he could hire people to do the things he'd previously left undone. He'd always believed that money needed to be spent as quickly as possible; it was just harder work now. He lived big, a lot bigger than I did, because he made more and because some of my father's lessons had stuck with me and I believed in banks as places to increase my fortune, not merely as vaults to keep my cold hard cash, as Rocky said, warm.

Not that I played the ant to Rocky's grasshopper. A better man than me would have watched Rock's spendthrift ways and shaken his head sadly: *Don't you know there's a war on?* I watched that grasshopping and thought it looked like fun. I frowned at the endless supply of gas ration coupons he'd got his hands on—he seemed to know a counterfeiter— but I happily bought myself a jukebox that, when plugged in, bubbled at the edges like a hysterical carpenter's level. Rock installed an entire game room, including a roulette wheel. I bought a restaurant; Rock took over a nightclub on Sunset and called it the Rock Club. Rock bought himself a trailer to relax in between takes; I had his trailer towed into my driveway; he hired a guy to come around on the set to hit me with a pie; I hired a pretty girl in a low-cut dress to hit him with three pies; he bought a Rolls-Royce and hired a driver; I bought myself a diamond ring; he bought his wife a diamond necklace that made my ring look like dust; I slept with his wife, though not the necklace.

Okay, so as pranks go, that last one goes too far. It wasn't entirely my fault.

Hear me out. Excuse number one: they were estranged, they'd both told me so. Rocky had taken an apartment and left Penny at the house while they sorted things out. "This time it's for good," said Rocky. "Born a bachelor, might as well die one." "You'll never," I said, and he bet me two thousand dollars that he'd stay single. But he hadn't divorced Penny yet, and now I know that this is exactly when you *shouldn't* sleep with your best friend's wife, because it means too much. Then, though, it seemed as though I might as well, the way that Rocky in restaurants would eat my leftovers when I was finished with my meal. That sounds awful. It probably is. All I mean is: the line between what was his and what was mine sometimes seemed pretty blurry.

Excuse number two: Rocky was sleeping around then, so he said, and how could he complain?

Excuse number three: it wasn't my idea.

Rocky loved his nightclub. He had an idea that he was meant to be an impresario, enamored as he was of liquor, company, smoke, music, and girl singers. "I'm only being patriotic," he said. "Servicemen drink free." Nearly everyone drank free. All you had to do was shake Rocky's hand: instant cocktail. If you were sufficiently grateful, you got a line of credit. Anyhow, it was late. Penny and I were sitting in a banquette in the back; she and Rock had recently resolved to be buddies. Across the room, Rock stood behind the bar, talking to a young woman whose blond hair was more aluminum than platinum. Then Rocky cocked his elbow for her to take and they left together. I was glad Penny's eyesight was so bad. We'd become buddies too: she was simultaneously the deepest and most shallow person I'd ever met. She had an abandoned child's need to be the center of attention, and then she'd get suddenly wise.

"They gone?" she said.

"Who?"

"Rock and the magician's assistant."

"They're gone. You can see that far?"

"I got radar for girls like that," said Penny. "I should get a part-time job on the vice squad."

"Penny!" I said, and clucked my tongue. "I thought there were no hard feelings between you and Rock."

"I'm drunk," she explained, leaning back on the quilted banquette. "You know, I always liked you."

"I never thought otherwise. Drink?"

"Nah. No: sure." She sat thinking for a while, then closed one eye and looked at me, then swapped and looked again.

"How many?" I asked.

"One drink's *fine*."

"No," I said. "How many of everything are you seeing?"

"Dozens. None of them clearly. You look like a whole orchestra, sitting there."

"What'll you have to drink."

"A julep," she said, which was what she now called all drinks. "A tall cold julep. Is it true that you slept with one?"

"A julep? Does that mean something I don't know about?"

She giggled. "Should. No: an orchestra. That's the rumor that I heard, is that you slept with an all-girl orchestra."

Ah. This was one of Rocky's favorite myths: *The week we played Syracuse, the Professor worked his way through the whole Cherry Red Orchestra, starting with the percussioness.* I wished he hadn't spread it to Penny.

"No," I said. "They loved their instruments too much. When a girl gets to know a tuba real well, she's pretty much spoiled for human company."

"You know . . ." Penny said confidentially. She reclined sideways and tossed her calves across my thighs, making a hash mark of my lap. "Where's my julep, Julep?"

"Let me free, and I'll get you one."

"Any minute now." Penny's dress was a bright emerald green, gathered with rhinestone clips at either point of her collarbone. "You know," she said again, "when I started hanging around with you boys, it wasn't Rocky I liked."

"No?"

"*No.*" She nodded.

"Okay," I said. "So you grew to love him."

"Yes!" she said. "He talked me into it. I figured the two of you had a conversation and decided he'd get me."

I decided to be polite. "He always did get the lion's share of everything."

"Sixty-forty," she said, and that was another thing I resented, Rocky telling her the terms of our agreement. "So, you want to collect?"

"What?" I said.

"Your forty percent." One of her green shoes fell off her foot onto the banquette next to me. I picked it up, slipped my hand inside. I could feel the row of elliptical indentations like little stones where her toes had settled into the leather.

"Listen," I said.

"You listen, Julep." The other shoe fell off. "You're going to have to carry me home. The all-julep orchestra. I mean, I always liked you. And I could tell you always liked me. I'm not really drunk, I mean, not much. Not more than you are, if that's what you're worried about—"

What *had* Rocky been telling her? That was what I always told him:

Never sleep with anyone drunker than you are. True enough, I was drunk, and that would have been excuse number four except that I never did anything I regretted simply because I was drunk. Rocky liked to say, "Too bad, the way you always keep your wits about you."

"—and besides," Penny said, and she looked like she wished she had a third shoe to kick off, "you don't want to hurt my feelings."

Excuse number four: I didn't want to hurt her feelings.

In the movies, I never so much as kissed a girl. These days they give even the fattest and least appealing comedians their own love interests, a pretty girl who has nothing to do with the business at hand. Our movies had the pretty girl plus her dull handsome gentleman friend. Now and then Rocky would be in love with a girl comedian, because Rocky was made even less than I for Romance, and therefore was a funnier Romeo. A kiss between them was a spoof, a giant zealous puckering sound like a zipper going, as though for Rocky even kissing was slapstick, slightly painful, unserious. In *Ghost of a Chance* I had a fiancée who was so much a foregone conclusion that we barely appeared on-screen together, though she did beg me not to go into a haunted house with only the Wee Willie Winkie candle on a plate I clutched in my hand. The joke was that girls frightened the Professor more than any old ghost.

In real life, I hadn't been afraid of a girl in a long time, not even Sukey, but Penny spooked me. Drunk as we were, we didn't get much sleep that night. Penny seemed always to have just brushed her teeth, her kisses all canines and peppermint. Why on earth was I doing this? She seemed amazed that I guessed that her dress unzipped on the side. Maybe she hoped that I'd give up if I didn't know the secret. That part was easy; her underthings were complicated, a camisole over a long-line brassiere, a half slip over a girdle and garters, hooks and eyes everywhere. Despite this bracing assortment of garments, she seemed smaller undressed. One knee was childishly skinned, rough and hot. Everywhere I touched felt like a different temperature: her narrow shoulders, her slightly wider hips. She took her hair down, and suddenly looked even more naked.

What unnerved me was watching this woman I knew perfectly well, this woman I'd grown fond of, turn, by degrees, into a woman about to have sex. I hadn't ever slept with someone I'd really known before, I mean, not for the first time. There was Mimi, but Mimi in bed was Mimi out of bed; I'd never known a woman who changed less in the act of love. As for Sukey: I'd never known a woman who changed more. Penny was somewhere in between. I hadn't seen her make that expression before, but it was familiar. Her hand went fluttering under my chin.

I bit the insides of her thighs, and she almost squirmed away but moved my hands with her own to her waist to keep her steady. I thought I was betraying everyone, Rocky and Sukey and Penny herself, and maybe the only difference the drink made was that I couldn't tell how much I cared. I had crossed over: I was no longer a man of discretion, I was a lousy goddamn sneak. She was his *wife*. She was living in his *house*.

Such a squirming girl. I am changing the subject.

"Do you think—" I began, but she shushed me with a shudder, sat up and kissed my shoulder and bit my collarbone. Where had her legs gone all of a sudden? Ah. They were around my waist, and I was sitting up on my heels, and Penny slid her lips across my chin and down my throat. My heart felt like a ball bearing in a child's maze, moved around by her mouth.

We'd gone to Penny's house, which is to say Rocky's, which was why I missed the telegram from the former Valley Junction, now West Des Moines. I found it slid beneath my door when I went home at four in the morning, just after Penny and I swore not to tell anyone, especially Rocky.

March 3, 1943
Michael Sharp
1123 Belmont Drive
Sherman Oaks, Calif.

darling Papa died today come home if you can all love Annie.

Beautiful frugal Annie, who wouldn't have said *died* but all the euphemisms cost more, and she'd already wasted forty cents on *darling*. I wondered who Michael Sharp was, and then realized she wanted to be both respectful of my stage name and formal. That was what I concentrated on, because my father's death seemed made up. I hadn't seen him in four years, not since Rocky had tricked me into going home. *You've come home once*, Annie said to me then. *Now you can do it over and over.*

I'd agreed with her. But then the war came, and Carter and Sharp were a hit, and it was hard to travel in wartime, and we were a hit, and I'd meant to and meant to . . . but I didn't, because we were a hit. Busy. *Come back.* Those were his last words to me. He'd gotten too deaf to use the phones. All I knew of his life from the past four years I got from Annie. *His appetite is good. He doesn't mention the war. He's grown fond of crossword puzzles. He adores his grandchildren. He thanks you for the necktie, he thanks you for the bottle of wine, he thanks you for the new radio.* What a failure I was. Bad enough to run away from home once, but twice?

I wondered whether I could catch a plane so I could make the funeral, which was probably today and if not today, then tomorrow. Most of the spots on planes were saved for servicemen, but I sat down and wrote several telegrams—one to Rocky, one to Tansy, and one to Annie, explaining where I'd gone, where I'd be, and I drove to the airport and waited for a flight, and there I remembered Penny, and sent her a wire too.

9

He Called Everyone Goldie

As I walked up Eighth Street to the house in Vee Jay, I could see a young woman sitting on the front steps, despite the late winter nip. She stood up as I got closer, a young woman in a brown dress with black piping and very red lipstick. Some niece, or great-niece, or unaccounted in-law. She met me halfway across the lawn, and I realized two things: I was about to be hugged; the woman was Rose, grown up.

"Mose!" she said in the sandy voice all my sisters had inherited from my mother, a kind of *yiddishe* Gene Kelly.

"You look different," I said, almost laughing.

"I stopped being twelve years old."

"Well, it suits you," I said, and it did. She looked like my other sisters, with her dark hair and blue eyes, but somehow more beautiful: her skin was pinker, her waist more emphatic. The whole town must have thought of her as the prettiest of the Sharp girls. No wonder some Quigley had kidnapped her.

She put her arm around my waist and pointed at the front stairs. "I was just thinking," she said. "About you and Hattie the day after Mama died. You stepped in all the food."

"We did. How can you remember that? You were a baby."

She stopped for a second. "You're right," she said, rubbing her chin with her free hand. "I shouldn't remember it, but I do. Annie was furious."

"She was?"

"Sure. What a waste!" She sighed. We still stood off the walk. "It's not so bad from here," she said. "The house. Not so bad altogether, I guess. But right now, I want to run away."

I kissed her temple. "Me too," I said.

"You're better at it than me," said Rose, and then the front door opened, and Annie waved us in.

"I found him on the floor," Annie told me. "I got up and came downstairs and went to the kitchen because I didn't want to wake him. I made some tea. I sorted and soaked some beans for dinner. Then I thought I'd make him some milktoast. He hadn't been feeling well. Stomach. Head, too, I guess. He called me Goldie. He called the little boys Goldie. I mean, he didn't think they were, but it was the only name he could remember, and that made him mad, and he'd point at whoever he meant, and say, Goldie, that Goldie. Got to be in a wheelchair, it's behind the door now. Doctor said strokes, maybe lots of little ones. He was ninety-four, the oldest man in Valley Junction, did you know? Doctor said he died in his sleep and then fell out of bed, but he didn't. He was reaching for something. Us. That's what I think: he knew he was dying, and he wanted to get to us!"

By *us* she meant herself and Rose, both sleeping upstairs. Now the house was filled with sisters and nieces and nephews, all those fascinating strangers.

Your people are barbaric, I'd said to Rocky when he'd told me what a wake was. Now I understood. I wished I had seen him. I wished he was as vivid to me as he was to my sisters: the crime scene, his last known whereabouts. His eyes were open. His beard was tangled. His right arm was over his head, and he had his hand out as though in the dark he'd seen the rabbi's face in the portrait over the mantel and had said, "Stranger, help an old man up, I beg you." Maybe he said it in Yiddish or Lithuanian. In the dark, the rabbi would have looked underwater; to be in black and white, then, was only sensible. Perhaps the rabbi had called my father out of bed. Pop sleeps, and wakes, and wants to look at his friend's face, but all he can see is a ball of light where the moonbeams from the kitchen window hit the curved glass. Something feels wrong, as though one of the children has been trying to scrape out his heart with a spoon. He leans out of bed, and he falls to the floor.

Nothing hurts except the wool of the carpet under his cheek. Then he realizes: he can feel that cheek again. He can nearly count the petals of the flowered carpet. Still, he can hear his friend, the man behind the glass who calls to that fine old gentleman on the floor—for a few seconds more, the oldest living citizen in Valley Junction—by every name he's ever been called in his life: *Jake, Jacob, Papa, Pop, darling, darling Mr. Sharp, sir, sir, Zayde, Jakov Shmuel—tell me, what is your name?*

Not anymore, here's a new one, good luck.

We said how lucky we were to have had him so long. A man who died well loved, well kissed, well fed. A life of sadness, but not of regret. Front-page news in the *West Des Moines Express*. All that food I'd imagined before: the neighbors brought covered dishes and platters of meat and dozens of muffins. Step in it, I thought, but instead I ate an entire coffee cake from the point of a knife. *Mose, what are you doing?* someone asked me as I polished it off, and I said, *Cleaning up.*

My father's will left the store for me if I agreed to come home and run it. If I refused, Sharp's Gents' would be sold to Ed Dubuque at a very reasonable price.

"Well?" Annie asked.

For thirty seconds I imagined myself giving up on the movies, coming back to Valley Junction, working with Ed Dubuque and Annie. I could feel the cloth tape measure slip between my fingers as I encircled the customers, telling them their size as though I were predicting a pleasant fortune. Then I might ease my guilt: I'd finally do what my father, my dead father, had always wanted. But I couldn't stop myself, and in my head I filled the store with chorus girls who flew back and forth on the sliding ladders; they did a dance with the metal measures for feet; some disguised themselves as mannequins and some as customers.

I shook my head.

"He could have left it to me!" said Annie, and burst into tears.

Well, I was shocked, first by Annie's greediness, and then, moments later, by the realization that she was right: poor, devoted firstborn Annie, who'd done everything an heir should have except been born a boy.

The sympathy in that house was like the coffee cake: too much, too sweet, too familiar. I wearied of all those sisterly embraces. The service at B'nai Jeshurun was packed with Jews and Gentiles. The one place I least wanted to be famous was the one place I was most: "It's the movie star!"

said old school friends, and minor cousins, and men to whom I'd as a teenager sold underwear. In the *temple*, at my father's *memorial*. All I wanted was to forget myself and remember my father, but I automatically shook hands and smiled, and then was sickened from smiling. *This is not a personal appearance. This is a personal disappearance.* Ed Dubuque finally rescued me, his nose red from weeping. "Master Sharp," he said solemnly. The rabbi of my youth was still there, and he threw his arms around me and rubbed my bald head (I left my hairpiece in California, I suddenly realized, I hoped not in Penny's—Rocky's!—bed).

At the graveside I stood with the shovel, planning to turn over the usual three spadefuls of dirt onto my father's pine coffin, but somehow, I lost track. He'd called everyone Goldie. Maybe he'd forgotten my name, too. Of course he had. When the dirt hit the pine, tiny white rocks revealed themselves there, and I wanted to jump down and pick them out. Hattie's grave was next to us; Mama's next to hers. I would not even look in that direction. When the family turned from my father's grave to head back home, they'd stop and leave stones for Hattie and Mama, to show they remembered. Not me. I'd lose track then, too, I'd heap so many rocks up you wouldn't be able to find the graves at all. Across from me, one son-in-law handed his shovel to another, but I was making up my own ritual, a spadeful of dirt for every year I'd stayed gone, proof of my regret. The only thing I could do for my father now was bury him.

"Mose?" said the rabbi, who stood behind me. His voice was both bewildered and educational. "Mose? You do know that it's only symbolic?"

Pop's old Jewett was full of gas despite all shortages: no one ever drove it. That night I took it coughing up Fifth Street to downtown Vee Jay. Someone had tacked a memorial wreath to the door of Sharp's Gents'. If I crossed Railroad Avenue, I'd get to Johnny's Vets' Club, a disreputable bootleg joint that maybe my father had never heard of. I'd killed him, I decided, though it took a lot of work even for me to figure out how. What I came up with: he realized, at last, that I wasn't coming home to run the store, that the next time I came to Des Moines would be to bury him, and he thought, Let the boy have his wish. Oh, that wasn't true. But I also knew that my father had spent his life assembling and perfecting Sharp's Gents' as a gift for me—who knew what he'd given up over fifty years to make it a going concern?—and every time he offered it, I turned him down. As though he were offering money, or an exploding cigar. Sitting in the Jewett at the end of Fifth Street, I tried to imagine how my refusal would have felt to him.

No: I wouldn't go to Johnny's, where the town toughs might be toasting to my father. I'd swing into Des Moines, maybe go to Babe's (another bootlegging restaurant; Iowa still held on to Prohibition), maybe find myself one of those nice WACs. We'd check into a downtown hotel, a grand one—I chose the Fort Des Moines, in honor of her home base. I wouldn't bother to call my sisters. Understand: I knew I would do nothing of the kind. I decided to do these things so that I could then decide not to.

So I drove past Greenwood Park, up Grand Avenue to Babe's, and around the state capitol, past the Soldiers' and Sailors' Monument, back toward downtown, then north. I went past the Jewish Community Center, where Hattie and I had gone to dances at my father's urging. As a matter of fact, there was a dance going on that very night; couples strolled in through the front door. They looked cheerful and full of pep. I parked the Jewett and stared at the place. It was as though I'd been talking to my father: *Pop, I'm going to Johnny's Vets', maybe Babe's.*

Mose, no nice girl will ever be in those places, because no nice boy would take her there. Why not go to the Community Center? You like to dance, so dance. Have a soft drink. Talk to nice people.

So in I went.

Most of the people inside seemed to know each other—they attended the Temple, or Tifereth Israel, the Conservative synagogue. I got myself a glass of lemonade from a plump girl in a tight pink dress. It was weird to see people dancing like this, earnestly, as though they'd studied dancing for a test. The band was two fat men in blue suits, one a piano player, the other a saxophonist. They played on a small stage near the lemonade girl.

Was dancing allowed during mourning? I flexed my toes in my funeral shoes, and thought I could maybe work it in.

When I first saw the woman, she was trying to avoid having her shoes trampled by an old guy whose bald head shone with sweat. I touched my own forehead in sympathetic embarrassment. They were doing the Castle Walk, an ancient dance. Probably it was the only one he knew. The woman wore her black hair in a Spanish bun, with curls on either side. You could tell she thought she came off as taller than she was, but actually she was tiny, with a long nose and white skin and I had

never, never seen anyone who looked like her, so unlikely and so beautiful. She was bossy when she danced. If they were the Castles, Castle-
walking, she was certainly Vernon, and he Irene.

The saxophonist was giving the pianist room to do some fancy stuff
on the keyboard. He leaned over to me and said, a mind-reader, "Go
ahead, ask her to dance. What's the worst that could happen?"

So I walked off to do that very thing. Later I found out he was the
lemonade girl's father, and that's probably who he meant.

But the woman I had my eye on was with yet another man, this one
skinny and pimple faced, with an active Adam's apple—was he talking,
or swallowing nervously? She made the way she dodged his jabbing elbows into a little ballet. I lost heart. She was too good, and though I
knew I could outdance any of the men here, I couldn't outdance her.
Who could?

I caught up with her at the refreshment table.

"May I?" I asked. The lemonade was free. My offer was only to accept
the drink from the fat girl and hand it over.

My woman smiled. "Surely. Thank you."

The lemonade girl handed me a dripping glass, though earlier her
aim had been faultless.

"My name is Mike Sharp," I told the dark-haired woman. I waited for
her recognition. The saxophonist said to the piano player, "See?"

"I'm Jessica Howard," she said. She wiped the glass with a handful of
her black skirt, which was made of bands of lace you could see light
through: it was a Roman Colosseum of a skirt. Beneath it, she wore a
dark red slip. "That guy I was dancing with?" she said. "Voice like a
saltine cracker. Made me thirsty."

The sax player pulled his instrument apart and laid it in its velvet
lined case.

"No more music," Jessica said sadly.

"Next time," the saxophonist told her, despite himself, "I'll play you a
flamenco."

She winked at him. Oh God, I thought, I need a wink like that myself. I said, "May I give you a ride home?"

"I don't get in strange cars with men."

"I don't have a car," I said, renouncing anything she might not like.
"May I walk you home?"

She was looking at me with what was either contempt or the earliest
stages of affection. "Why?"

"Why," I repeated. "I've been away from Des Moines for a while. I'd like to take a walk. We could keep each other company."

"Well, then," she said. "Let's walk."

The air outside felt damp and cool, like something laid across the chest of an ailing child. I felt cured already. She had a kind of skipping stride. Maybe she was thinking of how she'd attack the flamenco at the next dance. I couldn't decide if I liked the fact that she didn't know I was the Movie Star. I was pretty sure I did.

"You dance beautifully," I told her.

"Should," she said. "It's my business."

"You dance professionally?"

"Have. Now I teach. But I danced with the Chicago Opera Company for two years."

"Ah," I said. "You teach ballet?"

"*Everything*. Ballet, tap, social. I could teach you."

"I sort of already know," I said, modest as I could. "People tell me I'm a pretty fair dancer."

"Didn't tonight," she said.

The short sentences kept catching me by surprise. *My turn? Already?* "I just got into town. I guess I'm still tired."

"Too tired to dance," she said musingly. "So then: where?"

"I was in a dance marathon." True enough: for a few days in 1929 when I was between bookings, I'd entered (and lost) a marathon. I hoped that would explain my enthusiasm and weariness.

"Good grief, *that's* not dancing. That's just"—she moved her shoulders around, imitating someone who mistakenly believed he *was* dancing—"that's foolishness set to music. Dancing isn't a race. You can't do a marathon of it."

"Well, then, I'll come for a lesson."

She smiled then, delightedly. "Do!" she said. "Here we are." She turned to face me. She seemed to have her feet arranged in one of the five positions; I didn't know which one. "Mr. Sharp," she said, and that she'd remembered my name for a whole five blocks thrilled me. "Thank you." She tipped an imaginary hat.

"When?" I asked.

"When what?"

"The lesson. When should I come?"

"An eager student!" She stuck a fist on one hip. "Tomorrow? Two-thirty? Call—it's 9-0427—and make sure." Then she turned and walked up the path to a brick house with a green door. Like my California house, it had a red Spanish-style roof; I nearly ran up the path and pointed that out to her. One strand of her black hair had come unwoven from her bun; it nearly reached her waist, and I wanted to fix it. I touched the corner of my mouth, as if she had kissed me. She hadn't. She hadn't touched me at all.

I walked back to Valley Junction, a considerable distance. I imagined I looked like Dick Powell, besotted with a girl, about to kick a can and burst into song. For a moment I thought: my father died two days ago. But on that long walk home it seemed I could remember one thing at a time—either Jessica dancing, or my father, and I chose. Every time I thought of Pop, I willed myself not to, so thoroughly that the next morning I had to take the streetcar into Des Moines to pick up the car.

I Could Keep Time by You

When I arrived the next day for my lesson, Jessica was dressed in leotards, a small flippy skirt tied around her waist. The girls in Hollywood, in vaude, wore next to nothing, sometimes, but in a house in Des Moines Jessica's immodesty seemed revolutionary. She invited me in. Our houses, apart from the roofs, had nothing in common: the room I stepped into—her dance studio—was all wood, honey-polished from ballet slippers and dimpled from taps. In the corner a young man with dark hair that fell into his eyes sat at a grand piano, his shoulders already up to his ears, his hands above the keyboard, as though he was a character in a Swiss clock, waiting for the hour to strike.

"This is my brother Joseph," she said. "Joseph, this is Mr. Sharp."

He nodded and looked up at me through the hair. I could just make out one glinting navy-blue eye and three ugly pimples.

A Spanish poster advertising a bullfight was taped to the wall. A stout man, a dancer, frowned from a Lucite frame on top of the piano; he'd autographed his portrait to Jessica in Italian, and though I couldn't read the words I knew they meant something fond and excessive.

"Well, Mr. Sharp," Jessica said to me, "what can I teach you?"

"That's what I've come to find out."

"Let's see what you know, then." She put out her hands to indicate that I should step into them, and her brother began to play in waltz time. After a moment, Jessica laughed. "You can dance. Whoever told you that you couldn't?"

"Whoever told me that I could?"

"I did."

"Well, then," I said. I tried to arrange my stupid smile into something suave, and stepped on her foot.

"That," she said, "I can work with. To the left, dear. You keep wanting to dance me into the dining room. You're not a clock. You may change directions, if it suits the dance."

Oh, it suits me, I thought, though mostly it was being called dear. Mostly it was seeing her dining room right there, off the studio, the walls done up in a Polynesian-style paper, somebody's toast plate still on the table, butter lumped in a cut-glass dish. Mostly it was my hand on her back, her leotard a little rough but lovely: *she* was a clock, I could tell by her thin black-clad arms and the steadiness of her feet and the ticking in her wrist. (I'd secretly slipped my thumb down, to feel her pulse as we danced. It was perfectly steady, and wreaking havoc with mine.) I could keep time by you, I thought.

"Your feet are fine," said Jessica. "Now we have to work on your face."

"It's the only one I have." I wasn't the least bit insulted.

"Who told you that? Any dancer has more than one. First off, keep your mouth closed. You've got it hanging open. You look like you're frightened of something happening in the other room. Concentrate on your partner. Make her think that *she's* the one who's moving your feet. That's the way it works: she moves your feet, and your feet move her feet, and you're both in charge of the dance that way."

I knew who was in charge. I hadn't felt so deliciously bossed since Hattie, who I missed all over again, but you know? That sorrow was almost pleasant. I missed my father, too, in the same way: *look, Pop, a nice Jewish girl I wish you could meet*. All mourning should take place in waltz time. Des Moines was not so bad. I loved everyone: Annie, who had pressed my clothing this morning as she cried over my father; my mother, another small black-haired woman who sang under her breath.

Oh, my father would love you.

"What's that?" Jessica said.

"Just counting," I answered.

I wrote a check for my lesson, and said I wanted another. She consulted the calendar on her desk. "Next week—" she began.

"I'm much worse than that," I said. "What do you have for tomorrow?"

My sisters thought my absentmindedness came of grief. Maybe it did. My mother died when I was a child, Hattie died when I was a teenager, and I had mourned like a child and like a teenager, first without understanding, and then with too much. Now I was a man with a job and money, and my father was dead, and maybe that meant it was time for me to take a wife after all.

Because all of a sudden that was what I wanted. I believed in my desire to marry Jessica as deeply as any skeptic converted by a miracle. Problem was, I had to go back to California soon. Rocky wired four times my first day in Iowa, and six times the second, notes full of condolences and information and requests for phone calls when I had time but not a moment before. Jimmy Durante would fill in for me on radio that Tuesday—two days after my father's funeral—but then I needed to wrap things up. Our latest picture, *Fly Boys*, still needed its chase scene, though I was hardly necessary, since it involved Rocky escaping from an amusement park in a bumper car and driving down the boardwalk, where every plank made him blink. They needed me for reaction shots, flinging down my mortarboard, trying to get my own bumper car free from the bumper-car rink. I couldn't dawdle in Des Moines.

You might think a guy like me would never meet a woman and want to marry her so quickly, but I ask you: can you imagine me *dating* her, me in California, she in Iowa? Can you imagine me waiting? I couldn't go home with a phone number and a promise. I needed to bring back Jessica herself.

My secret. Nobody else knew. Sometimes I asked myself questions in Pop's voice, and then in Rocky's. Was she Jewish? Yes. Her father had been secretery at the same Orthodox shul that had employed my grandfather the rabbi. Cousins of mine had married cousins of hers, in that endless way of the Jews of Des Moines. She was only two years younger than me, but try as we might, we could not manage to come up with a single social event that we might have attended together as kids, not even weddings and funerals of mutual friends and distant relatives, or dances at the community center: she'd only gone to those after the death of her strict father.

Well then, my father would have said, she can work in the store. After all, I was going to stay. I couldn't take a nice girl away from her home, could I? An orphaned girl, after all. Look after her.

Rocky would get me on the other side. He had told me, when we first met, that I should be ambitious in love, but I could hear in my head his questions, and I didn't want to have to answer them. No, I hadn't kissed her. No, I hadn't asked her on a date. We'd only danced for educational purposes. She might have no idea of how I felt.

I could not wait to see her again; I did not think I could *bear* to see her again. She flat-out terrified me. She might upset that perfect romantic feeling, a pan of warm water inside my chest almost shoulder high, filled but perilous. It was the balancing that amazed me. Every time I thought of when I'd see her, the pan wobbled, but didn't spill, and the feat of carrying it astounded me again.

"How did you know you loved Mommy?" one of my daughters asked years later. "I just knew," I answered, which was not the truth. I realized I loved Jessica the day after I met her, when I mistakenly thought I saw her walking down the street toward me and I wanted to dive into a nearby bush and tremble with happiness, watching her pass.

The day after my father's funeral, I sat in the kitchen with Rose and Annie, amid the ruins of the neighbors' offerings. For lunch Annie had simply plunked a pie plate or Dutch oven in front of each of us: I had a chicken casserole, which I would have rather stepped in than eaten. Rose's adventures with Quigley had made her slightly bawdy, given to elbow nudges. Annie played schoolmarm, but fondly. There were twenty-three years between them; there had only been seventeen between Annie and Mama. Two women of different generations: Annie still wore long dark skirts—she looked like Carry Nation, inconsolable over the loss of her hatchet—but modern Rose wore blue jeans and a western-style shirt. Now they kept house together, and I guessed they would for the rest of their lives. I worried that Rose, raised by a spinster, was doomed to become one.

"He never even saw one of my movies," I said, running my fork across the ribbed edge of the white casserole dish.

"What are you talking about," said Annie.

"Of course he did," said Rose.

I looked at them. "Which one?"

"All of them," said Annie.

"We took him," said Rose. She pointed out the window. Annie took her finger and pushed it like a turnstile toward downtown. Rose laughed. "We took him. The Lyric removed a seat for us, to make room for his chair."

"Some we saw twice," said Annie.

"Three times," said Rose.

"No kidding?" I said.

"He wouldn't miss them!" said Annie.

"He *loved* you," said Rose, who knew the limits of our father's love.

I didn't know that my father had ever been to a movie in his life. "No kidding," I said, my voice cracking like a teenager's. Pop at the Lyric in the front row, in a parking space made just for him, watching me, a kid who never graduated from anything, jump around in a mortarboard.

"No kidding!" my sisters said together.

Annie and Rose indulged me. They'd lived with my father, had seen him get sick. They might have seen him wish to die soon; they might have wished it themselves in some small way. He was ninety-four after all. Rose began slicing a rhubarb pie with the side of her fork. "I hate rhubarb," she said, taking a bite.

"So what happened to Quigley?" I asked. Annie frowned, Rose smiled. They both shook their heads.

"That bad?" I asked.

"He hit me," said Rose. "Once."

I nodded. A terrible man, now gone.

"I mean, I might not have left anyhow, but I called Annie and told her."

"I said, 'Stay right there. I'm coming to get you.' "

Rose nodded. "So I packed my bags and waited. We lived in Kansas City, and Annie came on the train, which is not such a great way to make an escape. Billy figured it out and came to the station and begged me to stay. Sobbed, right there in Union Station."

"Ugly," said Annie. "Embarrassing."

"But Annie carted me away. She was right. It was a mistake, marrying Billy."

"You're still in love with him," I said.

"No!" said Annie.

"No," said Rose. She was twenty-eight years old and had failed at running away from home. She smoothed her blue jeans nostalgically, not the least bit heartbroken. "Heavens, no. But some days I'm still in love with the mistake."

Whose Dog Are You?

After my second lesson, Jessica looked at the clock on the mantelpiece, which was flanked by two porcelain dancers. "Would you like a glass of water?" she asked.

"I *am* thirsty," I said, as though my thirst was proof of something.

Joseph sat with us on the back porch, drinking coffee. (When she offered me water, she really meant coffee, which was the only thing Jessica ever drank.)

"Genevieve Gold can't dance at all," Joseph said suddenly.

"That's true," said Jessica. "She dances like a half-filled gallon jug."

Poor Genevieve, whoever she was.

"So," Joseph asked. "What do you do for a living?"

"I'm in show business," I said.

He laughed and ladled the hair off his forehead with a hand. "I'm kidding. I've seen your pictures."

I waited hopefully for some adjective.

"Doing?" Jessica said at last.

"I'm a comedian," I said. "Part of a team."

"He has a radio show," Joseph said.

"I listen to music," said Jessica.

"There's music sometimes. He lives in Hollywood."

"Right now," I said, though I had no plans to leave it.

"I don't like comedy," said Jessica.

"I do," Joseph said.

Okay, a setback, but maybe we could work around it. "Why not?"

She shrugged. I later found out that this was simply Jessica: there were plenty of things she didn't like. Olives, for instance. Mothers, except for her own. Omaha.

She shrugged again. "Don't. What kind are you?"

"Oh. Ordinary, I guess. My partner and I have a knockabout act. Sometimes I do a little singing."

"That's silly," said Jessica. She didn't sound mad, just certain. "And what brings you to town?"

"My father died," I said.

"I'm sorry." She took my empty coffee cup and examined it seriously, holding it, I imagined, as though it were my hand.

"How old was he?" Joseph asked.

I said, mournfully (I would go for sympathy if I couldn't get laughs), "Ninety-four."

But that, it turned out, was a punch line. They both laughed. *"Really?"* said Joseph.

I'd been looking at Jessica's hand, her thumb on the lip of the cup where my mouth had been, and when I saw their faces I was confused. They looked oddly delighted: *Not as sad a story as we thought.* I was a young man, and they'd assumed that Pop's death was premature, as their own father's had been.

"Ninety-four!" said Jessica. And though I felt a little flood of grief— here I was with Jessica, thinking of my father—the grief began to turn to something else. My sisters had said we were lucky, but they didn't believe it. Jessica and Joseph did, and I was convinced. I thought of my father and Rose and Annie at the Lyric, every few months suiting up to see another movie: what other proof did I need of my father's love? My father had never renounced me. He lived a long life. Luck. Later I would understand that my guilt had been a kind of egotism: if I couldn't be the hero of my father's life, then I could be the villain of his death.

The Howards owned a clumsy spaniel who looked like an old man, liver spotted and red eyed. The weather was fine, and the dog wanted to play catch with a fabric ball, which, when I inspected it, turned out to be a pair of tights rolled around themselves. They were wet and smelled like the dog, but I thought about stealing them. Instead, I sat on the back steps and talked through the screen to the Howards. They told me about their beloved parents. We gossiped a little about piano players we knew around town. They asked me how I'd gotten into show business, and instead of my life with Rocky I told them about my partnership with Hattie, because it was true, and because I thought they'd like a story about an Iowan brother-and-sister act, even one that broke up before its debut.

Jessica sat on a folding chair behind me, and every now and then she kicked me in the small of my back through the screen with a pointed toe. I couldn't tell whether this was on purpose until I said something slightly mean about a neighbor lady. Then she kicked me lightly at the ticklish part of my waist, which felt fond and primitive, as though this was how they courted in modest foreign countries: through wire mesh. Joseph, after a bit, went to bed, and Jess and I stayed there, swapping family stories. I waited for her to invite me back into the porch, but she didn't, so I sat on the step and threw the ball to the dog, who joylessly caught it and brought it back, brought it back, like a milkman longing for retirement. I threw it again, hoping the dog would love me. Then I might manage the rest of the house. I worried it wasn't working. The dog admired my tirelessness, which was doglike, but it didn't seem to think that was anything special. Dogs are not impressed with what dogs do.

A Wartime Wedding

"Mr. Sharp," she said when I showed up for a lesson the next afternoon. "I've never had such an enthusiastic student."

"I expect you haven't," I said.

She wore a scarf in her hair, so long it nearly trailed on the floor. "Today I'm Isadora Duncan, I hope with better luck."

We danced. Joseph played. I must have stepped on her feet plenty as I thought of California. Another Tuesday was on its way, and Durante wouldn't be free forever while I courted a girl in Des Moines. "To the left," said Jessica. I watched her, not her real self, but her back, her scarf—she'd bought it in Paris, she said—like water-soaked flowers in the mirror.

"What's the matter?" she asked.

I said, "I want . . ." What a lousy way to start. I dropped my hands and stared at my shoes. I wanted to cry. I hadn't even *kissed* her yet. "I don't know," I said. "I feel ridiculous. I can't believe—"

"What do you want, Mr. Sharp?" asked Jessica.

I said, "I want you to marry me."

At the piano Joseph burst into laughter. He must have overheard ten proposals a month; it was liable to get comic. All right. My hat was on the Victrola cabinet by the door. I'd just get it and leave.

But Jessica was looking at me. Her eyes were cherrywood brown. "That's it?" she asked. She took my hands again, businesslike. "That's easy. The way you were going on, I thought you wanted the moon."

I wondered whether I'd heard her right. She seemed to be proceeding with the lesson, even though her brother had stopped playing. Instead he stroked the keys in a mumbling way, as though the piano was their father, who didn't approve of the match.

"It's easy?" I said cautiously.

"Perfectly easy," Jessica said, and for a moment lifted her right hand to my cheekbone—she was still dancing—and said, "We can make plans later."

"Oh, brother," said Joseph, still laughing, still playing with the piano keys. "I suppose these things get easier with practice. But *him?*"

So I stopped dancing again, and Jessica frowned in a teacherly way. I'd thought he liked me. I kept expecting him to run out of the room, but he didn't. It was his house too. He suddenly began to play something fancy and classical, which was what he preferred to play anyhow, he said, not this ridiculous popular stuff where you had to listen to the words to know whether it was a happy or unhappy song.

Where do you take a total stranger, once you've proposed to her? We went to the screened porch, listening to Joseph pummel the ivories. In half an hour Jessica had a group tap-dancing lesson.

"He won't forgive me," she said, and then, "Of course he will."

"Of course he will," I said. I was holding her hand.

She turned it over to look at her wristwatch. "Oy. The tap dancers will be here any minute."

I turned her hand back over. "Cancel them."

"Oh, I can't do that," she said. "Bad business." But she was smiling at me, smiling at me, out in the sun for me, both of us sitting on the back steps. Inside, Joseph played music to go mad by.

"Tomorrow's lessons, I'll cancel," said Jessica. "California?"

"If that's okay with you."

"I'm portable," she said.

"We could take Joseph, with us, you know." I didn't *want* to take

him, but I lived in a big house, and he could play piano at Rocky's parties. We'd cheer the guy up some, find him jobs, then move him out.

"No," said Jessica. "Joe should be leading his own life. He lives too
much for me these days."

"But you won't change your mind?" I said. "You can change your
mind. But please, please, don't change your mind."

She was holding my hat in her free hand; she twirled it around and
around. The dog was asleep. The outside of her right foot just touched
the outside of my left foot. I had been engaged to be married for fifteen
minutes, and I still hadn't kissed her, and I could not imagine how I got
here, her knee swinging back and forth and sometimes hitting mine. She
tossed the hat in the air and caught it by the brim. "I once did a dance
with a hat, a Chinese one. I never change my mind," she said. "Ask anyone. I'll give you references." Then she put the hat on my head, and
kissed me on the cheek. *Time for you to go.* Just then I heard the clatter of
taps on the brick walk in front of the house.

"I want you to know I'm very happy," she said. "I'm sad that Joe's
sad, but mostly I'm happy. You're very dear to me, all of a sudden."

I didn't think she loved me then, exactly. My feelings for her were so
grand they couldn't possibly be mutual. Maybe she was making a mistake. Still, I'd take advantage. I'd bring her to California. I'd build her a
dance studio, buy a piano. We'd go to hear the best music. Joe would
come for visits. We'd redecorate my house with things she liked, posters
of bullfighters and Balinese masks and dark wallpaper full of birds. I'd
trick her, slowly, into loving the air around me, and she could work her
way in. In other words, I hoped—as Rose had said—that if Jessica was
making a mistake, I could turn it into a lovable blunder.

Grief, guilt, true love—I didn't know whether love was a hole you'd
have fallen into anyhow, or a trapdoor that sprung open only under certain conditions. A hole, I think now: an orchestra pit. An ungodly canyon
that makes an ugly noise something like music when you tumble in.
Your job, then, is to make it seem as though you did it on purpose.

I hadn't told Rocky about Jessica. I had a feeling he might be jealous;
he'd always adored my devotion to him. In the past, I'd toss aside any
girl if he wanted to go out drinking. I didn't think Jessica had anything to
do with how I felt about Rock, but I well knew he was a guy who compared the slices of cake on an arriving dessert tray and got disappointed,
really disappointed, when the largest was delivered to somebody who

wasn't him. He measured everything that way, glasses of liquor and applause and billing. Just a little more, please. Give me a little more than you think I could possibly want.

Love, like a hanging, concentrates the mind. Rocky would tell you it's for the same reason.

I told my sisters they'd have to get ready for a wedding. I cabled Rock: *Am engaged to be married but don't worry will be taking the girl out of Iowa you know the rest.*

He cabled back: *A wife? Only Moses Sharensky could sit shiva with a girl in his lap.*

All week long I'd been wearing the hodgepodge of clothing I'd managed to toss into my suitcase in California; the only good suit I'd brought still had cemetery mud across the knee. Who else to help me with my wedding duds: I went to Sharp's to talk to Ed.

"No time for alterations," I told him. "Wedding's tomorrow."

"You always do things suddenly," Ed told me, "and I always get you dressed in time. Look at the way the jacket bags at the waist! I'll take it in tonight."

I looked around the store. The old-fashioned headless mannequins wore some pretty slick jackets. "You'll be making some changes around here, huh?"

"Some," he said, turning back my cuffs, chalking them. The pins threaded through his lapel looked like medals of valor for service in some parsimonious war. "It'll still be your father's shop. It'll still be Sharp's."

"No," I said. "You're going to buy it. If it were up to me, I'd give it away, but there's my sisters to worry about. Hey," I said suddenly, "how 'bout I buy it and give it to you?"

Ed tugged at my lapels affectionately. "Silly. No. But thank you."

"There's no dishonor to it. If I'd inherited the store outright, I'd give it to you."

"Go like this." He flapped his arms and I imitated him. The jacket felt fine. "I'm going to buy the store," he said. "There's something else I want to do, but I have to ask your permission. I'll probably do it anyway, but I need to ask."

"Anything, Ed. You know that."

"Stop flapping," he said, catching me by the elbows. "Does it fit? Good. I'm going to marry your sister."

This made me flap one more time, to escape the hands still holding my arms, so I could clap him on the shoulders. "No kidding! My sister! One question?"

"Oh!" he said. "Rose!"

How long had they been in love? Well, he'd been in love with her almost forever, at least since she was sixteen; she'd fallen for him definitely post-Quigley, and possibly even pre-. Annie hadn't known until the day after the funeral, but had since given her blessing; Ed wanted mine, though Rose didn't care.

"I didn't tell your father, because I didn't want him to think I was marrying his daughter to get the store," Ed said gallantly, though we both knew the real reason: neither one had wanted to test my father's love again.

The same rabbi who'd eulogized my father married Jess and me four days later. I'd worried that my sisters would think it ghoulish, marrying mere days after burying my father, but they were thrilled: I'd done the right thing, I'd found a nice Jewish girl, an Iowan, no less. "I thought I'd have to read about your marriage in the paper," said Annie, taking a brisket out of the oven. (Her recipe: Coca-Cola, ketchup; cook forever.) Our wedding was furnished by my sisters and their husbands, the midwestern merchants: the brisket had come from Ida and Morris's butcher shop; Sadie and Abe brought chocolates and paper streamers from the dime store; Fannie and Ben brought tablecloths, and pajamas for me and a nightgown for Jess. Even surly Joe managed to smile, with all of my sisters making a fuss over him. Everything was easy, and beautiful. All weddings should be so spur-of-the-moment; leastways, all wartime weddings.

Then the sweetest thing: they filled our laps with gas ration stamps so we could drive back to Hollywood. They must have petitioned everyone in the neighborhood. It would take us days and days, what with the thirty-five-mile-per-hour victory speed limit, and we'd have to hope the gas station attendants wouldn't check our license numbers against the backs of the coupons, but it turned out that Jessica was terrified of flying, would not do it, not ever. At least the coupons weren't counterfeit. Durante would just have to stick around for another week.

And then Annie walked up to Rabbi Kipple's portrait and took it off the wall, wrapped it in brown paper, and handed it over.

"How did you know?" I asked.

"You always loved it," she said, though I knew that we'd all always loved it.

It was March, and the night before our wedding there had been a freak snowstorm, and so Jessica had come to her wedding dinner with a toboggan under her arm—she'd asked me if there was a hill—and wearing slacks.

"Slacks!" Annie said to me, and then, "They suit her."

We'd been married in the morning of March 9, 1943. Jessica spent the afternoon sliding down the Eighth Street hill, and then came through the back door in her wedding slacks, dappled with snow. Dripping, really, on the clean kitchen floor, and so she took off the offending slacks, and walked through the house in her leotard and tights. She sat down to dinner that way.

And the Sharp family, all of us, gaped.

Our Honeymoon Song

We left after dinner—no time to waste—and drove out of town between the fallow cornfields patterned with pig houses and melting snow. The freakish cold had turned to ordinary warmth. It's easy to forget the beauty of Iowan skies, especially when you're keen to leave them: they have the look of reverse glass paintings, backlit and full of a kind of smudged clarity. Our honeymoon sky was blue-jay blue, blueberry blue, mellowing slowly into serge black. The horizon seemed precisely as close as the stars over our heads.

I drove Jessica's car; she seemed to think that my sisters should see me at the wheel as we went off to our new life. Ahead of us the empty road stretched steady as a sharpshooter's arm. "Here," I said to my wife, "take the wheel a minute." She reached over and held it with one hand, and I leaned over and put my fingers at the back of her hair and kissed her. With her free hand she braced herself against my right hip. We were still driving. I'd thought it would be a momentary kiss, a silly thing, because though we'd been married ten hours, we hadn't kissed seriously yet: by which I mean, without a rabbi watching us. But we continued to drive and we continued to kiss, my foot on the gas and her hand on the wheel. I could see the barest edge of the road in my peripheral vision.

"Mmmmm," she said through the kiss, and I understood this meant that we planned to pull over. I felt the steering wheel turn against the left side of my waist, and I put my foot on the brake, and we narrowly avoided tipping into the ditch that fronted the fields. I'm sure we wouldn't have cared if we had.

We kissed in the car awhile.

"What I don't get," I said, "is why you were willing to marry me so fast."

She shrugged, my practical wife. "I knew I was going to marry you someday," she said. "That much was clear. Might as well be sooner than later."

I laughed.

"I'm dead serious," she said. "Best advice my father ever gave me: never do anything for the principle of the thing. I knew I was going to marry you, and then you asked, and saying anything but yes would have been for the principle of the thing."

Before this year—my thirty-second on earth—if you'd asked me about romantic love, I would have told you that I believed in it after a fashion. I knew about longing and affection; certainly I believed that people fell in love with other people, and that this state caused them to do stupid, heroic things. But in all of my study of the subject, it seemed that love was a table tennis game: you swung your paddle at the ball, or your partner did, but physics demanded that you waited your turn. One player would eventually pull ahead. Sure, people fell in love, of course they did, but for two people to fall at the same time and to the same depth seemed like the kind of unbelievable coincidence that movie comedy was made of: the keys are in the car you need to steal; the guy who chases you will find you, even six counties away from the start of the pursuit; you sit on the button of the tape recorder just as the villain starts to confess.

With other girls—those girls I was forgetting, just the way songs say you will (though they never mention that eventually your memory returns)—I could think of her, or I could think of me, and I believed that much of my romantic success was my ability and willingness to think more often of my date than myself. Why not? She was mesmerizing, I was not. But with Jessica—once we were married, in hotel rooms from Vee Jay to L.A. and ever after—I somehow kept both of us in mind at once. This seemed more a trick of the mind than of the body, as though for years I'd had to write down the simplest mathematical equation and carry ones and twos and threes and count on my fingers, and then one day discovered that I could multiply ten-digit numbers in my head without even trying.

"Should we find a place to stay the night?" Jessica asked when we went bumping out of the edge of the ditch and back onto the road. I shook my head. All that night we drove, Jessica leaning on my shoulder, kissing it sometimes, my hand on her knee, her knuckles brushing the bottom of my ear, and every time we came to a town she suggested that we stop and I drove past it. I couldn't explain. I think I needed to turn my longing for her into something noble, a state I withstood for as long as I could. I loved even that. I wasn't quite done loving it. Maybe that's why she insisted on driving for most of the rest of the trip. Just because she was now technically a wife didn't mean she liked being subject to a smitten husband's whims. It was two in the morning when we pulled off in a town on the far side of Nebraska, where we had to wake the gaunt desk clerk. He wheezed like a bulldog and he sniffed the air like a bulldog but he looked like a collie awakened from a coma, all nose and no brain. He squinted as though we were the most brightly lit things he had ever seen.

"I'm sorry," I told him. "We're newlyweds."

He said, "Then I think you would have gotten here earlier."

The next morning I took my place in the passenger's seat. I couldn't shut up. I told Jessica about my parents, my sisters, every detail I could remember. I told her about Rocky, and how much they'd love each other. "And California!" I said.

"California I know," she answered. "I studied with Agnes de Mille and Ted Shawn there, when I was younger, before I moved to New York."

"New York?"

"You'll catch up." She drove like a dancer, holding the wheel lovingly but lightly, as if to remind the car that it needed to do its own part. How *had* I talked her into this? I felt like I'd bribed the rabbi to sneak into Jessica's bedroom and pronounce her my wife, as though he was tying her shoes together: not till she woke up would she notice the prank. As her passenger I had plenty of time to stare at her face, trying to see if she looked bamboozled or regretful, but every time she looked over and saw me, she smiled.

"You'll miss Des Moines," I said.

"We have family there. We'll be back."

Is *that* why I'd married her?

She hadn't been lying about not having seen any of my movies. "How many?" she asked.

"Eleven."

She whistled. (She could whistle!) "How old a man are you?"

"You know how old I am. What can I say? I've been keeping busy."

"Which is the best?" she asked.

"The next one. The next one is always the best."

"So I'll see the next one."

"If you're really interested, Rocky has a theater in his house. I don't know if he owns prints of our pictures, but he could get them."

"A theater? You mean, a projector."

"Well," I said, "there's a projector. It's in the theater. Which is next to the bar. Near the soda fountain and the Ferris wheel."

"A Ferris wheel. That's handy. How many children?"

"None."

"But he's married?"

"Married," I said. "Maybe."

Just then, Utah crawling past our window, I remembered everything I was headed for: not only Rocky, but Penny and Sukey. It wasn't that I'd forgotten about them, exactly; I'd forgotten that either one of them might care about me getting married. I'd made a hash of things, I saw that now, though I couldn't imagine that I'd have done anything differently since leaving California. Rocky would have told them about the telegram announcing my engagement, but I hadn't sent another one saying that we'd actually gotten married. (How could he complain? He'd set the precedent for secret weddings.) Before Jessica, I might have managed to get out of this mess, to get Penny alone and—well, not apologize, a gentleman never apologizes for sleeping with a young lady—I could have explained that despite my dearest wishes, we should simply be friends, that in a perfect world, etc., etc. Maybe it wasn't too late to try something like it. Sukey I didn't think would be so much of a problem. She'd shrug me off like she shrugged off everything.

What I needed was to keep my brain busy, in those moments Jessica and I fell into a companionable silence. I decided to write a song as a late wedding present. The title came first: "My Darling Lives in Des Moines." I did better with the lyrics when I drove, which was almost never; my concentration was less focused when I merely rode. Jessica let me have the wheel through a large chunk of Arizona, and I noodled around with the verse.

In the middle of the city
In the middle of the state
In the middle of the country
I count my dreams and wait

In the middle of my bedroom
In the middle of the night
In the middle of my dream of love
I hold my darling tight

I had a melody in mind, even though I wasn't so good at melodies and couldn't have transcribed it. We passed a sign that said, "When You Ride Alone, You Ride with Hitler."

"There's something wrong with the car!" Jessica said, sitting up in the passenger's seat.

I'd been tapping the gas with my foot.

The Store Was Fresh Out of Camels

"Earthquakes," said Jessica, when she first saw my breakable living room.

"It's not like we can't afford to replace things," I said.

She laughed. "Broken *glass*. That's what I'm worried about. How long would it take to dig out glass from this carpet?"

I shrugged. She had a point, and still, all I could think of was how I didn't know, exactly, what everything in this room had cost me. A glorious feeling: I could smash a martini glass every hour, and it wouldn't make the slightest dent in my bank account. The difference between me and Rocky is that he might have thought the same thing, and then would have gone ahead and shattered the glasses.

I still live in this house, alone now, and somehow it's darkened over the years. Dirt? My own failing eyesight? A slight change in the earth's rotation? When the children were little, the house seemed full of light, and I don't mean metaphorically: the mirrors seemed as deep as rooms themselves, the window blinds glowed. Eventually we bought rugs the children could spill anything on, we put away the crystal and covered the sofas and chairs in dark green paisley, but still it was brighter than it ever was when I lived alone. On the table, glossy chicken soup or pale warm cream of wheat. In every patch of sunshine was a child, or our calico cat, or my wife the dancer who viewed the floor as a piece of furniture except more practical. Maybe bodies stop sunlight in its tracks. Without them it stumbles through the house and out the back door.

Rocky arrived at 8:30 that evening. (I'd called him from the California border. He made hurt noises over not being invited to the wedding, but I made it sound as though the marriage had been an emergency: a nice girl, after all. She wouldn't have come with me otherwise. I have no idea of whether this was true.) First he threw his arms around me, and then he went after Jessica. For a moment, I was afraid that he planned to scoop her up, but instead he took her hand. He said, "You're a dancer." She nodded. I didn't think I'd told him that.

"You know," he said, "I can't even *tell* you what a pleasure it is to meet you, Jessica." And *then* he whooped and scooped her up in his arms and kissed her. *"Tour jeté!"* he said.

Meanwhile, I realized he had stuck something in my breast pocket when he embraced me: a giant roll of money. I pulled it out. "Really, Rock," I said. "A wedding present? Why didn't you get me something I didn't already have?"

"Oh, for your wedding I got you a llama," he said breezily. He set Jessica down again, just as she said, "A *what?*" She'd already seen the jukebox, which might have seemed as unlikely a piece of living-room furniture.

I said, "Joke!"

"A nice llama," said Rocky. "Barely spits at all, for a llama. Someone for us to get drunk with. But: am I not an honest man? Didn't we have a bet going?"

"Usually several," I said, though I was hoping to introduce my wife to my bad habits one at a time. I already had the notion—and hope—that she might try to break me of them.

"We only had one two-thousand-dollar bet," he said. "The matrimonial one."

Penny's gone, I hoped. *To a beautiful foreign country where she's carried on a litter like Cleopatra. Rocky's remarried and has already forgotten Penny's forwarding address, because she's so gone she's never coming back.*

"Penny's come back to me!" he said.

Rocky threw a party for us the next week. I couldn't refuse, and I couldn't, of course, suggest that he not invite his wife and her best friend. Clearly Penny hadn't told Rocky about Our Secret (as I, a newly married man, decorously thought of it); he was being entirely too sentimental about me. Would I be able to get Penny alone and explain things? With a few insinuations, maybe I could get her to jump to a flattering conclusion: I married Jessie because I could not marry her.

At the party Jessica was whisked away immediately by Tansy. Penny spotted me outside the house and started to bound up. (Well, she didn't *spot* me; Rocky pointed.) Did the sight of me always make her so frolicsome? Probably she was thinking the same thing, because she slowed down and walked the rest of the way.

"Mike!" she said. "Congratulations! I could hardly believe it when Rocky told me! I said, Mike? Mike *Sharp*? Married? Good grief, then there's hope for anyone! I said, Rocky, if *Mike* can get married, then there's hope for us too! Where is she? That's her? She's *beautiful*. And from Des Moines? Beautiful *and* from Des Moines? Not that it surprises me, it's just that I've never been to Des Moines. We'll go sometime. Dancer? She's a dancer, right? Well, you'll put her in your movies. Of course you will, but don't you *dare* put her in before you put *me* in. I've been twisting Rock's arm for four years now, I won't give up that easy. Maybe we can do a scene together, me and your wife. Your *wife*. You're married! Do I have a surprise for *you*." And then she slapped me on the seat of my pants, hard, kissed me on the nose, and left.

So I stood for a moment, feeling both the slap and the kiss and hoping that one of them was the surprise. She thought Jessie was beautiful, huh? Penny couldn't fool me: she couldn't possibly have seen my beauteous wife from that distance. Red Shaw's band was there, and they struck up some dance music.

When I recall nearly any story from those first weeks with Jessica, I decide of every single one, *That's when I knew I was in love with her,* even though I don't remember any surrounding doubt. Here's another one:

that night, we danced. We'd only ever danced during my lessons, but now we jitterbugged. Then double time. Then quadruple. I couldn't tell whose idea it was to speed up, mine or hers or the band's, but I realized that everyone else had stopped dancing and had cleared space for us. I've always wanted to be that guy, I thought. Maybe they were just doing it because it was our party, but I didn't care. I spun her from me and then back. I missed her when a step took her farther away, and I tried to prevent sweat from dripping off my nose and onto her face when she was near. We were both laughing, even though laughing was an effort. I could feel my back suddenly soppy wet. Surely the song was nearly over. It wasn't. I'd never danced this hard in my life, and I couldn't tell whether I was giddy because I danced or vice versa. People around us clapped, which would have given us permission to stop, but I couldn't imagine doing that until the end of the song, which in my mind had become our wedding itself, and would I walk out on that? My lungs hurt. My heart felt slightly bruised.

Finally. End of song (were those sons of bitches putting on all those extra flourishes to *kill* me?). Applause. Lovely. I collapsed onto a nearby chair. For a second Jessica stood, fanning the backs of her legs with her skirt. Then she sat down primly on my knees. Despite myself, I took her by the waist and slid her closer to me, both of us still panting. When she leaned I could feel that her shirt was soaked through, too.

She arched her back away from me for a minute, and then settled the backs of her shoulders onto the front of mine. She said, "I'm afraid I'm sticking to you."

I said, "Please."

Later that night Rocky danced with both Penny and Jessica, twirled one from each wrist. How could a guy who danced that well have any trouble with woman at all? I didn't like having Penny and Jessica that close together, but at least they weren't talking.

Penny's secret turned out to be completely endearing, if odd. I'd shown Rocky the words to "My Darling Lives in Des Moines," asking for advice, and his photographic memory had snapped a picture, and his friend Red Shaw had set the lyrics to music—he must have had a spare tune lying around, he managed it so fast. Penny was going to sing with the band. I didn't recognize it till she began the verse. There was betrayal in her voice, but there was always betrayal in Penny's voice:

Indianola, Osceola,
Cedar Rapids, Cedar Falls,
But the city I love most
Is the city that she calls

Home—
(Don't need a map at all)
Home—
(To the State Capitol)
Home—
My darling lives in Des Moines.

When it was done, and Jessica kissed me, and we went to thank Penny, she simply shook our hands. "I'm taking this *so* well," she said to me, and then, to Jessica, "I might as well admit it, I've always had a crush on your husband."

"He's pretty adorable," Jessie said. Then she turned to me, and yawned in an informational way. "It's midnight," she said. "I think I'll go home."

"Okay," I said. "I'll get the car."

"No," she answered. She touched my cheek. "You're having a good time. I want to go, you want to stay, nothing wrong with that. Somebody will drive you. Wake me when you get back."

I couldn't decide if I was delighted by our independence from each other, or crushed. But I'd hardly seen Rocky at the party, so I kissed her and stayed. I ended up in the basement bar, Sukey between me and Rock.

"So I hear," Sukey said, "that you got yourself a housewife."

"Ain't it great?" Rocky asked.

I didn't know the etiquette. I tried, "She's not—"

"A nice Jewish girl, like he always wanted," said Rocky, though I'd never said that. But he was right, I reflected: that *was* what I always wanted. "From his hometown," said Rocky.

"A city girl," I corrected. "Next town over."

"Forgive me," said Rocky. "She's from Des Moines. He's from West Des Moines."

"And who could blame him?" said Sukey. "Lights of Des Moines are liable to dazzle a boy."

"Indeed," said Rocky.

"It's what they all want." Sukey stared into her drink. I worried that I was about to hear the answer to *And who could blame him?* "They all pretend that they're big sophisticated men, but then they see a simple little girl and they turn into simple little boys."

"Now, wait a minute," I said.

"It's true." The bartender had gone home, and Sukey knelt on her barstool and grabbed a bottle and poured herself another drink. Whatever she'd snagged colored what was left in her glass green. "They act like big men, but in the end they just want to play house."

"Who's them?" asked Rocky.

"All of y'all," said Sukey, suddenly southern with drink. "All of you boys. You want housewives. You're not *real* men."

"I'm married to Penny," he said. "You don't think she's—"

"Well, Jesus Christ," said Sukey. "*I've* been to bed with Penny. How much of a man am I?"

There was a silence you could have wrapped in a bedsheet then. Finally, Rocky scratched the back of his head and said, hopefully, "By go to bed, you mean—"

"You know what I mean, funnyman," Sukey said.

Rocky shook his head.

"A waterstain birthmark the shape of Spain on her left hip," said Sukey, and—whoops!—I said, "Yes." Rocky didn't notice. He said, "You mean Italy."

"Italy," she said. "And cold feet."

"Yes," said Rocky.

"And she likes her waist to be held—"

"*Okay*," Rocky and I said.

After she left, Rocky said, sadly, "Nobody remembers the shape of Spain."

10

Biblical Slapstick

I wanted to show my midwestern sweetheart everything about California, but she'd already seen it all. She didn't like Hollywood Boulevard, which still staggered me so you would have guessed I was a tourist, not a guy whose name appeared with almost mind-numbing regularity on the marquees of the movie palaces, whose footprints could be seen in the cement in front of Grauman's Chinese. (I swear Rocky wore bigger shoes that day, so that his feet would dwarf mine in perpetuity.) "The ocean!" I said. "It's nice," said Jess. "The mountains!" I explained. "I've climbed them," she told me. One day I dragged her out into the backyard. "Hummingbirds!" I instructed. "Look!"

She did. She was silent a long time, and then she said, "There are hummingbirds in Iowa."

"Never," I said, looking at the little mechanical genius that now backed out of one flower and hung in the air like a cartoon fairy, looking over what the other blooms offered.

"I'll get you a bird book," she said, "and you can look it up. But isn't he beautiful?"

"Beautiful," I said sadly. "Iowa?"

"Yes, Mr. Audubon. Iowa."

Despite having climbed a mountain, she viewed Nature as mostly an inconsistently lit corridor that led from one building to another. She adored music: Tchaikovsky and Mendelssohn, and big bands, and jazz, anything you could dance to, anything you might—with the right people—reproduce in your living room. She could not sing at all, but she loved to, so she did—not like Hattie, who flaunted her pitchless vibrating alto voice, but softly, so you could hardly hear how wrong she was. She loved in general the works of man, painting and poetry and architecture.

And she loved me.

This was a fascinating prospect. She really did love me, my Jessica. I kept thinking that she'd notice she didn't. Sometimes she could be almost dismissive of my behavior, if it displeased her—sniffing the air for a snuck cigarette, shaking her head as I tried to memorize lines to movies that she never would have gone to, had her husband not been one of the stars—and would give me a look that I well remembered from my days as a boarder under the gaze of a disappointed landlady: *Mr. Sharp, is this how you act in your own home?* But that was just Jessica: she loved me, but that didn't mean she'd put up with all sorts of nonsense. Minutes later—she was not mad, she would not brood—she'd call me her boy (how did she know this is what I would want to be?) and outline my ear with her finger. Or she'd sit in a chair across from me, and ask me about my childhood. I told her different stories than I told Rocky: at least, the telling was different. With Rock the point was to be funny, to pump tragedy full of slapstick. You knew that there were awful things in this world—what people had to bear!—but God had rigged up one kind of consolation: you could get a good story out of it. "This," said Rock, "is the lesson of the Bible." Jessica did not love comedy, despite loving a comedian; she wanted to be moved by stories unadorned by wisecracks. The sadder the better, and so I told her the whole story of Hattie's death, a story I had not told at all since I first met Rocky, and only an abridged version then.

"She died with me angry at her," I said to Jessica.

"Do you think so? Sounds like you had forgiven her."

No, I said, I hadn't. Jessica shrugged. She'd never argue about that sort of thing. But her eyes darkened, which meant they were damp, and she laid a hand upon me—more people should have this knack—that was somehow less about comfort, which I couldn't have stood, and more about just wanting to touch me. She did not pat, she did not hug, she did not *there-there*. She just set her hand on my arm. That's what she always did, she'd touch my elbow or stomach or the back of my neck, as though she wondered what a sad man felt like, so we could be sad together.

And generally, when she did this, no matter what time it was, we'd go to bed.

On the other hand, we went to bed when we were happy, too. She was amused by my constant willingness, and I grateful for hers, which in those years was what I believed marriage was. Years of vaudeville meant I never gave a thought to when decent people embarked on carnal embraces: I'd worked nights, and besides, I didn't know any decent people. Not that I told her this. I mentioned Mimi, but otherwise my past was my past. It was scattered across the middle of the country, and here we were at the edge. Maybe some days in Dayton, Dubuque, Duluth (dear Duluth!), part of my past would walk into a theater, and see me: *So that's what happened to that guy.* I felt no need to go likewise looking.

I had Jessica. In the mornings she stood in the bathroom, naked, winding her hair on the back of her head and fixing it with a two-part contraption, a long skewer and a curved bar; the pieces worked together, like an arrow drawn in a bow, at her nape. The bathroom was so porcelain-white that even pale Jessica looked pink in it. In fact, if I came to the door without my glasses on, I saw an impressionist painting: white, with a smudge of slightly ruddier white; a curl of black; some silver-blue bursting in through the pebbled glass window. In some ways she was fastidious and in others filthy. She showered and powdered herself with talcum and then she'd put on an unwashed leotard covered in fuzzy fabric blemishes and would dance all day. By evening she would smell like something burning—a small something, a thing that shouldn't be burned. Not consumed, just a spark at the heart of something densely packed.

What was marriage to me, a guy who had, historically, gotten around? Favors granted endlessly, cheerfully, complicatedly. A certain relaxation of good manners. Permission to stick my nose anywhere. My knuckles had already grazed every part of her body as we danced, as we stepped away from dancing. This was marriage: sticking my nose into every alcove of her body. A skinny ballerina. She had tiny biceps, though her legs were decidedly muscly. You could see her ribs above and below her small breasts. Her sweat smelled like rain-barrel water, sun-warmed and touched with rust.

"My feet are ugly," she told me once, a single moment of self-deprecation. They weren't. They were just covered with the evidence of her work, the bottoms thick and darker than the rest of her skin, a gray lampshade over a white light. The lines of her footprint were slightly darker than that. Her big toes cocked over, and her little toes were beveled: they had distinct edges where they tucked in against the rest of her foot. The grain of her toenails ran side to side, unlike her fingernails, but in this she was probably not unique. Only her arches resembled the rest of her, resembled the talc she doused herself with. I kissed them. Why was a foot curved except for kisses?

Her hands were well trained, maybe from years of describing things while dancing. Now, they described me. Was my back really my back, before Jessica swept one hand from the top of my head to the hinge of my knees? No, it had been a jumble of parts, the nape of my neck to keep my necktie up, a pair of chummy shoulders, a length of spine, a prat for pratfalls, legs for hightailing it out of there, all certainly previously kissed and bitten and even spanked, but not this: all me. I felt like I could think great thoughts with my skin. She curled her fists into my armpits, then ran her hands (opening) down the underside of my arms past my elbows, till we were chest to chest and her fingers were around my faulty wrists and I wished I could bend them, to take her hands, maybe if I just tried, and then she stretched her arms a little wider, and suddenly we were palm to palm, palm to palm. She had quite a wingspan, my wife. She nudged my nose with her nose, she fluttered her lashes on my eyelids. *Eskimo kiss, butterfly kiss, soul kiss,* when I was a young man I collected these kisses the way some daft old women amass spoons from every state in the union, acquiring, until they run out of holes in the collection, dozens of miniature spoons with symbols on the end to pledge their allegiances, a beehive for the beehive state, a keystone for Pennsylvania, a full set and nothing to eat dinner with. Jessica rubbed her forehead against mine, as though she were a patient foreign-language instructor: how would I know what a chin was, unless I felt another chin upon it? Repeat after me: cheekbone, temple, left ear, right ear, toes. I hadn't known. Really she was three inches shorter than me, but in bed she could make herself my height. In vaudeville I'd seen an act like this, a guy who stood beside a taller man—the short guy slowly elongated himself, put a fraction of an inch between each vertebra, a fraction of an inch at the top of his kneecap and another at the bottom, until he stood next to a shorter man, the same one. The audience blinked, then applauded. That was the whole trick, and it didn't seem much till Jessica did it: she rubbed her instep over my ankle, then my instep, then the bottom of my foot, never losing track of our kiss, the pulses in our wrists against each other.

———

She signed up at the Hollywood Canteen as a hostess, of course—we all had to do our part, and Jessica's specialty was dancing. We went together: I served drinks and dinner, and Jessica danced with soldiers and sailors and flyers: you could see guys walk away from her, delighted by the dance and confused by the conversation. Did she have a boyfriend? they'd ask. Married, she'd answer. Pretend you're my girl, they'd say, and she'd smile and say she couldn't. Sure you can, they'd say, but she couldn't, she was incapable. In some ways she had nearly no imagination, but I can't say it bothered me much in this instance.

"You let your wife dance with *anybody*," Rocky said, on one of the nights he showed up at the Canteen; we'd performed earlier in the evening.

"Only with guys in uniform," I told him. Well, if the most valuable thing I had to give to the war effort was my wife, I'd do it, as long as she came home with me at night. And danced in sight of me at all times. And never, ever got talked into a game of make-believe, not with the suavist officer or the most innocent about-to-be-shipped-out sailor boy.

Still, soon enough she got pregnant and even the sailor and soldier boys had a hard time pretending she wasn't another guy's girl.

At one elbow, excessive Rocky; at the other, my abstemious wife. When Jessica and I settled into married bliss, it was all I could do not to compare her to Rocky, and not always favorably. She had plenty of rules. She didn't drink; she hated rich foods; she could deliver a lecture against gravy that made it sound as though gravy had invaded Poland. She couldn't bear to hear people rhapsodize about food. She strictly forbade indoor smoking.

"This is just a little cigar," Rocky told her one night, when he'd come over and demanded an old-fashioned midwestern meal; Jess cooked him a cheese omelette, *oeufs Des Moines*. She'd sent home the cook, an Irish nineteen-year-old named Nora who specialized in rich cream sauces— liquid gout, said Rocky—and mashed turnips. Jess barely tolerated her, torn between hating hired help and despising housework.

"Nevertheless," Jess said.

"This cigar is next to nothing," said Rock. But he was already genially sliding it into his jacket pocket. He'd brought over three bottles of champagne and two of wine, all for the three of us, and kept pouring glasses for Jess that she never touched. He emptied his water glass and tried again, as though if he booby-trapped the table with enough vessels she'd eventually fall in.

"Mr. Carter," Jessica said. From the very start that was their joke, a cheerful and annoyed formality. "I don't drink wine."

"A whiskey woman, then. No? Martinis. Gimlets?"

"Coffee," said Jessica.

"I'm just curious," he said. "If you wanted to have a drink, what would you have? I'll buy you the best. Vodka? Or kirsch: I bet kirsch. I once knew a ballerina—"

"I haven't the slightest," said Jess. "I've never tasted alcohol."

"Really?" I said. I mean, I knew she didn't drink, I just didn't know she never had. I snagged the bottom of one of the glasses Rocky had poured her and sloshed some wine onto the tablecloth, a gift from my sister Ida. Jess got up and went to the bar for some club soda to sop up the stain.

"You married this guy *sober?*" Rocky said.

"Drunk with love," Jess said wryly, which even so delighted me.

"You've been to *Paris,*" said Rocky. "You lived in *New York.* Sometime, somewhere, a toast, a prayer—"

"Never," Jess said.

"Grounds for divorce," Rocky told me, but of course I loved it: I loved any new thing I learned about her.

I stood up from the table. "We'll smoke outside."

"Oh, goody," he said, "that's allowed?"

From the lanai, he surveyed my grounds, as if he couldn't quite figure out what the place was missing. "She's something. Is she ever something."

"She's got ideas," I offered.

"I noticed."

I crossed my legs on my chaise longe. "I was hoping the two of you would hit it off."

He laughed then. "We *are.* Can't you tell? We adore each other."

"Good," I said dubiously.

"No! Ask her. Jess—" he called.

"Don't do that. She'll lie. She's very polite. . . ."

"No she isn't," he said.

"No she isn't," I agreed.

"But okay. You ask her. Later tonight." He pulled out the cigar and looked at it. "Oh," he said, "if only someone would make *me* straighten up and fly right."

"Penny's not the girl for that," I told him.

"She's not the girl for anything." He twirled the cigar with the tips of his fingers, let it slide down the back of his hand, caught it, twirled it again. "She's gone for good, this time."

"She'll be back."

"Not this time. I told her not to. Penny can take anything except a lack of admiration. I told her"—he sighed—"told her I wasn't attracted to her. Not after that Sukey business."

"That Sukey business."

"Well, really. It's not that she slept with a girl. It's that it was *Sukey*. If Penny was looking, I would have found her a nice date. No, I would have! Some dancer. But Sukey Decker? Who *hates* me?"

"You finally figured that out, huh? Well, look at it this way. With Penny's eyesight she probably didn't realize it wasn't you till it was too late."

He pursed his lips.

"Rocky?"

"You'll pardon me, you son of a bitch, if that doesn't make me feel any better."

"Sorry."

"Sorry and laughing, sure. Anyhow, it's not all Sukey's fault. Penny's moved in and out so often I should install a turnstile. Charge admission."

"Offer to sell her a season pass."

"You misunderstand. She's *gone*. You know, I thought the one advantage of marrying a simple woman was that I'd be able to understand her."

"You think Penny's simple?"

"Not dumb. Just not complicated. I *thought*."

"You were wrong. She's plenty complicated."

"Tell me more."

"Uh-uh. I'm drunk. I'm liable to say things I don't mean."

"Fair enough. Educate me some other way, Professor. Tell me about your wife."

"She's not simple either."

"No kidding. Tell me—tell me what the two of you talk about. It's late. You're in the living room. What happens next?"

"Depends."

"You love her?"

"Yes. I do. Did I forget to tell you that's important in a marriage?"

"There's always been plenty of love in my marriage, kid. It's just that me and the missus have lousy *aim*. Okay: so you're in the living room. She's sitting in her chair. You're on the sofa. You look at her. What do you think?"

"Mostly, I think it would be nice to crawl across the room on my hands and knees and sit by her feet."

"Jesus. Well, that's you. I don't kowtow to women."

"You just kowtow with money. You just throw money at the problem. Anyhow, I don't want to crawl across the floor to kowtow, I don't think."

"Then what?"

"I don't know. It's a big room. I think maybe I just want to get across it."

"Walk."

"I want to get across it without her asking me where I'm going, and would I get her something while I'm up, and is it time for bed already? I want to get from one side of the room to the other without her noticing."

"Yeah, but what do you want to do once you get to the other side?"

"I don't know. Sit there. Put my hand on her ankle." (Put my hand on her ankle, and feel that tendon at the back of her heel, as subtly lined as a run in a stocking. Put my head in her lap.)

"You just want attention, old dog."

"No. I mean: no. It's like I want to be near her without her really noticing. Sneak across the room. Put my head on her lap. Maybe she pushes her hand through what's left of my hair, but she doesn't even look up from her book. Like she's used to me being there."

"Like you're a dog."

"Have it your way. Maybe. A good dog. A loved dog."

"Yeah. Sure." He stroked his cigar as though he was Aladdin, thinking carefully before he summoned the genie. "That'd be okay."

I'm Light on Your Feet

Rocky discovered Jessica's sweet tooth, and liked to try to stuff her full as a piñata. Usually he succeeded: his taste in chocolates, said Jessica, was nothing short of genius, and even during the war managed huge smuggled boxes of European bonbons.

Wasn't it unseemly for a man other than her husband to supply her with candy?

So I'd top him: I'd build her a candy box of her own, a music box: a dance studio. I hired some set guys from the studio to design and build it at the far end of the back lawn. I told Jessica I was working on a game room, a place for Rock and me to play cards and smoke. The way I figured it, the studio was for her solitary dancing pleasure; I would be her audience. I really was thinking of a music box, my mother's, where the celluloid ballerina who lived inside sprang up only when someone wanted to see her twirl.

The set guys got fancy: dramatic masks above the entrance, a mirror trimmed in painted velvet ribbon. I took her to it when they were done.

She walked over the threshold. For thirty seconds, I think, she wondered what kind of clubhouse this was. Then she figured it out, and kissed me. "Oh, Mose," she said. "This is a wonderful place for lessons."

I managed not to say, "For *what?*" (Sometimes I had to work not to be a straight man, not to say every little thing that crossed my mind so that my comic could respond to it.) I looked at the wood floors, the blond untouched barres. "That's what I thought."

She inspected the mirror, the small dressing room at the back, the latticed Swiss-style windows, the bathroom, the record player and radio. Her brother, Joseph, still lived in their house; otherwise I'd have paid to have certain details of her old studio (the fireplace, the peach-colored flame-shaped lighting sconces) flown in.

"Wonderful," she said again. "The barres are too high, but other than that. Easy to fix." She sat down in the middle of the floor. Her stomach—she was six months pregnant—hid the angles of her crossed legs. She asked if I would leave.

"Sure," I said. I tried to make it a question.

When I got back to the house, I heard the music. I hadn't bought any records for the player; she must have snapped on the radio. From the kitchen I could see only one small slice of a studio window, and realized that if I had wanted to watch her, I'd built the place badly. You couldn't see anything from here, just Jessie occasionally spinning into view and out again. She must have danced through commercials, *Ballet Pepsodent*, *Ballet Lucky Strike*. A mistake, I thought: I'd given her something that would keep her from me. That's the kind of guy I was. She was so happy, and I, kept from her happiness, was miserable.

Soon enough, Jessica offered lessons. In Des Moines, a dance lesson with her was glamorous. Not that she worked to make it so: still, she was the only Bohemian her students ever met, a single woman in leotards, forbidden jazz on the gramophone. A professional dancer, here in our city. You knew you'd never be one yourself, but for an hour a week you could pretend. Then you'd go back to your parents, or husband, or wife. You wouldn't even tell them how much you'd loved your time in the Ninth Street studio.

But in Hollywood, professional dancers were common as bedbugs. Who *hadn't* danced professionally? See that woman crossing the street? She scissored her legs in the two-o'clock spot in a Busby Berkeley kaleidoscope, and she was nothing special. Well, that was the point, to look like all the other girls angling identically for the camera that came in overhead on a crane. From below in the front row, a mother might see a certain turn of ankle. But to everyone else, you looked like the girl on either side, and how would you ever become a star *that* way? So you took more lessons, while privately assuming you were better than your teacher.

Even the children—Jessica's specialty—were not impressed. They took dance lessons as a matter of course, even though most of them hated to. They were the children of the rich and famous, and they had one woman who cooked them breakfast and another who buttoned their coats and another who helped them correct their turnout and posture and faulty rhythm. All the world was hired help, wasn't it? Jess would have taught adults, but they generally studied with people more directly connected to a studio. If I'd been a musical star, they might have signed up with my wife so they could dance loudly, hoping I was hungry for discoveries. Years later she got choreography work in television, and loved it. "All that time with those awful, awful, awful children!" she said.

"What a waste!" But it was good for us, like eating loaf after loaf of lousy bread—you pick up some tips on how to get your own dough to rise.

Her only grown-ups were my old pal Johnny Atkinson and his roommate, Alan. Johnny managed to find a part in most of our movies—we always needed a blustery tough-guy to frown at our high jinks. I figured they took tap classes together.

"How'd the lesson go?" I asked Jessica one night when we were in bed.

She sighed. "Well, fine, except that John finally dropped Alan."

"What?"

"Not hard, dear. Toward the end of the lesson. But he needs to train so it won't happen again. You know. Adagio is hard work. John's not the youngest man in the world. Not the thinnest. A person should be one or the other or both. With two men, we must be inventive."

"One or the other for what?"

"For *adagio*," she said. She gestured with her hands. Then she did it a little more emphatically, and I saw her hands gripped an imaginary waist and tossed an imaginary dancer in the air. "That's what we're doing."

I said, "I didn't know two men ever danced adagio together."

"I didn't, either, until they asked. John and Alan want to dance adagio, so. John's too heavy to lift, so he lifts Alan, and so he'll have to get stronger. That's how it works. You look shocked, dear. They *sleep* together, I don't think dancing together is such a surprise."

I furrowed my brow at her.

"They're dancers," she said. "Very common among dancers."

"Johnny's not a dancer. He's a second banana."

"To you he's a second banana. To Alan and me, he's a dancer."

I sat up and stuffed my pillow behind my back. "I don't like the idea," I said. Adagio? Two guys? In front of my *wife*?

"Well then," said Jess, arranging my pillow better, just the way I liked it, in fact, "I suppose he can't be your friend anymore."

Most of my life, my education has come this way: someone else being nonchalant about things I had never dreamed of. I don't mean men who slept with men—plenty of those in Hollywood and vaudeville; the previous Savant had been a nance—I mean friends of mine who were men who slept with men. Johnny and Alan? I sighed. "Invite me to the recital," I told Jess.

She kissed me. "You're invited."

(How had I not known about Johnny? Rocky did. Once I mentioned it, he referred to them as Romeo and Julius, which ended up being the title of one of our movies, though with a different plot than Johnny and Alan's life.)

There never was a recital, though I did imagine it: Johnny in his white shirt and striped tie, a cigar in his mouth, dancing with little Alan, struggling only momentarily to get him airborne.

In March of 1943, I had been a man-about-town in Hollywood, promised to no one (but Rocky), responsible for no one (but Rocky), enamored of no one (but Rocky). By New Year's, I was a father, besotted by my new life, save for the few moments it absolutely terrified me. Jessica had our first child, Jacob, named for my father, on the last day of December. He seemed as good a resolution as any. Before, I had never wanted to be a father, particularly. I'd have been happy to honeymoon for the rest of my life. In this I was perhaps like my own father, who hadn't even started on the enterprise until he was in his forties, and then he never stopped.

But a baby! What a fascinating invention. They were so sleek and new and cunning, I wanted to believe that they too must be native only to California. Jake, for instance, was a shrugging, squinch-faced, black-haired newborn. I held him; he touched his fist to his chin, and then to mine. A communicator, is what I mean. When he got older, he liked to untuck my tie, like a girl in one of our movies.

"My hummingbird," Jess called him when he cried, reading my mind as usual. He was a tightly wound kid, florid, a flapper, worried already. A regular hummingbird.

Nathan was born a year later. "How're things in the Fertile Crescent?" Rocky asked Jessica. "Mind your business, Mr. Carter," she said, blushing for once. "Your neighborhood, I meant!" he said with a whoop. "Not your own *personal* Fertile Crescent. I would *never* ask about that. Not in front of your husband." Natey was Jake's opposite, mild mannered, white-skinned where his brother was ruddy, a baby you could tuck under your arm like a football while you attended to the business of the day. Jessica refused a nanny, but we had plenty of help by then, a housekeeper, a gardener, a cook, a driver, and Nathan was passed from arm to arm. He could sleep anywhere, he smiled all the time, but he only laughed while he was around his mother.

"She's not so funny," I told him. "Me, *I'm* funny. Everyone says so."

"Give!" Rocky said, putting out his arms. So I did. "I'll make him laugh." He tried everything, surefire bits from *1,000 Jokes for Infants* and *Calvacade of Silly Faces*. Nothing worked. He put Nathan back in Jessica's arms, where he began to chuckle.

"My laugh!" said Rocky, pointing. But everyone knew it wasn't true. He sat on the sofa morosely. "She always was the funny one."

"Ain't it the truth," I said.

That was the night before V-J Day. Neddy and I had planned to meet at Musso's for lunch that noon, but there was no going anywhere on Hollywood Boulevard. We decided to meet there anyhow, not knowing it would be impossible. You couldn't call it a crowd, or a throng, or a mob—all those people, all that flittering paper, all that *joy*: from storefront to storefront, a giant animal made up of hands and arms and kissing mouths. I stood on one of the side streets, looked for Neddy, and laughed at the thought of finding him, and then stepped in. How long had it been since I'd been a part of a crowd? Usually I stood in front of one at personal appearances, walked down a center aisle at premieres. No one knew me here, sans toup, sans mortarboard, sans flashing egghead glasses and prissy fussbudget expression. A man in kitchen whites slapped my flank; a woman in a tweed suit kissed my cheekbone, then moved away, still kissing, as though she were a fish that moved by suction, a rare Angeleno smooch fish, except everywhere you looked there they were: women and men, their mouths tilted up and down and sideways. *And no one knew me.* All we knew was that we'd won! All of us! Standing on the sidewalk or the gutter or smack in the center of Hollywood Boulevard, we'd done it, we'd given things up and we'd *slaughtered* them, Hitler first and now the Japs and we loved ourselves, we loved each other, every elbowing, kissing, caressing stranger on the street. I began to lose a sense of myself. Just another guy on the street, his mouth full of lipstick and damp confetti. The people in this world who actually knew me were back at my house, my sons and my wife, and who else's attention did I need? Maybe even then I knew, surrounded by ecstasy, that my work here, by which I mean as a Hollywood headliner, was done: Carter and Sharp had won the war, too, we'd contributed everything we could to the effort. We were soldiers; we'd done our country proud. Soon enough, we'd be discharged, though not right away, when there was so much peacetime celebrating to do.

Loaded for Bear

First scene: a double bed in a boardinghouse. Snoring beneath a crazy quilt, two men. Right side of the bed: a thin man sleeping at attention in striped pajamas. Left side: a plump lump, a pair of plump feet resting on the pillows where a head should be. The thin man's snores are orderly and girlish; the fat man gerphlumphs like a clogged drain.

The alarm clock rings. The two men sit up—the fat man is wearing a top hat—and manage to bump heads. The top hat flies into the air with a champagne-cork *pop*.

In silence, they dress. The fat guy is wearing a full-length nightshirt with a ruffled front; a pair of tuxedo pants hang by their suspenders from one bedpost. What a good idea: first he finds his hat and puts it back on, then he drags one side of the suspenders to the other bedpost, and jumps from the foot of the bed into the trousers. The hat pops off, the suspenders ricochet onto his shoulders like slingshots. He finds a bow tie on an elastic string, snaps it around the collar of his nightshirt, his hat pops off, he dons it again, locates a pair of tails, struggles into them, loses the hat, picks it up, reaches in, finds an elastic string, which he snugs under his double chin as he lowers the hat on his head.

Meanwhile, the other guy is doing deep knee-bends, deep breathing exercises. His pajamas look silk but are actually an awful nylon. He gargles. He gargles. He tilts his head, not gargling, just thinking, then gargles again. He steps out of the room for five seconds and reenters in a tux and a mortarboard.

"Barry," the thin man says, "it's your big day."

"I got cold feet," says the little man.

"Let's take a look." The thin man drops to his friend's feet, discovers a pair of bunny slippers, and takes them off angrily. Then he catches himself, and tries to warm the fat man's toes with his hands. "Sit down, why dontcha? Here, sit down. Cold feet? You're marrying a beautiful girl, a beautiful rich girl. With all that money you could buy a million pairs of shoes! You could buy *me* a million pairs of shoes! Don't louse this up for me, Barry. I've been waiting forever for this wedding." By now he's practically throttling his friend's feet. "After all I've done for you, and now *this*? Cold feet?"

"She is beautiful, isn't she?"

"And rich!"

"Oh," says the little fat man, "my mama told me never to marry for money. Only love."

The thin man stands up. "Fair enough. You take the love. I'll take the money."

We never made a serious picture, but *Marry Me, Barry* was the silliest, giddy with its own jokes and costume changes and slamming doors. The war was over, and we could do whatever we wanted. I've always loved a wedding: *Marry Me, Barry* featured seven. Neddy Jefferson wrote it, our first flick made for just us alone, not an old script or a retread of an old script. Neddy even put in private jokes: Professor Mervin keeps betting Barry that he won't get married again. (In real life, Rocky'd bet me a post-Penny three thousand dollars.) Soon Barry's handing over bags of cash, sorrowfully, because every time he tries to marry the girl of his dreams—the poor-but-honest daughter of a greengrocer—he somehow ends up standing in front of an altar or a justice of the peace or, in one case, a movie of a justice of the peace, at his side a different bucktoothed harridan. At the end, of course, he finally weds his girl, who carries a bouquet of carrots. When she tosses them over her shoulder, I catch and share them with his third wife, the jilted pony.

Marry Me, Barry came out the first week of 1946, my favorite year ever. Rocky arrived at Jake's second birthday party with a bottom-heavy dishwater-blond woman in a Chinese dress that made her look more Ming vase than Suzie Wong. "This is Lillian," he said. Lillian cleared her throat and raised a set of eyebrows so plucked they looked like two columns of marching ants. Rocky slapped her shoulder. She cleared her throat again. "Oh!" said Rocky. "Of course. My current wife." *Current*, Lillian mouthed to herself, and hooked her arm through his arm. He'd married the interior decorator he'd hired to spiff up his now obsolete bachelor pad. I put out my hand for my money, and Rock obliged.

The war was over, and Carter and Sharp—like everyone else—were out of uniform and full of optimism. I was a father in peacetime: I'd won the war for them, hadn't I? A father of three—in May, we brought home our postwar boom baby, Betty. Okay, then: three kids, just right.

I loved my sons, no mistake, but I'd never longed for an heir. What I wanted was a girl baby, a baby girl, and that's what we called her: the baby. Where's the baby? How are you, baby? Hey, over there, you know who you are? The baby.

"I want one of those," Rocky said, when he came to meet her, bringing with him a box of chocolates and a giant, scowling teddy bear that looked like Lon Chaney, Jr.

"Not this one." The baby was cuddled into the crook of my arm. Already I'd decided we were each other's favorite. She liked to slip her fingers between my shirt buttons, and she had a luxurious sigh when she was happy. In her crib, she'd sob; all she wanted was to be held, all the time, round the clock, and I obliged her. "Let her cry it out," Jessie suggested. "Your mother's heartless," I told the baby, rescuing her from her misery.

I bought Jess a fur coat to celebrate. I hadn't planned to: I'd just gone to the Wilshire Bullock's, looking for a present, and I was assured that any woman's dearest wish was a fur. "Really?" I said.

"Sir," said the salesgirl. That was all she said, but she made it sound significant.

Who knew? I was out of the habit of women, so maybe I'd once known this fact and forgotten. The salesgirl offered me a pink-upholstered chair, and then she had other girls—models? store employees? aspiring actresses who'd happened by and heard I was there?—don the coats in the dressing room and then parade in front of my chair. Well, I'd have to shop for women's clothing more often. Who knew the merchandise would have actual women in it? Pretty girls in fur coats, trying their best to act rich and privileged.

I knew, at least, that Jessica would not wear a full-length fur coat. She'd want something a little more eccentric, something you could use as a prop. Out came a blond girl in a short white coat, ermine, I think, though it could have been Samoyed.

"Let me see that one on a brunette," I asked. So the girl turned around and left. They thought it more elegant not to let me see them put the furs on, and I couldn't think of a way to ask without sounding filthy. They merely walked out of the dressing room as though they'd been born wearing fur, and opened one wing of the coat to display the satin lining: camel or black or silvery white. Just one wing: a woman in a fur coat did not fly, she was chauffered. I would have loved to have seen the blond girl take off that pale fur made of whatever unfortunate animal, careful not to let her ring snag the satin, and hand it over to the brunette, help her on with it, let the weight and the leftover warmth settle.

But I couldn't ask. I just bought the coat.

When Jessica lifted the lid off the box, she said, "Oh, for God's sake."

"What?" I said.

She saw how she'd hurt my feelings, and said, softly, "A fur coat? We live in California. It's summer."

"So?"

"I can't." She pulled the coat from its box and laid it on her lap, as though it were a dead beloved pet. Several of them. She stroked the fur. My wife was not someone who made nice over unsuccessful gifts: she believed that was both dishonest and wasteful. "We'll send it to Annie. Iowa winters are cold." We'd visited Des Moines summers since the end of the war, and Jessie, an older sister herself, was particularly fond of the oldest Sharp girl.

"Do you recall how many sisters I have? If I send one to her, I have to send one to everybody."

"Then return it," she said. "The store will take it back."

She knew I never would.

"Okay," I told her. "We'll send it to Annie. I'll swing by Bullock's and buy out the department. You work on commission, or something?"

I imagined my oldest sister, by then in her fifties, in this coat that had been modeled that very day by two pretty girls. Annie would wear it to Friday-night services at the temple, explaining that it was a gift from her brother. She'd offer up an arm to any interested party: *go ahead, feel.* Annie had, as she had aged, developed a weakness for foolishness and grandeur. Her roommate, Bessie Mackintosh, an old school chum, was foolish and grand herself. She'd moved in after Rose had married Ed, and now Annie and Bessie lived in my childhood home, two plump midwestern ladies who had pooled their money and their family china.

"It's so practical of Annie," my sister Ida wrote; we were all glad that Annie did not have to live alone. Practical, yes, I agreed. Our last visit home, when I kissed Annie—who'd always seemed perfumed by boiled parsnips—I noticed that she smelled wonderful, like hot spice. Then I kissed Bessie, who did too. Annie told me, looking fondly at her friend, "Bessie is my best girl." I knew that she would not believe that they smelled the same, that she was in any way like Bessie: who, Annie would say to me, was anything like Bessie?

I sent Annie the original fur, and my other sisters near duplicates. "Thank you for the beautiful coat," Annie wrote back to me. "We take turns wearing it." And so I went back to the store—I must have been a running joke by then, it's amazing my habits didn't turn up in the gossip columns—and bought the same style in a different, darker animal, and sent it to Bessie. I wasn't thinking, of course: taking turns was part of the pleasure of the fur, the settling weight, the leftover warmth.

I Will Be a Sister to You

Tuesday nights I kissed my kids and wife and then drove down to the radio studio for the Carter and Sharp Show. A show-business father has access to all kinds of magic working stiffs don't: my family turned on the radio and—though they'd seen me walk out the door minutes before!—heard my voice in the playroom (or living room, or kitchen, or dance studio; our house was crazy for radios). There he is, plain as day: Daddy.

Jessica tried to explain it to them. Jake, at three, was scientifically inclined and understood how my voice could make it through a bramble of electrical wires and atmosphere and arrive at our house, but was puzzled by the things I said; Nate, two, knew I was pretending but figured I must be hiding in a closet as a joke. As for the baby, she crawled across the floor and tried to turn up the volume, smart girl. Jessica was never sure about letting them listen to their old man talking such nonsense with their uncle Rocky—at home we all got along, so why did I always sound so angry with him Tuesday nights at seven? Sometimes when I got home, they'd grill me.

"How come, Daddy, did you do that?" Jake asked.

"Do what, sweetheart?"

"Hit him?"

"I didn't," I said, and he, the literal kid, gave me a dirty look, and said, "I *heard*."

At least they weren't the kids of a matinee idol or screen siren, which would have been worse, according to Jessica: you'd have to watch your parents necking with all kinds of strangers and family friends. That was before Rocky cooked up a romance for me on the radio show: he decided that we'd invite on one of his fake sisters, Ida, who'd always been described as the beauty of the family. (My own Ida was vain, and

I'd hoped she'd like this piece of flattery.) The Professor would develop a crush on her from afar: "Tell me, Rocky, is she single?" he'd ask.

"Is she ever!" Rocky would answer, and then, when she showed up (according to the script) she'd be so fat I'd say that calling her single was stretching the truth. Rocky wanted a fat actress, so that the moment she stepped onto the stage the folks in the studio would start laughing, which would set off the audience at home.

"You know someone?" Rocky asked me. "Someone who needs steady work? Could be a regular character. Here's your chance to cast your own Heloise, Abelard."

I didn't.

"I'll take care of it," said Rocky, who usually left everything up to the writers and studio bosses. "Someone good," he mused. "Someone funny and fat."

Well, of course he was playing a trick on me. I'd show up, and there he'd be in drag—that would make perfect sense, of course. In a movie, who else would play Rocky's sister but Rocky? Not much of a joke, sure, but he and I were busy married men these days, and we'd take our laughs when we could.

But when I arrived at the afternoon run-through, there was Rock in his street clothes, and, with her back turned to me, a terrifically fat blonde. She was shaped like a fir tree, fatter the farther down you looked. Her ankles seemed to almost cover her tiny black pumps; her hair was platinum, nearly translucent. She and Rocky were reading from the script already, and I could hear that her timing was good, that her voice could go from sultry seductive purr to angry foghorn blare in the same sentence. I felt even worse than usual that we'd given Rocky's sisters my own sisters' names.

I walked across the stage to introduce myself. Rocky said to the woman, "Don't take it hard, Ida honey, you're just too much woman for a guy like the Professor."

"No, I'm not, I'm just *enough.*"

"Hello," I said. The woman turned and looked at me. She was younger than I'd expected, and her face wasn't as fat as the rest of her. I couldn't decide whether this was lucky or a mean trick. "I'm Mike Sharp. Your love interest."

She laughed, and set her hand on my arm. It reminded me of something. "Is *that* what you are?"

"So they tell me."

The woman flexed her eyebrows at me. She had a thin nose that sprang from her face like a swan dive. Otherwise, she looked like a giant, bratty, lovable baby. "Mose," she said. "Mose. Don't tell me you've forgotten me."

And at that I almost fainted like my on-screen self would have, to be reunited with someone he'd thought dead. It took some looking, but there she was: Miriam, Mimi, my giant bratty lovable lost child.

Still, I was the real Mike Sharp, not the celluloid one, and I had my wits about me: I kissed her cheek. I tried to get my arms around her, but I couldn't. I felt like crying.

She said, "You probably didn't recognize me because I got my nose fixed."

"That must be it," I said gallantly.

She burst out into her beautiful raucous laugh, and that was the moment I did fully, completely recognize her. "*Must* be," she said, "because I can't imagine how *else* I've changed."

I looked at Rocky, who was beaming, either evilly or paternally: I couldn't tell. "She's got the part," I told him.

"Of course she does!" he said. "Let's go out to lunch!"

"Sure," said Mimi.

Her curls were a parody of her old blond wig; I could see how short hair would no longer have suited her. All I could think was, Is lunch a good idea? But I offered her an elbow and said to Rocky, "You're not invited."

"No?" Rocky thought he was invited to every meal in the world. "Oh, okay. Old times. I understand."

"Good," I said.

I took her to Musso's, my favorite spot, to a table up front.

"So," she said, as she struggled into the booth, "I don't have to ask what *you've* been up to."

"Don't believe everything you hear on the radio."

"Carter's hijacked your sisters, has he?"

"For the time being. Listen, I'm a smart date. What have *you* been up to?"

She set her fingers on the table. The backs of her hands were dimpled like a baby's. "Radio work. In New York, mostly. I moved here a few months ago. Carter recognized me on the street. How about that? Saw me play Boston twenty years and a hundred pounds ago, picks me out

walking down Sunset, comes up with a role for me. I don't usually play
fat women, so this is a stretch. You're married," she said.

"Is that a question?"

"Of course not. Can't I read the magazines? You're married."

"You?" I said, though I'd already noticed her ringless fingers.

"Not anymore. I was married to Savant for a while."

"You mean a new Savant."

"Same old Savant."

"I thought he liked the saxophone player."

"Did. Does. All I can say is it seemed like a good idea at the time. He
was a good husband, but a lousy lay. According to me, I mean. The saxophone player might think he's a *great* fuck."

I'd forgotten how she could scandalize me, and how much I liked it.
All though our conversation, I kept losing the thread of her, of my
Miriam, until she did something in particular—laugh, bawl me out mer-
rily, touch the bottom of her hair with her fingertips—and then I'd recognize her, and then I'd lose her again. It was like hearing slightly
familiar music coming from another room and thinking, *Oh, that's what
the song is . . . hold on, no, it's not.* I couldn't decide what made me sadder: all the weight or the butchered nose. The surgeon had just scooped
out the center like a grapefruit.

"It's not fair," she said. "Look at me, and then look at you."

"What?"

"You haven't changed! We're both eighteen years older, and you look
exactly the same! And you're *older* than me. You still're older than me,
aren't you?"

"I've changed," I said.

"You haven't."

And so, sitting in Musso's, I dipped my fingers in my water glass and
put them to my hairline and softened the glue, and took off my toupee. I
dropped it over the bread basket. Surely I looked like hell, bits of glue
still stuck to my scalp.

"Well," I said, "I haven't changed much," but Miriam couldn't hear
me, she was laughing so hard. God knows I was ready to drop my pants
to keep her laughing like that, to hear that wonderful mocking noise.

She applauded me, as though she was—well, what she really was: my
first teacher, pleased that her student has finally extravagantly succeeded
at his course of study. "Jesus, Mose," she said. "Jesus Christ. Look at us!"

She was wonderful on the show that night, eerie though it was to stand next to her on a stage. We were cheek to cheek at the same mike, though this time she played voracious and I played prim. She seemed taller to me. Her current boyfriend, a nice-looking man with a hysterical infectious giggle, sat in the audience, good as gold; I don't know when we got bigger laughs. Back during my old days on the road, I thought any girl I'd ever slept with was mine to sleep with forever, so long as I charmed her, and I could see that the statute of limitations might never have expired. If I wasn't married. If I wasn't a father. If she wasn't so heavy. If I wasn't very, very careful. She had the same charismatic crackle as always, the same perfect unlined skin, the same pink round cleft tongue that flashed when she spoke. When Ida embraced the Professor over the air, Miriam embraced me in front of the audience, and because of her size and a well-deployed script, nobody could see her proprietary upstage fingers and where, exactly, they tickled me. She wore the same sinful cologne she'd favored as a teen, and she'd grown into it.

"Now," Rocky said after the broadcast, "it's time for a cocktail, and I *am* invited." He had his arm around Miriam's waist. Twenty years ago they would have looked nothing alike, a dark-haired exotic beauty and a pie-faced, snub-nosed Irish comedian. But, boy, she did look like his sister now. "Where shall we go? The Mocambo?"

"I need to go home," I said, yawning. "Promised the kids. Rock? Could I talk to you a second? Business?"

"Now?"

"Now," I said. I backed off the stage, beckoning him with one hand, waving good-bye to Miriam with the other. I could see her face change when she realized that this was our farewell; she lifted one hand and gave a toodling wave with the ends of her fingers, like the little girl she once pretended to be. I kept backing away till we turned the corner into a hallway and we couldn't see her.

"Not bad, huh?" said Rock. "She'll be a regular, I think. There she was, walking out of the pancake house, and I almost told you a million times, but—"

"She's fired," I said.

"What? She was great. Did you hear those laughs?"

"I don't care," I said. "My heart can't take it. I guess I'm lucky you didn't bring her over to the house, but Rock, listen: I can't do this."

"But *why*?"

I shrugged. It was sadness over what seemed to me her ruin. Fear over turning into the kid she'd dumped in Madison, Wisconsin, someone so completely abandoned he'd forget all the people who *hadn't* left him. A little bit of habitual desperate lust. Years ago, I'd convinced myself that I'd only wanted to be friends with her, but I didn't know how to do that now. I'd never had even a day's practice.

"Okay," said Rock, pulling at his ear. "I think it's *mean*—"

"I don't care," I said. "Kiss her for me."

When I got home, the kids were already asleep. "I put them to bed early," said Jessica. "Too much of Daddy's girlfriend on the show tonight." She was sitting on the floor in her usual spot, her back against the sofa. I sat down next to her.

"They would have understood."

"Maybe." She turned and gave me a kiss on the cheek, an impersonation of our sound guy's drawn-out ultrasuction pucker. Then she said, "You *do* have a girlfriend! Lipstick on your collar."

I pulled up my collar to see. Pink. A guy in the movies could always say, "Can't you tell? It's my own shade."

"I must have bumped the actress," I said.

"Who was she?" she asked. "She was awfully good. You know me, I don't laugh for just anyone. She really had you going, though. I mean, *you* were awfully good too."

"Thanks," I said. "The actress was just someone Rocky dug up."

She mussed my hair fondly. "They have credits on your show, you know, at the end. 'Playing the part of Ida Carter, Miriam Veblen.' It's all right." She got up—she always stood up from the floor like she was levitating, as though it took nothing—and then pulled me to my feet. "She scared the hell out of you, huh? Come on, Romeo. I'll fix you a snack."

My Platinum Blonde

Children, like all of us, are sensitive to class differences. They love two kinds of grown-ups: those who address children as genuine equals, and those who act like large children themselves. Rocky was the second sort.

Children could wrestle him to the ground in seconds. My own kids adored him. The rest of our sophisticated friends would say to Jake, now age five, "Are you married?" Jake was the kind of serious boy who took this kind of joking for what it was, a polite but preposterous lie. "Not yet," he'd say. "Maybe when I'm *thirty*." That left his inquisitor with nothing to do with his next line. ("Handsome guy like you? Got a girl, at least?")

Jake's seriousness evaporated at the first sight of Rock. He flat-out loved the guy. He even stole chocolates from his mother's supply (she noticed, of course), to press, only slightly melted, into Rocky's pocket. Rocky in turn brought firecrackers and comic books.

"For me?" said Jake, hopeful.

Rocky flopped on the ground and tiredly pushed his hair off his forehead so it would flop right back down, juvenile-delinquent style. "I dunno. You like these things?"

Jake nodded cautiously.

"Whattya got to trade?"

"Hey," I said. "Are you gambling with my child?"

"I am *bartering*," said Rock. "I am trading away these very fine, hardly thumbed comic books for your *house*. There is no gambling involved."

"The house is pretty big," Jake offered. "You don't have *too* many comics."

"I'll just take your bed," Rocky told him, "and I'll throw in the fireworks. The kid owns his bed, right?" he asked me.

Rock sat in the front row for all of Jessie's recitals—usually just our kids clowning around for our friends—and applauded loudest. I couldn't figure out how he could have been so often married without kids of his own. When we went to visit Tansy and his wife and children—talk about a fertile crescent! they had seven—Rocky brought individual presents. It took some talking to wrangle an invite, though.

"Why are you keeping your kids from us?" Rocky asked.

"Who says I'm keeping *them* from *you*?"

If Tansy himself was small, Mrs. Tansy could hardly be seen with the naked eye. Rocky said that Jessica and I looked ready to stand on top of a wedding cake for a full-sized couple; the Tansys could have stood on *ours*.

Small, small people, Mr. and Mrs. T. A screen door wouldn't keep them out of your kitchen. The children seemed normal sized, though there were so many of them it was hard to keep track of ages.

"How do you manage?" I asked Mrs. T., a good-humored, slouch-shouldered woman who loved to feign grumpiness and absentminded-ness.

"Who manages?" she said. "I just figure we keep production at this level, we're bound to turn a profit eventually."

"Aren't there seven kids in your family?" Tansy asked me.

"Sure, but that's different."

"Why? We like children. They keep showing up. We should send them to the pound?"

"I'll take your surplus," Rocky said. There was a set of twin Tansy girls, and they were riding around on Rocky's feet, one twin per shoe, holding on to his belt.

"When are you going to have your own?" said Tansy.

"These're good. They match each other, and I think they'll spruce up the living room. I'll take them. Fifty cents a pound sound okay?"

"We're using those," said Mrs. Tansy.

"We all have to pitch in, Mrs. T. I have no kids, you have extras."

"Stop bothering Tansy's wife," I told him. "Bother your own wife. That's where babies come from."

"You better *not* bother me," said Mrs. Tansy.

Later, when Mrs. Tansy had gone to put the kids to bed, which in-volved rounding them up as though she were a Border collie, Rocky and Tansy and I went to their dining room to smoke. The table was covered with white rings from the kids' milk glasses, burn marks from hot dishes—the Tansys took everything casually. We sat at one end. Rocky poured himself a glass from a decanter that wore a little nameplate that said *Gin*, though the liquid was brown.

"Don't think I don't want kids," he said. "It's just not working out that way for Lillian."

"Oh," said Tansy.

"She gets pregnant, but then . . ." He sighed with the hopeless mys-tery of it. "Four times. Probably we should—"

"You leave that poor girl alone!" said Tansy. His passion surprised both of us, probably the way Rocky's casual confession had surprised him, and me. Rocky and I stared at him, and finally I cleared my throat and said, "You're a fine one to talk, Mr. T."

"The sadness, I mean." Tansy settled back in his chair. His feet didn't touch the ground. "No woman should have to bear that sadness."

It hadn't occurred to Rocky to blame himself in any way until Tansy yelled at him. What was he if not an innocent bystander? Nevertheless, within a few months, Lillian and he had adopted Rocky junior, a fat, chortling black-haired baby. Rocky senior joked to the press that in order to keep up with the Sharps, he and Lil had considered taking home half the ward at the Marymount Orphanage, but for now they were just keeping up with Rocky junior.

"We picked out the one who'll laugh at *anything*," Rocky told me. He'd brought the baby over so Lillian could get some beauty rest. She required a great deal of beauty rest, apparently—she turned down all invitations that involved leaving her own house, though she liked throwing theme parties. Rocky made it sound as though she spent hours every day rearranging the furniture.

Junior was ten months old when they brought him home, an excellent age for a baby. Our own baby, nine months older, was fascinated by him. They sat together on the grass where our back lawn sloped down toward the gated swimming pool I'd had installed for Jessica, shaped like a heart because in California you couldn't have a swimming pool shaped like a mere swimming pool. (I'd suggested the state of Iowa, itself nearly swimming-pool shaped, but Jessica vetoed that.) Our two babies poked at each other and laughed—our baby, like Rocky and Lil's, was a prodigious giggler.

"This kid—" said Rocky. But then he stopped. "He's a *good* kid. Probably above average, but I don't care if he's a dope. I hope he is one."

"He's not a dope," I said.

"I just hope he doesn't remember too much, you know?"

"No," I said. "You mean whoever his actual mother was? Who remembers that far back?" Rocky junior turned over in the grass and began to graze. His father seemed unconcerned, but I went and flipped him back sunny-side up.

"Me," said Rocky. "I remember the crib, sure. My father once dropped a slice of meat loaf on my head. You know, that's my problem. No, no, don't say it, not the meat loaf: I just remember too much. Everything, every single embarrassing thing I ever did, every rotten name anyone ever called me, every rotten name I ever called someone else . . ."

I sat back down. "Comes in handy, that memory."

"I'd trade it away in a minute if I could. That's why I want the kid to be forgetful. Happy."

"He won't have any bad memories to wish away," I said, "his childhood will be milk and chocolate cake—"

"He'll find a way to fuck it up," said Rocky. "It's human nature. All's that matters is how quick you get over it. If you're lucky, you'll forget what you need to and revise what you can't."

"What a philosophy!" I said. I looked at our kids, both now dozing in the shade of a midget palm tree. Maybe he couldn't tell, but I knew they were both geniuses, beloved, as lucky as a pair of loaded dice.

Compared to Rocky junior, our own baby was not really a baby any-more: she was nearly two, though she was still as plump and milky as an infant. One day you look at your kid and see that she's become a child, a little person, but it happens to every kid at a different time. Thinner arms and legs, a more muscular mouth, hair that needs cutting. The whole world of noninfant expressions: babies do not smirk, but toddlers can. Our baby had not outgrown her baby ways, though her older broth-ers had become actual little people by the time they were one year old. Betty—I love that name, the way it sounds like Hattie but luckier—did not talk much. She gestured. She waved like a starlet. And then there was her giggle, God how she giggled, slow at other things but at laughter a genius!

"An audience," said Jessica, dryly.

So what if the baby was not in a hurry to be a kid, a toddler, a refuser of fatherly advice? Maybe she just enjoyed the condition of infancy. In my own childhood home we'd always known that there were good ba-bies and bad babies. There wasn't any pattern: good babies could grow up to be miserable people, and bad babies saints. My father always said that Fannie, the mildest and quietest of my sisters, had been such a squalling vomiting bundle that sometimes he threatened to take her to the store and put her in the case that held smaller accessories, white handkerchiefs for businessmen, bandanas for the railroad men. "I could have gotten a good price for her," my father said, and Fannie smiled, and apologized for her earlier behavior.

Just as I'd planned, Betty was my favorite and I was hers. The boys preferred their mother, and who could blame them? The baby stuck to me. She gave her mother what I called the House Detective Glare, a kind of polite suspicion. Jessica *probably* wasn't stealing the towels, but she bore watching. I sat on the sofa, and the baby backed up between my knees and slung her arms across my thighs, watching her mother stretching on the floor.

"Where did you come from, my little blondie?" I asked her. It seemed impossible that Jess and I could have produced such a creature.

"She'll darken," said Jess. "I was blond as a child."

"What?" That seemed even more impossible.

"Sure. My hair didn't turn this dark till I was a teenager."

"A former blonde," I said musingly. "No kidding. All the women I know are former brunettes." Already I felt sad that Betty might become like the rest of us. I loved her this way, different, my changeling, my little bubblehead. Don't darken, I thought, and of course later I could hear my sister Annie whispering in my ear, See? See? Things you wish for will be granted, in the worst possible way. Wishes are fatal.

11

Better than a Backdrop

By 1948 Rocky and I had made a dozen and a half movies, so many that the oscillations on our careers happened very quickly. Still, we'd been on a downswing, box-office-wise, for a couple of years. We suffered—like most comedians—from the very thing that had made us. We reminded people of the war, and the war was over.

Why not take some time off? I said. Give the audience a year to miss us. Give Neddy and the studio more time with the scripts. We were saturating the market all by ourselves. I wasn't talking retirement—we had the radio show, there were some murmurs about getting into television, we could play Vegas or London. Just no more movies for a while, no more holding my mortarboard to my head as I turned corners one-legged or jumped down a manhole. On our last picture, *Slaphappy Saps*, I'd been chided by wardrobe, and then the studio: Jess, a champion of all sorts of exercise (a pioneer, I think now), had presented me with a set of dumbbells for my birthday, which she installed in the corner of her studio so I could watch myself in the mirror, and by developing a couple of muscles I'd done the unthinkable and monkeyed with the Professor's chickenhearted scrawniness. "Leave off the weights, Adonis," a studio exec warned me, and that seemed too much to bear.

We met with Tansy to discuss the future. Tansy loved his office, where he could always be seated when people were ushered in, though to show off his prosperity he'd bought a desk that could have seated twenty for dinner, which made him look more than ever like a mouse peeping out of a hole to see if the coast was clear of cats. Even the pencil holder was enormous. Rocky paced the room; I settled into one of the huge leather armchairs for guests, which made me feel agreeably like a snagged pop fly.

"It's not like we need the money," I told Rocky.

"You don't," said Rocky. I didn't point out that he still made sixty percent to my forty. "I need all the money I can get. We have our entire lives to slow down! Tansy," Rocky pleaded. "Tell him: we have a contract with the studio, and—"

Tansy smiled apologetically. "I don't think the studio'll mind, if you lay off a little. The last few pictures . . ."

"That's their fault," Rocky said.

"Maybe it's time to move along on TV, that's all I mean," said Tansy. "You could rest a little more. Spend time with your kids."

"I'll spend time with my kid when I'm retired." Rocky frowned and tried to peek under Tansy's blotter. "In twenty or thirty years. Meantime I'm going to make movies, with whoever wants to make them with me."

"Go ahead," I told him. "I'm too old for this nonsense. I'm done."

Rocky slowly sat down on the edge of Tansy's gargantuan desk. "You're *quitting?*" he said.

Was that what I'd meant? I only knew I was done with the dumb argument that we couldn't stop making movies because we couldn't stop making movies. But quitting? Out of the business? Surely not, and yet— what was that I felt? Elation? Why not retire, before we ended up like Skipper Moran, with his skid-row clothes and trembling fingers. We didn't have our dignity—that we'd sold off at the start of our careers— but at least we had all our teeth, and I had plenty of money, and three kids who'd love to roll around on the carpet with their pop.

"He's not quitting," said Tansy.

Rocky stared down at him, then at me. That's why he stood up, for the height advantage. "Are you quitting?" he asked.

"I'm tired. I'm an old man." I was thirty-seven. Rocky was forty-three.

"Toughen up!" he barked at me. "Jesus Christ. What would your father think of you, too tired to work?"

"I hate the movies we're making," I said. "So does the moviegoing public, apparently."

"The next one will be better. Look," he said, kinder now, "I know you pretty well, huh? Today you're tired, tomorrow you'll be fine. You're like your old man: you don't know how *not* to work. Right? Don't give me a heart attack, Mosey. I got alimony and a kid and maybe more alimony in my future—no, I'm kidding, but who knows. I need to work, and I need you to work. I'm not ashamed to say it." He had his hands together, fingers down, prayerlike but not too showy about it. He was taking this more seriously than I was. "Tell me you're not quitting."

"Rocky—"

"Tell me."

I'd never seen him so earnest. "I'm not quitting," I said dubiously.

"The kid's not quitting," said Tansy. "Sit down in a chair like a human being, would you?"

But I'd spooked him pretty bad. Rocky claimed not to read his own press, but I did, and a couple of months and one above-average but still lousy movie later—*What, Us Haunted?*—I picked up a movie magazine with an interview with Rocky.

Q. *What have been the most important parts of your success?*

A. *Burlesque, the navy, vaudeville. My lovely wife, of course, and our son.*

Q. *And your partner?*

A. *Mike's a nice guy.*

Q. *But where would you be without him?*

A. *Oh, probably somewhere close to where I am, but it wouldn't be as much fun.*

Maybe he was just trying to suggest to the general public that Carter was the essential ingredient of Carter and Sharp, and that, should Sharp devote himself to his family instead of show business, things could go on as they had without him. Chances are the world believed that already. But I had thought I could count on Rock as the one person who didn't think so. Now I could practically hear him shrug me off. I was *fun.* Not for the audience, just for him.

I went that night to the Rock Club, with the magazine in hand; there was a painting of Hedy Lamarr looking gorgeous on the cover, her head tipped back to show off her white neck. Rocky was sitting at his favorite banquette in the corner, where Penny had thrown her legs across my lap six years before. The club was half filled. Onstage, a trio of Spanish girl singers tragically harmonized on "Enjoy Yourself—It's Later Than You Think." They had red roses tucked behind their ears; the girl in the center held the neck of the mike stand like she couldn't decide whether to kiss or strangle it.

I shook the magazine at Rocky. "What's this?"

"Hedy Lamarr," he said.

"I've been reading your press," I told him.

"Yeah? How'd it come out? The reporter got me a little drunk." He snuffed his cigar. As though it *took* someone to get Rocky a little drunk.

"I'm a nice *guy*?" I said.

He must not have read the article; he was authentically confused. "Are you trying to establish a reputation as a son of a bitch I don't know about yet?"

I read him the pertinent passage, then tossed the magazine down on the table, where it careened into the candle. Fine. Let the whole place burn.

"They used that, huh," said Rock, staring at Hedy Lamarr's throat. "That's not so bad."

"This success," I said. "This is all your doing?"

He thought for a second. I assumed he was mustering up an apology. Then he looked at me. "This success? This success you're not so impressed with? Probably not. That doesn't mean I wouldn't have had a different, possibly more interesting success without you. Why do you think I get paid more?"

"That's a good question. That's a very good question. Because we have a contract together. And the contract says it's my turn to get more money. In fact, I'm long overdue. I figure, you owe *me*."

The singers finished their song. Rocky clapped, still looking at me. "You know, kid," he said, "you were more interesting when you didn't talk about yourself so much."

"What?"

"When I first met you. You shut up all the time. You never said anything except to ask a question."

"And I was interesting then."

"You were fascinating."

"Watch me shut up," I told him, and stalked out of the club.

He could have at least lied and said he'd been misquoted. Maybe I'd quit after all! Rocky could find one of those dime-a-dozen straight men. Just lean over and pick one up off the sidewalk, if it was that easy.

It might have been, I think now. Maybe I should have quit the team then, taken that early retirement. We could have been friends for the rest of our lives. I would have forgiven him. He was drunk. He was scared.

But at the moment it felt like Rock had been beating me at an eighteen-year game of poker. If I quit now, I'd never get even. I still had the orginal contract, the one that said that Rocky would get sixty percent more for the first ten years, and then the terms would reverse. He owed me eight years in back wages, the way I figured it. I steamed the page out of my scrapbook and took it to Tansy, who doubted it was legal. He urged me to calm down. "I'll talk to Rock," he said. "How's fifty-fifty? That's fair, right?"

"Barely," I said.

But Rocky wouldn't budge, and then he stopped talking to me completely.

We were shooting a racetrack picture—I played a tout, Rocky a jockey—and he only looked at me when the cameras were rolling. Then he was exuberant. The scene ended, and he walked away in disgust. It made me crazy. *You do not exist, you do not exist.* "Rocky, this is foolishness," I told him. He didn't care. Okay, then. If I didn't exist, then he didn't either.

Our first major falling out. After a while, it was almost like we weren't mad with each other, just shy. We declared nothing. We just stopped talking. For our radio show, we picked up our scripts; for the picture, we hit our marks and said our lines. I don't think the audience noticed the difference. Everyone was on my side, but everyone humored Rock. Jessica told me I should apologize, if not for me, then for our kids, who missed him.

"What am I apologizing for? Making less money? Being a sucker?"

"We have all the money we need," she said. "You know Rocky. He won't apologize. Don't drag your heels just to punish him."

"That sounds very wise," I said, "but I'm not going to roll over. I do it for every single other thing."

She sighed. "He's an unhappy man. If a little money makes him happier—"

"It isn't the money," I insisted.

"So you keep saying, dear, and then you explain how it *is*."

Those couple of months were our first silence: not the longest one, but the deepest. Once you've stopped speaking to someone, no matter how sincerely you then make up, there's a new chance that you'll stop speaking again. Every time, though, is different: sometimes you're furious and sometimes merely peevish; sometimes you struggle not to call the other person up in the middle of the night to yell or apologize, and sometimes it's just something that you do, like the morning crossword or calisthenics. After that first time it was easy: mad? Stop talking.

But that time, of course, we made it up.

Baby in Bright Water

Where was I? At the studio. I figured it out later, I mean, I wrote down everywhere I'd gone that day, and at just what time, accounting for travel, for conversations in hallways, for visits to the canteen and the men's room. I was sitting in one of those canvas-backed director's chairs that civilians believe movie people spend all their time in, my name stenciled across the back. We were posing for stills. The most hackneyed shot in the world, both of us leaning back, one careful elbow hooked over the canvas so that we would not obscure our names or the little drawings—mortarboard on my chair, Rocky's striped shirt (empty of Rocky) on his. In real life we hadn't spoken to each other in a month, but in publicity photos we were the best of friends, smiling at the camera, our elbows nearly touching. It was supposed to look as though the photographer, strolling up behind us, had said, "Heya, boys!" and snapped the picture. That took two hours.

Then I went to Musso's with Neddy. We ate tongue sandwiches; that's what I remember. (Tongue was one of the only things Rocky would not eat. "I only like human tongues in my mouth," he said, "but past that I'm not particular.")

"He'll cool down," said Neddy. "He never stays mad for long."

"Maybe *I* won't cool down. How come nobody ever worries about that?"

Neddy got the look on his face that meant that if he were a laughing man, by now he'd be in hysterics. He gestured at my sandwich with his sandwich. "Bite your tongue. Because you've always cooled down. What do you think is the secret of Carter and Sharp? You're the only son of a bitch who can take him. You're the only one who'll never walk out."

"That's all?" I said. "Good God, Neddy, I'd like to think that's not it. I'd like to think I had some *talent*. I'd like to think—"

And then the waiter came to our table, and handed me the phone, and it was Jessica saying, "Come home."

"What is it?" I asked, and she said, "The Baby," and hung up.

She hung up because she could not bear me asking for specifics. The specifics were this: my beautiful family was in its beautiful home. They had everything they could want, including, behind the house, that heart-shaped swimming pool with the wrought-iron fence. Jessica was the only one who swam; I still didn't know how. She complained about the shape. You could not travel one long line across the heart without bumping into a point or a curve. Every morning, nearly, she dove into the pool for a few irregular laps, and then she'd get out, and she'd shut the iron gates.

Maybe sometimes she forgot to shut them.

The baby had wandered out of the house. Look: a beautiful shimmering heart in the backyard, glittering romance to a baby girl. There were always little wavelets in our pool, the water holding coins of light between its fingers. The baby doesn't know the difference between water and light, unless it's on her skin: one is cold, and the other warm, but how can you tell if you don't touch? So she tries to touch. She is a magpie; she steals all the shiny things in the house and hides them in her bed, butter knives and costume jewelry and the foil from packs of cigarettes. She walks to the edge of the pool. She doesn't look around. She doesn't know this is forbidden. She leans over the water, and now the flash is beyond her reach, so she leans farther, and she is so small there is no splash, and she is so round that she floats, and she is so surprised that she does nothing, nothing at all, and when her mother finds her—only minutes later, says the doctor—she is still floating, little jellyfish, greedy little jellyfish, her hands empty and her face, when they turn her over, disappointed.

You cannot save the dead, though I'd spent years in dreams trying, catching Hattie and catching Hattie and every morning she was still dead. Now, I dreamt I dove into the pool until I remembered that this was a good way to kill myself as well, and then I thought that wasn't such a bad idea: it didn't count as suicide if it was accidental, did it?

Then I told myself, uncertainly, that I did not want to kill myself. I had responsibilities, so then I tried out other rescues: the net on the long pole that the pool man used to fish out flotsam. A call for help. Too long. Eventually, over and over, I merely locked the gate, with a giant padlock on a chain like a sunken treasure chest.

"If the gate was locked," I said to Jessica. This was cruelty, I knew even as I said it. Those days after the accident—the gates now actually locked—I wept, and she didn't. She curled up on the sofa with the boys, or walked into the kitchen, or sat on the floor cross-legged. My slight wife dwindled. She looked as though she'd wandered into another person's closet to dress, someone bigger and more optimistic. I regret to say that she grew oddly more beautiful: the few pictures I have from those days prove it. Skinny, too skinny to live, but gorgeous.

As for me, I wept, nearly all the time. It's come to this, I thought: I'd believed that as I got older I got more sentimental, but really I was losing my mind day by day, and this blow knocked me right out of it. "Mike Sharp's Tragedy," said the newspapers and magazines. "Tears of a Funny-man." Documentation everywhere, and well-meaning but horrific bouquets of flowers. Soon the florists knew to deliver to the local hospitals instead. All these years later, I can imagine how it would have been for Jessica, this great interest from the outside world in how *I* felt, what *I* had lost, as though by not being famous her own grief was not so compelling. Then, though, I agreed. My grief was as engrossing, as vivid, as unremitting as a hallucination.

I'd fallen into a pool once. I could have drowned! And yet I'd had one installed, I'd never learned to swim, I ignored *everything*.

Tell us what to do, my sisters said, in telegrams and phone calls. Say the word. I told them to stay home, that Jessica and I were doing our best for the boys now, and that a whole houseful of mourning grown-ups would only make things worse. My sisters agreed: that was how we'd been raised. But Jessica's brother, Joseph, arrived without warning; he'd heard the news on the radio and drove straight to the airport and once in Hollywood talked his way past the maid, who'd been instructed not to let anyone in. He was the one who arranged the burial—we had no funeral—and bought a plot in Forest Lawn at Babyland, which (I learned this later, though I still have never been by the grave) is a heart-shaped plinth of grass in the center of the park, a place in every way so tasteful that it's tasteless beyond imagining.

The maid was a poor guard dog. The day after the accident—Joseph already at the Forest Lawn—we had another visitor who slipped past.

"Mosey," Rock said as he stood in the door of my den, and I burst into tears and threw myself into his arms. I'd been crying by myself for so long. "Ah, sweetheart," he said to me. "Oh, babe."

We never officially made up, unless you call me weeping in his arms making up. Ask anyone: a tragedy will drive two people apart or together. In my case both things happened.

The first thing Rocky did was get me drunk. Terrible man, you think, but no, it was exactly what I needed. We sat in my study on the leather sofa Lillian, Rocky's decorator wife, had talked me into—if you napped on it, you woke up red faced and button printed—and he handed me glass after glass of brandy until I stopped weeping and could talk. The brandy slowed me down. Drunk, I could almost think. I couldn't remember the last time I'd been drunk. Surely it had been with Rocky, him pressing drinks on me, talking me into just one more.

"Just one more," I said now, and handed him back the glass.

"What can I do for you?" he asked. "What do you need?"

"I don't know."

The sofa made a fussy noise as he rearranged his weight. He wasn't drinking himself. "You know what I think? You need to get back to work."

I shook my head. But what I said was "Yes." My father's cure: keeping busy. Who knew more about such things than my father? We'd wrap the racetrack pic, which was nearly done—that's why we'd been posing for stills—and there was the radio show on Thursday night. They'd already arranged for Eddie Cantor to replace me. There would have been jokes about all of Rocky's mythical sisters and Cantor's very real daughters: he had five. "Five daughters," I said to Rocky on the sofa, the way he used to say, *Six sisters!* He just patted my back. Maybe he thought I was making plans for the future.

"Work," he said to me. "It's not a cure, but it will help."

That first radio show was torture, not funny in the least. You will find it on no tape of *The Best of Carter and Sharp.* Cantor showed up anyhow, just in case I couldn't go on. The script seemed especially stupid to me, but radio work was perfect for the state I was in: I could sit down when they didn't need me, just listen to Loretta sing her ballad, sounding ready to burst into tears herself. The writers hadn't changed anything; they probably should have given her something upbeat. On the other hand, that might have been worse, sniffling through "The Sunny Side of the Street."

The audience gave me a standing ovation. The papers marveled at my bravery, as though my greatest duty in the world was entertaining people (not that I was the least bit entertaining that night: I flubbed my lines, I stepped on cues). I was a trooper, like the soldier I'd once thought I should be, charging ahead despite my fear. The only people who didn't admire me were Jessica and Joseph. When I got home that night, Joseph said, "Your wife needs you." He looked like he was working on his resemblance to Mahler.

I shrugged, and started for our room.

"Not *now*," he said. "She needed you to be home. Now she's asleep."

"Good," I said. "I'm glad she can sleep."

"The doctor gave her a sedative," he told me. I remembered when I thought he had liked me, and then finding out that he didn't. He was eating this up. See, he seemed to say, what my sister needs is *me*. You, she's not even related to.

"Where are the boys?"

"Everyone's asleep."

"Didn't they listen to the show?" They always listened to the show.

"No," he said. "They weren't in the mood for comedy."

"Me neither. Sometimes you have to force yourself."

"Forced laughter," said Joseph, "is no kind of laughter at all."

When we were kids, Hattie and I sometimes talked about what our mother had been like before we were born. Annie would tell us to remember the babies that had died. We couldn't understand why Annie was so bitter, when she was the lucky one, the firstborn, before our mother started all that grieving: Annie in her arms. Full of love in those days, surely. Full of health and dumb rhymes, ready for anything that might happen. Ordinary, in other words. Six dead children would change any woman. Hattie and I hadn't forgotten those siblings, but we hadn't forgiven them either. They had been bad for Mama. They were ancestors who had never done anything. I never understood it fully, until the accident. A lost child means—in a way a living child never does—a little less love for those who are left. A dead baby is a bank failing: you'll never get that particular fortune back.

Maybe my own youngest child, Gilda, wonders what it would have been like to know her mother and me before Betty. She's such a good girl, Gilda. (Girl! She's in her late forties.) She runs the Carter and Sharp fan club, and wrote a book about my career that mentions nearly none of my faults and sold nearly no copies. Probably it makes sense that of all of the children, she was the one who tied up her life with Carter and Sharp: she needed to believe in partnerships.

"It's different for me!" I yelled at Jessica the week after Betty died. She looked at me. "Because I've lost *everybody!*"

"Oh? And who am I? And who," she said, the orphaned girl who'd been spirited away from home by a wandering husband, "haven't I lost?"

She wanted to fill in the swimming pool. I refused, though we drained it. This, too, might have been cruelty, might have been me wanting her to look at her mistake every day. But I couldn't bear the idea of men coming to throw dirt into that impractical heart, as though we wanted to pretend that it never existed. Of course it existed. Why bury the baby twice? I imagined that even if we'd planted it over, like a curse some sign of it would always remain: grass would refuse to grow right, a brown heart, worse than a swimming pool ever was.

"It's dangerous," Jessica said, and I said, "Not if you lock the gates."

12

Anything Without a View

Rocky and I started on a movie that took place, sort of, in ancient Egypt. That is, Rocky gets clobbered by a crate of bananas in the first scene, and the screen goes wavy and when he wakes up he's suddenly a pharaoh. How can he tell? A crowd of people surround him and sing:

For he's a jolly good pharaoh
For he's a jolly good pharaoh
For he's a jolly good pha-a-a-raoh—

and he, of course, answers, "Which nobody can deny!"

I played his loyal minister of something-or-other. A long tunic, sandals, a mortarboard. "Moses in the desert," said Rocky. Mummies chased us: that was the plot. All those movies, and the only thing that changed was what the guys chasing us were wearing, and how fast they moved. The mummies stumbled and were easily tricked.

Our twenty-fifth picture, fuller of song parodies than a Jewish family reunion. *Mummy, how I love you, how I love you/My dear old Mummy./I'd give the world to be/Right there with you in E-G-Y-P-T, oh, Mummy.*

Rocky never mentioned the money to me again, but Tansy had to. "How about fifty-five/forty-five?" he asked.

"Who gets what?"

He stared miserably into the giant pencil holder. It looked like the Holy Grail in his hand.

"Okay," I said, feeling both bullied and grateful.

So I worked, radio and the movie and personal appearances. Then I went home, where, every single day, Betty was still dead. Sometimes Jess and I managed to be tender with each other, but mostly we were not: money does not buy happiness, but it does buy a great expanse of real estate, and in our house you could avoid the other occupants without much effort. I spent time in my den. Jess and the boys hung around her studio, or the playroom by the solarium. She did her best to be cheery around them, and I could not bear to see such love aimed at anyone in the world, because the world did not deserve it even if the boys did.

I hope my sons have forgiven me now for the strange barking nasty man I was for the year after Betty died. I wouldn't blame them if they haven't. I was an angry father. I can hardly remember what I was thinking, though I can recall my actions, the things I said.

Not everything got me mad. My temper took them by surprise; me too. Lies always enraged me, though now I know that children always lie: in fact, they lie because they're afraid of their father's anger. Then, though: whose muddy footprints were these? Not mine, said Jake, though we were a movie family and knew a detective's ways: here's the print. Here's the shoe. Here's the foot that fits that shoe. Who left this ukelele out on the sofa? I held the neck of the uke and swung it through the air. Only Nathan played the ukelele, and yet he swore he didn't do it. He believed that I'd believe him. I flung it onto the ceramic tiles in the entranceway so it would shatter. I remember the pleasure in my shoulder as I overhanded the uke into the foyer; I remember Nathan, curled into a ball on the sofa, as though I'd go for his neck next.

"Natie," I said. He had his head pressed into a pillow, sure I meant to do him harm. Never. The anger itself was the point, the scrim of flames the magician draws to hide himself. But really, why did he lie?

"Go to your room," I told him. He ran at top speed.

Suddenly it was June again. In two weeks it would be the Baby's *yahrzeit*, the anniversary of her death. We all could feel it coming. I came home one day to what I thought was an empty house—the boys were at a birthday party—and found Jessie in bed, two o'clock in the afternoon. She was weeping. I'd known her seven years and I'd never seen her cry like that. Our bedclothes were heirlooms: pillow shams trimmed in lace made by Jessica's mother, a quilt stitched by an aunt. Lillian, Rock's wife, was scandalized. Surely we could afford new sheets.

I sat down. Jessica did not look at me. "I've been in bed three hours," she said. "I don't think I can get out."

"You're missing her, that's all."

"No. I mean yes, but I'm in bed because I miss *you*."

"I'm right here," I said.

"But you know, my darling, that I have to leave you."

I knew no such thing.

"I feel like a bad person," she said. "I used to think I was a good person. I prided myself on it. I thought, no matter how mean someone is to me, I won't be mean back."

"Who's mean to you?"

"You are. I don't care about that. People have been mean to me before. But not the boys. Not the boys. I need to take them someplace where people won't be mean to them."

"People," I said.

"You can't forgive me, that's obvious, but they haven't done anything to anyone, and now we have to go."

"No, you don't—"

"Yes," she said. "We're going to Des Moines. My studio's still there, Joseph hasn't changed a thing. It's a big house. You'll come and see them."

"Jessica," I said. "Jessie."

"Maybe you can stay with Rocky and Lillian for a while. It'll take me a week to pack. To arrange things."

She was still under the covers. I tried to get beneath them too. She wouldn't let me. I lifted one of her arms.

"*Mose,*" she said, "I can't."

I could feel her hand trying to make up its mind. She hadn't opened her eyes. I stared at her, trying to will her to look at me. She had something gray caught in her hair, and I brushed it out with the tips of my fingers. She had stopped crying, and I was about to start. "Where did you find a cobweb?" I asked.

She gave a swallowing smile. "Before I was in bed, I was under it."

"Why?"

"I don't know. I thought it would make me feel better. All day long I crawl into places, beneath the sofa cushions, under your desk. There isn't a closet in the house small enough. I can't bear to live here and I can't bear to leave and everywhere I go I turn around and see myself and pretty soon I'm going to try to sleep in dresser drawers or in the sink and it's time to go."

I held her one hand in my two hands. "Things will get better!"

"Sweetheart, if I believed that for a moment, would I feel this way? You think I don't miss her."

"I never said that."

"I don't do anything else. I love her. And I love Jacob and Nathan. I love them all the same, still, and I can't do anything for her. And I can't do anything for you, the way you hate me now."

"I don't—"

That's when she finally turned her head and opened her eyes. "Go to Rocky and Lil's," she said. "I'll call you when we get settled."

I did. She'd already packed me a little suitcase.

First, though, I drove around in my car. Should I go back? There had to be something I could say, even though I now understood the whole past year from her point of view: she'd been waiting for me to say something to her forever. I laughed, thinking that Rock had told me years before that I should come to him if I wanted divorce advice. *You'll fuck around*, he'd said, and I hadn't. I'd figured that was the only rule.

I drove past our house again. What should I do? I could go back in and put my foot down, *You will not leave me, you will not take my sons*, but that was what had gotten me into this trouble in the first place. I could cry, but I already had. I could plead, but I'd done that too. My fault, I told myself, *my fault*, and every time I tried to split the blame between me and someone else—Jessica or God or even Rocky, who'd told me that work would solve my problems—I realized again it was my fault.

In the morning I would know what to do.

The Lodger

Lillian and Rock took me in right away; Jessica had called them ahead of time. They moved me into a guest room that overlooked the swimming pool. I crawled into bed. The sheets were still warm from the iron.

That whole week might have been comic, if I had been in a laughing mood. Actually, that first day I often laughed, inappropriately. Every time I saw her, Lillian was wearing one cosmetic mask or another, blue or brown or surgical white. Her vanity in such things was double, I think: she wanted to improve her complexion, but she also knew that for some reason those masks suited her. They highlighted her two best features—large light brown eyes, and lovely full lips—and minimized her puggish nose and her wide wrinkled forehead. In fact, she always looked quite beautiful that way, a strange apparition bringing me tomato soup, tomato juice, pitchers of lemon-clogged ice water.

I felt pretty bad that first day, but I believed I would live. In the morning I realized I was one of those people who'd been kicked in the head and managed to get up and walk around for twelve hours, rubbing his noggin and saying, A little headache, that's all, only to wake up an invalid.

"You want to call her?" Rocky asked.

I shook my head.

"We'll call her." He sat on a chair by the bed, his knees up against the nightstand. The phone was a confection that Lillian had installed, all gold scroll and black inlay, better suited for a pinup to hold to her ear, saucily shocked at her caller. The receiver looked too small in Rocky's hand. "No answer," he said.

"Didn't think so."

"Buddy," he told me, "you need to do something."

Our radio show was on summer replacements—our bandleader, West Thompson, had taken over—and we weren't shooting a picture.

"We'll go out," he said.

I shook my head. Actually, I did nothing so athletic, I just stirred the air in front of my face lightly with my nose.

"Say the word," Rock said. He stood up to leave.

I said, "Thanks."

She'd been under the bed. I understood. Back when I boarded in other people's homes, I often had the same dream: I'd been out of the house, and when I returned, there was some guy—sometimes more than one— sleeping in my bed or reading the paper in my chair. *Excuse me*, I'd say, *wrong door*, but then it turned out that I'd been sharing my quarters all along: we'd just never happened to be in the same room at the same time.

I wanted to do that now. I wanted to haunt the house, so that I could be around my family without them ever noticing. Couldn't we live together that way? I'd sleep under the bed and only get up in the middle of the night, make my rounds, look at my boys sleeping, maybe lay out their clothes for the morning, fill the front room with flowers, stick handfuls of candy in their empty shoes. That way, I couldn't hurt them. I got under Rocky's guest bed to test. Apparently his maids were more thorough: no cobwebs here. Light came through the sheer bedskirt, and I put my hands up and felt the slats of the bedframe, and then the flimsier slats of the box spring, and I tried to imagine the sweet outline of Jessica over me, the princess and the pea in reverse: a small shape layers and layers above whose tiniest edge lacerated me, from the knot in her sneakers to the buckle on her watchband.

Mostly, though, I spent my time on the sleeping side of the bed, like my wife, fully dressed and half paralyzed. I kept my back straight, my elbows tucked in at my sides, as though I'd been dropped into a swimming pool again, but this time I wasn't going to fight, this time I wanted to sink to the bottom, I swear I had bruises at my waist from my elbows digging in, my toes were pointed, my hands in a ball at my stomach, but no matter how heavy I tried to make myself, I was buoyant, I was buoyant, something was letting me breathe when I only longed to be drowned. How could I make myself sinkable? Keep your eyes closed. Keep your toes pointed. Keep your mouth shut.

Rocky knocked on the door. "Do you want anything?"

I'd just been picturing somebody—not Rocky, someone in better shape, and without a face—snatching me out of bed and throwing me through the window (not made of sugar in this vision, unlike the panes of glass Carter and Sharp dove through in the movies) and into the swimming pool.

I didn't think I could ask for that, though.

I said, "I don't want to die, but I wouldn't turn down a coma."

A few hours later—or the next day, or the day after that—I thought, *After the baby died, I could move, but now I can't, and that means I miss Jessica more than I miss the baby,* and I ran to the window I'd imagined sailing through and opened it and spent the next five minutes vomiting and then doing a painful impression of vomiting. The recent contents of my stomach (tomato juice, ice water) ran down the pitched roof onto— must be the kitchen, if I remembered the floor plan right. Someone should clean that up. If I'd been drinking, this would be a story we'd tell, the night I got sick and clogged the gutters.

I blamed gravity, which pulled at the hems of everyone I loved: first Hattie, then Betty. What did a guy like me do, except in my movies defy gravity over and over again? If I fell, I bounced back unhurt. I was always sitting on the end of a plank balanced on a barrel, so someone could sit on the other side and launch me into the air, pulled up to the rafters by invisible guy wires. Offscreen, there was nothing for gravity to do but take its revenge. Those days in Rocky's house I gave in to my fear of the stuff, got as low as I could get so gravity couldn't knock me farther down, into beds and under them, away from the dangers of pavement and airplanes and cliffs.

People aren't afraid of heights: they're afraid of depths.

Every day Rock came in and called Jessica. No answer ever. Was she already gone? No, he said, he'd driven by the house that morning and had seen her through a window. It was like Rocky knew how this was done: your wife is going to leave you, you don't let her. I told myself that in a few weeks I'd go to Iowa. I'd be better. I could put together a good argument. Now, though, I thought of Jessica with the cobwebs in her hair, and I agreed with her, I was mean, and I did not see how insisting that my family live with me would ease their troubles.

"I'm the problem," I told Rocky.

"Kiddo, that's not the case. Do me a favor and give yourself a break."

"I'd like to give myself several."

He sat on the bed and bounced. "Let's go out. Let's get drunk. Let's find some pretty girls to be the death of us."

"I'm a married man!" I said, and I burst into tears.

At the end of the week, I was invited to a party. Initially I suspected that Rocky and Lillian threw it to cheer me up, which made me want to kick them, but then I realized Lil was too much of a worrier to put together anything on three days' notice. This was another of her horrible theme parties. Just before the baby's accident, Jessica and I had gone to her Artists and Models Ball, husbands as famous painters, wives as their subjects. I decided on Gauguin—a pair of ragged pants and an old white dress shirt, a little French moustache, a paintbrush in my fist—and Jessica rolled herself in a sarong and filed a hibiscus behind her ear. Lillian kept knocking things over with her petticoats—she was somebody out of Toulouse-Lautrec—and Rocky went around on his knees, sneaking under his wife's skirt until he got drunk, and then under any skirt he pleased. Mrs. Tansy was the real surprise: she came as a tiny Vargas girl, holding a prop cigar and stretching out on sofas.

This one would be a hobo party. What fun! We'd all dress as though we had no money at all, and we'd eat casseroles cooked for us outside in coffee cans. Boiled coffee laced with cognac; good wine decanted into plonk bottles. I tried to get out of it. Rocky insisted.

"It'll do you good," he said.

"I don't want to be cheered up."

"Of course not," he said. "But you'll have to act human for a few hours, and that won't kill you. I got no expectations of you. Maybe it's time to deal with expectations."

It didn't take much to turn me into a vagrant: I hadn't shaved in several days, I'd been sleeping in my clothes. Lillian put some mascara on my face for coal dust. I didn't know half the people at the party, and the other half I didn't recognize. Lots of bandanas around, the kind Sharp's used to sell when the Rock Island roundhouse was still in Valley Junction. The guests were supposed to look like boxcar riders. Lil, as hostess, puttered around nervously. She wore a patched skirt over about a dozen cotton petticoats, not so different from her Toulouse-Lautrec outfit but more ginghamy.

"Mike!" she said. "Are you having a good time?"

"No."

She tried to look sympathetic. "Are other people?"

I surveyed the room. "I think so."

She held a napkin with a small slice of beef Wellington on it. *How very Rock Island line*, I thought. "I don't know most of them," she said. "There's one little bum who gives me the creeps, though. Won't talk. Stands by the food."

"Probably Tansy."

"No, Tansy's over there. See? That's the guy I mean."

The guy in question was slight, with a giant false beard covering most of his face and a giant hat pulled down over his ears, big greasy gloves, dark glasses, torn overalls, a soiled suit jacket. You could hardly see an inch of skin. Suddenly, I felt cheered: maybe an actual bum had crashed the party.

"I think I recognize him," I lied. "Some burlesque friend of Rock's."

"You think?"

"Either that, or the genuine article, looking for a handout."

Lillian shivered so elaborately her petticoats rattled.

People were getting drunk. I wanted no part of it. Fact was, Rocky was right—standing up did make me feel better, and I didn't want to. They'd hired a boxcar and parked it next to the pool. I wondered what had happened to the Ferris wheel. Left behind at the old place in the hills, probably. I wandered through the house, stepped out onto balconies I'd never seen before, surprised an off-duty maid and apologized, watched Rocky junior sleeping and nearly burst into tears. What I wanted to do was crawl into bed next to him, but I realized this would not be interpreted as polite behavior from a guest. I ended up going into Rocky's den, and lying down on a leather sofa identical to the one at my house. My house. Soon to be empty of my family. Maybe I'd have to burn it down when they left. "That's a joke," I said out loud.

No good. I got up and went downstairs to the basement. The party roared on above my head. Rocky—out of sentiment or sheer perversity—had duplicated, here in the new house, the bar he and Penny had had in the old place. I wondered if Lillian knew. In the old days, this room would have been filled, but Lillian loved elegance even when slumming, and a cellar didn't qualify. I don't know what I was looking for. Some ghost from 1941 or '46. A patch of air like amnesia that I could walk through.

Same old bar, same black stools with ribbed metal edging. Rock owned a jukebox, too, though not one that bubbled like mine. Pool table, dartboard. I gave the roulette wheel a small sluttering spin.

Suddenly I became aware of someone else in the room. There, in the farthest corner, back against some bookshelves, was Rocky, in his arms the realistic little bum, a coil of chestnut hair falling from the flea-bitten hat. They were necking. Ah, the ghost I'd wanted. I cleared my throat.

The little bum turned to me, Rocky still holding on to one shoulder. Rock looked bewildered: *I think I was just kissing someone, but now I appear not to be.* The books behind him had been pushed in, a rough outline of a heavy man.

"Mike!" said the little bum, her breath fluttering her false beard—how did you kiss through *that*? "Mike! I've missed you!"

Someone had told Penny about the party and she'd driven down from San Francisco, where she'd been living, to crash. "Take her out to the pool house, will you, Mosey?" Rocky asked. "I need to make an appearance. I'll be out in a bit." Upstairs, the guests had sat down to dinner—we could hear the chairs scraping against the marble floor of the dining room—eating the coffee-can casserole, a layer of potatoes, a layer of meat, a layer of beans.

Penny and I crept along the edge of the swimming pool hand-in-hand like Hansel and Gretel. I tried not to look at it. The boxcar was abandoned. The pool house looked like an oversized ice-cream stand, complete with striped crank-down awnings. We moved with cartoon caution, tiptoed so the heels of our wingtips wouldn't clonk on the tile, pulled on the door so the latch wouldn't click. "I feel like I'm harboring a runaway," I said.

"You are," Penny told me. "I'm sleeping out here tonight. Rock says it's okay, so long as I'm quiet as a mouse."

"You?" I said. "You won't sing?"

"No singing. Only squeaking."

The moon cast its silver-dollar glow across the water and into the pool house. Apparently Rock and Lillian were using it for storage: I could make out the shapes of things left over from parties and stolen off sets. A series of easels like lanky birds leaned in one corner, props from the Artists and Models Ball; one wore a damp-looking feather boa. There was a deflated gorilla suit from a jungle picture, and Rocky's souped-up bumper car from *Fly Boys*, which Penny eased into.

"The key's gone, dammit," she said. She leaned her bony chest against the padded steering wheel.

We couldn't turn on the light, but I found a pair of beach chairs, striped like the awnings, and unfolded them. I gestured at one for Penny: Madam. She stepped out of the bumper car, and we both stretched out. A couple of tramps on the Riviera. I leaned back and crossed my ankles. Penny pulled off her beard and doffed her fedora; she hung the hat on one of her feet, and the beard on one of mine.

"Look!" she said. She held up the dark glasses. "I finally got specs, the way you told me to."

"I meant glasses to help you see," I said. "I didn't mean any old pair."

"These do!" She put them on and turned her face from side to side. "Prescription," she declared. "Do they suit me?"

"They do," I said. She gave me a delighted smile and kept them on.

"You sweet sneak," I said admiringly. "Poor Lillian."

"Whose side are you on?"

"Yours," I said. "Of course, Penny. But she thought you might be an actual hobo."

"I'll kill her," said Penny, "though if you were a gentleman, you'd offer to kill her for me."

"Well, I was the one who might have put the thought in her head. You're very convincing. I think she'd rather a gate-crashing hobo than an ex-wife."

"I'll kill you," she said warmly. "Really? Convincing? See, I *told* Rocky he should give me a part in a movie."

We could hear the music and laughter across the pool; it felt like a shrunk-down version of the kind of beach resort Rocky and I had played summers at the start of our career. If you'd asked me an hour before whether anything could cheer me up, I would have said no, but Penny's arrival did. What romantic stupidity! Besides, she was someone I had known back before: before Jessica had left me, before the baby died. It was so dark and moonplated inside that we both seemed black and white. Penny looked wonderful, and I told her so.

"*You* look like hell," she said.

"The lady of the house put mascara on my face."

"Did she make you lose ten pounds? Has she been waking you up every hour on the hour? Tough hostess."

"I've had some hard times lately."

"I know," she said. She looked at the hat that tilted on her foot, wiggled her ankle, and spun it around. "I'm so sorry about your daughter, Mike."

I nodded.

"How's everybody else?" she asked. "How's your wife?"

I thought about not telling her. We could sit out here and look at the house, at the rich people dressed as paupers who got drunk on good liquor while making jokes about rotgut. See, Penny had it right: the only reason in the world to dress up like that was so you could pass for someone else. So you could walk into a house where you weren't wanted. Could I go home if I wore a costume? A French maid's outfit, maybe. *Monsieur Sharp haz hired me to help wiz ze packing for ze treep to De Mwainh. He haz azked me to zmell your hair before you go.*

"Everything else is not so good," I said. "My wife is leaving me. Any moment, she will have left me." And I told her the whole story: my conversation with Jess, what I'd done that week, what I hadn't done.

Penny kicked her hat in the air and caught it in her hands. Then she flipped her dark glasses on the top of her head. I couldn't see the expression on her face, though I imagined it was sympathetic. She said, with great sadness, "He gave away my Ferris wheel."

"I figured you got it in the divorce."

"Honey," Penny said to me. Then she tried Rocky's old pet name: "Darling boy." That made me smile. "Why would you throw away your family like that?"

That floored me. Hadn't she been listening? Her beard fell from my foot. "I'm being thrown."

"No, you're not." She slid to the very edge of her chaise and pinned the false beard to the floor beneath her toe. "Of course you're not. Why a week? Why on earth would she wait a week to leave?"

"She needed to pack."

"Take it from me, Mike. Take it from one with years of experience. Nobody *needs* to pack. Especially if you've been thinking about it. Even if it's just the smallest niggling thought, I might leave, you somehow walk around with escape supplies: money, passport, car keys. Extra underwear in your purse. Why let her go?"

"I'm not. She's going anyhow."

"Don't *let* her," Penny said. She crossed her arms under the bib of her overalls. "You're one of those people who can't be alone. Anyone can see it. You know," she said, "you're not near so suave as you think you are."

"My suavity's at an all-time low, Penn."

"You never were. Girls wanted to take care of you, that's why they like you. They think, he'll starve to death without me. I know I did. Nobody ever looked at Rock and thought that, and I don't just mean his weight. But he's the same as you, he just doesn't know it. He can't be alone. Can't take care of himself. Doesn't like his own company. I had to be married to him for a while before I saw that. And once I did, he started picking fights with me. He throws people away, Mike. You're the only one he doesn't. You know he's going to leave Lillian? He wrote me a letter. Take a lesson from your partner. Whatever he does matrimonially, do the opposite."

"Which is?"

" 'Faint heart ne'er won fair lady.' *You* know that. Maybe you're not so slick as you believe, but you never were fainthearted. Go home. Tonight. Talk to her. Don't let pride make you stupid."

"Do I look like a proud person?" I spread my arms to display my sorry self.

"It's pride or cowardice," said Penny.

The door opened, and Rocky walked in, his arms around a stack of bedclothes. He switched on the light with his elbow. "Why're you sitting around in the dark, children?" he asked. Lillian had darkened his chin with a slightly opalescent eye shadow. He was drunk; he probably hadn't noticed at the main house, among his sozzled peers. You could tell, though, that here in the sober outpost he felt a little self-conscious.

"The head hobo." Penny gave him a little salute.

"You'll be okay out here, Penn? I told Lil some buddies of mine are sleeping off a few too many drinks, so she won't bother you. I'll come out at breakfast time."

"Sure. Thanks. And in the morning you'll toss me out on the street?"

"Don't say that, Penny," said Rocky. "You can stay as long as you want, if you lay low. And anyhow, you keep turning up."

"Like a bad Penny," she said.

He said, cheerfully, "*Very* bad."

He set the sheets behind her on the chaise, then sat upon them. He looked at both of us, then, sighing, set his cheek on the back of his ex-wife's shoulder. "Don't mention it. We'll harbor anyone. The Carter Home for Little Wanderers."

This little wanderer, however, wandered home. Rocky shook my hand, bewildered, and Penny kissed my cheek and said, "Nobody ever takes my advice!" *Faint heart ne'er won fair lady.* I did feel fainthearted. I'd felt that way all week. Not brokenhearted, which suggests that you know that your life is over, but faint, which is why I'd spent so much time in bed. Should I get some flowers to court my wife? No, it was late, no florist would be open, and in my hobofied state, if I crawled through someone's garden I'd probably be arrested. I considered this: would it be romantic to be taken in and tell the desk sergeant to call my wife to make my bail? *Look what trouble I get into without you.* Then I remembered that it would be written up in the papers—Mike Sharp Arrested for Pinching Peonies—and that would be hard to explain to our sponsors.

Even though I'd spent the past week repenting the misery I'd inflicted on my wife and my boys, I hadn't really fathomed it. In the car, as I drove to the house, I began to. I tried to plan what I would say to Jessica, but no matter what I came up with, I saw her frowning at me. I nearly turned around at one point, so I could ask Penny, Okay, so I'm going back, but what do I say?

Fact was, Jess had been right a week ago: I hadn't forgiven her. Now I somehow had. (I knew better than to make this the thesis of my speech.) I'd spent a week suffering like she had for a year: inconsolable, and in private.

There was my driveway. At the end was my house. Inside was my family.

Everyone was asleep when I went prowling in, the boys in their beds, and Jessica in a nest of blankets on the carpet at the foot of ours. I heard a voice—my father's, actually—bawling me out: *What did you do to that girl? Apologize, right now.* On the way over, I'd imagined her the way we'd last met, in bed, lying like a tin soldier beneath the covers, plenty of room for me to crawl in next to her. Instead she lay on her side, knees tucked up and heels behind, soapy water going down a drain. I didn't recognize that blanket; she'd probably packed her aunt's quilt. The moonlight at Rocky's was cheap nickel, but the light from our hallway was rose gold. I got down on my hands and knees and crawled toward her. I tried to fold myself into that swirl.

She woke up. She looked at me. I'd gotten a long streak of fake coal dust on her pillow. She said, "Where have you been?"

"Out riding the rails," I answered. "Tramped around. Saw this place and figured the lady of the house was softhearted. Can you spare something?"

"Always with the jokes," she said, but with some love. We both knew: for the past year, it had not been *always with the jokes.* It had been ages since I cracked wise unless paid to do so.

"This leaving," I said.

"Whose?"

"Everyone's." I brushed the hair at the back of her neck, and then just kept brushing, at the feathery edge at one side of her nape, then the place at the very back where her hair came down in a point. Not a widow's peak: that was the V of hair on the other side of her head. What was this called? "Cancel everything," I said. I couldn't tell if she didn't argue because she was so sleepy. Then she turned around underneath the blankets and looked at me.

"You're in a good mood," she said. "I hardly recognize you."

I nodded. If that's what she thought, I could ease into one.

All through that night, I made promises, I explained things, I swore to be better, less angry. She stayed under the covers, and eventually I wormed my way under them, too, in my wrinkled suit. I kept talking. In the morning, I went to the boys' room and woke them up and kissed them. They seemed mostly confused that I had been away on a trip and had come back without any presents, an unheard-of thing in our house.

For a while, I believed that I'd apologized my way back into the house, that my eloquence convinced Jess not to go. That wasn't it, though. She only let me talk to make me feel better. It was that first joke, she said, and the way I brushed the hair off her neck: she could tell my misery had broken like a fever, and it had been my misery that she planned to leave.

Not that all was forgiven, of course, on either side. Still, we vowed to be kinder to each other. It's amazing how far a vow can go. I had the pool filled in, and the entire back lawn torn out and then reseeded. We started a foundation in Betty's name, for underprivileged children, and Rock and I did a benefit to get it going.

"How'd you do it?" he asked me, looking at Jess and the boys.

"Do what?"

"Go back in time," he said.

Rock himself was going forward. He'd left Lillian, just as Penny had said he would, though he hadn't fully realized that this meant leaving Junior too. So he rented a beach house in Malibu, thinking the kid would like that, forgetting that his estranged wife knew some people who'd recently lost a child to drowning: no swimming for Rocky junior. They'd have to meet in town. So he stayed in the house by himself, and called me up to say that he couldn't figure out where to put the sofa, as though what he missed most about Lil was her good sense concerning furniture.

"Let's go out," he'd say, but I was sticking close to home. These days, I mostly saw him on movie sets and at the radio studio. I thought a lot about what Penny had said the night of the hobo party: that Rocky threw people away, even as he kept their photographs—"I suffer," he once told me, "from memoraphilia." Sometimes I thought she'd been right: here was a man about to go through his fourth divorce, who wouldn't visit his own parents. Other times I thought, Well, I'm still here, aren't I? So's Tansy, and so's Neddy. I wanted to talk to Penny about it, as though she were a friendly, reasonable devil, and we were negotiating for Rocky's soul. If I put up a sound enough defense, he'd be saved.

But I don't know when Penny moved out of the pool house. I didn't see her again, not for years.

Every day, Rocky drove around for hours: up the coast, to see Junior, to his lawyers, to the nearly bankrupt nightclub, to Tansy's office. They were talking about TV again.

"What do you think, Mosey?" Rock asked.

"You and Tansy fight it out," I said. "I'll go along."

In the meantime, I was a homebody, maybe for the first time in my life. Up until then, I'd looked for ways to sneak out, wherever I lived: to downtown Des Moines with Hattie, and then to vaudeville without her; to bars and restaurants and strange girls' rooms; to Sukey's, back in my bachelor days. Even during my marriage I'd done my share of nightclub-bing. Jessica wanted to stay home with the kids, away from the smokers and drinkers. I loved going out. I loved walking into a room full of strangers, a party, a club. I loved watching other people perform. Don't get me wrong, movies were the luckiest break I ever got, but I'd still rather see the clumsiest comic fiddle player struggle in the flesh with "The Flight of the Bumblebee" than watch Heifetz on a screen. People are so dear, in person. They implicate you in their talent. I know I keep talking about luck, but I never felt luckier than when I was anywhere—a hole-in-the-wall bar, someone's living room, some swank joint that cheated you on the drinks—and heard someone really good sing. Or dance or do magic tricks or jump, suddenly, onto a table. Even the things I could do seemed better done by someone else—and to think, if I'd stayed home I would have missed it.

But after my strange week at Rocky's, anyplace that wasn't my house, with my family, couldn't hold my interest. "Your spirit's been broken," Rock said to me, newly bachelored and looking for company. No: I'd had a taste of my own medicine. Maybe I hadn't been in the habit of throwing people away, but I'd left plenty behind in my long wandering career. I'd always hated to say good-bye to people—which isn't anything special, of course, most people are miserable failures at farewells. I'd do anything to get out of them. Even now, when Jess and I and the kids went to Des Moines to see family, I'd get anxious the day of our exit, because I'd have to say good-bye to all my sisters, to Ed Dubuque, who I loved, to Jessica's Joseph, who I didn't. Bad luck to say,

This is the end. Better: *Soon. Still.* I made it, you see, a nearly religious belief, a twist on my mother's curses. If you never say good-bye, no one will ever leave you.

Then Jessica said she would, and though she decided against it I developed a fear of the thing itself, and not just the word.

Gilda was born a year later, nearly prescribed by Jessica's doctor. That's what doctors did in those days: when a woman lost a child, they told her to have another, a make-up baby, as quickly as possible, to help you over the grief. We named her for my mother, and after that I barely went out at all.

Looking back, I think the team died that week I spent at Rocky's. I'd thrown myself into work; now I wanted to throw myself into family.

"A couple years more," said Rocky. "Then we can retire. We gotta crack TV, for instance. You gotta let the boys see you on TV."

"I guess," I said, though privately I believed that television was a fad, a waste of material; between the radio show and the movies, we barely had enough anyhow. We'd look awful, too, shrunk down and fishy. Who'd want to watch that?

Remember, I'm the guy who thought vaudeville would never die.

13

Live from Hollywood

Ladies and gentlemen, welcome—
  (FANFARE)
  It's the *Carr Oil Comedy Hour*!
  (FANFARE)
  Starring this week's hosts—
  (DOUBLE FANFARE)
  Rocky Carter and Mike Sharp—
  with their guests
  (HORNS)
  Don Ameche!
  Martha Raye!
  The Dove City Dancers!
  And now, ladies and gentlemen—
  (HORNS)
  Carter and Sharp!
  (THE BAND BREAKS INTO "MY DARLING LIVES IN DES
    MOINES")
  (THE CAMERA SHOWS AN EMPTY STAGE, A CRUDELY
    PAINTED BACKDROP OF A PARK)
  Carter and Sharp!
  (HORNS. BAND STARTS AGAIN)
  Where are those guys!
  (A WHISTLE FROM THE HOUSE)
  ROCKY: Camera three! Over here, camera three!
  (APPLAUSE)

And the camera swivels to find two mugs in the audience, Carter and Sharp, hands in pockets, the surrounding crowd cracking up for no reason.

I'd been wrong. I loved TV.

We broke into television as the once-a-month hosts of a weekly hour-long live variety show. By 1951, our movie career was mostly over, and we were back where we'd begun, except famous, rich, and middle-aged: a thin man and a fat man on a stage, willing to do anything for a laugh. We were shameless. We insulted the band leader, we knocked down scenery on purpose, we tried to crack each other up. We broke props we'd need later, just so we could improvise first about the breakage, and then about the lack of props. Our old wheezing vaudeville jokes were new again, thanks to the postwar baby boom: the country was full of brand-new people with blissfully unsophisticated senses of humor. You could see Rocky search for the red light that told us which camera was paying attention, doing a slow burn and then saying, "Watch me, camera two," and tipping his hat. You could see me shove an extra cream puff in his mouth in a banquet scene, so he couldn't deliver his next line.

Sometimes we laughed so hard we ended up in each other's arms, even if offstage we weren't speaking. We spent a lot of time not speaking.

I can't remember what tipped off that round of fights. No, wait, I do: yes. He'd wanted to talk, and called me up. "Come out to the club," he said, meaning his own.

"Can't you come here?"

"No," he said. "It makes me too sad. You got your happy family there, and what have I got?"

So I went to the Rock Club, into which Rock now poured all of his spare money. He couldn't stand the idea of it closing—a guy can spend all day in his own bar drinking, and it's business; a guy drinking in another man's bar is bad behavior. Chances are Rock deducted his martinis off his taxes. That night, he wore a light brown gabardine suit, a mustard-colored shirt, and a yellow tie. He probably thought he looked spiffy, but mostly he resembled a large cheese sandwich. A cigarette burned in his hand, a bad sign: he favored cigars unless he was upset enough to chain-smoke.

"Friend, Hebrew, countryman," he said. "Lend me your ear."

"Have both," I offered.

He waved to a waiter, who brought us whiskeys. I sipped mine; I'd been drinking so little lately I'd lost all capacity.

"I've missed you, Professor," he said.

"Where have I been?"

"You tell me. Lying in bed, is my guess."

"Rocky, I see you all the time."

He tilted his head to let what seemed to him a lie pass. "Anyhow. Drink your bourbon, it's good for you. I'm just lonely. Just want some company. How are the kids?"

"Swell," I said. "Wonderful."

He nodded. "I miss being married."

"When you're married you want to be a bachelor, when you're single you want a wife."

He got a thinking look on his face, and I realized he'd misinterpreted me: I meant *he* wanted to be a bachelor, *he* wanted a wife, but he'd taken this as some universal wisdom, as though I suffered from the same desires.

"You need to make up your mind, Rocky," I said.

He'd taken ahold of the salt and pepper shakers, made them dance across the white cloth of the table and then kiss, silver top to silver top. I watched this puppet show. Finally he sighed, as though he'd learned another universal truth from the condiments: even salt and pepper belonged together, but he'd never have anyone to own, to own him, except maybe his straight man. "You know me, Professor. I have such lousy luck."

For some reason, I saw this all of a sudden for the preposterous lie it was: Rocky had plenty of luck with women. I thought of his four wives; of the landladies, all those years ago, who loved him; of the chorus girls on our show I knew would be happy to cheer him up, at least momentarily. He could charm any woman who didn't particularly interest him, and even some who did. Long ago, though, he'd decided that he was a failure at love, and had held on to that fact as though it were the striped shirt he still, at forty-seven, wore professionally: a vaudeville prop. He once told me that to be a star, you had to have a spectacular romantic life, or a miserable one. "No one with average luck in love has ever made it big," he said. "Look it up."

"So go back to Lillian," I said now. "She'll take you."

"Whatever my problems are, Lillian's not the solution."

"So when you say you miss being married, you're looking for a *fifth* wife?"

"Oh, who keeps count?"

I could tell he expected me to laugh, the way I would have once. Instead, I told him what his third wife had said to me two years before: "You *have* a family. Go home to it."

He looked at me almost hatefully. Go home? In this suit? Then he sighed again, as though he had explained this to me dozens of times but I was too dumb to absorb it. "Well, in the fairy-tale world of Moses Sharensky, maybe that works. You leave, you come back, all is forgiven. Life isn't so fucking *easy* for the rest of us."

"You make yourself miserable, Rock," I said. I didn't yell. I didn't contradict him. "You pick up the hammer and hit your thumb, over and over, and after a while, it gets boring. And maybe that was okay before you had a kid, but now you need to think about him."

Rocky didn't say anything. We must have sat there silently for five minutes, and I was proud to think he was considering my advice. Then I said, "Rock?" and he didn't look at me, and I realized it had happened again. Probably he'd stopped listening when I uttered the word *boring*. His club, his banquette: he wouldn't leave. "For Pete's sake, Rocky," I said, but he didn't look at me, he just picked up the salt and pepper shakers and clonked them together, the glass toe of the salt to the silver hat of the pepper, which left dents. Good old salt, surely, was the comic, kicking its highfalutin straight man in the head.

But he forgave me again, on the set of our next rotten motion picture. He needed to complain to someone without being argued with: there's nothing as dispiriting as making garbage and having some well-meaning person assure you that it's gold.

God knows we made a of lot movies, garbage and aluminum and fool's gold if not real gold. Twenty-eight features in thirteen years. Our fan club—oh, our fan club, full of men (mostly) who memorize our statistics the way other men learn baseball scores—has arguments in their newsletter about which of our pictures was best. My daughter Gilda, who reads all that stuff, tells me. "There's a guy who loves *Rock and Roll Rock*," she said once, naming Rocky's last movie, a solo effort, middle-aged Rocky in an Elvis Presley–styled pompadour. "Isn't that interesting?"

"It's unconscionable," I said.

The club spends a great deal of time defending my reputation. "A great straight man," they say. "The greatest!" They write long annotations of our pictures, full of cross-references and games: find Shemp Howard. Look for this flubbed line. And they also mention the saddest fact of all: that everyone knows that Rocky Carter was funnier (*even* funnier, they put it) offscreen than on. They wish, more fervently than Carter and Sharp themselves ever did, that just once The Boys had been given a top-notch script to work with. They try to make themselves feel better with *Marry Me, Barry,* the best of the lot.

Despite the fact that we never made a good picture, they nevertheless over the years got even worse. A little research reveals that most people who've wasted time thinking about it would rate *Red, White, and Who; Marry Me, Barry;* and *Ghost of a Chance* as our best pictures, all of them made in the first six of our Hollywood years. Problem is, we kept going. We'd always done ghost stories, but after a while our scripts got less and less realistic, probably because the shtick was always to get us in trouble with some unforgiving group, and we'd already antagonized every possible demographic of our time on this earth. So the writers went looking elsewhere: how about pirates? *Yo Ho Ho.* Mummies? The aforementioned *For He's a Jolly Good Pharaoh.* Men from Mars? Elves? Naughty children?

Carter and Sharp Meet Mother Goose was our second color picture. Personally I thought it was pandering, but then our kid fans never particularly cottoned to me, just another grown-up flitting around that large child, Rocky. Rocky played the Piper's son, Bobby Shaftoe, Little Jack Horner, and Jack Spratt; I appeared as the Piper, Jack Horner's father, and—in my only drag screen roles—both Mrs. Spratt and Mother Goose herself. Tansy claimed the picture tanked because it came out the same year as *Hans Christian Andersen,* with Danny Kaye playing so sugary and pure you wanted to bop him in the nose and steal his wooden shoes. But our movie was awful, and we knew it, before we'd even finished filming. Our budget was nothing. I still remember sitting on a hill overlooking a fake lake on the studio back lot; Rocky was wearing his Bobby Shaftoe outfit, not actually silver buckles slightly below his actual knees. He said to me, "I should have been a silent comedian."

I said, "What?"

"I would have been famous."

"You *are* famous."

"I would have been great."

"You are—" I began.

"Like Chaplin," said Rocky. "Great like that. I'm a B comic. A kid's comic. I should never have opened my big goddamn mouth."

But what could have kept him quiet? Nothing. I knew the guy: nothing. Okay, maybe imagine he worked harder, was born a few years earlier, hitchhiked to Hollywood in the teens and talked his way onto a set and then into a movie and then into a scene: All right, the director says, give the kid five minutes of film, let's see what he can do. The movie's set in a department store, and Rocky tangos with a tailor's dummy. Across town, there are men trying to figure out, by means of science, how to make people speak from the screen. For now the fat kid is silent, but dancing. He wants to tell you everything, but he can't.

And then somehow he does.

The fact is, if Rocky Carter had made it to Hollywood before the invention of sound movies, he would have invented sound movies by force of will. Suddenly, a miracle. Dateline New York City, Duluth, Valley Junction: today in movie theaters across the nation, the image of a comic actor suddenly looked at the camera and therefore the audience, and spoke. "Some stuff, huh?" the comic said, as the audience searched the seats for a ventriloquist. "No, up here, it's me: I'm the one." No sliding dialogue card trimmed in white lilies, just the voice, his celluloid co-stars still mute and damp-eyed and milk-skinned.

But for now Rocky adjusted his sailor's hat. It had a pom-pom on top, like Buster Brown's. "Who'll remember me?" he asked. Then he sighed. "It's okay. I like kids. They just don't remember anything."

"There's no music in silent movies," I said. *Carter and Sharp Meet Mother Goose* was a putative musical. We wanted to do a real one; all around us glorious musicals were being made, *An American in Paris*, *Singin' in the Rain*. I do not believe in reincarnation, but if it exists, please, God, let me come back as Gene Kelly.

"Silent movies are all music," said Rocky.

"Local music." I tried to sneer. "The lady organist from the Lutheran church. The idiot cousin of the theater manager."

"But music," said Rocky. He got up. His silver buckles were made of tin foil. He walked back to the artificial lake, where he would later be bitten by one of the bad-mannered geese in residence there. Rocky always had bad luck with animals.

In the books about us, Rock's praised for his pantomime, those moments he dummies up and dances with a mop, savors a single grape as though it was his mother's home-cooked pot roast. Once he speaks, you can tell that he's a smart man who knows more than he'll admit to, miming foolishness and sweetness and hope because they're funnier than all the education of all the professors—real or imagined—in the wide world. Remember, I was married to a ballerina. People who move beautifully will tell you a million things, they will convey notions with one tilt of the wrist that you can't imagine successfully hinting at in a ten-page letter. Watching, you will echo their gestures with a hand across your mouth or at the back of your neck, and every single minute, every ankle turn, chin point, elbow tuck, they will be keeping secrets from you.

He had to speak. Still, I wish he'd stayed black and white. Color was bad for Rocky; it's why we managed to do okay in television when our movies were bombing. In black and white, a guy in his late forties could look like a guy of no age at all, acting like a ten-year-old—round, fretful, slightly slowed. In color, you could see that his double chin had lost some of its bounce; his eyes looked less like buttons and more like metal snaps about to pop. The flush on his face showed through his makeup, which is to say that you could also clearly see his makeup. We switched back into black and white for our next picture, and he looked better. More substantial, less real. Perfect for a baggy-pants comedian.

That was the last picture we made: *The Great Stocking Caper.*

Certainly there was a part of me that wanted to say, when he dreamed of out-Chaplining Chaplin, but what about me? Where would I have been? I was not a physical comedian. All the laughs I ever got on-screen were through double talk, handy with a malaprop if not an actual prop. I couldn't have been even the least significant Keystone Kop, the one who runs and stumbles around corners only because the assistant director says, "You guys in the back, just follow the guys in the front."

As if I would have gone to Hollywood without Rocky. As if the worst thing that could have happened to me is becoming an obscure comedian instead of a famous one. It's completely possible that had Freddy Fabian waited another night to overdrink, Rocky would have found some other straight man, and I would have spent the rest of my life, one way or the other, behind a cash register, in Valley Junction, in Chicago, wherever my dreams of fame finally died. My children would still have had photographs, they would tell their friends, their future husbands and wives, *my old man was in show business, once.*

There ought to be a law. There ought to be an act of Congress blocking the rebroadcast of *Carter and Sharp Meet Mother Goose* and *Carter and Sharp Meet Santa Claus.* Those are the movies that you've most likely seen, because they appeal to kids. More people on this earth have seen them than have seen *City Lights.* Don't think I'm proud: more people have seen Buster Keaton as an elderly man impersonating Buster Keaton in *How to Stuff a Wild Bikini* than the real brilliant thing in *The General* or *Steamboat Bill, Jr.* More people can do a Charlie Chaplin impression than have ever seen a Charlie Chaplin movie. If you're a comedian, all you hope for is that some bit of your act sticks to the shoe of history: a twirled cane, a bent-over walk, a three-word catchphrase. If you're lucky, you'll end up a Halloween costume, a rubber mask, a bigheaded statue, the kind of two-bit impression anyone can do.

Slowly I Turned

I'd hoped the TV show would let us go out on a high note—not *Mother Goose,* but laughing onstage surrounded by flung pies and smashed vases. But it took us only months to run out of material. Worse, Rocky started showing up for broadcasts pretty well plastered. Not fallingdown drunk, just distractible, and he tried to laugh off missed cues the way we laughed off any mistake—live television, folks! No telling what'll happen! Now that he lived alone, there was no one to tell him to stop drinking, and so he never did. His face had turned an alcoholic red; Neddy said, "It's a shame the way Carter's gone prematurely crimson."

Rocky, like plenty of show-biz types, was two people: the guy he played, and the guy he was out in the world. I was two people myself, the Professor on-screen, and my wife's husband back at the house, a family man, an Iowan, and a Jew. (I didn't give much thought to the Professor's background, but I knew he wasn't Jewish.) In the real world, Rocky was a bully, a man about town, a bluff and hearty barker of commands. And then there was the patsy he played in the movies, a big baby in too-small clothes who'd take anything, pies to the face and blows across the head, who only wanted love and ice cream and good cheer from more manly men.

Except, in Rocky's case, it was like this second guy, the childish one, followed him wherever he went. He couldn't shake himself. He went out to his club and turned around; there was the fat guy in the tight suit, his hat in his hand, tagging along and smiling. And so Rocky began to bully himself, throwing first food and then glasses of liquor and then lit cigarettes and cigars, and then ashtrays and filled bottles and entire tables of food and silverware, and still the fat man stood, smiling, ready for more. You had to hate a guy who took abuse like that and kept his feet. You wanted to see what would knock him to the floor. And so Rocky ate and drank and smoked, trying to smack himself down. But the fat guy couldn't take a hint! There he was again, swaying, but on his feet! *He won't fall down.*

We lost our TV spot in 1953. Audiences got a whiff of the whiskey over the ether, is what I think: no charming feigned harmless drunk, but the real thing.

Forced retirement. Rocky wouldn't rest. He cooked up an idea for a situation comedy. Lots of comics just transferred their radio shows to TV—Burns and Allen, Jack Benny, Eve Arden—but our radio show really had no plot. So Rocky strung something together. Gas station attendants, I think, who lived across the hall from each other. Nice wives. Maybe some kids.

"A change of pace," said Rocky.

"I don't want one," I told him.

What I wanted was out. We had plenty of money; I'd invested pretty well over the years. I was getting too old—correction, I'd *gotten*—though I'd dive through a store window for old times' sake, and I could still stand next to a table, then suddenly jump on top of it. In fact, under the iron hand of my health-nut wife, I was in fine physical condition: I just thought a man of forty-two should find more dignified work. I didn't tell Rocky this; he'd take it as an insult, since he was even older, and even sillier.

And besides, something had to change. The guy was destroying himself.

Well, then, why didn't I save him?

I couldn't have.

Why didn't I try?

Good question. Now it seems obvious: I just should have said something. As it was, I spent hours in bars and restaurants with him, always a fraction of a second from saying, *You know, Rocky, that you drink too much.*

And then I'd imagine what he'd say in return.

I know. (Still, he takes a gulp of his fresh drink.)

Come on, move in with us, stay in the guest suite. We'll keep you busy. Jess will whip you into shape in no time. Spinach, deep knee bends—

Sounds great. (He takes another gulp.)

You'll love it.

No really, says Rocky, his finger in the ice cubes at the bottom of his now empty glass, *it sounds terrific. But I'd rather die.*

And I couldn't watch. I wanted no part of it.

I believed then—as almost everyone believed—that if one of us went on to have a solo career, it wouldn't be me. Sometimes, when I thought of stepping down, I imagined the comeback we'd make later, staid, cleverer. A sophisticated double act. Other times I thought that without the Professor hectoring him, Rocky could finally become, as he wanted, great. A guy who could speak that many languages could do something with his own, once he had to, write movies, become an auteur. Go abroad, hang out with brooding comic Englishmen—he loved *The Lavender Hill Mob*. Hang up the damn striped shirt and act his age, in other words. I believed that I'd have to orphan the on-screen childish Rocky to push him out into the world. Okay, I'd be selfless and walk away. Like many a guardian, I tried to leave in degrees. Like many a juvenile delinquent, he clung and misbehaved, longing for attention and punishment.

Six years before, I'd threatened to quit the act, but waffled. This time I stood my ground: I wanted to take a break, at the very least. Jake was ten, Nathan nine, and Gilda three. Betty would have been seven. Rocky called all the time to twist my arm. The last time was March 17, 1954. The kids and Jess and I were in her studio, watching Jake practice a Western dance—he had a cowboy outfit he loved, with chaps and a holster and a hat he wore slung back on his shoulders, its string across the hollow of his throat. I could hear the phone ring in the house. By that time we had no live-in help to answer, just a maid who came in the mornings and a cook who came at night. Normally I would have let it alone, but my sister Sadie's husband, Abe, had been sick, and I worried she might be calling with bad news. I took the call in my study, so if we needed to fly to Des Moines for a funeral I could check my calendar to see what I'd have to cancel.

"I want to talk about this television thing," Rocky said without prelude.

"You never rest," I said.

"You hang around the house enough as it is." He said this like it was a new argument, though we'd been having it since 1943. Used to persuade me.

"We've been working for almost twenty-five years steady," I said. "Don't you want to take some time off?"

That was a stupid question.

He said, "How much time?"

I pretended to think carefully. "Three years."

"In three years," Rocky said, "every jerk's going to have a show. In three years, *Tansy*'ll have a program. Live, from Hollywood: the *Buddy Tansy Hour.* He'll look at the camera and bare his teeth and pull down millions."

"I'll be happy for him. All that thwarted promise, finally realized."

"But it should be *us*." He tried to appeal to the actor in me. "Same character, every week. You can develop it. You'll be married. Hey," he said, and lowered his voice, "—I bet we could swing it so Jess can play your wife, and your kids can play themselves. How about that?"

Once upon a time this might have sounded swell to me. In the early days of our radio show, I listened to our competitors—at home, of course, never around Rock—and got jealous. Not of the laughs: of the on-air marriages. George Burns, Jack Benny, Fred Allen, Goodman Ace, Fibber McGee—those guys got to work with their wives, got to broadcast to the country that they were married, even if they didn't play married. I loved to hear Portland Hoffa on the Fred Allen program say, in her slightly stiff, slightly boop-oop-a-doop voice, "Oh, Mister A-a-a-allen." He'd answer, and the audience would applaud, as though both he and the people in the studio had had no idea she'd show up that night. I knew that an on-air romance resembles an off-mike one only in the names, but through the radio it sounded wonderful.

But now Jess had a job: she'd just started choreographing variety-show dance numbers at the networks. She had no interest in being in front of the camera. Besides, I couldn't think of anything worse, my whole family on TV. "I'm not putting my kids to work," I said. "Who am I, Fagin?"

"I was thinking Ozzie Nelson," said Rocky, "but okay. We'll get kid actors."

"No, Rock. I don't want to do this."

"Tell me why, and I'll tell you why you're wrong."

My den was in the back of our house, on the first floor so I could shuffle papers without being disturbed. The window looked out on a little patch of foliage. Fifteen years in California, and I still couldn't identify the flora. I wished I could see Jess's studio, though I thought I could hear Gilda and Nate and Jessica applauding Jake. Yes, there was Nate, yelling in his oddly husky voice, "Brava," which was what I called out to his mother when she danced. Jess must have corrected him, because now he yelled, "Bravo, Bravo, Braveeeeeessssssimo!" How had I come up with a kid so smart? I thought about telling Rock this story, but he was after business and it had been years—I realized with a start—since I'd told him such things. It felt like bragging.

"Two guys, two wives," I said instead, "one guy, one wife. What's the difference? Call it *The Rocky Carter Show*. Who'll notice that I'm gone?"

He said, brusquely, "If that's the way you want it," and hung up.

Two hours later he drove over. He found us in the yard. Jake was on his back, idly firing his toy guns in the air; Nathan, our critic, was telling his mother a long story about a little girl at school who liked to lick other people's sandwiches. Gilda had put on Jake's hat and was rattling it around on her head. Everyone but me wore blue jeans. *The Mike Sharps at Home*, the picture in a movie magazine would have said, though we hadn't posed for any such stories since Betty died. Before then, we did a couple, plus a newsreel piece of Jake's fourth birthday party, Rocky standing by the heart-shaped pool and waving, me threatening fiercely to push him into the pool, then kissing him on the cheek.

"Mike," said Rocky, which gave me a shock—he never called me Mike. "Spare a moment?"

"Hey!" said Jake, still Rocky's particular favorite.

"Howdy pardner," Rock said with no real enthusiasm. "Mike?"

So we went inside the house.

"I need to talk to you about this TV thing," he said.

"I thought it was settled. *The Rocky Carter Show*. Solo billing. Hundred percent of the salary. Nice TV wife—get a single girl and maybe marry her off-camera too."

"The sponsors want both of us or neither."

"Gotta be neither, then, Rocky. I'm telling you: I need time off."

I don't think I really understood his desperation then. He looked awful—he'd been gaining weight steadily since he and Lil broke up, from the drink and too many breakfasts. He rarely ate anything but ham and eggs and buttered toast, up to five times a day. He had a scratch under one eyebrow, and his hair needed dyeing, and if I'd been thinking about it I would have known something was wrong, because he was so vain about his hair: he had it colored every two weeks and, for the TV show and movies, painted his scalp black beneath to cut down on the glare. Now I could see a little border of sandy brown at his hairline, like a curtain starting to rise.

He bit his upper lip, and then ran his tongue over his front teeth. I couldn't tell whether he planned to threaten or beg me.

"Look," he said. "Commit to a year. One year of the show, and then you're out. By then it'll be on its way and they won't even miss you."

"No," I said.

"You son of a bitch," he said. "After all you've done to me?"

He must have meant, *after all I've done for you.*

We stared at each other while we both deliberated over how much of a joke he was making. I could hear Jake knocking with the butt of his gun on the French doors behind me. "Daddy," he said, his voice muffled through the glass. "Mom says can I have some ice cream."

I didn't turn around. "In a minute, honey."

For some reason, I felt like we were in some ridiculous Western, maybe because I'd watched Jake's cowboy dance earlier. Rocky and I faced each other. He had the advantage: he could look out on my family sitting on the grass. No telling what he'd do if I let my guard down. I couldn't tell whether this was a comic Western or a real one, whether I'd be saved by the cavalry or a pull-apart horse.

I said, with some forced kindness, "How's Junior?"

"He could use the money, same as me. I guess. His mother won't let me see him. But, see, if I was on TV again, he could watch—"

Good God, what fancy thinking. "Rocky," I said. "Do not make this about *me* keeping you from your kid. Okay? You left. Right? And if your life has not been what you wanted since you and Lil—"

"Since Penny," he said. "My life's not been what I wanted since Penny. Look at you. Look at your own life, and look at mine. Your gorgeous children. Your brilliant wife. Do me one fucking favor in your life. Mike," he said, because I was turning away from him, "wait. *Mike.* I can make it so you don't have a choice."

"Get out your handcuffs," I said, "and I'll hire a locksmith. Threaten me with lawyers, and I'll go abroad. *I will not do this show.* I don't know how else to put it."

He stuck his hands in his pockets and shook them, polished one shoe on the back of the opposite calf. "It's nice Jess is working," he offered.

"It's lovely," I said, exasperated.

"At the networks." He said this helpfully, as though I'd misunderstood. "Doing her dance stuff. She likes that, right?"

"Sure," I said.

"Well, then, I'll blackball her."

Poor Rock, to have such a high opinion of himself. This was 1954, not 1944, and though he could convince one or two people not to hire my wife as a personal favor to him, he wasn't exactly the most powerful man in Hollywood. If he was, he'd be on TV by himself now, wouldn't he?

And that's what I told him, laughing.

He flinched a little, as though this was news. Then he said, "That's not what I meant. I mean, I'll bring up her past."

I had no idea of what he was talking about, but I didn't care. Certainly I'd never known him to make up stories about anyone other than himself, but that must be what he was doing now, he was working on some fake scandal about Jessica, something just awful enough. He would have threatened me directly, but he needed to keep me employable.

Was I going to have to push him out the door? He was heavy, but I'd been building my biceps in my time off. "Rocky," I said, "go home. Sleep off whatever it is that's making you this way. Get Tansy to find you some jobs, work on your act, *leave me alone.*"

He said, "You know what will happen if people find out she's a communist."

I laughed again. "Current events, is it? That's the best story you can come up with? My wife's a commie." I turned and pointed through the window. "Is it the blue jeans? No, I get it: you have pictures of her in a red dress. She loves Tchaikovsky?"

He looked puzzled. "She never told you?"

"She doesn't keep me up to date on your delusions, no."

Jake had gone back to sit with his siblings, who watched their mother. She was dancing on the grass—she told me later she could hear the two of us fighting, and wanted to distract them. She didn't know we were arguing about her. An ordinary dance wouldn't do: Jessica, forty-one, was turning cartwheels, doing back bends, all of those things children think make for really fine ballet.

"I'll bet you," Rocky said. "I'll bet you one year of work." He swung open one of the French doors and called to her. "Jessie," he said, and his voice was suddenly more reasonable than it had been all day, or all year. "Would you come in for a minute?"

She walked to the threshold. Rock waved her in like a maître d', with a small bow and a sweeping hand. "We've called you in to settle a bet."

"What he wants to know, dear," I said, taking hold of my all-American sweetheart's hand, "is are you now, or have you ever been, a member of the Communist party?"

There was a pause while she cocked her head at me, then at Rocky. The cartwheels had styled her hair into something island-girlish; she wore it lately to her shoulders, where it hung in lovely waves. The right knee of her blue jeans was grass stained.

She said to me, "You knew that."

All these decades later, the issue of the hearings seems simple: bad men asked questions they shouldn't have. What goes on in someone else's head is none of your business, cannot hurt you. *Asking* is un-American.

It wasn't that easy at the time. I turned my back on Rocky because he threatened my wife, yes. He menaced us with a truth instead of a lie, but that made no difference. I felt the way I had when someone in a wartime crowd shouted, "Slacker!" *You lack character,* he seemed to be saying. *I'll expose you, and your so-called patriotism, Mr. So-called Sharp.* If I were a character in a movie, I would have delivered a speech, my eyes shining, about my immigrant father who'd come to this country with nothing and had built up a business, a man who so loved his new home and opportunities that he never mentioned his past life in Lithuania, never spoke his own language again—at this there might be a double exposure of my father, eyes similarly shining, and then another of a waving flag.

"Aha!" said Rocky, like some lawyer who'd been trying to break her for five years.

I still held Jess's hand, a little tighter now, though of course I didn't care about her politics, which to be sure had always been left of mine. "*What* did I know?" I asked her.

"You were here. When Rocky and I talked about New York. All of my friends in the city were members of the Party. We were artists," she said. "We wanted great things for the world."

The city, of course. The Party. Maybe I had known this, ten years ago. Rocky was a member of the Swans' Club; Jessica was a member of the Communist party. Now she combed her hair with her hands and re-aligned a bobby pin above one ear. She wasn't contrite, of course. Years later, the threat might sound silly—who cares whether someone's wife was slightly pink as a kid? Romantic, even: Jessica with her dark hair, testifying. She might miss her TV choreography a little, but not enough to lie or apologize. TV work was not artistic, not a great thing you planned for the world.

Oh, yes. After they called her, they'd call me.

I was a bigger star than anyone who'd been ruined by the hearings so far, sort of a dream name for HUAC: famous, but not beloved. Known, but past my prime. A fine example. A lovely scandal. People could deny me work and not feel like they'd been cheated out of anything.

I organized a few thoughts. Rocky was smart enough to know that if he informed on Jessica, he would ruin both her career and mine, which wouldn't do him any good. If he did it out of spite anyhow, well, I'd wanted to retire, hadn't I? I'd rather choose the terms myself, but we had money, and if it got unpleasant to live in North Hollywood, then we'd move somewhere else—to New York. To Des Moines. We were hardly the Rosenbergs. What kept me in California?

Only Rocky, who had his hand in his hair, as though he'd just become self-conscious of the creeping blond in it. All in all, an impressive display of betrayal: threaten my wife, her livelihood, mine. Years ago, maybe even months ago, maybe even last week, I would have begged him not to do such a thing. I would have been driven crazy, like the straight man in that old bit about Niagara Falls, who hears the words and clenches his fists and advances on the comic, all because his wife ran off with his best friend to Niagara. Those two words remind him of all he's lost and still desires. Not a bad part for a straight man. Maybe Rocky thought if he couldn't make me bend, he could make me rage. If he said the right words, I would turn around like a trouper and walk toward him, feeding him setups for panicked punch lines. Revenge, after all, is a kind of love.

But this? He broke my heart, as brutally as anyone or anything had ever broken it, and now I was too old to throw myself at his silly two-toned shoes and beg him to stay. Heartbreak makes you plead and weep, or else it shuts you up. Who was I to him? The Professor. As Mose Sharp I was useless.

Rocky said, uncertainly, "I won the bet."

"There was no bet," I said. "No bet, no show, no team. Nothing."

Suddenly he seemed afraid of what he'd done. Thinking back, I believe he'd tried to get out of his threats by calling it a gamble. He didn't care about politics any more than I did. Just another story we'd tell: one day, in 1954, we wagered over some ridiculous thing, and that's how *Life with Rocky* began.

"Mose," he said. "Professor."

But I had my back turned to him. My kids were in the yard—Jake and Nate had heaped all of the cowboy costumes on Gilda, and died gloriously as she shot the pistols into the tree, over the roof of Jess's studio. All those times we stopped talking, and this was the first time I'd begun it. I could see the appeal. I hadn't known before, when I'd borne the brunt, that it was the worst thing you could do to someone. I felt cruel and happy. Rocky said, "Mosey."

I am not talking to you.

Rocky said, "Okay, listen, wait."

I am not talking.

If I'd opened my mouth, I would have said, over and over, *You broke my heart, can't you see you broke my heart?* I kept my back turned. Jessica murmured something to him, and led him to the front door, and then I didn't see him again for a long time.

14

Instead of Me

In Greenwood Park, when I was fourteen and Hattie sixteen, I got mad and sat on the grass and refused to speak to her. "The little man has a temper," said Hattie, which is what my sisters always said when I fell into a sulk, almost admiringly. A boy could get away with that kind of moodiness, and though I never yelled or threw punches or used my teeth (Rose, at age two, went through a brief biting period), my silences seemed full of manly anger to them, or so I was happy to think. I liked to be cajoled the way some kids liked to be tickled: I held very still and waited for someone to tease me into cheerfulness.

Not this day in Greenwood Park, though. Hattie and I had gone to a picnic, on one of those July days so hot your brain poaches in your skull and your blood turns to mucky syrup. This was nine months before Hattie died. We'd packed a lunch and taken the streetcar in. Some kids had made a fire and thrown in potatoes and corn to roast, and Hattie wanted to stand near it to talk to people, and I wanted to lie in the grass as far away from any kind of extra heat as possible.

So we each did what we wanted, and I might have been annoyed that she preferred to joke with strangers instead of me, but that's not what got me so mad. I found a tree for shade. The best ones had already been taken: this was a scrubby maple, not much of a parasol, roots braiding through the dirt at its feet. It took me a while to get comfortable. When I looked at the cook-fire, some huge freckle-faced teenager had speared an ear of corn for Hattie at the end of a stick; he blew across it gallantly and—to my eyes—lasciviously. His breath was probably too hot to do much good. Then he stripped off the husk and burned his fingers. Good. He stuck them in his mouth and looked at Hattie, who laughed and touched the back of his wrist. Bad.

I ate my chicken sandwich—mustard, no mayonnaise, because of the heat. How long would Hattie want to stay? Maybe I should just go back to Vee Jay by myself. Drowned by the heat, I napped.

When I woke up, I looked: no Hattie. No big teen boy.

I waited. I scanned the park. Had I lost her? Was she my responsibility, or her own? Should I call someone, or sit tight and hope the guy wasn't a white slaver?

God. A white slaver. I wished I hadn't thought of that. Annie believed in white slavers so completely she made me want never to leave the house, even though she didn't think I was at peril. (In that trade, boys weren't precious.) She even kept a pamphlet in the kitchen drawer, with other instructive tracts, Annie's version of motherly advice. There was a fascinating one published by the Kotex company that I wasn't supposed to read, and another on using electricity safely, and another on baking. "If you have a question, just read the pamphlet," Annie said, and so the contents of the drawer were so jumbled together in my memory that I sometimes believed my sisters were visited every month by Reddy Kilowatt or—because there was also a tract a religious person had left at the door, angrily annotated by Annie—that we should be careful not to be converted to Christianity, possibly by Aunt Jemima.

White slavers. Were they freckle-faced? High-school students? As imaginary as Aunt Jemima? Maybe they hired high schoolers as agents. I couldn't figure out what to do. I looked at the edge of the woods and considered storming them. The only person who'd give me good advice was Hattie, and I'd let her be kidnapped.

Then suddenly Hattie walked out of the woods with her gangly friend. At first I thought they were holding hands, but instead they each gripped a hat. Then they exchanged the hats, because they'd been holding each other's. The boy put his cap on his head, and then tipped it and walked away, and Hattie came up the slant of the park, adjusting the men's straw boater from Sharp's Gents' that she had covered with silk flowers. Bigheaded Hattie.

She kicked the bottom of my shoe, but it was too late: I was furious at her. Not shanghaied at all, worse, just walking in the woods with a boy.

"What's the matter with you?" she asked.

"Nothing."

"Ready to go home?"

I shrugged.

"Are you mad at me?"

Another shrug.

"The little man has a temper," she said.

All the way home she examined my face. She'd say something cheerful. I'd grunt, or shrug. Why couldn't she just guess why I was mad? I wanted her to know, so we could forgive each other, but it seemed impossible to explain myself, and I got angrier the longer she failed to read my mind.

I'd never been that upset with Hattie before. Soon enough, that anger was forgotten, eclipsed by her death. Now, of course, I can see it plainly: months before she announced she'd be going to Iowa City, I realized Hattie might leave me. I saw how easily she talked to someone who wasn't me, how handsome she looked next to a kid happy to burn his fingers for her. How ordinary it felt to be watching her from a distance: *That's how she talks, without me. That's how she walks. That's how she laughs.*

I thought Rocky's threats came out of something similar. He might have worried when I first got married, but I stayed in the picture, up for nightclubs and movies, all the trappings of our success. He might have eyed each of my children, wondering whether a person who might take me away from him had finally arrived. Still, I hung around, I donned my mortarboard, I hit my mark. Then, suddenly, I planned to walk away into the woods, my arm around that girl from Des Moines after all. Obviously, he would have to deal with her.

Stuck in his ways, I thought. Devoted to the shadow I cast on him, because he needed a shadow to dance around. I wanted for someone to talk me out of my anger—I didn't think I could be cajoled this time, but someone would tell me, as they always did, to cut the guy some slack.

Nobody did.

While Jessica didn't indulge me, she did think I should give him some air. Tansy hadn't thought much of the situation-comedy idea anyhow, didn't think the public would buy Carter and Sharp as family men. Neddy—now working for Milton Berle, another famous pain-in-the-neck—said I was better off.

As for Rocky himself: he wrote a few letters, and then a few telegrams. Maybe he apologized, and maybe he told me to go to hell. I don't know. I never read them. I was working on forgetting him.

Of course, it wasn't that easy.

I wondered whether Rocky went through this when he divorced a wife. Do you take the pictures down, or would that mean you cared too much? Do you call and explain exactly what you meant, when you said it was over? How do you stop thinking of someone, when you're accustomed to thinking of that someone all the time?

"He won't actually do anything," Jess told me. "He won't make a report. He told me so, when I showed him out."

I was in my office, trying to decide what came next. In every drawer in every piece of furniture—selected by Lillian a few years before—was nothing but documents pertaining to the careers of Carter and Sharp: contracts, scripts, comic books.

"He would have told you anything," I said.

"My point." She sat cross-legged on the leather sofa. "He'd *say* anything. He wouldn't *do* anything."

"You don't understand."

I found, on my desk, a folder of publicity photos, waiting for a pair of signatures. Carter and Sharp in a mock fight; Carter and Sharp doing their radio show; Carter and Sharp leaning on their canvas-backed chairs, not speaking to each other but looking like the best of pals. It had been years since I'd been photographed alone.

"What don't I understand?" asked Jessica.

"He threatened my *wife*."

"Okay," she said reasonably. "You're mad. Be mad a while, that's fine. And the act's broken up, that's fine too. You're too old, the two of you, if not this year, then the next. But what you have to remember is, it's going to be easier for you. It's going to be hell on him."

I turned back to my desk and shrugged. A little hell would be the least that he deserved.

"He's my friend too," she said.

I said, "He's not anyone's friend."

Shortly after the fight, in April of 1954, my sister Sadie's husband died, and we went to Des Moines for the funeral. He'd had a heart attack, and then another—the second, according to Sadie, because he was so worried over the first. The service was the right amount of sad: Abe, sixty-five, had gone prematurely but not tragically. He'd had four weeks after the first attack to spend with his wife and his kids and his grandkids. Enough time for sentiment and good-byes. We'd miss him, we would, we'd already told him so. Still, I wished I'd given him a part in a movie, the way I'd promised all those years ago.

April in Iowa. It wasn't Paris, but it would do. I took a snapshot of Jessica in front of the State Capitol, the wind in her hair and four-year-old Gilda in her arms. Jess is wearing a dark jacket with white piping, a little scarf tied at her neck; you can see the breeze trying to peek under Gilda's Peter Pan collar. They look as though they're in Rome, in front of a building filled with old masters. I couldn't remember what Hattie had looked like at Gilda's age, but I imagined it had been like this, the same copper curls, the same slight baby overbite and soft cheeks. A kid in love with her parents. She can't decide which way to look, at her mother who holds her or her father who says, "Gilda, will you smile?" even though she already is. Sometimes I had to remind myself not to blame Gilda for all the people she made me miss: my mother, Hattie, Betty. She was an altogether goofier kid than her sister (she did not even know she'd had a sister then), made happier by goofier things. A make-up baby. She took the job seriously.

"Look at the birdie," I said. What birdie? She looked at the sky. I snapped the picture. Then she jumped from her mother's arms and ran up the State House lawn to join her brothers, who were rolling down the hill like loose barrels. I had Jake's glasses in my breast pocket, so they wouldn't be crushed.

"You know," I said to Jess, "we could move back here."

"Don't be silly," she said. She took the camera from my hands and looked around, not taking pictures, as though it was a pair of binoculars.

"I'm not. We have a family. You could reopen your studio. We could join the temple. Our kids could roll down hills."

"You're not going to stay retired. You know that."

"Depends on what Rocky does."

She lowered the camera and sighed. She had told me and told me he'd never see through his threats. My believing otherwise could only be stubbornness.

The kids came down in the same order, chronological, every time: Jake, Nathan, Gilda, picking up speed till they ended up in a pile at our feet, then running away to tumble again. Gilda rolled up onto the toes of my shoes. I lifted her by the ankles. "What's this?" I said. I answered one of her saddle shoes like a telephone. "Hello? Hello? This is a very poor connection." Then I swung her back and forth like a pendulum.

"You're a man without hobbies," said Jessica. "What will you do with yourself if you don't work?"

"I'll take up golfing," I said darkly, and she laughed. Gilda laughed, too, her curls brushing the ground.

"I'll take up knitting," I said, and Jess snorted. Gilda snorted in response.

"I'll take up sailing," I said, and Jessica said, "Please love, don't get lost at sea."

"Don't!" squealed Gilda, and I tossed her in the air and grabbed her, upright, by the tummy. "No!" she said. "Swing me more!"

How could Jessica forgive Rocky that easily? Now I understand: she felt sorry for him the same way (though she never would have said so) she felt sorry for herself. She saw a man at the end of a career, desperate to extend it. Physical comedians have performing lives as brief as ballerinas'. The very thing you do—falling down stairs, going en pointe—gives you arthritis, so you can no longer do the very thing you do. An aging singer is still gorgeous. She can't hit all those familiar notes, but she reminds you of their lost beauty, and her new, narrow voice is as lovely as any ruin, the Venus de Milo, the Colosseum. What's left is the same, just simpler.

But an old guy who flubs a pratfall only resembles the young guy he used to be in what he can't do. A vague gesture toward funny is the opposite of funny. It's cruel to laugh at a man that old, pretending to be that young.

A flexible straight man, though, can just move on. That much I knew, as I stood at the foot of the State House, flipping Gilda over again. We'd been Siamese twins, I'd often thought: our appeal was how utterly stuck together we were. I'd tried more than once over the past few years to run away, but every time I did, the other guy—Rocky, bending over at the waist to muscle me off my feet—ran me back.

Now I was free. Three weeks before, when I was smack in the middle of it, Carter and Sharp appeared to be all of Hollywood. One part of my career was over, but I could probably work. I wanted to. "Aren't you dizzy?" I asked upside-down Gilda, and she nodded while laughing. I'd forgotten that was the point.

"Yeah," I said to Jessica. "I'll call Tansy when we get back."

At home, there was a pile of communications from Rocky waiting for us, including one hand-marked FINAL NOTICE. I flung them in the trash. It looked like anger, but I knew the moment I read a single word, I'd be back in the act. Tearing them in half: that would be anger. I considered it.

"Mose," said Jess.

I shook my head.

"You'll forgive him," she said, and I couldn't tell if this was a prediction, a question, a command.

Jessica was right: Rocky did not go to the government with his information, though he did have to go to the government plenty, the Treasury Department instead of the Senate: he owed the IRS pretty big. Later I heard that he blamed a crooked accountant, but I think he balled it up himself. He was one of those guys so bad with money he wouldn't trust a professional—how would he notice any funny dealings? He never invested in anything. He kept all his cash in his checking account.

I called Tansy when we got back. He alluded to Rock's money problems, believing we were fighting over salaries again. I didn't say otherwise. Rocky's finances didn't soften me at all: he wasn't desperate for my company. The guy needed cash.

"But you're finding him work?" I asked Tansy.

"Sure. Here and there. People want to see if he's a team player. If he behaves himself, he'll be fine."

I said, "Then he's in serious trouble."

Greasepaint

My first post-Carter-and-Sharp break came two months after the fight. Johnny Atkinson invited me over to the bungalow he and Alan shared near Venice Beach. The place was crammed with memorabilia—Alan, who worked in the billing department of Bullock's, was crazy about the movies. You'd think he'd had no idea of how they were made. Even the end tables were covered with signed head-shots of starlets and frilled china figurines of silent-movie actresses. The furniture had been arranged around the inventory, as though it, too, was part of a museum exhibition. For all I knew, it was, the coffee table a souvenir from *Dark Victory*, the cabinet from a corner of a Ma and Pa Kettle flick.

And there, in a Sydney Greenstreet peacock chair, wedged between end tables as though he was part of the collection, was Ripley Davidson, a movie director. A real movie director. Even though our pictures (at least early on) did great at the box office, for directors we were the minor leagues, what you did on your way up or down when you, too, were only B material. This guy had actually directed well-reviewed movies. He balanced a coffee cup on one knee, tried to put it on a table, but clonked it into a framed still of Pola Negri, and so brought it back to his knee. He was a tall man in his thirties. A youngster.

Turned out he was working on a drama about a bunch of vaudevillians and was looking for a few genuine articles. I was game. Johnny had talked me up.

I balanced on the arm of the sofa, which seemed like the most convenient spot. I held my breath. Directors had always hated Carter and Sharp, who had such scorn for order.

"So," he said. "What did you do in vaude?"

"I was a straight man," I answered, puzzled. Could he never have heard of me? The idea appalled, then cheered me.

"Oh, I thought Johnny said you did some other acts before. Acrobatics, maybe?"

"Dancing," I whispered. I cleared my throat so I'd sound confident. "I was a song-and-dance man."

"Yeah?" Davidson said, perking up. He set the coffee cup on the floor. "Were you any good?"

I said, "You should have seen me."

Why had I even paused? That was how you got jobs in vaudeville: someone asked, "Can you?" and you answered, "Are you kidding me?" Many a trouper nearly drowned in a tank act or got thrown from a horse, doing what they'd sworn they were old hands at. The movie already had a double act, but they could use a hoofer, someone old enough to give advice to the young folks. At first I worried that I'd be playing an old-timer, a failed singer who died a never-was, but actually it was a pretty jaunty role, and not beyond my talents. *Greasepaint*, they called the picture. I played Cecil Dockery, song-and-dance man.

"You won't mind not being the star?" Tansy asked me later, when I asked him to okay the deal. He drummed his fingers on the script. "It's a good part, but not huge. One musical number."

"Sign me up," I said, and he did.

Be vigilant, I told myself. Don't let the Professor's mannerisms come creeping in. Don't jump too high, or fidget, or become overly involved with your necktie. Don't spoonerize or malaprop. Don't keep looking to your right, for a fat little man ready with a punch line.

I didn't. It was as though my fight with Rocky had burned out any sentiment or reliance I'd had on the Professor. Instead, I leaned on my bamboo cane like the swell I'd never been. The musical number was best: in-one, in front of the curtain, like Carter and Sharp in the old days, except I was allowed to cover the whole stage. My God, how had I endured it all those years, not moving? I posed patiently for stills, alone, rakish in my derby. I learned my dance steps overnight, and sang my song for hours around the house. I drove my family crazy. "Okay, Sinatra," Jessica said once, and then the kids started calling me that. Sinatra, can I have five bucks? Sinatra, can I go to the movies?

The picture wasn't a huge hit, but the critics who reviewed it always mentioned me as a minor revelation, someone they didn't recognize till the credits rolled. I looked different enough—no mortarboard or specs, no oversized scowl. No hairpiece. No comic, who'd absorb all my light and work it over and then throw it out to the audience, like fish to trained seals, flashing, luminous, something else entirely. Something, I now believed, cheap.

Meanwhile, Rocky worked some, too, mostly on television. He tried his hand at straight parts on TV dramas, and showed up on variety shows, shooting pistols with Spike Jones, singing a duet with an annoyed Eddy Arnold. I didn't watch him, but it was impossible not to hear some news, especially from my kids, who missed him. Jessica took them to see his first—and last—solo movie, *Rock and Roll Rock*. I spotted a publicity shot at Tansy's office, Rock in a pompadour that looked like a black plastic mold. I groaned when I saw it.

Tansy shrugged. "He's trying to cash in on that Elvis Presley fad."

"Uh-huh. Rebel without a comb." (It was 1956. Presley had just made it big. I didn't think *that* would last either.)

"That's the *look*," Tansy said. "He's supposed to."

"Okay."

"I still can't believe the two of you split," said Tansy. "I always thought you'd be like Smith and Dale, together forever. No way you'll reteam? Not even for a one-time thing? He could use the money. I've got some offers from Vegas."

"No," I said. Then I thought, and said more tentatively, "No, I don't think so. How bad is it, the money thing?"

Tansy grimaced, shook his head. To say anything aloud would be indiscreet, which seemed silly since I'd known for years what the guy made. Twenty percent more of the salary than me, that's what he made.

Still, I sometimes pined for him. Not the act, the fat guy in the striped shirt, but Rocky himself. Occasionally, Jessica or Tansy would drop his name, and I'd simply shake my head, because I realized I could be talked into seeing him, and if I saw him I'd forgive him, and if I forgave him, he'd whip out the mortarboard he'd just happened to be holding behind his back. No. *He'd threatened my wife.* I had to keep myself stubborn.

"Not yet," I said.

"Yet!" said Tansy, as happy as I'd seen him since he landed us the Broadway show.

"No time soon," I said quickly.

"Mose." Tansy took off his glasses. Of all the people I knew, he had aged the least; he'd been such a middle-aged little man all his life. The squintiness that had made him mouse-ish when I met him now made him look shrewd. Like an honest lawyer. A prosperous one. Now he had dozens of clients. I always liked to think he loved me best, because he had known me longest. I would have done anything for the guy. "Mose," he said again, "call him."

"Tansy—"

"Not for business. Just as a friend. He needs it these days. He'd call you, but he's afraid you'll snap his head off."

"I might." I played with a giant crystal paperweight on Tansy's desk. It weighed about a billion pounds, though it looked like plain old glass to me. "Snap his head off, I mean. Okay. All right. I guess."

"You'll call?"

"I'll call."

He wrote down Rock's new phone number on a piece of paper and slid it across the blotter.

So I did call, after several hours of approaching the phone in my den and then walking away. What could it hurt? I asked. Everything, I replied. A hotel operator answered the number. She put me through. He was in. I yanked the phone away from my ear to hang it up, and immediately brought it back, clonking myself in the temple. I cleared my throat.

The guy recognized even that. "Mose," he said, "what's wrong," as though he was still the person I'd call in an emergency.

"Hey, Rock," I said.

"What's wrong," he repeated.

"Nothing. Everything's fine." I cleared my throat again. I'd expected to ease into a casual conversation. "It's just that I was over at Tansy's office."

"Yeah?" Rock said.

This was a stupid thing to do on the telephone. I should have had Tansy arrange a lunch. Even that might have been too much: I should have had Tansy tell Rock, "Mose hopes you're okay." We could have worked up from there.

"Well," I said, "Tansy and I got to talking."

"That'll happen," said Rocky.

"Yes, and—well, he was just saying it was a shame we broke up—"

"Professor," said Rocky excitedly. I could hear him pacing in his hotel room. I wondered how swank or low a place it was. "You're killing me here. Just tell me what you guys came up with. A movie? A TV special? Christ, I'm willing to start out with a benefit, even though I can tell you I could use some charity myself. I haven't had steady work in—"

"Oh, God, Rock," I said. "Nothing like that. I just wanted to see how you were. That's all."

"Ah!" he said. Then he fell silent. "Sure," he said. "You could have told me. . . ."

"I didn't think you'd be home."

"I'm not home," he said. "I'm in a fucking hotel." I listened to the background noise, trying to figure out what he was doing. I couldn't hear anything. "No chance, huh?" he said.

The last time I'd talked to him on the phone, I was exactly here, staring at the bush outside my window. He'd been on the line doing what he was doing now, trying to talk me into work. I closed my eyes and rubbed my ear with the phone. "Later, maybe. I don't know. A benefit, like you said. It's just now—"

"Now you have work," he said.

"Well, and the kids—"

"And you have work," he said breezily. "Obligations. I understand. I got some projects too."

"Tansy told me," I said, though Tansy hadn't. "But really. In a couple of years—"

"Keep me in mind," said Rocky. "Later, kid." He hung up the phone.

Carter and Sharp Go to Hell in a Handbasket

Who's my favorite piggy-wig?
Who's my favorite pig?
Who has such lovely pork chops
That she makes me flip my lid?

It's Sadie Sow, it's Sadie Sow,
I'm happy to report!
With a grunt and an oink and a grunt and an oink
And a grunt and an oink and a snort!

Voilà. Rocky had a regular job, without title billing: the host of *The Sadie Sow Show*. He'd probably had the offer when I called, and hoped I'd save him from it. Instead I'd driven him into the arms of a pig, a puppet operated by a temperamental man named Marcus; when Rocky made a slightly blue comment to Sadie, Marcus turned his wrist and Sadie turned her back. Still, it was a national show, and kids had always loved Rocky. He wore his striped shirt and changed hats every five minutes to suit the theme of the segment.

Gilda made me watch it with her. She was six, and had hardly any memories of Rocky at all, though the boys talked about him still. I kept thinking they'd grow out of it. (Later, when someone was trying to put together a documentary about the team, Jake described his childhood this way: "It was like having two fathers." At first I though he meant me as both, the screen version and the at-home guy who acted the part, but then he said, "I was devastated when they broke up. It was like a divorce.") Jessica made herself scarce when Sadie Sow was on. She wanted me to be the one who kept Gilda company.

At our house, Rocky laid 'em in the aisles, Gilda at least. Everything he did slayed her: kiss Sadie on the snout, pour a bucket of water over his head, fall down the stairs, sing, *You must have been a beautiful piglet* or *I found a million-dollar piglet*. The first time she called me to the sofa— "Here, Daddy," she said, pointing to a cushion—I didn't go right away. I stood at the back of the family room, and looked at Rocky on the TV screen. *He's in our furniture*, I thought. I hadn't seen him in two years. How had I avoided it? Now he wore a beret and his striped shirt, a narrow moustache, a broad French accent.

"Daddy, *here*," said Gilda, pounding on the sofa. So I settled down, and she snuggled up to me. I told her I knew that guy pretty well, and she developed a whole new appreciation for her old man. You could have seen the show two ways: A. Rocky had been reduced to teaming up with a felt and cotton-batting pig. B. I had been easily replaced, by a felt and cotton-batting pig.

Despite everything, I vacillated between A and B.

Rock and I hadn't announced our breakup. Nobody noticed for a while: in the early fifties we made only one movie a year, and the radio show had been canceled, and people weren't so used to seeing us on TV that they noticed when we didn't show up. *TV Guide* finally asked Rocky about it when he guested on the *Texaco Star Theater* in a semiserious role, and he made it sound like we'd just taken a breather from each other. "No dramatic story," he said. "Working apart for a while, that's all."

I landed a couple of other movie roles playing fathers of teenagers— nothing as good as *Greasepaint*, but nothing as bad as the last few Carter and Sharp flicks. The rest of my time I spent at home with the kids, writing letters to my sisters, reading magazines and newspapers and books of history. I didn't see much of my old friends, so when Neddy Jefferson invited me out to dinner at the Brown Derby, I said sure, even though I didn't much like the place, being devoted to the less splashy Musso's down the street.

"Dress up," said Neddy. "Boys' night out."

"I always dress up," I told him.

"Well," said Neddy, "you're in semiretirement. I just didn't want you to show up in your bathrobe and carpet slippers. We'll invite Tansy, hey? No wives."

"Boys' night out," I assured him.

So I spiffed up and went to the Derby the next week and scanned the dining room for Neddy's giant head. There it was in the corner, there was the rest of him underneath it, next to him tiny Tansy, and next to him: Rocky.

I stood, holding between two fingers the green plastic chip the coat-check girl had just dealt me. I could leave without redeeming it. The three of them conferred around a half-moon table, heads tilted toward the relish plate. They looked like something out of Lewis Carroll: tall, short, fat, waiting for something unlikely to deliver a speech. A parker house roll, the pitcher of cream. Then Tansy glanced up, and waved me over. I gave a faint finger-wiggle in return, and he tried to reel me in. Neddy and Rocky lifted their chins.

Did my heart melt? Did I forgive him instantly? Did I want to throw myself into his arms and suggest we that minute start filming a movie?

Well, yes.

Like me, he'd let his hair fade to its natural color, which was mostly sandy gray. He was in his early fifties by now, and he didn't look great but he didn't look as bad as he might: roses in his cheeks, for instance. The hair suited him. He wore a pretty snazzy suit, a subtle tattersall plaid. Between his fingers he pinched the stem of a martini fresh from the shaker, still with its sheen of ice, which held still while he twirled the glass around it.

"Fellas," I said when I got to the table, and Rocky said, "Darling boy. You never call, you never write. I'm beginning to think you don't love me." He lifted the martini like a flower he meant to sniff and then stick in his buttonhole.

He'd had all the time in the world to think of an opening line. I just looked at him.

"Sit down, Professor," he said gently. "Have a drink."

I think I was about to do that very thing, but that was when the television cameras showed up, and we heard the hearty disembodied voice of Ralph Edwards explaining, redundantly, that This Was Our Life.

Have you seen this show, ever? A televised prank, and you had to take it, and smile. They sit you on a couch. A voice you either recognize or don't comes over the speaker and tells half an anecdote, and then the voice's owner comes out of the wings, a person whose entrance to a party might, under other circumstances, cause you to hide in the kitchen.

A sweet idea, it must have seemed, when the producers had originally come up with the plans for such a show. You're back in touch with the people you love. A foretaste of heaven: everyone you've lost over the years comes through a door and hugs you and tells one fond story. You peer over their shoulders to see who's next. When that door opens, you think you recognize someone deep in the wings, though of course that's impossible. Even through the magic of, as they say, television, they can't bring the people you really want to see, your beloved dead.

But what a show *that* would be, huh?

I'm sure somebody's working on it.

We walked across the street to the Roosevelt Hotel, where the show was taped—hurry, hurry, the audience waits—up the stairs and into the Magnolia Room. A huge jumble, and then we were onstage, under the lights, and the people in the seats applauded us, and Rocky slapped me on the back. He hadn't known ahead of time, either, but he probably had hoped every day that a television crew would show up to tell him the story of his life, no matter how abridged.

They sat us down on the love seat, which normally held only one honoree; I had the spot closer to stage center. "Mike," the host said jovially, "got enough room left over for you there?" I almost corrected his manners—why insult the weight of an invited guest—but smiled. I could feel the warmth of Rocky's knee near mine, but I concentrated on the show.

Rocky first. They showed a chubby baby photo that caused the audience to coo, then brought out a seventy-year-old showgirl who'd known Rock at the Old Howard Theater in Boston. Then a baby picture of me, buck naked on a bearskin rug. How had they got hold of that? I would have blamed Jessica, but I didn't think I'd seen that picture in years.

"Mike," the host said, "you were born in Valley Junction, Iowa, in 1911." It seemed like the kind of thing you'd say to a stroke victim. Then a voice: Ed Dubuque's, and he came through the door. All over again I was surprised that Ed was a man not much older than me. He hugged me first with one arm, and then the other. The host told me to sit back down on the sofa, and Ed began to talk. He was stiff; he must have rehearsed.

"One summer, Mose worked at his family's store after he'd broken both wrists." Ed gestured to his own. "His father told him to go over the stock with a feather duster, and one day, when he was holding the duster between his casts"—Ed demonstrated—"he started to sing to it. And then he began to dance. He moved all through the store, singing and dancing. When he was finished, we applauded, customers and everything. Loveliest thing you ever saw, and all for a feather duster." Ed's nose and ears were bright red. That's how he always blushed. Then he was whisked backstage again.

I wanted to call him back. Dancing with a feather duster? I didn't remember, though as soon as he'd said it, I could see myself, the way I slid and nearly went down on one knee, a clot of dust in one cuff of my pants, my thick hair that needed cutting as usual. Then I realized I saw it as though I'd been filmed. If it really happened, if I really remembered, what I would see would be the gray head of the duster, the handle like a turned table leg between my plastered arms. Come back, Ed. Are you sure you're not thinking of some other kid?

Meanwhile, Ralph Edwards had skipped back to Rocky. I tried to pay attention. This disembodied voice said, "Hello, son." And then, out walked Professor and Professor Carter, Rocky's parents.

They looked unbelievably aged and sour. Arthritis had left his father like some flat-out-of-luck dinosaur whose ancestors had been able to fly and whose descendants would be able to walk upright. You expected his wife to help her husband across the stage, but she didn't, she held the clasp of her white pocketbook as though she were about to start rummaging through it. It might have been the most suspenseful moment in the history of *This Is Your Life:* would Rocky Carter's parents make it to center stage without expiring?

Rocky got up and shook his father's hand and kissed his mother's cheek, and then sat back down. This time, I could feel his knee vibrate with nerves; he was agitating his whole leg with rapid minuscule bounces of his heel. He probably thought nobody would notice, but over the air the tattersall pattern of his pants would pulsate.

Twenty-six years I'd known this guy. Never in all that time—not once, no matter the venue, no matter the size of the crowd—had anything like this ever happened. Not what we were doing, though we sat hip-to-hip, and that was strange, both the posture and the proximity. (Usually if he was close enough to touch, I was smacking him over the head, removing his hat to use it as a weapon on his cranium.) Not the man holding a microphone and our prop biography. Not even the two terrifying elderly people, glowering at the mixed marriage before them, unlikely to deliver their blessing.

The unprecedented thing: Rocky was frightened in front of a crowd. He was onstage and silent, wedged in next to me, and contemplated—I could tell, I'd worked with him and knew his ways, even this one thing that had never happened before—running from the stage without an apology. Stage fright. Nerves like an amateur's.

I don't remember what the Professors Carter said. Some scrap of a story, told without much affection. Then they were gone too.

I tried to hold body and mind together, but it was hard. There was Mimi, and she was almost thin again but not quite, and her nose was still all wrong; she kissed me and pinched my upstage ear. Here comes Tansy, shaking both our hands. They had to rush to fit two lives in one half hour, and it was over so quick there was no more time for suspense. Only later I would think: I wish they'd found Penny, it would have been nice to see Sukey Decker, why didn't they ask Johnny Atkinson? They mentioned Betty's death (though not Hattie's), and I wish they hadn't: anyone who couldn't come shouldn't be invited to the party. At the very end, they called out Jessica and then Rocky's new wife, a very tall young blonde named Ella, who kissed her husband on the top of his head. My kids came out. Rock and I both looked around for Rocky junior, but he didn't show up. My sisters flooded the stage, and that's when I began to cry—I'd been to see them six months before, but that was in Iowa, and here they were, Annie, Ida, Fannie, Sadie, Rose, dressed up and on television, as though it was the most ordinary thing in the world.

Why *not* get back together, I thought, sitting on the *This Is Your Life* love seat. Nothing big. A TV appearance where we actually had some lines. A week of club work in Vegas. I got a kick out of my new movies, but I missed thinking on my feet. No, I didn't miss that: I missed Rock. After the show I'd talk to Tansy—

"Well, boys," Ralph Edwards said, "we've got fifteen seconds. Any words you'd like to leave us with?"

We stood up. I was still crying and waved away the microphone. Rocky threw one arm around me, which for him was always a gesture equal parts fond and hostile. "This has been wonderful," he said, not looking at me. "Mike and I had such a long, happy ride together. This show is a perfect end to a perfect partnership. I can't think of a better going-away party."

"Oh?" said Edwards, confused.

"Didn't you know?" said Rocky. "Carter and Sharp have broken up."

They threw a party for us afterward in the hotel's dining room. Rock and I were seated at either end of the table, twin fathers, with our extended families all around us. I wanted to talk to him, but not here. *You didn't have to do that.* I believed he'd thought he'd done me a favor. What insanity, to see your longtime partner on national television after an extended silence. How happy I was to see him anyhow. What a bad idea this all was. Rocky talked to Tansy and Neddy and Mimi and Jessica and our kids, especially Jake, who hadn't forgotten his favorite wayward uncle. I talked to Mimi and Ed and Ida and Fannie and Sadie and Annie and Mrs. Rose Dubuque, proprietress now of Sharp's Apparel of West Des Moines. Annie still did the books. They'd decided to stock women's clothing, she told me, and I felt like a club member whose old haunt has gone coed without his permission. Ladies' frocks in Sharp's Gents'! Ladies' underthings, even!

Why hadn't I thought of that?

Professor and Professor Carter spoke to no one. As I suspected, Mrs. Professor Carter cared only for the contents of her purse, which she emptied onto the tabletop. I worried that she'd eventually pull out a gun. Instead, she began to fill the purse with sugar cubes and silverware.

Plenty of mingling all around—my sisters approached Rocky and said, "I don't know if you remember me, but we had dinner together sixteen years ago." He greeted them all warmly, by name. Gilda sat on everybody's lap. I thought she'd be shy around her idol, Sadie Sow's best friend, but instead she leaned on one of his knees and asked him to do something funny.

By the end of the evening, Rocky was as drunk as I'd ever seen him. Strange as it sounds, I took that as almost good news: maybe sturdy Ella made him drink less, and therefore he was more susceptible to the martinis. She sat next to the Carters, who seemed to be berating her for not knowing what the Bayeux Tapestry was. "The Babe Ruth what?" she asked. I sat down next to Rocky.

"So how's the boy?" I inquired.

I watched him try to piece together a clever answer. I watched him fail.

"Money troubles," he said. "You probably heard."

"You know," I told him, "if I can help you out with a loan . . ."

He raised his head, and gave me a look that went from haughty to embarrassed to grateful to defeated in the space of two seconds: I could almost chart each reaction as it arrived at his forehead and tumbled down his face and into his drink.

"I don't think it's come to that," he said.

"I like Ella. She's a very giant woman."

"I'm playing Vegas next week."

"That's good."

"Tonight I have to see my folks." He pointed them out to me, in case I'd forgotten. He laughed. "They haven't changed a bit. Forty years. You know," he said. The waiter set down a new martini in front of him. He started to turn it, and we both looked at the thin layer of ice doing its steady trick despite the revolutions of the glass. I couldn't imagine what he would say. It seemed an apology was in order, but I didn't know who was owed. "You know, Professor," he said, "not many people realize this"—he nodded at his glass—"but the ice in a martini always points to true north."

"So," I said to Jessica as she drove us home, "that was a surprise."

"It seemed like a good idea at the time." She made it sound as though she still thought it wasn't a bad idea. "Did you get a chance to talk to Rocky?"

"He was fried. As usual."

"I didn't know they'd brought in his parents."

"Of course they did. That's what the show is about."

From the backseat, Jake wondered how many people watched *This Is Your Life*.

"Too many," I told him. He was thirteen, just the age vanity would get the best of him, one way or the other. "You looked like a prince. The new teen heartthrob. Across North America, girls are burning their pictures of Pat Boone."

"They should," said Nathan, "but over *him*?"

"All we wanted was for the two of you to talk a little," said Jessica.

"He pulled a fast one, huh? Shocked the hell out of Tansy. I'm sure he thought we'd get back together after tonight. Neddy probably had a script all ready: *Carter and Sharp Collect Social Security Benefits*."

We pulled into the drive and then into the garage. Jess put the car into park with a clunk. "Nobody wanted anything but for you guys to talk. You miss him. You don't realize it, but you miss him."

Of course I realized it. For instance, he would have laughed at *Carter and Sharp Collect Social Security Benefits*. I didn't know anyone else who'd find that really funny. We might have gone on making up geriatric slapstick titles. *Carter and Sharp Break a Hip. Carter and Sharp Wander Off. Carter and—What Was Your Name Again?*

"Darling boy," he'd called me, when he saw me at the restaurant.

But I hadn't begun to fully bend until his parents took the stage. Ah, thought the audience, his parents: how proud they must be! I understood *exactly* how proud they were. All the years I'd known Rocky, Mrs. Carter's motherly correspondence consisted of requests for money when the fictional Mrs. Carter showed up on the radio. They couldn't profit from the sisters, since they belonged rightfully to me, but I had in my head several paragraphs written in case Father Professor Carter decided that because I wore a mortarboard I was patterned after him. He never made a claim. "My father doesn't care for show business," Rocky used to tell me before we hit it big, "but he adores money. I have a little plan cooked up to buy his love. . . ." Then he discovered that his father would cash the checks and welsh on Rocky's dreamt-up deal. In other words, I had followed the whole complicated plot of the past twenty-six years: I'd had a major role. I would have known not to invite those people who happened to share his name. *This,* I knew, *is not his life.*

The thing was, all he had were those awful parents, the most recent wife. They wouldn't call up the exes, and I guess Lillian wouldn't release Rocky junior. If somebody kept track—by which I mean, Rocky—it would be hard not to notice: my first partner, my wife, my children, my sisters. Me, who had never once been called lovable in a review. Me, who never walked into a bar full of strangers and dazzled them. Me. The straight man. No matter how you counted it up, somehow I'd gotten the lion's share after all. I could hear him practically whine about it: sure, you get all this love, and what do I get?

Of all the people they'd excavated for Rocky up onstage, I was the one he'd always loved most. Most stubbornly. Most irrevocably. Despite all his best interests. I should have been the one walking through the door, Ralph Edwards saying, Now, this is a voice you haven't heard in a while. And when Rocky recognized who was speaking, I'd come through that door so fast I'd bust the hinges, and we'd fall into each other's arms, and the audience, quite rightly, would give us an ovation.

The show got that right. You always needed a door. Reunions, goodbyes, anything, you had to have a door to do it right.

My next couple of days were taken up by my sisters, a gaggle of middle-aged and elderly women who were acting like teenagers. I mean, they giggled for a solid three days. They wanted to stand in footprints outside of Grauman's; they wanted to eat at the Brown Derby and Cantor's; they wanted to drive through Beverly Hills and sit in hotel lobbies and go to Trader Vic's for mai tais.

"Only rubes do that," I said. Then I examined them more closely. What do you know? Rubes!

I planned to call Rock once they flew home. Already I looked forward to him trying to scandalize me with stories of Ella and where he'd found her. I'd even started to think he'd been smart announcing our breakup on the show. By now, even Rocky knew we were too old. When you were eulogized on TV, it was probably time to throw the dirt on the coffin. So once my sisters had filled their suitcases with souvenirs and swizzle sticks, I'd call.

I never got the chance. Something strange happened: Rocky Carter disappeared. He walked out on Ella, and Rocky junior, and even Sadie Sow. He left a short note saying he was leaving on purpose. He didn't want any time or money wasted on a search.

"Good-bye," said the note, which had been addressed to no one in particular. "I'm sure we'll meet again someday."

15

He Left a Hole in Sadie Sow

I thought I'd gotten used to life without Rocky. Two years practice, though, turned out to be *nothing*. We hadn't been speaking, but he was around, everywhere, really, in stories my kids told each other, in sly questions from Tansy and offers from Vegas, stored in the box we called television in the family room. I snubbed him at every turn, but he'd been available.

Then he wasn't.

The morning papers covered his disappearance, coming as it did five days after he'd announced the end of Carter and Sharp. Do you know where he went? reporters asked me. Surely he must have told *you*. They'd seen us together on *This Is Your Life*, looking like the best of chums. Nobody had asked me about Rocky in some time, but now I spent several hours a day discussing his whereabouts. And so Rock, in leaving, had managed what he'd failed to do in staying: he reteamed Carter and Sharp. Suddenly, I was responsible for the guy again, and I'd let him slip through my fingers.

People kept asking why we'd split. I should have come up with a consistent story. We were old. I wanted to retire. Rocky had always wanted to do something especially for children. He left me for a pig. We'd gone as far with the act as we could. When asked, I chose the answer that seemed most true at the time.

I continued to make movies after Rocky left. I played fathers and grandfathers and mayors of small towns, men who glanced, befuddled, over the tops of newspapers. In *Fair Warning*, I played an elderly junkie who tells the hero it's not too late, he can change, he doesn't have to die of dope; then I died of dope. I always had work. Jessica too: she continued to choreograph for TV, and then when variety began to die on the tube (as it had years before in real life) she took up choreographing for a local theater company, where she was beloved and feared. When I went to opening nights with her, I held her hand, jealous of all the young people who brought her bouquets of flowers.

Tansy took on more clients and two assistants. Sadie Sow found a young fellow in a sport shirt with whom she seemed quite smitten. Old movie stars disappeared every day, of course. Obscurity was not front-page news. A year passed, and then another. People forgot that Rocky had gone missing. He was just gone.

Our kids got older, the way kids will. Rocky junior, too, who we took under our wing some; Lillian thought we were good influences, I guess. He and the boys were about the same age, and here he was, a fatherless kid. A really nice kid, too, a little heavy (like his father he ate when nervous, which was often), but completely at ease around grown-ups. He called us Aunt Jess and Uncle Mose, as our kids had called his father Uncle Rocky.

The freeway came through Los Angeles. The freeway came through Des Moines. Jess's hair turned snow white all of a sudden, and I had some idea of what she must have looked like, all those years ago, as a blonde: spectacular. Jake went to college, then Nathan, and then they both went to medical school, and before long—it felt like no time at all—Jess and I were the parents of a gynecologist and a dentist. They did not appreciate the jokes I made about this pairing. Two practical young men! They married nice Jewish girls and settled in southern California and began to have children: Nathan, for some reason I still cannot fathom, changed his last name to Sharensky, to honor the grandfather he'd never met. These boys had been taught at an early age how to do a spit take, how to tap-dance and project when they sang, and so they both ran away and joined the circus, by which I mean ordinary life.

Gilda, however, wanted to follow her father's footsteps. I'd been right, all those years ago: she grew up to look like Hattie, long limbed and red-haired. She danced on television, and wrote some sitcom scripts. She never got married. I thought she clung to us, the way children born to older parents sometimes will: there was hardly a gap between us taking care of her and her taking care of us. A charming, pushy young woman; our make-up baby. When she visited, she'd go through our medicine cabinets and come out with the prescription bottles.

"What's this for?" she'd demand. "Oh, and it says it's supposed to be stored away from the *damp*."

When Jess got sick in '74, Gilda wanted to do everything, and so did I. We fought all the time. So she moved into her old bedroom, and took over the invisible, thankless jobs that I couldn't remember to do and therefore didn't notice when they were done. I drove Jess to the doctor's, for the diagnosis, and then the mastectomy, then the chemo. I did not care about the breast, but I wanted to shake the doctor, who seemed to think my tiny wife, ninety pounds now, had a single ounce of weight to spare.

I'd always thought of myself as the most competent of men. I could patch, hem, darn; I could even take in and let out suits, thanks to childhood lessons from Ed Dubuque. I could starch and iron a shirt till it glowed like a snowy lawn, capable of bending but not creasing. I could clean. I had beautiful manners. My wife had never once had to straighten my tie.

But I could not cook. I'd never had to. For years during my vaudeville days, I never so much as switched on a stove. And then Jess got sick, and I wanted to cook for her.

"Anyone can make bouillon," said Gilda. Not me. I snatched the kettle off the burner and poured the water, lukewarm, over the cube, where it managed to suck off a little flavoring but nothing else. Or I forgot to stir, and left a nugget at the bottom. All of the things the world claims you can cook if you can boil water, I failed at. The water would boil eventually, sure; the laws of thermodynamics would not bend to my incompetence. I brewed coffee you could read magazines through. I forgot to latch the tea ball, and poured cups of what looked like a river that had jumped its banks.

Then I'd walk around the house. Somehow, I would have slipped two bouillon cubes in my pants pocket. I'd shake them like dice. Why square, I'd wonder, why not round? A question like that could absorb me for hours. My aluminum palate seemed a colossal character flaw: I should have prepared. I should have taken lessons.

Jessica thanked me for everything. She couldn't eat anyhow: the chemo was poison, of course. I should have sent out for prop meals every day, set them on the nightstand beside her bed, and saved the trouble. She spent two months in bed; I spent two months looking at her profile, the long nose, the thinning hair combed up off her forehead, that Roman-coin beauty. Then she got sicker, and even her beauty was gone.

I took care of my wife, though when I think back on the months she was really sick, I remember all the time I spent in other rooms, putting off going back to her side. She was so sick it left me gasping.

People had died before, of course, and people would die hence. But really, but really, hadn't I—shouldn't the one person—

—I know I had a warning this time, but the *one* person—

—just this once—

A Double Act

At the memorial service, Gilda gave a eulogy. I could not. Her words made everyone cry, but she got it wrong. She said: "It was like my parents were one person."

No, I thought. We were like two people. We did not share one soul, or one mind: simple division shows you the folly of that. Before Jessica, I'd wandered around, very much like one person, no matter whose company I was in. It wasn't always fun. She did the same thing. Every now and then, maybe we'd find someone to be the disappointment act, to fill out the bill for the evening, or a week. Then Jess and I met, and were never, not for one moment, anything like one person.

But Rocky and I were. I think that was the problem. Onstage, in front of the cameras, we knew exactly what the other guy was thinking. No: we just thought the same thing at the same time, a comic animal with four legs and four arms and two heads bumping, bumping. The animal slaps itself across the face, throws itself over a balustrade. Time to step this way. Time to pause. No surprise, *how did you know?* We knew. It was our job.

One person, yes, but the one person we were like was Rocky.

When Jess died, all of us—my kids, and me, and Tansy—thought Rocky might show up. What a eulogy he could have given! The phone rang and rang, and it was never him. My sisters stayed in Des Moines again, at my request. I'd be out there soon enough and they could comfort me then, because I was bringing Jess's body back to be buried at Greenwood Cemetery.

"Shall we come with you?" the kids asked. "We'll come."

"No," I said. We'd already had the memorial in L.A., and while I'd wanted it to be small, barely noticeable, it was filled with weeping dancers and amateur actors, all the people she'd choreographed over the years. They seemed to shudder and sob in unison, as though they'd been instructed, and they unfurled their hankerchiefs with unsettling grace.

"I just promised her," I told my kids, which was a lie. Jessica did not care where she was buried. I couldn't bury her by Betty, who was still in Babyland, and I had no interest in an exhumation, a word that made me want to throw myself in an open grave. I couldn't bury her by Joseph, who like his father had died of a heart attack in his fifties: Joseph, or his ashes, were in our front hall in a tin can. This had bothered me at first. "One of these days we'll scatter him," Jessica had said. "We'll think of a nice place." So we stuck the can in the cloak closet. After a while, I got used to the idea—I started calling him Prince Albert—and then even jealous. I would have liked Hattie's ashes, something so homely and ridiculous. Where's Hattie? Ah, yes: behind that door, up on the shelf, among the hats.

But I could bury Jessica beside her parents. So in September of 1975, the Howard kids traveled back to Iowa together in one box: Jessica, intact, in a casket; Joseph tucked at her feet. Her parents' graves were in the Jewish section of Greenwood, a stone or three's throw from my parents' and Hattie's—Rabbi Kipple had been interred across town, in a tiny Jewish graveyard that now had a view of the interstate.

Really, that's why I brought Jessica back: I could think, *She lives in Des Moines now.* Far away and safe. No graveside service, and the day I buried her I wished I'd had her cremated: the ground was so cold, and the sky was so blue.

I stayed in Vee Jay with Annie, who was in her early eighties and in remarkable health. Sweet Bessie Mackintosh, her friend, had died the year before. I figured maybe Annie would be a distraction from my grief—she was an old woman, and lonely, and I could look after her—but in fact she was in better shape than me. All of the oldest girls had become sturdy old women. But Little Rose, our baby, had spent the past two years having nearly everything removed—her uterus, then part of her stomach, then her ovaries. Annie spent most of the time at the Dubuques' house, since Ed frequently ran away to the store. "You know how men are," Annie said. "He can't take the fact that she's in pain."

"No," I said.

Then Annie looked sympathetic. "Rose'll love to see you. You'll go over to their place today?"

"Of course."

"Can you be cheery? I hate to ask you. I know this isn't a cheery time for you. But we have to keep her in good spirits, doctor says. So can you?"

"I'm an actor," I said, "I can be cheerful no matter what."

She pursed her mouth cynically then, which I took as a comment on my talents.

Once again to downtown Valley Junction. The Lyric Theater had become a theatrical shop, with rubber masks of Nixon and Agnew in the window, gorilla suits, feather boas: it looked like Rocky's pool house. Down the street, antique-store windows glittered with cut glass and old china cups; a few new restaurants had been decked out to look old-timey. There wasn't a pool hall anywhere. And Sharp's Gents' was now Sharp's Ladies'. All they stocked for men were handkerchiefs and pocket flashlights in the front case. Ed Dubuque looked like a Dutch farmer, his hair gone white but still sticking up. "Master Sharp," he said to me when I came in. "I hope you're not looking for clothes."

"I'm thinking of doing a drag act," I said. "I always looked good in lilac."

"We have several things in a nice wash and wear," he said seriously.

I leaned on the counter. The wooden sign on the back wall still said SHOES in thirties flat-topped serpentine script, but the footwear on the stands were sandals and high-heeled pumps, a few kids' sneakers. *This is where I spent my childhood*, I thought, but of course it wasn't: the place had moved, the railroad men were dead or retired, my father was gone. I tried to remember the smell of the old original building, a kind of leathery tang tamped down by dust, a hint of whiskey blown in from the tavern next door. "Don't you miss the menswear?"

"It's what Rose wanted," he said. "I'm happier surrounded by ladies than she was by men."

"How is she?"

"Not well, Master Sharp. Annie's over there now. I'll go home after lunch, when my high school kid comes in. I should stay with her all the time, but work . . ."

"Helps," I offered. He nodded.

I went to their house on Sixth Street, an old property of my father's that he'd signed over to Ed in the thirties. Rose was on their screened-in porch on the front of the house, Annie beside her. She'd seen Rose come into this world. Now she'd see her go out.

They'd moved a wheeled hospital bed onto the porch; it must have been Rose's main form of transportation these days. Annie's nursing hadn't changed. The bed had been made up in white sheets and a pink blanket so neatly that Rose looked like a love letter waiting to be sealed and sent. A child's Mickey Mouse doll with a plush body and a plastic face had been slid under the covers next to her, his head on the edge of the pillow. That embarrassed me more than anything else.

"Hey, kiddo," I said. "How're you feeling?"

"Like springtime."

"You look it."

She coughed, but her voice didn't sound so bad. Annie gave me her chair, then went into the house to get another.

Rose said, "Now if I could only get that doctor to leave me alone."

"He bothering you, kid? Point him out and I'll take care of him for you."

"He just got ahold of my ovaries. I told him, 'Put them in a jar so we can keep them on the mantelpiece.' "

"Rose!" Annie said, from inside the house.

"Well, I miss them," Rose muttered. "I suppose I was done with them, but still."

"I'll punch his lights out," I said.

"Thanks. Hand me that glass of water on the table? I think he's got one of those treasure maps left over from your movies, except it's of me, so he keeps digging." She accepted the water with one hand, and with the other traced two lines on the blanket above her torso. "X marks the spot. What movie was that?"

"*Yo Ho Ho.*"

"*Yo Ho Ho,*" she said. "I liked that one. I wish you'd make movies like that one again."

"Like what?"

"You know. Silly. Broad jokes. People falling down. Whales blowing water in your face. You were good at that. Oh, I've hurt your feelings. I mean, I like the movies you make now, but I liked the old ones too. Nobody makes stupid funny movies anymore."

Annie's face appeared briefly at the window; she was giving the two littlest kids some time alone. I never palled around with Rose when we were young—Hattie, of course—and now I wished I had. She'd offered to be my vaudeville partner once, and now, partnerless, I wanted her to offer again.

"You didn't hurt my feelings," I said. "I'm serious about punching your doctor. He's not a big guy, is he?"

She shrugged in slow motion. "Who knows? I haven't met him when we've both been standing up. *Oh!*" she said. I jumped to my feet.

"What's the matter?"

She began to cry, just slightly and silently, and I thought she must be in terrible pain. Where was Annie?

But Rose said, "Jessica died. Annie *told* me, and then somehow I *forgot*, and I've been sitting here talking about myself like some *jerk*. What is wrong with me?"

"It's okay, Rose," I said.

"You must really *hate* me." She picked up Mickey Mouse and threw him across the porch into a screen, where he frightened several insects.

"Rose, Rose, of course not." Actually I liked it (though I never would have said so)—I'd found a place where it seemed possible for minutes at a time for me and anybody else to forget that Jess had died. I had work here. Grief makes you do things, pick up knitting, weed the yard, keep your hands busy, but best is talk, jokes, X marks the spot. She was *funny*, my kid sister. Surely Rose was the one we couldn't spare. I remembered her wanting to be on the radio as a teenager, how I'd teased her, how she'd put the idea of vaudeville back in my head. She'd run away from home, but only got as far as Kansas City before being snatched back by Annie. *You didn't run far enough*, I wanted to tell her. *You should have come with me.* That wasn't fair: now she had Ed, and dying in California was no more picturesque than dying in Valley Junction, I knew that much.

I picked up the doll and tucked him back into bed. Of course I didn't hate her. "I love you," I said, smoothing the sheet over the doll's disturbingly pink stomach.

This took her by surprise. She said, somewhere between laughing and crying, "You love Mickey Mouse?"

"I love Mickey Mouse," I said. "And I love you, Minnie Mouse Dubuque."

"Who is," she said, wincing but definitely laughing, "a pain in the *ass*."

I said, "Rose, ssshh. Don't give your doctor any ideas."

When Jessica was sick—

I can't.

When Jessica died, when she died, when the nurse came out of her hospital room, from which I had been banished minutes before (one o'clock in the morning, they let me sleep there) and told me she was dead, I got in the car and drove around and then I called my children and then I was occupied for a great deal of time, which was good, because while she was sick I kept extremely busy all the time doing things for her and at one in the morning what seemed terrible was that I had suddenly run out of things to do, as though I'd been handed my pictures. Fired. Let me cut down on the euphemisms. This isn't a vaudeville house, I can say anything I fucking well please, as Rocky would tell me. Then we had the service and then I arranged for her to be flown back to Des Moines, which was the first time Jessica had ever been on an airplane—she once said, "The only way I will ever get on a plane is if I drive somewhere far away and die and they have to fly my body back," and I'd always loved this fear, even though it made travel difficult—we drove and took trains and steamers and ferries, and sometimes I flew and she and the kids would catch up in the car. *My darling, let me kiss your phobia.*

I remember everything. Her shoe size, her dress size, the seventeen times she winked at me in our thirty-two years of marriage—"Only seventeen?" Rocky, a spendthrift winker himself, would have said, but Jess knew if she did it more often it wouldn't mean anything, each time I had forgotten that it was something she did, but then we'd be separated in a crowd, and maybe I was bored or maybe I missed her, and she'd look at me and wink.

I just always had a crush on her.

"I'm going, my darling," she'd said the day she died. "Where are you going?" I asked. She took my hand and said, "Out the window on gossamer wings."

And now here I was alone in Iowa, an out-of-work actor. I considered staying. "I could help with Rose," I told Annie later that afternoon. "I've picked up a few nursing skills lately." And I could make jokes, I thought, all day long. I'd dig up every slapstick routine I could.

Annie kissed my cheek. "Sweet boy. No. If you stay around she'll think she's dying for sure."

"I'm sure she knows."

"Don't say that. She's better some days. Go on home to your kids. How many times a day do they call here? And you think they can spare you?"

"I guess not," I said, and she said, "Ed'll drive you to the airport."

I packed my little leather bag in my father's empty house. Years of vaudeville had made me proud of how little I needed to travel. Ed picked me up in a new Chevy, which I admired.

"I'll park and come in," he said at the airport curb, but I waved him away.

"No more big good-byes," I told him.

Inside the airport, a tired young woman in an airline uniform leaned on the ticket desk, a red cloth flower in her buttonhole. Apparently, I was the only person leaving Des Moines today. I thought of Rocky—I often thought of Rocky—running away from home. He'd been gone eighteen years now, and had stayed in touch with people just enough to make it clear that somewhere he was alive. He'd called Tansy, drunk, from a pay phone four years ago, mumbling about a comeback. He sent Rocky junior postcards that had been hand canceled, no legible city. ("Do you think he's in town, and just slips them into my mailbox?" Junior asked. "I think he's charmed a postmistress," I answered.) He never called me. He never wrote. "I'm beginning to think you don't love me," I said aloud.

Maybe I'd pull a Rocky. I wouldn't go home. I'd write my kids: *Off traveling. I'm sure we'll meet again someday.*

I imagined stepping onto the tarmac and hailing a plane like you'd hail a taxi, a gag we'd pulled in *Fly Boys*, though this was the Des Moines International Airport, which meant I could only get as far away as nearest Canada. Who was I kidding, anyway? Of course I'd go home.

Not right away, though.

Nearly two decades before, when people asked me my theories on Rocky's whereabouts, I couldn't think of an answer. Mexico, I thought sometimes, speaking Spanish and getting brown as a berry. London: he loved the pubs there. Some big city where no one knows him. He's gotten a crew cut, wears glasses. Once I'd outfitted him, I had to employ him. Bartender? Handyman? Gigolo? I remained unconvinced.

No: Las Vegas. Naturally Las Vegas. What kind of idiot had I been? He'd even said so, sort of, after *This Is Your Life*: he claimed he'd been booked there. Las Vegas was perfect for Rock, a twenty-four-hour town, free drinks, gambling, endless strangers. Girl singers in every casino. Strippers.

I bought a ticket from the weary agent in Des Moines, and on the flight to Chicago, and then to Las Vegas, I constructed his new existence. The crew cut and the glasses could stay. He worked at a casino, probably as a dealer. He told jokes as he took people's money. Though he'd just turned seventy, he couldn't afford to retire. After all, he'd recently been married for the twelfth time.

I almost expected him to meet my plane. "You figured it out!" he'd say, and he'd tow me to the airport bar and order me a drink. "What took you so long? Any day now, I kept thinking." The bartender would set down two bright pink drinks and Rocky would pay in chips and soon we'd be two bright pink drunks and he'd raise his glass:

"To us! To me! Especially to me!"

There was nobody looking for me at the gate in Vegas. I took a taxicab to the strip, undeterred.

Picture me going from joint to joint, a double exposure of bubbly neon and bubblier cocktails across my increasingly bewildered face. Any cliché you choose will probably fit. At some point it occurred to me that I had come to Vegas so that I could get as drunk as I wanted, which is to say extremely. No: Rocky. He was here somewhere. I examined every dealer, every bartender, every cigarette girl. Mostly, I knew this was a delusion. I needed to keep my mind busy, that was all, so I'd invented this one-object scavenger hunt. What's more: whenever someone died, I suffered from the belief that he or she was actually alive and living elsewhere. Well someone had died, that was true, but Rocky—as far as we could tell—*was* alive, *did* live elsewhere. Might be, in fact, found! How crazy was that?

To one confused but pretty cocktail waitress I claimed to be a private eye trying to locate an unsuspecting heir to a million-dollar fortune. I sat down at a roulette table and instantly won $350. Someone brought me another drink, and I threw half the chips on her tray and filled my pockets with the rest and stumbled on to the next casino, where I was sure I'd find Rocky. I went from the Dunes to the Sands to the Sahara: Moses in the desert.

According to my watch it was somewhere after midnight. I had to hold my wrist steady to see. Just this morning I'd been in Iowa. I'd buried my wife. I'd realized I would soon bury another sister. Only hours ago I'd been responsible and sober, a loved father and grandfather and brother. But not a husband, not a husband, and I sat down on the edge of a fountain in the lobby of a hotel and rubbed my face. That water would sober me up if I jumped in. Across the lurid carpet a security guard sized me up, wondering if I was a dangerous drunk or just an ordinary one. Dangerous, I wanted to say, because I was, and unlocatable, and drunker than I'd ever been in my life, looking for a man who seemed to be my only friend in the world even though we hadn't spoken in nearly two decades.

It had taken years for Rocky to hit bottom; it had taken me fifteen hours.

I reached behind me to wet my fingers, splashed my forehead, and then somehow stood up and launched myself through the hotel lobby and into the casino behind it. I could hear a woman singing in a middle-aged and sexy voice.

My kisses are like cigarettes
Try one, you'll want a pack
But you'll find they're killing kisses
I need a warning printed on my back
When the doctor cuts you open
He won't know what turned your heart so black.

I tried to locate the source. Ah: tucked in a corner, a small bar and a stage, entertainment for people who wanted to sit down but weren't willing to cough up the dough for the show. Me. I squinted at the figure onstage. Her chestnut hair shone cherryish from the red gels on the lights, and the microphone she gripped cast a shadow like a port-wine birthmark across her face. Sequins, of course, emerald-green against her pale skin.

The space between me and the stage was packed with small round tables on stalks and big round chairs on wheels. Barely any floor space at all, but the chairs were so huge you wouldn't feel crowded once you sat, though it might be hard to get up if you'd arrived sober and stayed through a couple of sets: you could lose track of how drunk you were.

I knew precisely how drunk I was. *See that old man? Pathetic. Where's his wife? She should take him home.* I instructed myself to marshal up some dignity, then found that I had none, so I held on to the backs of the chairs, apologizing to the few occupants I encountered, all the way to the little stage, at which point I fell over at the singer's feet. I grabbed her by the ankle and looked up: Penny O'Hanian Carter.

A bouncer came to remove me. I was seconds away from being thrown out of a casino at one in the morning. Penny shook her head at him: I was fine, I could stay. She sang her next verse to me.

> *My love is just like bourbon*
> *It's so smooth that it's a sin*
> *The thirst runs in your family*
> *Your parents called again.*
> *They swear they'll leave each other*
> *Long as I will take them in.*

Wotta professional. She made me part of her act.

Penny must have checked me into the hotel room. Everything was red and braided; it felt like waking up in somebody else's stomach. Better his than mine. I went to the bathroom to vomit.

Hadn't I grown up any? I found a note taped to my shirtsleeve from Penny, suggesting that if I was able, I should meet her downstairs at the buffet nearest the elevators, the elevators nearest my room, at ten o'clock. I wondered whether Rocky had ever told her of pinning a similar note with similar directions some forty years before. Okay, I had enough time to call downstairs to have a razor and toothbrush sent up. I'd have to go in the wretched clothes I was wearing, because I'd managed to lose my case. Thank God I had buried Joseph's ashes in Des Moines. I saw myself placing the tin can on the roulette board. What would you win if you bet a corpse?

My sense of humor was getting very black indeed.

"You're vertical!" said Penny when she saw me.

"Barely," I said.

"Let's start again," said Penny. "Mikey!" She half stood up to greet me. "Buddy!"

Good old Penny. I'd been feeling a little embarrassed, but she treated me like a returning astronaut. I tumbled into the red booth across from her. I'd thought I'd ended the night at the Sahara, but the elevators had opened on Circus Circus, and I expected then to see Penny in clown drag. Instead, she wore a knit pant suit that wrapped around her thin waist. As a young woman, she'd aged badly, but then she stopped. I couldn't remember how old she was. She looked forty, but that was impossible.

"So," I said. "We meet again."

"Always in the most awkward places," she said. "What are you doing out here? Performing?"

"No," I said. I'd slept off any delusions I had about finding Rocky, although here was his ex-wife. That should count for something. What *was* I doing here?

"Jess died," I said. "I don't know. I guess I'm avoiding going back to the house."

"Oh, Mike," she said. "I'm sorry."

"Somehow I got it into my head—well, I'd gotten to miss Rocky. Instead of missing Jess. It seemed easier. So I came here. Started looking." I laughed at myself. "I'd leave one place, and I'd be absolutely positive he'd be in the next."

"But he wasn't," she said.

"No."

Penny shook her head. "He's not in Vegas."

"It's a big town," I said.

"He's not here," she said.

"Have you been looking too?"

"I'm going to get you some breakfast." She stood up suddenly and edged her way out of the booth. I noticed she hadn't answered my question. "You're in a delicate condition. Eggs? Eggs will be good. Toast," she said very certainly.

Penny had always liked buffets, because that way she didn't have to read menus. I wondered whether she wore contact lenses now. When she came back, I said, "If he's not in Vegas, do you know where he is?"

She'd shored up whatever she'd almost let slip before. "Of course not."

"Are you sure?"

"Well." She spread some jam on a triangular piece of toast for me. "I did. I'll admit it. I saw him maybe three years back."

"Where?"

She thought. "Here."

"Las Vegas?"

"Sure, that's what I said. He was coming through, he looked me up, we had a few drinks, he went on."

"Why didn't you tell me?"

"I beg your pardon," she said. "I haven't seen *you* for thirty years. *Thirty years*. We're twice as old as we used to be. Suddenly I'm supposed to know that you're looking for Rocky? The way he told it, you guys weren't speaking to each other."

The math confused me. Weren't you always twice as old as you used to be? She shuffled then stacked the toast on my plate. It, too, looked like something internal. When she held the ketchup over my eggs, I had to catch her by the wrist before she slaughtered the entire plate. I had a headache. I wondered if a screwdriver would help.

"We were talking to each other," I said. "I mean, the last time I saw him we were talking to each other."

"How long ago was that?"

"Nineteen fifty-seven."

"I'd say if you hadn't talked to him from 1957 till 1972, which is when I saw him—face it, you weren't talking to each other."

"No," I said. "I guess we weren't. Do you know where he was living?"

"He wouldn't say. Somewhere warm, I think. He had a pretty good tan."

Then we didn't say anything.

"So," she said. "When did your wife die?"

"Three days ago."

She gasped. Then she leaned forward and looked at me. She seemed about to check me for fever. "I figured you meant months—" Very slowly, she said, "Your children. Still in California?"

"Yes," I said.

"Okay," she said. "You'll give me Jake's number. You remember Jake's number?"

"Of course," I said, irritated.

And she drove me back to the airport, and packed me in a plane.

I thought about this conversation all the way back to L.A., examining it for lies and evasions. If you play a character in a movie, sometimes you later confuse it with job experience, and Rocky and I had been detectives—lousy ones, sure, but in the end we always figured it out—in three of our pictures. *She knows something.* I wasn't sure what, but I saw the holes, the way she mostly just agreed with what I said. Another time, maybe I could have talked her out of the information. *Come on, Penny, aren't we friends?* But then my plane landed, and this time there was somebody there to meet me, Jake, his hands stuffed in his pockets, looking for all the world like he'd lost his best friend in the world, like he had terrible news to break to me, and then I remembered what it was, and I let him drive me home and put me in bed and for the next year I let my kids—chiefly Gilda, as always—take care of me, and then the trail went cold.

16

Living History

Rose and Ed never had kids. He died a month after she did. They'd been married thirty-two years, same as Jess and me. In some ways I thought his death showed the depth of his character: he couldn't live without her, he wouldn't even try. They left the store to Ida's grandson, Paul Schloss, who'd worked in the store every summer and loved it. A family business, after all. My father's wishes were granted, though Paul and his wife changed the name to Schloss's Boutique.

Valley Junction is called Valley Junction again, except the name refers to the neighborhood: the city of West Des Moines sprawls all around it, strip malls and housing developments. Fifth Street has become fashionable, in its way, antiques stores and kitchen shops and restaurants, a historic district, a tourist site, if such things can exist in West Des Moines. On the other hand, if a *boutique* can . . .

My sisters died, one by one. Annie, the eldest, went last: she was 102. Like her father before her, she was the oldest citizen in town, and the local schools invited her once a year to deliver a lecture on Valley Junction's rough-and-tumble childhood.

All this is summary. I'm from the theater, I'd rather: Act Three, ten years later, a house in North Hollywood.

Because that's where we are now. You know the house.

Hollywood is not such a bad place to grow old. Everything they built back in the thirties was made to be a monument: a newsstand here is not just a newsstand, but an homage to the genre. They never changed a

single thing at Musso's, except the prices, and when I go there for lunch
twice a week, I can pretend that all sorts of people who are otherwise
disposed might be walking through the door. Outside, I drive around—
though my kids wish I wouldn't—past the billboards that are now, often
as not, in Spanish, and I feel like my father, the immigrant, except I
haven't gone anywhere, not in years.

I live alone. I have a comic cat, a little tortoiseshell named Thisbe.
(Gilda, always theatrical, named her.) On my lap, she throws her head
back. I know just where she likes to be scratched, and her eyes close and
her mouth opens in rapture. Never have I seen a being so absolutely in
love with what is happening to her at the moment. She doesn't remember the last time she felt this good. She doesn't worry that it's me and
my fingers. And after a while, at her highest point of ecstasy, she'll snap
and bite me, and I'll knock her to the ground. Minutes later she comes
back, she's forgotten. Me too. Clean slate always, me and the cat.

Ah, this cat. Halfway between Rocky and Jessica: in her body, given
over to pleasure, self-centered, fussy about the details. She'll bite me, we
both know that. In the meantime, we love each other.

I once knew a girl who said that the cat you owned was like you. A
daughter of a lady who ran a boardinghouse, this girl, and some other
man had told her so. For instance, she liked food too much, she liked to
cook and eat, and her cat liked food too much too. When fed, the cat
was loving; otherwise, under the sofa. "Oh," I said, emptying the box of
chocolates that had prompted this confession into my pockets (all of my
pockets, though who had the money for laundry?), "is that true?"

"Yes," said the girl, reaching.

And so maybe Thisbe and I are alike. Still, cats are like horoscopes in
this way: any interpretation is relevant, if you look.

What started me thinking: Rocky junior came to the house six years
ago. He calls himself Charles now, since both "Junior" and "Rocky"
sounded too childish for a guy in his forties. Somehow he's grown to
look just like his old man, despite his adoption: a good bit taller, black
hair that's his own, but heavyset and snub-nosed.

"I'm making a movie about you guys," he told me. He was a director
of commercials, but I knew he had other aspirations. We sat out back of
the house, drinking coffee. Like Rocky, he couldn't sit still. He turned
the cup around in his hands, laced one index finger through the handle,
then the other. My good cast-iron lawn furniture had been stored in the
shed—somebody had mowed the lawn and hadn't moved it back—but I

had a couple of cheap webbed lawn chairs in the trunk of my car, and those I could lift myself.

Rocky junior's creaked as though it would fold up. "Well, I haven't decided whether it's going to be about my dad, or the act, but either way: would you be willing to help me?"

"Sure," I said. "I'll even play myself."

"A documentary," he said quickly. *Joking,* I thought. "But it just goes to show you: the two of you still think alike. That's what my dad said, when I told him."

"Your dad." Had Junior sought out his birth parents? "Your *dad*—"

He said, "I found him."

I'd been warm, ten years before: Rocky had been living in Reno, which Penny knew perfectly well. A twenty-four-hour town, strippers, drinks, gambling, girl singers. I'd forgotten that there was more than one town in Nevada.

He lived, his son told me, in a trailer outside the city limits, and had indeed worked in a casino as a dealer for a while, though eventually arthritis made him quit. Like his son, he'd taken a new first name, the same one, and through no fault of his own Junior was a junior again, though his father went by Charlie as much as anything.

The lawn was very green and confusing.

"How is he?" I asked.

"Old," said Charles. "Not in the best of health, but who thought he'd live this long? I guess only the good die young. No offense."

I waved aside the insult, though I didn't know if it was about my age or my goodness. "None taken. Is he married?"

"There's a lady," said Charles diplomatically. He crossed his legs and stretched out in his chair, which tilted to the right. I tried to remember whether he'd played football in school, because he looked like a prosperous retired athlete. "We didn't delve into the legalities. Her name is Gertrude. She's tough. Very German."

"Does she know who he is?"

"Actually, I think she thought he was lying until I showed up with my video camera. Then she seemed impressed."

We had our backs to the house; suddenly its presence felt oppressive. My kids kept telling me I should sell it, move to an upscale condo nearer stores and restaurants. That and the car: they wanted me to give up things. Their caution made me more reckless. "Let's go," I said to Rocky junior.

"Where?"

"Take me to Reno. I'd like to see him."

"I'm not sure," he said, though he sounded sure: *No.*

"We won't ask. You know how he is—he'll say don't come, and by the time we get there, he'll have the door barred out of pride." The more I spoke, the better this idea sounded to me. Sure. One thing to sit around when I didn't know where he was, but now I was ready to ride off into the sunset looking for him. No, sunrise, I knew my geography. Riding off into the sunset in California would only get you wet. "We'll take my car," I said.

"Thing is," said Rocky junior. "Hmmm. I interviewed him when I was down there. Asked him questions about his life and the act. He was pretty hard on you."

"Of course he was," I said. "That's Rocky. And then things didn't go well for him, and they went well for me—I know he'd have a hard time swallowing that. I don't care what he said. Look, I've already forgiven him, and I don't even know what he said."

"I'll give you the tape. You can watch it. Then decide. If you still want to go—"

"We're old men," I said. "We haven't seen each other in thirty years. What could he possibly have said?"

"Watch the tape," said Rocky junior, "and then call me."

The Interview

Q: So where did you go when you left Hollywood in 1957?

A: I went to drink.

Q: To drink?

A: To drink? Yes, that's what I said: I went away to drink. Young men drink so they can be around people. Old men drink to be alone.

Q: But couldn't you—

A: I went away to drink *unimpeded*. People kept telling me to stop. And if they didn't tell me to stop, then they just avoided me. I mean, I was drinking a lot already, sure, and I'd call people up in the middle of the night.

Q: I remember. Why'd you do that?

A: I missed them, I guess. Or I wanted to settle scores. Bad behavior. So I emptied my bank account, and I went to live where there were no phones.

Q: Which was where?

A: You're too literal minded. But, okay, cheap hotels. There are hotels where you don't have a phone in your room. And in bars there are pay phones, but I never had change. I went out of my way not to have change. I tipped the bartender with it. I gave it away to panhandlers. I always hated loose change anyhow. I thought it was an insult to my pocket. Later I'd be mad at myself, when I was running out of money—all those quarters would have added up to—well, to a lot of whiskey.

Q: Why did you drink so much, do you think?

A: I guess I was thirsty.

(SILENCE)

Q: What did you do during the days, then?

A: I drank. I drank all the time. I slept, and drank. Maybe something interesting happened to me in there, but I've forgotten. I forgot most things. I got beat up once, but I only know that because my nose was broken, in a way—said the doctor who set it, I met him in a bar the next morning—that was caused by a fist.

Q: You could have been killed.

A: Yes, I could have been. Wasn't.

Q: You're smiling.

A: I didn't care. I still don't. It wouldn't have been the worst thing, some has-been gets killed in a barroom.

Q: It wouldn't have been the worst thing if your life ended in tragedy?

A: Ah, but you see: it already had.

Q: But—

A: It's a long end. It's a very, very, very long end. Longer than I would have liked, and longer than anyone would have guessed. It feels endless, but that's probably the nature of unhappy endings, right? Don't kid yourself. The past thirty years have not been the rest of my life, they've been the end of my life, and as it happened my life has ended in tragedy.

Look: I don't buy that bullshit, that life is precious. This planet's full of life, overfull of life, if you believe what the papers say. Everywhere you go, there it is, Human Life, walking down the street smug and stupid. A thing is precious—by definition, look it up in the dictionary—by being scarce. People call life precious because some of them like it too much. I could claim whiskey's precious. But life? More to the point, my life? The market's glutted.

Q: You say that, but you're crying.

A: I guess I'm thirsty. That usually makes me cry. Anyhow, Gert found me and I'm fine. You've got questions there. Ask me another one.

Q: Everyone wonders why Carter and Sharp broke up. I've heard a lot of theories.

A: Sure, there are a lot of 'em.

Q: But I've never really known why. Was there one reason?

(PAUSE)

Q: If you don't remember—

A: Don't you know? Mike slept with my wife.

(PAUSE)

Q: Mom?

A: No, no. Not that I know of. I mean Penny.

Q: While you were married to her?

A: Sure, while I was married to her. That's the kind of guy he was. In some cultures, if your enemy has something you want, you tear out his heart and eat it. Mike just fucked your wife. The guy had no loyalty.

Q: I always thought he and Aunt Jess—

A: Maybe he was faithful to his own wife. Maybe he believed in the sanctity of marriage, as long as it was *his* marriage. And maybe he fucked around on her too. I don't know. I tried to forgive him, but I guess in the end I couldn't. But we didn't break up right away.

Q: Are you sure about this?

A: Of course I am. Ask him, maybe he'll tell you the truth. You know, I did everything for that guy. He was a green kid when I found him. He barely knew how to *walk*. And I liked him. Well, I've never been a good judge of character. I brought him into the act, and I taught him everything, and I mean every single thing. I guess he's a fancy actor now, but without me he'd be a shopkeeper.

I loved him. I trusted him.

Q: He loved you—

A: Yeah. Sure. No, I know he did.

The Family Business

"He was pretty hard on you," Charles the diplomat had said. Maybe he assumed his father was lying. *But you did.* Penny told him, she must have. Still he might have just jumped to a conclusion, might have believed I'd slept with Penny one of those many nights I didn't. *But you did.* Rocky and I were together for eleven years after that single, solitary night, and he never said a word. The statute of limitations for any crime except murder had run out. *But he was right. You did.* Even if he knew, knew the next day, it hadn't seemed to bother him, and maybe he only brought it up to take the blame off himself. *But*— Or maybe Penny told him after everything, their divorce and our divorce, at a casino in Reno or Vegas, and he thought: Ah, if I'm ever asked again—

Despite everything, guilty as charged.

Video unnerves me—I like the process, not the medium. I'm a film guy. Used to be I hated it because the quality was so bad, kinescoped copies especially: everyone came through blurry but harsh. Now—it's too good, I guess. You can see everything. Back when people believed in ghosts but had never seen one (not *Topper*, not Hugo from *What, Us Haunted?*) I don't know what they imagined, exactly. Then the spirit world started appearing in the movies, and people thought that made sense: if our loved ones managed to slip through the border patrol of heaven to hit the bricks of the real world, they'd look filmed, filmy. Like the movies projected on the walls of the buildings on Fifth Street in Valley Junction. That's how gentle film is. It looks like a version of heaven.

On video, though, people look like themselves. It's too painful. I could see a perfectly square chunk of skin on Rocky's lips, the burst capillaries near his nose. I could practically count the salt crystals in his tears.

Of course I wanted to see him. The guy had done everything for me.

Charles and I drove to Reno in my new Cadillac (not a convertible, I never cared for them the way Jess did), and got lost looking for the trailer park. Then we found it: *Reno Acres*. There was a small blond girl riding a plastic tricycle near the front gate, the big front wheel stuttering in the dust of the lot. She looked at us, then stood up, and picked up the bike and waddled off with it waggling between her legs.

"Reno *Acres*?" I asked.

"That's it," said Charles—I am working so hard to call him Charles—pointing at a 1940s silver Airstream trailer parked some distance from the others.

I'd dressed several times that day, as though I was going on a date, and had finally settled on a pair of black slacks and a green sport shirt. No hat. I didn't want to look like a fuddy-duddy, though in fact I'd never given up hats.

I made Charles knock on the door. A tall nicotine blonde with nervous eyes answered the door. She frowned until she saw Charles. "Sonny!" she said. Then she saw me. "Hello! You are . . . ?"

I shook her hand. "Mose Sharp," I said, and she recoiled slightly, then let us in.

Rocky sat just inside the door in an enormous reclining chair. For some reason I'd imagined him in an undershirt, just as I'd imagined Gertrude in curlers, according to some trailer-park dress code. But he wore a button-up-the-front short-sleeved shirt and polyester knit pants. I was an old man myself, but—a fop to the end—I'd told myself knit pants were a sure sign you'd given up. He'd shrunk. At first I interpreted the pale hair as sun bleached from years in the Nevada sun; I'd forgotten how old we both were. The shirt was butter-yellow, and the pants brown.

He turned to look at us. First he saw his son, and smiled. Then he saw his partner.

I watched him very carefully, waiting, as always, for my cue.

He looked at me, then at his hands. And then he beckoned me over.

Oh, God, he looked so bad. Old-mannish and sun cured. How presumptuous of me to pity him, when all of this was his choosing, even Gert, who'd gone outside to have a cigarette. But he was *thin*, for Christ's sake, all the folds in his chin had turned vertical instead of horizontal. How could I have let this happen to him?

Every other person I knew was dead, it seemed. I felt avalanched. I sat down at his knees on a hassock in front of his striped chair, the same colors as his clothes, butter and toast. I was ready to promise him everything: Money. A room in my house. A reunion—surely somebody would be interested in that, some late-night talk-show at least. I took hold of his hand, and then I burst into tears.

I don't know how long I sat there weeping. I didn't know why I was the one who cried. Every time I looked up, he was—not stony faced, but waiting, and I cried some more. After a while he put his free hand on top of my head, the way the pope—from what I knew about the pope—would to the head of a sinner.

He said, "You take things too seriously, Mosey. You always did."

The Long Shot

Gert came back in and served us tea and cookies. I felt slightly cheered when she brought out a whiskey bottle, and poured us both a tiny dram, the way Annie had given me coffee as a child, just enough to give my milk a sophisticated color. "Thank you, love," Rocky said. She tickled him under the chin with scarlet painted nails. The furniture was second-hand; the television antenna was bandaged in tin foil. In the corner was a cabinet of Hummel figurines, little brown boys and girls in lederhosen and caps and yellowish braids—who says Germans can't be simply darling? We spoke of not a goddamn thing. Well, we exchanged the information that any other old friends would think was crucial—deaths and marriages and births.

"I keep waiting for this one to make me a grandfather," he said, pointing at his son with a toe.

"Keep waiting," said Charles.

It was all very fucking civil, Rocky would have said in another life. Very fucking civil indeed.

"You working?" I asked.

"Sometimes. Every now and then I emcee a drag show downtown, and they pay me under the table."

"A what?" I asked, sure I'd misheard.

"Drag show. Female imps. I'm so old the only women who'll flirt with me are men. I like it, though. At a drag show, it's like *every*one's senile. *Nobody* knows what the hell is going on."

"I do not like this," Gertrude said, though I already had started eyeing her with suspicion. Then we fell silent again.

Well, what was I expecting? We hadn't seen each other in three decades, and if I'd called ahead he would have told me not to come. I finished the licorice-scented biscuit on my plate, and wondered if I'd hug Rocky before I left or solemnly shake his hand. Then Charles said, "Let's give them some time alone."

"Oh," Gert said. She put her hand on the kitchen counter, as though she'd have to be pulled out.

"It's all right, Gert," Rocky said.

"You know," Rocky said confidentially, once they were gone, "she's a Nazi."

"Yeah?" I said.

He nodded. "My own darling Nazi."

I felt my shoulders relax. This we'd done many times. Rocky's paranoia was one of our running jokes. "She's German," I said. "And won't let you drink that much. But that doesn't mean she's eyeing world domination. Besides, she's, I don't know, forty? She's too young."

He shrugged. "*You* try living with her. Today this trailer, tomorrow, the trailer next door. Younger women, boy. I think; soon I'll be dead, and I want to leave her something, but what have I got? Nothing."

"Oh," I said. I looked around the joint and couldn't argue. Anything posh he'd left in California thirty years before, or sold off for taxes and alimony. Maybe I had something at home, some award we'd gotten for fund-raising, a piece of Jessica's jewelry that I could claim somehow rightly belonged to him. "I'm sure—"

He interrupted me. "I think I thought up something." He leaned on his hand dreamily. "I have a little plan worked out."

"Is it legal?" I asked.

"This is Nevada," he said dismissively. Then he put his hands out, *voilà*. "Me."

"Why not give her something she doesn't already own?"

"You misunderstand me," he said. "*After* I'm dead. Some men leave their bodies to science. I'm leaving mine to Gert."

"That's some Catholic thing," I said. "Right? Lie around in a glass coffin, breath like roses? You told me about this once. Some saint you had a crush on. Let me think: if your body remains uncorrupted twenty days—I'm trying to remember this part—well, let's just say that would be a lifetime record."

"*Funny* man," he said, smiling.

"Or you were thinking maybe of taxidermy?"

"Nothing that fancy, no. I told you: she's a Nazi. Lampshades." He fingered his now half-sunk anchor tattoo. "Nautical theme, maybe. I figure, the place could use some sprucing up, right? I got enough skin for a whole chandelier. Maybe a couple of rings from the gold in my teeth—"

"*Jesus*, Rocky." I laughed and closed my eyes in happy horror.

Happy, no kidding. A happy ending: two old men joking about the worst thing in the world in an Airstream trailer. Another time I would have explained to him why there was nothing the least bit funny about what he'd just said, but right now I found it hilarious, may God and the Audience forgive me.

One of our ongoing fights: Rocky asserted that with enough diligence and joie de vivre, you could turn anything to comedy. If he'd been born twenty years later, he would have made completely different films. Farces. Movies with mean streaks. But he hit it big in the 1940s, when everybody—moviegoers, politicians, censors, and me—believed that certain things were *not* funny, could not be made funny, would not be made funny. The physics of censors meant that a funny joke about something unfunny was even less funny than a clunker.

When I'd asked Junior to bring me to Reno, the best I'd hoped for was something sentimental, apologies and forgiveness. A movie might have shown us launching into an old routine, a soft shoe choreographed for men who could no longer pick up their feet so well. Not this: both of us with senses of humor so funereal nobody young could even see the jokes. What kind of act would we work up now? *The Two Undertakers. The Ghouls. Black and Barry: Comedy with a Grievous Touch.*

"You know," I said, "I read where the chemicals in the human body are worth upwards of thirty-seven dollars."

He nodded. "I'm asking fifty a pint. I put a lot of money into this thing"—he slapped his missing belly—"and I'm not going to let anybody lowball me. Speaking of which—"

But then Gert and Junior walked back in, to find us laughing.

"You're in a good mood," Gert said accusingly. She probably thought we'd gotten into the liquor.

"We were just talking, my only love, about the human atrocities of your fatherland," said Rocky.

Junior looked at his shoes. "Socko stuff, I'm sure."

"I've *told* you," Gert said to Rocky, and he showed his palms in surrender.

Then he turned to me, as though his ladyfriend and son weren't there. He leaned forward out of his chair, and I realized he hadn't stood up the entire time. "I sort of hope she does it. What I said? Let the light go through me. Think of me when the sun goes down. Maybe you'd like one too."

"Rocky," I said, shuddering.

"You know?" he said. "Might as well make myself useful."

When we got up to leave, Rocky said, "This was nice."

"It was," I agreed.

"But you know, Professor," and that was the first time he'd called me by that name, the first time in ages anyone had, "we can't be buddies."

"What do you mean?" I asked, though I had some inkling.

"We can't be buddies. Glad you came down with the kid. Would have told you not to—you know that—glad you did it, but that's that, right? *This* is my life now." He gestured around the trailer to the TV, the Hummels, everything—and, I saw now, a total lack of memorabilia. No photos, no plaques, no souvenirs. No copies of his movies on tape. "This is *it*," he said, in a voice I couldn't interpret, *I don't want anything else*, or *Please don't make me want anything else.* "And," he said, though I'd already figured it out, I wanted to stop him, "you're not in it."

"I know."

"We're not picking up where we left off."

"Sure not."

"Don't want you going off and telling people where I am. Don't want—listen, this one's important—you telling any reporters, and the one guy whose editor maybe thinks I'm this human interest story actually sends him down to find me, already with the lead: 'You won't find Rocky Carter's place on any map of the stars' homes.' "

"Of course, Rock."

"Right? Right." He clapped his hands together.

I stood up to go. Rocky caught my eye, and said, "You understand me?"

"You know me, Rocky," I said. "I always do."

"So did you?" Rocky junior said on the way home.

"What?" I answered, playing dumb.

He sighed and tapped the steering wheel. His hands were mammoth. "Penny," he said at last.

I had never told anyone, not even Jessica. A drunken escapade; bad behavior, but hadn't I been mostly good? What could it matter, then or now?

"It's complicated," I said.

He ran a hand through his black hair, and switched on the radio. The Caddy had a fine radio, with big knobs that were a pleasure to turn. We drove twenty miles without talking before he said, "Well, then, I guess I'm provincial."

We drove another forty miles.

"So it *was* your fault the act broke up," he said. He turned his head to me one last time. How was it possible he looked so much like his father? I realized he cultivated the resemblance, combed his hair the same way, ate the same way, for all I knew drank the same way. I wanted to confess to him all the sins of my life: Hattie's death, my father's, Betty's, all the hours I should have been by Jess's sickbed when I paced the house, how I'd stomped in food when my mother died, danced the night my father died. Look, I would have said, you want to know about *guilt*?

Fancy thinking. A coward always feels guilt over the things he's not guilty of. The things he really did he never mentions.

My fault?

"Well, yes," I said to Rocky junior. "It certainly seems that way."

What's the difference between a comedy team and two people who happen to be funny together? Not just longevity, though that's part.

The movie starts: two people. Could be two men, two women, some of each, several of one or the other. You recognize them instantly, by their clothes and their silhouettes and the way they stand in relation to each other. Laurel will always cry; Hardy will always look at the camera in consternation; Gracie Allen will always gaze at her husband chin tilted up; George Burns will always look back at his wife, chin tucked to his chest. George will feed his wife a straight line. Gracie will say, "Don't be silly," and offer a punch line.

They will never change, and if they ever do, it's for a moment, and *that's* a joke: suddenly the comic is sensible and the straight man humiliated, but never for long. They are bound together. You will never see them meet for the first time. You will never see them part forever.

George Burns, for example. Next to tiny Gracie, he looked like a big guy, tall and broad shouldered and handsome enough. He combed his wavy hair straight back from his forehead. Age alone can't explain how his looks changed: the dumb wig (blond for a while, then silver) that he wore parted on the side like a kid, those round black glasses, the way his eyes narrowed to slits. How small he was. You could hardly recognize the guy. Sure, he was older, and eventually he was very old indeed, but plenty of it was his own choosing. After his wife died, he was no longer Gracie's straight man. If he looked the way he always had, audiences would know what was missing.

This is a comedy team: one person straightening the other's necktie, and it makes sense.

Soldiers with legs amputated suffer from phantom pain. Me, I've suffered forty years from phantom punch lines. For all the noise I made about being glad to get rid of him, the things I did afterward, the movies

I appeared in—being with Rocky was the best time of my life. I love my children, but they don't understand.

I waited for a phone call for a long time after Reno, until I realized the call wouldn't be from him, but from someone telling me what had happened. So I started to call, every six months or so. Gertrude answers. She's used to me. "Hello, Gert," I say, and there's the muffled sound of her smoky hand going over the receiver, and then she says, "Sorry, darling, no." The last time, though, the number had been disconnected. But I don't think he's dead. I'd know. The damnedest people live forever. Rocky, my father, Annie, pulling up the median age of my acquaintances. I mean, the people I loved. Rocky junior moved to Europe sometime in the late eighties—he never finished the documentary—and I don't much hear from him anymore. I thought maybe he'd be the one to call me.

I do the routines in my head, every single night. I go over our final routine, too, the one in his trailer. I thought I said some funny things myself. And everywhere I go, I hear his voice, pushing me around, giving me advice, yelling sometimes. *Have a drink. Cheer up, kid. Don't stand that way, nobody'll notice you. What the hell were you thinking—I did everything, everything, everything for you.* Sometimes I contradict all his advice on purpose, just so I can hear his correction.

Look, here we are on some black-and-white boulevard. An early movie, then, nothing supernatural about it. Walking down the street with suitcases in our hands. You can't tell yet whether we're running away or starting out fresh. My little fat friend has sat on his hat, it looks like; I'm wearing a mortarboard that by movie's end will spin like a top. We get closer and closer to the camera. Somewhere there's a policeman looking for us. Everything in this world is made to fall apart: breakaway pianos, breakaway bottles, breakaway pants, breakaway skirts, breakaway vases, breakaway chairs, breakaway windows—panes, mullions, sashes, everything. Soon enough there'll be sugar glass and balsa wood everywhere. Nothing is of consequence.

At first it sounds like Rocky is asking questions and I'm answering, but if you analyze it, you can see it's really the opposite, no matter the punctuation: I set up, he responds, I set up, he responds.

He says, "Where are we going?"

"Over there."

"What'll we do when we get over there?"

"Whatever's next."

"Could sitting down be next?"

"I'll decide when we get there."

"You'll decide when we get there, okay."

Whatever we're about to do is a very bad idea, three reels of hot water for sure. We can't help ourselves, though. I'm sitting here in my chair in Sherman Oaks, California, but really, I'm on a movie set, or on some vaudeville-house stage—not the Palace, we never played the Palace, but someplace nearly as good. He's skittering away from me, but soon he'll come back, I'm his only friend in the world, he has to trust me. I'm saying, *What's wrong with you, Rocky? Stand still. Pay attention. Whatever will we do with you?*

You see, I still miss the guy.

ACKNOWLEDGMENTS

Endless gratitude to:

my editor, Susan Kamil, whose patience and good sense about this book boggle my mind; my beloved agent, Henry Dunow; my darling big brother, Harry McCracken; my first reader forever, Ann Patchett, and my parents.

And also to:

Rob Phelps, Paul Abruzzo, Max Phillips, Bruce Holbert, Paul Lisicky and Mark Doty, Zoe Rice, Carla Riccio, Robin Robertson, Tim and Wendy DeVries, Hunter O'Hanian and Jeffry Cismoski, Fritz McDonald, Maurice Noble, Marguerite White, Frank Cullen of the American Vaudeville Museum (www.vaudeville.org), the Fine Arts Work Center in Provincetown, and the Guggenheim Foundation.

Many people talked to me about nineteenth- and twentieth-century life in Des Moines and West Des Moines, including Carolyn Matulef, Richard and Ellen Caplan, Chick and Helene Barricks, Ozzie and Carla Lucas, Mary Robinson, Henry Davitt, Ted Livingston, and those I miss: Sidney and Rose Pearlman, Estyre Hockenberg, Irene Sideman, Yetta Toubes, Harold Brody, Elizabeth Perowsky, and Norman Matulef.

ABOUT THE AUTHOR

ELIZABETH MCCRACKEN is a National Book Award finalist. She is recipient of the Harold Vursell Award from the American Academy of Arts and Letters and has received grants from the Guggenheim Foundation, the Michener Foundation, the Fine Arts Work Center in Provincetown, and the National Endowment for the Arts. She was also honored as one of *Granta*'s 20 Best American Writers Under 40. In addition to *The Giant's House*, a Barnes & Noble Discover Award winner, she is the author of *Here's Your Hat, What's Your Hurry*.